Welcome to Paradise, Flora Brock

Genevieve Flint

Copyright © 2023 Genevieve Flint

All rights reserved

The characters and events portrayed in this book are fictitious. Any similarity to real persons, living or dead, is coincidental and not intended by the author.

No part of this book may be reproduced, or stored in a retrieval system, or transmitted in any form or by any means, electronic, mechanical, photocopying, recording, or otherwise, without express written permission of the publisher.

ISBN-13: 9798853863767
Imprint: Independently Published
Cover design by: Genevieve Flint

For my family, both the blood ones and the chosen ones

"Freedom, in any case, is only possible by constantly struggling for it."
Albert Einstein

"The mind is its own place, and in itself can make a heaven of hell, a hell of heaven."
John Milton

CONTENTS

Title Page
Copyright
Dedication
Epigraph
Prologue
CHAPTER ONE	1
CHAPTER TWO	8
CHAPTER THREE	16
CHAPTER FOUR	23
CHAPTER FIVE	30
CHAPTER SIX	38
CHAPTER SEVEN	46
CHAPTER EIGHT	54
CHAPTER NINE	59
CHAPTER TEN	67
CHAPTER ELEVEN	77
CHAPTER TWELVE	83
CHAPTER THIRTEEN	97
CHAPTER FOURTEEN	103
CHAPTER FIFTEEN	112

CHAPTER SIXTEEN	119
CHAPTER SEVENTEEN	130
CHAPTER EIGHTEEN	137
CHAPTER NINETEEN	148
CHAPTER TWENTY	153
CHAPTER TWENTY-ONE	155
CHAPTER TWENTY-TWO	160
CHAPTER TWENTY-THREE	168
CHAPTER TWENTY	175
CHAPTER TWENTY-FIVE	183
CHAPTER TWENTY-SIX	185
CHAPTER TWENTY-SEVEN	195
CHAPTER TWENTY-EIGHT	202
CHAPTER TWENTY-NINE	210
CHAPTER THIRTY	218
CHAPTER THIRTY-ONE	227
CHAPTER THIRTY-TWO	238
CHAPTER THIRTY-THREE	244
CHAPTER THIRTY-FOUR	253
CHAPTER THIRTY-FIVE	259
CHAPTER THIRTY-SIX	263
CHAPTER THIRTY-SEVEN	267
CHAPTER THIRTY-EIGHT	272
CHAPTER THIRTY-NINE	279
CHAPTER FORTY	284
CHAPTER FORTY-ONE	290
CHAPTER FORTY-TWO	296
CHAPTER FORTY-THREE	300

CHAPTER FORTY-FOUR	301
CHAPTER FORTY-FIVE	304
CHAPTER FORTY-SIX	306
CHAPTER FORTY-SEVEN	314
CHAPTER FORTY-EIGHT	320
CHAPTER FORTY-NINE	328
CHAPTER FIFTY	334
CHAPTER FIFTY-ONE	337
CHAPTER FIFTY-TWO	339
EPILOGUE	342
GET READY FOR THE NEXT INSTALLMENT…	345
About The Author	347

PROLOGUE

"Lana," Tane screamed, as his feet beat the earth. Flora heard only blood; her heartbeat thundering in her ears. The fire heaved, spewing flames like curses.

She was faster. The terracotta mud was her home now; her senses were alive to each rip in the terrain, her bare feet moving like a cheetah across the savanna.

She crouched down. Shook Lana's body until the older girl's sprained wrist lolled to one side.

Crimson trickled into a pool on the floor. The hot earth looked to be crying.

Flora expelled a guttural, animalistic noise.

Let this be me.

She glanced at Tane. Her hand pushed Lana's hair back, smearing red across that perfect forehead.

Did we do this?

"You're too late," Lana whispered. She opened her eyes; the slits reflected flames. Nearby, a lone giddyfruit rolled from the wreckage, charred, smoking, abandoned from a game of Jungleball, from back when everything was ok.

"What happened?" Flora said, or perhaps she just screamed, because an inhumane noise was rolling from someone's tongue. She tried to pull Lana's hand away so that she could see the damage, see past the blood-sodden t-shirt. It felt as if the remnants of Flora's heart had been peeled and butchered and spliced above Lana's belly button.

Lana's vest had a skull and crossbones on the front. One of the bones had disappeared. Flora's eyes weren't working. She blinked rapidly. A joke, surely. A joke.

"He escaped."

Silence. The blaze raged on. The words were pithy. Cauterised.

"He escaped," Lana repeated. "I'm sorry."

More silence.

"I love you."

Flora blinked. A tear fell.

You never know that it's the last time, that you've missed your shot, that there are so many words that should have been spoken, until it's too late.

CHAPTER ONE
WOEBEGONE

Marks & Spencer was boring. Flora's scuffed-up, knock-off trainers abused the freshly cleaned linoleum of the big store in town. Her dad's new wife was striding in front of her. Why was she walking so quickly? She wished her dad had sacked off his daytime nap for some quality family time.

The smell of bath bombs trailed after them from the expensive shop in the lobby. Flora didn't particularly like nice smells, because it made her house smell even worse when she got home. It wasn't dirt that filled their nostrils while they slept, it was all the stuff Abbie had brought along with her: hemp seed smoothies, hessian cushions, incense sticks.

Rubbish, basically.

Abbie ploughed on ahead. Around them, worried parents paced the floors with Back-to-School basics clutched in carrier bags, as if they weren't two weeks late. A few kids from Flora's school had sat in the Burger King food court earlier. She'd let her hair fall over her face as she passed.

Shopping for baby clothes was not high up on Flora's list of interesting things to do on a Saturday, or areas that she was skilled in. Perhaps if it was buying a new skin for her avatar, or buying a game upgrade, then it would be more scintillating. Either way, Abbie had insisted, in a way that basically said that Flora didn't have to go, but she'd be a terrible future older sister if she didn't.

Abbie was surprisingly nimble, given the size of her stomach. She was already asking Flora what she thought the offspring should be called and whether they should find out the gender and whether Flora was excited.

"'Course," Flora would reply, sounding rude, but really she was still shy of Abbie and didn't know who to be around her. She'd barely mastered the personality of 'daughter', let alone 'stepdaughter'.

Flora would sound impetuous and Abbie would pretend not to go pink around the ears and would inevitably hum something by One Direction, as if that hadn't become an obvious anxious tic. Flora liked to imagine that she could read Abbie's mind. She'd noticed that if you looked at someone carefully enough for the first few seconds that they looked at you, the truth often flickered across their eyes before they had a chance to hide it.

She practised this on Abbie.

Abbie can't stand me.

A rack of beanie hats caught her attention. It was too soon for it, surely? It was September, but the picture of the model wearing them, a gorgeous girl with thick black hair, caught Flora's attention. She couldn't look away. The girl looked like she would belong in Arlo's gang at school, and the hat looked designer. She picked one up in a charcoal grey, glancing first at its price tag. £11. That might be asking a bit much. Abbie was only able to shop in M&S because her sister gave her a gift voucher.

Flora rubbed the soft, woollen fabric and imagined smelling it. It would smell like the plastic air of department stores, a smell she found fairly pleasant because it reminded her of cleanliness and order, but not in an arrogant way. It merely said, 'We bothered to clean'.

But even here, where no one from her school was likely to shop, she wasn't about to go sniffing the accessories. Besides, she might struggle to fit it over her mass of dirty blonde hair. Curly, some people called it. Scarecrow-like, Arlo's ex-girlfriend called it.

"Do they do haircuts at the local farm now?" Natalia asked her once, in mock surprise, tossing her stunningly straight locks over her shoulder. Flora wanted to stroke her hair, but since Natalia was a total a-hole, it was easy to resist.

"You were conceived there, you tell me," Flora retorted, her face hot. Natalia almost smiled at that one, and Flora felt electricity shoot through her veins.

Natalia wouldn't be seen dead shopping with her pregnant step mum in Marks and Spencer. Flora sighed, setting the hat back down.

She breathed in, not quite letting it go, her reluctant fingers tracing the ridged detailing. If she could only turn up to school wearing something cool for once-

"Just take it."

She froze. Her hand was still touching the soft beanie.

Did I imagine that?

She turned around. A boy was standing right behind her, his teeth shining and his eyes grinning wickedly. He had his hands in his pockets, pockets that were stitched onto a huge shirt, far too big for him, and he was wearing a hat, but one of those flat cap types that old men wear. In one ear he had a hoop earring with a metal star dangling from the rim, and between missing shirt buttons she could see the flash of a studded belt.

His look sat firmly between 'punk' and 'charity-shop-chic'. This somehow suited him. He had a nose that turned up slightly, showing a flash of nostril, and eyes that were curved into half-moons. He looked to be around twelve - four years younger than Flora - but a hint of eyeliner made him look older.

"I can't just steal it, idiot," she said. Defence was her usual form of communication. She automatically felt self-conscious, even though the boy was dressed in such an odd way. She tugged at her oversized black jumper, pulling it down further over her skinny white legs, shuffling her dirty trainers.

The jumper was sold as a 'jumper dress', but she suddenly realised that it was too short to wear without leggings. Especially in September.

What was I thinking?

"Why not? It's a huge company, they won't miss it."

"It's wrong."

"Says who?"

"Says general intuition. And post-adolescent morality."

He looked at her for a moment and she could tell he was vaguely impressed, even if his mouth hadn't stopped its grin, which was beginning to look less friendly and more taunting.

"You sound like Tane."

"Great," Flora said. She had no intention of finding out who 'Tane' was.

"Is that your step mum?" he asked, nodding towards Abbie, who was studying the Floor Plan.

"How d'you know that?"

"Easy," he replied, watching Abbie. The older woman turned, revealing her huge belly. "Ah, right." He said it in a distasteful way, as if in apology.

"Right, what? She's pregnant, if that's what you mean." Flora felt a sudden flash of loyalty for Abbie. Who was this guy and why was he judging them?

"Must be hard for you," he said, looking back at Flora with surprising intensity. His smile had dropped, his half-moon eyes turning into almonds.

He clearly thought that he was irresistible. He looked like the lead singer in a band that was taking a break, busy shopping in a supermarket wearing his band gear, incongruous in the clean surroundings, having missed the memo that they were no longer on tour.

"What's it to you?" Flora asked, once again regretting how harsh she sounded. Her body was thrumming, her heart that of a hummingbird, and his judgement felt like it poured petrol over an already burning fire. She'd put one of her trainers onto the toes of the other foot and it hurt, but she stayed frozen in place.

"Nothing to me, I'm just saying: I get it. I've got a good read of people, you know. I can tell you'd fit right in." He looked at her for a long moment, during which she slowly felt more uncomfortable. "Please can I borrow your phone to send a quick text?"

"What?"

"Yeah, I left my phone... at home, and I need to tell my family that I'll be heading back later."

"Right, ok," Flora said, still feeling uncomfortable, but glad to distract him from staring at her. She handed him her phone and watched as he typed away.

He gave the phone back.

"Thanks," he said brightly, as if sending the message had answered all of his worldly problems. "That's that, then." His smile made her uneasy; she looked at Abbie to anchor her. "Anyway, I need some socks. Maybe we'll see you round..."

She didn't reply and he cleared his throat before he said one final statement: "I feel like you need some adventure in your life, Flora."

With that, he strode off. His walk was something of an exaggerated swagger, which made him seem three feet taller than he was.

Had she told him her name? She must have done. She couldn't remember.

What a weird boy. And as for the idea of 'fitting in', well... Flora could only imagine that he was from some sort of gaming convention.

She didn't have much time to ponder anything, because, without warning, Abbie yelled "FLORA!"

She'd found the right floor for the baby rompers and suits and tiny shoes and little hats that she'd been blabbering on about. Flora joined her on the escalator, taking the steps two at a time to catch up with her bulbous step mum. Her nerves were still pumping her heart rate into the back of her ears.

"Who was that boy?"

"No one," Flora replied, but she'd replied too quickly and only cemented Abbie's mistaken suspicions. *Flora's seeing some boy in a band.*

Flora wasn't even sure that boys were 'her thing', but Abbie just gave her a wry glance and dropped the conversation, saving her the trouble of pointing this out.

Flora just wasn't sure about Abbie. On the wall in the living room, Abbie had taken down the picture of Flora on her first day at secondary school, when she had chunky braces and a nervous disposition, back when it was just Flora and her dad, and replaced it with a stitched canvas that read: *Family is the most important Thing.*

Flora liked the idea that you could choose your family, that actually your *Chosen Family is the most important Thing.*

△△△

While Abbie waltzed off to the tills to pay, Flora did her usual anxiety-reducing ritual, touching her thumb to her forefinger, then her middle finger, then her ring finger and finally her little finger, counting as she went: one, two, three, four, one, two, three, four...

Had she told that boy her name? And if not, how did he know to call her Flora?

△△△

On Sunday evening, she talked to Stu from Bolton, who wasn't nearly as good as her at Pictopia, but who was interesting to chat to nonetheless.

"Good job," he boomed.

Her avatar had just defeated the giant - *again, how many times will this guy show up?* - and she'd arrived at the edge of a lake. Flora paused the game and a black stripe appeared across the screen. Behind the stripe, she could see blue: azure water, hazy skies. Tropical flowers and digital fish. Bright white sunlight. She breathed in and could almost smell the verdant petals on the flowers, the clean, crisp air.

She resumed play and the fish jumped up with newly-born fangs and crimson eyes. She fled the lake.

The elephant enclosure in the abandoned zoo caught her eye. There was an odd reflective pixel towards the bottom of it. She looked at it and smirked.

That had been a major achievement.

"Flo, you good over there?" Stu from Bolton asked. That was literally his handle – StuFromBolton.

She didn't reply.

"Look, I hope you don't mind, but I told TheEagle about you."

"What?" Flora's spit landed on her computer screen in exaggerated globules.

"Yeah, well he's always asking about talented kids from broken homes. He asked what I knew about you, WestCountryFlo, think he wants to help, or get you into the conventions. Don't worry about it. Doubt you'd ever talk to him, you know."

"I...what... go away Stu," Flora gasped, her voice catching on all of the things that she'd like to say, her eyes reflecting her own face in the spit-laden screen. She killed Stu.

So TheEagle had been asking about her, even after the elephant enclosure?

CHAPTER TWO
SCINTILLA

About a month ago, Flora had spotted something interesting behind the abandoned elephant enclosure in Pictopia. A solid black square, tiny, almost invisible to the gaming eye. Every so often, it glimmered.

She tried to click on it. No luck. She tried to shoot it, to blow it up, to fire a bazooka at it. Nothing happened. It frustrated her. She went to sleep thinking about it, struggling to believe that the game designers would have made such an error. It frustrated her, thinking that there might be a flaw in the game. It devalued it.

One night, when she'd tried everything else, she started researching online. Down in the deep, dark web, she managed to find a server-side hack for the game developers that would allow her to access the Java source code. She then used a profiler to find the parts of the code that took the longest time to execute. She found the square.

Only, it wasn't just a square. There, in almost indecipherable code, which had taken her an age to reverse to recognition, as it was obfuscated (but not irreversibly so – *idiot developers*), were instructions for getting into the gateway.

The black square was a door.

She managed to get in. Inside were a small scattering of chatrooms, hosting encrypted conversations, shadowy deals, and debates about malware and the illegitimate roots of evil.

That is where she met TheEagle. The gamer who was

always ahead of her, the one that she could never beat, no matter how quick her fingers were. She followed him almost obsessively on streaming sites; she would often dream of being as good as, or even beating, TheEagle.

She asked him how to beat the undead witch. He ignored her. She asked him how he'd made it past the Blue Mine. He ignored her.

Instead, he asked her for her name. She repeated her username.

He asked her where she lived, and she told him Plymouth, but that was all. She wasn't about to give out her home address, even to a gaming legend. He asked so many questions that she wondered if it was flirtatious.

Most likely, TheEagle was a middle-aged groomer, spending his time in dark web chatrooms rather than living his life. It was disappointing.

Never meet your heroes.

He threw a few random coding questions at her, which she immediately responded to, wanting to show that she was the real deal, impressive.

But that was it. The first time meeting him.

She left the chat room, dissatisfied.

And now? It bugged Flora that Stu had told TheEagle about her home life. She'd told Stu about her mum once, but also the important part, that she'd got help. Her dad had done an alright job since those turbulent years, so the situation was hardly "broken".

Eventually, she couldn't stand the game any longer and she got into bed, seeking solace in other pixels. Pictures of people on the beach, baby pink bikinis and beautiful faces.

Social media played to its strengths and distracted her: *do I want to be rich? Do I need plastic surgery? Do I need friends?*

△△△

At school the next day, Flora managed to avoid the attention of the Balenciaga kids, who spent their weekends at festivals and whom her best friend Jen admired a little too much. Natalia was always sniping at Flora, and Arlo... well, he was too cocky for his own good. At lunchtime, she made a beeline for Jen.

Around them, the cafeteria teamed with life and stank of cauliflower.

Flora, feeling tired and fed up – she'd heard her dad and Abbie arguing into the early hours – projected this annoyance onto Jen, who was fiddling with a can of Diet Coke and watching Arlo.

"Dude, stop staring over there. Look, are you going to be in Pictopia tonight? Because you've missed a shedload now. I've got to Lost Grace, I've found a new map, but you're going to need to hurry up if you want to join me."

Truth be told, Flora's thumbs were actually hurting from how much she was playing. With her dad and Abbie turning the house into a tense battleground, she felt more relaxed in the world of Pictopia, where she had a horse and armour. There were limitations with the magic, and she didn't get as much time as she liked on it, but she didn't have to worry about real life as much.

"Look, Flor," Jen said, using the endearing name that she always started bad news with, "I'm not going to Pict anymore. I'm a bit over it. It's just a bit, you know... I don't want to be one of those stereotypes who just abandons the game when life gets more interesting, it's just..."

"It's just what?"

"It's just not very cool, is it? Like, when you post screenshots and stuff on your socials, you're the only one doing it. No one else is."

"So now you're bowing down to conformity?" Flora asked, voice flat. Her heart hadn't stopped thrumming like a drummer on steroids.

"Being like other people isn't such a bad thing, you

know," Jen said, standing up and picking up her uneaten salad. She rolled her eyes and sauntered off to dump her food in the bin.

Here is the problem. Real, strong girls changing into pretty, quiet women. That could stay in the world of fiction, as far as Flora was concerned.

Because otherwise, who was left to talk to? Who was she going to talk to about actual, interesting things?

Stu from Bolton. He was the only one who would listen, and she didn't even know what he looked like.

And probably Mrs White their stern but nurturing Head of Year, who had given out more advice than Flora could ever possibly remember. Mrs White might listen; indeed she frequently did in Flora's head, where she also tended to don a fur coat and an extravagant hat.

Flora: I feel like Jen is my only friend, and yet most of the time I can't stand to be around her. But if I'm not friends with her, then I have literally got no one.

Mrs White: Do you think that's nice?

Flora: Nice? No.

As she cleared up her nearly empty pasta bowl, one sad bit of broccoli left, she remembered the boy in Marks & Spencer. The one in the baggy shirt and old man cap and hooped earring, with the turned-up nose and cheeky grin. He wasn't into conformity, of that she was sure. *One in a million.*

△△△

Jen didn't sit next to her on the bus on the way home. Flora struggled to remember why she was upset; they'd had Science and Geography since lunch. *She's annoyed because I'm not cool,* Flora remembered, thinking back to Jen's claim that *being like other people isn't such a bad thing.*

Remembering their fight made Flora tap her leg in agitation. If she lost Jen then she wouldn't have anyone to hang with. *I am maybe more than a bit weird, and awkward. Maybe I don't fit in and maybe most people don't understand me, but at least I'm being real.*

She got Flick up on her phone, an app with livestreamed gaming. She immediately went on TheEagle's profile.

He was making his way through Pictopia, ducking potential blows and death spells, avoiding the hidden mines, knowing how to release the undead elephant from the not-so-abandoned enclosure, riding it without a moment's hesitation.

TheEagle was ridiculous. *No one's that good.* Perhaps he was an AI robot. Occasionally he would talk through his moves, and his voice sounded so flat that it could have been faked. Plus, he never had his video on.

He was way ahead of her, but she spent the journey watching anyway, learning what was in Lost Grace, which weapons she would need, where she was going to need help. By Pictopia standards, Flora was ahead of ninety-nine percent of the other gamers, she knew she was good. But this guy, TheEagle, well... he was better.

I need to spend more time on it, Flora thought to herself. There was no way she'd keep up if she could only get a few hours in a night. And her fingers were already in pain; how did TheEagle do it?

She glanced down at her thumbs, hating them.

She considered calling in sick to school tomorrow. It was the type of exciting, forbidden thought that she enjoyed pretending might happen, even though she knew that she'd never have the guts. Besides, Abbie was at home all day; surely she'd notice if her 'sick' stepdaughter was sitting gaming? She wouldn't approve. She didn't approve anyway.

"Do you know how much that stuff adds to the electric bill?" she once heard Abbie complain to her dad.

"It's not that much. She could be growing marijuana up there," her Dad had joked.

"And it's really bad for her social skills, you know. She never goes out, she never sees anyone. I'm worried she's losing the ability to talk to people in real life, seriously. At her age I was going to house parties, getting drunk with the girls, sneaking back home at midnight. It's not good for her mental health, all this sitting at home on her own."

"Leave her alone, she's fine," her dad had said, and that was the end of that. Flora had tiptoed back to her room and put her gaming headphones back on, silently seething, feeling the rage tip over into her thumbs, which attacked an unruly giant until its head exploded.

△△△

She had a dream about skipping school and getting a bus to Pictopia. Not the game, but an actual place, where it had become a reality, somewhere behind the walls of her city. In her waking world, she lived in Plymouth, a city by the sea, and it did have citadel walls, but nothing like the ones in her dream; great towers that split Plymouth Hoe, a huge park, from the world of Pictopia. In her dream she was a warrior, an adventurer, with knotted hair and a real sword, scaling the walls with ease, slaying druids.

She awoke with the sounds of Pictopia still in her ears, the adrenaline coursing through her veins as if she'd temporarily teleported. She also awoke to the sound of Abbie shouting at her dad, something about him getting her bag. They were both running around the house, the noise of their feet slamming against the cheap carpets.

"What's going on?" Flora yelled from her bed, realising that it must be early in the morning and actually, it was all that stomping that had woken her up. No one replied and she heard the front door slam and then the house was filled with a silence that overtook the faint thrum of the boiler.

"Dad?" Flora called again, wondering whether one of them had killed the other and then fled.

Eventually, when no response arrived, she got out of

bed and wandered down the stairs, the early morning light turning the house a deep shade of orange. Neither of them were there and it was only when she looked at the table, where a note should have been, that she realised that Abbie must have gone into labour.

She's gone to give birth. And neither of them thought to tell me.

For some reason, Flora felt the same burning sensation that she had when she'd overheard Abbie telling her dad that basically, she needed to get a life. Sometimes, Abbie represented everyone else, everyone in the outside world. By judging Flora, the whole world was judging Flora. By deeming her not important enough to keep in the loop, the world was making her even more alone.

I should just run away, she thought. *See if they even notice.*

But that would be a lot of work. And then she'd never beat TheEagle, or finish school.

She wished that she could walk up to Plymouth Hoe and find the great wall of her dream; she'd scale it and land on a druid and watch as his body shattered into dust. She wished she could summon the right spells to ride the elephant, to enhance her energy, to turn all of those in her path into nothing but smoke and sighs. She wished she could use her body instead of just her fingers to finally feel powerful.

I feel hopeless. Literally, all hope has been lost. Because they weren't a normal family and she didn't really belong, even at home.

I think everyone feels lost during these crisis years, she mused. *They should name it something; there's the mid-life crisis, but this is when we have to decide who we want to be for the rest of our lives.*

She texted her dad. He didn't reply. She thought about calling her mum, but she definitely wouldn't be awake.

I can't just sit here all morning, Flora finally thought, feeling adrenaline spark up again in her veins. It was becoming a bit much: school and Jen and Arlo and now Abbie and the new baby.

Flora: I can't do it. I need a break.

Mrs White: That's fine, Flora. You take as long as you need to feel sane again.

CHAPTER THREE
INGÉNUE

Plymouth Hoe was serene in the cold morning air. The early sun glinted on the water, creating diamonds that rolled around on the navy palm of the ocean. The September grass glittered with dew, not yet muddied by deep winter, leading down to jagged boulders of rock and a brief slip of granite sand. Somewhere, a dog barked and an owner whistled.

Flora filled her lungs: salt and seaweed and morning mist. A bird trilled a tune from the dawning orange leaves of a nearby tree.

Far ahead of her, the horizon sat in stark, dark contrast to the milky blue of the early sky. The famous Plymouth Hoe lighthouse endured proudly, its red and white stripes a colourful manmade contrast to the craggy hill, the coruscating water, the raw and beautiful world.

I can breathe. Finally.

Flora inhaled again, deeply, smiling without really realising it. On the corner was the lido, the outdoor swimming pool in which she'd spent her youth, splashing about in the saltwater while her dad chatted to surrounding mums.

The pool was a mixture of two sources, the end of the winding river Tamar and the start of the vast ocean. She liked to pretend that she could tell the difference between the river water and the seawater, but in reality, it was the seawater that she craved. She loved the sea.

She imagined living in a lighthouse one day, perhaps somewhere in Scotland.

Flora didn't think that she was the typical 'hard home life and so I'm desperate for stability' personality type, because she loved adventure. Flora had decided that nurture versus nature had collided within her and she hadn't turned out as planned. Her nature was that of an adventurer; she longed to see the world, to ditch school, to turn the excitement from her games into real-life experiences. But her childhood had introduced a need for structure, safety, routine; something she was certain wasn't a natural, born part of her.

Either way, it was this level of introspection that led her *towards* anxiety, and not away from it.

Shut up, mind.

In the time that she'd stood by the lighthouse, the sun had already made a significant climb from the horizon, working its way upwards, bathing the sparkling sea in a pink glow. A row of houses along the water started to reflect the light in their windows as if they'd woken up, their previously dull eyes filling with wonder and illumination. Flora imagined all the different lives taking place behind those windows.

"Oh, hey." She was awoken from her daydream by a newly familiar voice. She spun around and there, wrapped in a leather overcoat, still wearing his flat cap hat, was the boy from M&S. He was grinning, looking more sheepish this time. He scratched his nose. "It's you again!"

"Have you been following me?"

Don't be a narcissist. The world doesn't revolve around me.

"Of course not, idiot," he said, laughing, his almost feline smile becoming even more pronounced. "A coincidence, a *remarkable concurrence,* as you and Tane might say."

Flora looked around. There were two police officers in the distance, their bright jackets bobbing beside the coffee stand.

"What do you want?"

"You're not very friendly, are you?"

"Depends who I'm talking to." Flora narrowed her eyes.

The boy sighed and stuck his hands into his pockets.

"I wanted to see if you… want to come and look at my boat."

"Is that a euphemism?" Flora asked, glancing towards the officers again. They were drinking coffee and talking animatedly. She was pretty sure that she could scream loudly enough to attract them, if she needed to.

"Ha, no. It's an actual boat. And like, we don't have much time, so do us a favour and come check it out? You'll like it."

Flora stared at him, this strangely dressed boy with his confident gaze and his dangling earrings and his androgenous make-up.

What have I got to lose? He's shorter than me and he doesn't seem too strong; I'd win in a fight. Besides, I can't stay here all day.

A new thought occurred to Flora. What if the police officers saw her and wondered why she wasn't at school?

"Alright," she agreed, wondering whether her brain had temporarily fallen out.

△△△

"You daydream a lot," Ritchie remarked, as they walked down the strip of concrete that separated the two grassy parts of Plymouth Hoe, passing pushchairs and skateboarders and people talking loudly into their phones. The day was bright now, the sun beaming out the last days of the September sunshine, and the noise of people was finally louder than the noise of the water. "Are you an only child?"

"No," Flora said quickly. She was always aware of the stigma that befell singular children. She was so aware of it that she went out of her way to share food with people, to not act spoilt. "My step mum is just in the hospital giving birth, actually."

"Wow," Ritchie exclaimed, eyes alight. "That's so cool."

Flora smiled. If it were anyone else that she were talking to, they'd probably be horrified that she was out strolling in the sunshine, instead of on the phone to her dad, the hospital, building a cot or laying out baby clothes.

"Mind you," Ritchie said, as they walked around the walls surrounding Plymouth's Royal Citadel, a historic fortress that Flora had only visited once, "it ties you down I suppose?"

"What do you mean?"

"Like, you have to stick around I suppose, having that baby around?"

"Well, Dad's there. Also, I feel like they want to turf me out of my room so that they can turn it into, like, a baby paradise."

"Oh cool," Ritchie said. "Hopefully."

She looked at him, confused, assuming that he must have misheard her. The slight wind was whipping around the walls of the citadel, taking some of their words with it.

"What's this boat called then?" Flora asked, raising her voice. The morning air was cold on her tongue.

Before replying, the boy looked around, evaluating who was close enough to hear them, his eyes becoming more excited, more cautious.

"Poukai," he whispered, his voice only just reaching her.

"Poukai," she repeated, trying the name out. She liked it.

"It's the name of a huge, formidable bird," he said, his voice still low. He rubbed his nose again, as if warming it up.

"What's your name, by the way?"

"My real name? Frances."

"Oh, that's funny."

"Why?"

"Well, it's funny that there are all these stories of Sir Frances Drake playing bowls on the Plymouth Hoe, and here you are. Our very own Frances on Plymouth Hoe."

"Oh right." He shrugged. "I had no idea."

"You're not from around here, are you?"

"Meh. Anyway, we have another Frances who keeps his

first name, so they call me Ritchie. It's my surname."
"Ritchie?"
"Yep."
"Cool."
"I'm glad you're coming, Flora."
"Right." She glanced at him. "And why's that?"
"We need you."

△△△

As they neared a series of jetties, hundreds of masts and flags and salty brown rigs grew from the ground. Flora realised that she was now, officially, skipping school. 9 am had been and gone and the school rush had subsided on the pavements. Now there were only parents, wandering home with buggies and takeaway coffees, and retired folks, setting off to watch the sea.

Flora knew that she should be feeling guilty, but instead she felt light, as if she were a balloon travelling high up into the sky. She wouldn't have to deal with Jen or think about exams or eat the watery broccoli in the school café. She'd miss assembly, which was a shame because that hour of the week was usually the most informative part of her whole life.

On the other hand, she felt like she could breathe. And she felt a bit like she had an interesting friend outside of Stu from Bolton, which was a positive life step.

"Don't you have school to get to?" she asked Ritchie. He was leading her past rows and rows of boats. There was a sunny silence over the whole place. Only a few of the vessels had accompanying humans, washing and fixing and emptying huge hoses. They didn't cast a glance at Flora.

If it wasn't so sunny, it might be a bit creepy here, she thought. All those masts raised like rib cages towards the sky, the sound of a thousand rusty hinges moaning on the breeze. But the sun expelled any sense of darkness, any sense that you could get murdered here and no one would hear.

"I don't go," Ritchie said, as if it were obvious. "I stopped a few years ago. It was a rubbish school, actually, over a thousand of us and they had to check us with metal detectors on the way in, in case we had contraband. And the teachers all hated it and left to go and work in the countryside, so the only ones left were the teaching assistants who *had* to be there, and they didn't know anything about real life. You know?"

"Not really." Flora was alarmed. It sounded a world away from her small school on the outskirts of Plymouth, where the worst that could happen was the polytunnel falling over. "Where was it?"

"North London." It was only now that he'd said as such that Flora suddenly heard London in his vowels. It also might explain the hat, she thought, wondering if she was being xenophobic.

"Wow, so, what, your family bought a boat and moved here?"

"Sort of," he said, sounding cheerful enough. She was glad; it seemed like a much better life for him here, working on the seas, than he could have had. Even if he didn't go to school. She wondered how his parents were getting away with that. Perhaps he was home-schooled. "Mum used to text into the radio every day, you know?"

"As in, to win competitions?" Flora asked, confused.

"Yeah," Ritchie said, as if that explained anything.

To the right of the jetty there was a shadowed cliff, jagged and white, that saw the start of the long wooden boards that eventually formed the walkway over the water. By the cliff, the land was littered with rubbish and rubble, sporadic weeds daring to grasp towards the light at the end of the shadows.

Flora only noticed this darkened part of the jetty because a movement caught the corner of her eye. She turned her head and squinted towards the cliffs. It was difficult to see with the sun shining brightly outside of the shadows, but she discovered a man in the shadows, leaning casually against the rock, legs crossed in front of him.

He was watching them.

He was wearing a baseball cap and reflective sunglasses, which caused a tiny pinprick of ice blue to dance in Flora's vision. She squinted harder and had time to glance a huge scar down one side of his face, pulling from the bottom of his sunglasses to his neck, before he swiftly pulled the cap down further and got out his phone.

As if he's telling someone that we've arrived.

"Here she is," Ritchie announced proudly, as they reached the end of the wooden walkway.

Flora looked up and gasped.

CHAPTER FOUR
EFFLORESCENCE

In front of them was a real, proper pirate ship. Not just a lacquered black replica, the miniature type that you might find in a museum, but the real thing; a towering, intricate ship of creaks and sighs, squares and circles, sails and nets.

The flags billowed and the mast stretched up towards the sun and the smell of salt and tales of the sea leaked from the gaps along the pockmarked wood.

There were ropes. Tens, maybe hundreds, of them, hooked to great iron rungs on the sides of the vessel, throwing themselves up towards the masts, dangling over the sides, as if the boat had been dipped into a huge spider's web.

"Wow," Flora whispered, rooted to the spot.

Wow didn't quite cut it. Lattices of rope were wrung together to make a towering hammock-like ladder from the floor of the boat up to the standing platform towards the top of the main mast. Painted black metalwork hung the parts of the ship together; great hulking bolts and flat metal plates. The paint was peeling, showing rust, flecked with orange, which made the overall effect even grander.

In the side of the boat were three man-made holes, where cannons would have once protruded, attacking enemy ships and keeping Poukai from mutinies. Only one cannon now remained, peeking meekly out of its jagged wooden cell.

Below this weapon and to the right was a ladder. A rickety wooden ladder, propped precariously between the walkway of the jetty and the main body of the ship.

"How big is this thing?" Flora asked.

"Our main mast is sixty feet tall," Ritchie said, strolling up to the ladder, his impish face smiling as if it were his handiwork, "see up there, where the ratlines take you to the crash deck? There are more than two miles of lines, that's all these ropes you can see," he pointed up towards the neat lines that seemed to be holding it all together, "and it's eighty-five foot long. A great size for nipping around in, not too big."

"Not too big?" Flora repeated, looking up at the imposing boat, so dramatic against the cornflower-blue September sky. "Ritchie, it's huge."

"Trust me, some of them are double that." Ritchie shrugged. "The merchant ships; you want to see those. We're a discovery vessel; much smaller, much quicker. Wanna come up?"

Flora wasn't sure. She absolutely wanted to try something new, but the ladder looked as if it wouldn't take a lot to fall over and, if not kill her, at least give her serious brain damage.

Is that ladder even legally safe?

She remembered Ritchie telling her that she was in her head too much.

"We don't invite tourists over, Ritchie," a voice said in a light American twang. Flora looked up to see a girl leaning out of the cannon hole, cigarette in hand, eyes fixed on the horizon. She blew a plume of green smoke into the air, where it hung.

Flora felt as if she'd been dropped into the ocean. Her heart fell into her feet; her throat seemed to snap closed. *Wow.*

The girl leaning out of the hole had a short shock of white blonde hair, strong eyebrows and huge blue eyes. She had thick pink lips and a toned bicep, which showed the hint of a spidery tattoo on her shoulder. Her clear gaze reflected the sky; her flawless skin had the slightest hint of tan.

She was stunning.

"Flora's not a tourist," Ritchie replied, his voice slightly meeker than before. He grabbed the ladder and it swung slightly on its feet. "She wants to join us. I've found some fresh blood."

"Oh really? She *wants* to join?" the girl said, and she ripped her eyes from the horizon and looked down at Flora. Her eyes were a brilliant blue, her hair the whitest blonde. Distracting Flora momentarily from both of these things was her nose, which had clearly been broken and reset badly, casting a box-shape shadow across her cheek. She looked a little older than Flora, but only by a year or two. Flora closed her mouth, but couldn't rip her eyes away.

Who is she?

Flora tried to work out what the girl had meant by her inflection on the word 'wants'; did she suspect that Ritchie had lured her here under false pretences, or was she suggesting that Flora had audacity in merely wanting to join?

The girl shifted and Flora could see that the tattoo was the bow of a ship, poking out from under her plain white vest. Below this, she wore a baggy pair of jeans. Her burgundy Doc Martin boot was hanging down by the side of Poukai. Her sock had a colourful flag badge pinned to it: pink, purple, blue.

She waved her hand towards Flora, the hand holding the cigarette, causing a spray of ash to fall through the air like fairy dust. "How come, New Girl?"

"Broken family," said Ritchie, before Flora had a chance to talk. The whole ship was rattling. Rattling and yawning and creaking in the breeze, the water making low slapping sounds against the stern.

"Are you talking about my family?" Flora asked, registering what Ritchie had said just a moment too late. She'd been distracted by the noises and the girl.

"Yeah, course," Ritchie replied, for all the world as if he wasn't casting huge aspersions on her life with very little information.

"I've no idea what you're talking about," Flora snapped.

"There's nothing wrong with my family, and I'm certainly not joining you, if by joining you, you mean coming to work for you on a tour ship. I have school and we're not all lucky enough to get home-schooled on a boat."

Silence would have followed her words, if not for the creaking, groaning noises of the ship, matching the pace of the wind.

"Home-schooled?" said the girl in the cannon hole, her lips creeping up into a half smile. Her eyes, now properly focused on Flora, started shining wickedly. Flora looked so bewildered that the other girl couldn't hold it in any longer. Her laugh cackled out into the air, loud, hysterical, followed by a hacking cough that saw her withdraw into the boat.

Where did she go?

"Well, that's what'll happen if you smoke," Flora muttered. She reached up to check that her hair was playing ball, or at least not as mad as it could get. That girl had been astonishing.

"You aren't half judgmental, are you?" Ritchie asked, one eyebrow raised, disappointment dragging his lips down by a few millimeters. He sighed and scratched his head as if he'd just lost a bet and half of his money in the process. "A righteous daydreamer."

"I'm not judgmental," replied Flora, feeling on solid ground again, even if his words stung. Of this, she was sure; she'd gamed against people from all walks of life and knew better than to cast any stone of judgement.

People smoking was different; it was a literal health risk.

"She's not even smoking a cigarette," Ritchie said, turning his attention back to the ladder and scraping it against the side of the boat until it felt secure. "It's just some weird spices she picked up when we stopped in Shanghai."

"You went to Shanghai?" Flora's eyebrows flew up. She'd assumed that the boat was a bit of a gimmick.

Sure, it looks great, but surely it couldn't cope out on the open ocean?

"Yeah, although it was a right pain to moor up. We paid a fortune and then had to leave sharpish, but Lana managed to raid the local market. Nearly had to leave her behind, mind. And meanwhile, McLarty was getting some kind of fire throwers."

"Fire throwers?"

"He's a pyromaniac," Ritchie said, matter-of-factly. "And Lana's Captain, so we couldn't leave without her if we wanted to."

"That girl is the captain of your ship?" Flora asked, wondering if Ritchie was constantly making jokes. It might get tiring.

"Yeah, why? Women can't be captains?" Ritchie swung onto his side on the ladder so naturally that it looked as if spent his life there.

"Not at that age, they can't."

"She's seventeen." Ritchie nodded, pursing his lips and raising his eyebrows as if to say that seventeen was equivalent to seventy. Perhaps it was, in boat years. "Fifteen when they got the boat. How old are you?"

"Sixteen. Seventeen in a few weeks."

"Nice," Ritchie said, showing no reaction, as if age was as interesting as watching planks dry. "So, are you coming up or not?"

Flora was still undecided and stinging from his comment about her coming from a broken home. Flung out so casually, it was as if her upbringing had been condensed into a strapline for strangers.

Flora Brock, Broken Home.

On the other hand, she was curious to see the rest of the boat, and not going on board because she was annoyed at Ritchie was a bit like cutting off her nose to spite her face.

"Fine," she shrugged, as if it were no big deal, as if her heart wasn't already pounding a chorus at the idea of climbing up that rickety ladder, the one Ritchie was jauntily swinging up, pulling each of the feet off of the floor for a millisecond with each hop. "How do I get up?"

"You not climbed a ladder before?" Ritchie called down. He'd arrived at the top now and was looking down at her with his face cast in the shadow of a sail.

"Err...no," she admitted, casting her memory back. They did have a loft, but she'd never been up in it. Mostly, her dad went up there to get the Christmas tree down and then to put it back up again in January. She'd never felt compelled to go exploring the cornucopia of spiders that lay in wait.

"Wow, you are a weird one," Ritchie called down, for all the world as if he didn't live on a pirate ship.

"Just help me, will you?"

"No problem, boss. Just literally climb it, and I'll hold the top, make sure you get up here."

She did as she was told, but the wood shuddered under her hands and the rungs didn't feel secure under her feet. It took her at least a minute to climb each rung, and when her shaking feet met on the same rung, she had a mild panic that the rung would break, and she didn't have a free foot to save her.

Eventually, she made it to the top, which was even worse because she had to leave the relative safety of the ladder to climb onto the wooden floorboards, but at least Ritchie was there to grip her arm.

"You're crazy." She rubbed a sweaty palm through her mass of hair.

Screw ever going back down. I guess I'm staying on the ship forever.

"It's not that high," Ritchie said, and allowed himself to laugh, straightening up and snorting. "You'll see; you'll be sliding down it in no time."

She ignored this comment. Once again, he seemed to assume that she was looking for a new job, a new life. And life aboard a ship, working all day touting tickets to tourists and presumably doing her school classes when the ship wasn't open to visitors, did not appeal to her. She knew she should probably get a job, should look for waitressing work or similar, but the idea of trying to fit that around her revision and exams made her mind go numb.

It just doesn't sound particularly exciting.

CHAPTER FIVE
IMBROGLIO

On board the ship, she could appreciate that it didn't seem quite as enormous as it had from the ground. Nearby, the wheel squealed like a pig.

"Where's your family?" Flora asked. She had been half expecting to see Ritchie's mum or dad or responsible carer wandering about, cleaning the floorboards or whatever one does on a tourist ship during downtime.

"They're getting supplies in town," Ritchie said. "Except Tane and McLarty who have to hide, and Lana. She wants us to leave Plymouth ASAP; she's getting annoyed that we're all having a good time here. Some of the others go home for the summer, so it's been pretty lonely, but this is our last stop. It was supposed to be a quick one, but it's been hard to… track down everything we need. And Bell's grandma died. We really lucked out that it was during Summer."

"What?" Flora asked, feeling as if she was getting whiplash from all of the random information that Ritchie piled on.

"Well, we were heading back anyway to get the Summer losers."

"Summer losers?"

"The people that had to go home for Summer. It's a pain, pretending they're at boarding school just because they have like… family. But they're the important ones, so Tane was pretty insistent that we bend over backwards and create this like, fake school for them, which is a massive pain in the giddy ball."

"Giddy ball?"

"You'll find out," he said, dismissively. "Just a shame you've got your dad, right? It's not like Lana's mum's hassling her to go home, you know what I mean?" He laughed.

Flora stared at him for a moment, thinking him incredibly glib about potentially quite cruel statements. Like saying that they lucked out that Bell's grandma died in Summer, and that Flora was unlucky to have a dad.

She wasn't sure that she liked Ritchie.

"Err, no," Flora said, eventually.

"I think you do," Ritchie said, flashing her a deep look that she couldn't decipher. She decided that it would be easier to let everything that Ritchie said just flow over her, rather than try to understand.

Flora looked out at the masts waving in the breeze, the billowing sails, the huge steel and wire breakwaters that had been built to manage the currents and form a safe haven for the vessels. Yachts and sailboats and even little rowing boats bobbed in the morning breeze, nodding awake above shoals of silvery fish and billowing crisp packets.

"How long have you been moored here?" Flora asked, remembering that 'moored' was the correct word. She'd been brought up by the sea; she'd picked up a few words that would allow her to sustain a very basic seafaring conversation.

"Five days," Ritchie said. "We're leaving the day after tomorrow. It helps us to buy food and keep busy, but they don't like to stay too long in one place. We usually avoid the UK and the US in case we're found."

"Who avoids them, your parents?" Flora asked, feeling like she wasn't learning any more about Ritchie's life as time went on. If anything, she felt like she knew less about him now than when they first met. Did he say that he didn't have parents, or was that someone else? Who were the people who definitely *did* have parents?

Her skull was starting to pang.

"Lana and Tane. They run the show. Captain and boat owner."

"Interesting jobs," Flora mused. They weren't quite the academic jobs that her school hoped that she'd get. They were already talking about Oxford or Cambridge, hinting to her that she should do something in IT or 'Computers'. They didn't understand that just because she liked to game, it didn't mean she wanted to monitor large data servers for multinational organisations. Or "upskill", as their careers advisor said. A lot.

Ritchie read her face.

"They don't just manage a ship," Ritchie said, scratching the wood next to him, his head cocked to one side so that the star swung on his hooped earring. "Tane's rich. Mega rich. You know Esmerelda Nuku?"

"The artist?"

"Right. She's like his great, great-grandmother or something. He's Tane Nuku."

Flora stared at him for a moment, before subconsciously nibbling at her lip until the iron taste of warm blood met her tongue.

Esmerelda Nuku had been a hugely successful artist. Flora had studied her work in art class and had tried to replicate her impressionist coves, her wild seas, her plumes of stars. She'd seen those pictures on phone cases, t-shirts, calendars. Her name was up there alongside the likes of Pablo Picasso, Vincent Van Gogh, Frida Kahlo.

Esmerelda had been obsessed with the sea, Flora remembered. Even in her stills of apples and fireplaces, their art teacher had taught them to find the echoes of the ocean's waves, the undercurrents of blue and teal and reckless foam.

How funny then that her great, great grandson now works on the sea.

"Why does Tane need to work then?" Flora asked, wondering why such a famous and presumably rich boy would need to come and work on a tourist boat. She licked a fleck of blood from her lip. *Tane's family would never bite their lips until they bleed.*

"Work? Where?"

"Here, on the boat. Selling tours…" Flora trailed off in response to Ritchie's quizzical face. She might have made some massive assumptions.

"We don't sell tours," Ritchie said, finally, and he rolled his expressive eyes and let out a manic burst of laughter. "You're a funny one, Flora Brock."

Had she told him her surname?

"A funny one indeed."

△△△

"I've gotta go find them."

"Find who?"

"Lana and Tane. He'll be in the Captain's Cabin." Ritchie suppressed a yawn. His burst of energy had taken the life out of him. He wandered towards an aged cabin, scratching his head through his greying hat, yanking up his dirty trousers using his studded belt

What on earth?

Left alone on deck, Flora took a deep breath, feeling the air from the river Tamar and the swell of the ocean mix in her inflated lungs. She breathed out and looked around, at the creaking mast, the dark, stained floorboards, the spindles that wound up into railings, old and yet new, rough and yet smooth, historic and yet flecked with chewing gum.

Excitement was growing inside her, whether she liked it or not. This might be the most exciting thing that she'd ever done. She'd skipped school and was standing on an imposing pirate ship. Flora had a sudden urge to throw herself off the back of the ship and into the harbour water, something she'd do if she was an avatar.

She suppressed the urge.

This boat is insane, she thought, then admonished herself for not thinking of something more eloquent. What would Mrs White, her Head of Year, say?

What a fine example of historic craftsmanship, probably. Or *This boat is the very definition of freedom. Freedom in the form of a hull, stern and mast, which took our forefathers to countries unknown.*

Or possibly none of those things. Flora admired the older woman deeply but couldn't admit to knowing her terribly well. What would Abbie say?

Uh, nice ship, but, like, it's really cold up here.

She walked over to a big square hole in the boards, where a trap door had been thrown open and pinned down. A set of stairs descended into the dark underbelly of the ship. Flora saw movement in the dark room below. Lana.

Flora's phone vibrated.

It was her Dad. She answered it without thinking about the fact that she was supposed to be in school.

"Dad?" she said, shouting slightly over the sound of the ropes, which were flinging themselves around in the breeze and causing a loud dinging where they met the iron rings.

"Flo?" he replied, his voice sounding far away and exhausted. "We're at the hospital, I've just popped out to call you. Where are you?"

"I'm, ah, just on the field," Flora replied, referring to the huge playing field behind their school. "We're doing Sport."

"Right, ok, I don't want to distract you from your class," her dad said, still sounding weary, and she wasn't sure why he'd phoned during the school day if he didn't want to disturb. But then usually she had her phone on Do Not Disturb; perhaps he was planning on leaving a message.

"I phoned to tell you that the baby has arrived safely and both mum and baby are doing really well. It was a short labour, just five hours, which the midwife said was very unusual for her first time, so I couldn't be prouder. It's been smooth sailing, as things go, and we're hoping that we'll be released today."

"Released to go home?" Flora asked, seeing Lana moving around at the bottom of the staircase, dragging a huge sack behind her.

"Yes, hopefully," her dad replied. There was a long silence during which Flora watched Lana walk back and drag another sack, before she remembered that she didn't yet know the sex of her new sibling.

"What was it, a boy or a girl?" she asked, wondering whether her dad found her horrifically rude.

"A boy," her dad said, his voice gaining in momentum and emotion, "and we've called him Albert. Well, Abbie has, it was her choice really; that was her uncle's name, and she likes that we're all A's: Andrew, Abbie, Albert."

And Flora.

"Wow, that's great news, Dad. A boy, you must be so happy."

"Absolutely," her dad replied, but his voice had grown tight. "Anyway, I'd better get back inside, but see you tonight. Oh, and while I remember…"

His voice trailed off, but Flora didn't notice as she'd crept down onto the first stair to watch Lana from a better vantage point. The older girl was zipping hundreds of strings into a sack-like bag. She worked neatly and methodically, zipping up each bag and then hauling it to the part of the room that was under Flora's feet.

Lana didn't look up, even though Flora's silhouette must have been obvious. Her beauty, in all of its angry glory, was distracting, even though Flora could barely see her in the gloom.

"Dad?" Flora muttered when she realised that he'd stopped talking.

"Where the hell is Tane?" she heard Ritchie ask from somewhere.

"Yes, sorry, I was just looking at- no, never mind. I was going to say that I think we might need to borrow your bedroom for a little while, just for a changing station. You can still sleep in there, but we need to move your computer for a while and put the nappy bits there, a changing mat and things."

"Move my computer?" Flora asked, scratching her scalp. "But how am I supposed to game?"

Lana looked up at her then. Their eyes locked and they stared at each other for a long moment. Flora felt her face start to burn, as Lana's eyes melted from confused back to indifferent. Flora coughed and spoke into the phone again. Lana looked away.

"That's fine, Dad. Of course, it is. You guys use it for your changing station, and I can always put my computer in the living room, and move the old fish tank out of the way."

There was a huge, empty fish tank in their living room which her Dad had bought Abbie one Christmas, with promises that they'd fill it full of exotic, colourful fish. He'd found it cheap on Gumtree and was so excited about the price that he'd forgotten that Abbie hated fish. She didn't like to eat them or look at them or even talk about them, with their big blank stares and their gasping mouths.

"Yeah, let's see, shall we? I'd better pop back in now hon, but you give me a call if you need anything, ok? I can't answer, but I'll check my phone for messages when I can."

"Ok, I will do," Flora started to say into the phone, but her Dad had already hung up.

She looked at the blank screen for a minute, processing everything. She had a new brother, called Albert. She had to move her computer. Her bedroom was going to stink of nappies. Lana clearly hated her. She didn't have anywhere to game.

It was a lot to take in.

"New Girl, can you help move the hammocks somewhere people won't trip over them?" Lana called up. Flora realised that Lana had been watching her.

"Sure," she replied, wondering whether she liked that

Lana was calling her "New Girl".
    She decided that she did.

CHAPTER SIX
DALLIANCE

Flora gingerly stepped down the stairs, which were much sturdier than the ladder had been. She felt nervous being in such proximity to Lana, as if she might trip over her own feet and vomit at the same time. Energy crackled through her.

She descended into a long, dimly lit room. The scent of salty driftwood hit her face. She breathed in deeply by default. It smelt like Autumn Saturdays, wandering down to abandoned beaches to see what had been washed up on the craggy bay, collecting fanned ivory shells, straggles of seaweed, mermaid purses.

The lengthy room played host to dark wood floors and dangling candelabras. Thick pillars were studded down the centre, holding the ceiling in a low bow. Trickles of daylight wove through the cannon holes, playing on a mess of bedding that was strewn across the floor. Dotted around the huge room were hammocks; big spidery mounds which Lana had been in the process of zipping into canvas bags.

"It's three to a bag," Lana said, dragging one of the hammocks over to add to a small pile she'd built. Lana's voice was American prep school interspersed with disdain.

"Ok," Flora replied, still feeling embarrassed that she'd been caught getting upset about not being able to game. She hoped Lana couldn't see her burning cheeks, her shining eyes. She bent over and started folding. "Do you do this every day?"

"When we're out, yeah. Some of the others are messy as anything, it's a real battle."

"Right." Flora couldn't get her head around the fact that presumably the family slash crew all slept together in the same room, in hammocks.

Who are they?

After a few minutes, she realised that she was glad to get stuck into some physical labour, to prove that she was more than just two thumbs and a penchant for pixels. Subconscious bias, she noted, hating herself for putting words to other people's assumed judgements.

Not that she cared what Lana thought.

Flora threaded her hands through the hammocks as she dragged, pulling them on top of one another and then rolling them up deftly, before collapsing each stringy sausage in on itself. Her hands shook as she zipped up the first bag.

"Nice," Lana commented, watching Flora's hands, which were struggling to manage the zip, conduits of the tension.

"Thanks," Flora said, her throat scratched by the word. She was glad for the dimness of the room, for the lack of electric bulbs.

Lana flashed Flora a genuine nod of approval, and she let out the breath that she'd been holding. The room felt too dark. She was glad of it.

After zipping up three bags, much of the awkwardness had melted away, and when they eventually got to the last few hammocks they knelt side-by-side, rolling the pile, their hands inches apart. Lana's fingers were laden with rings. Flora wanted to reach out and run her fingertips over the shining silver. She breathed hard and resisted.

If I just moved my hand an inch to the right...

She could barely breathe; she felt the heat from Lana's body press against her side. As they rolled the final few times, they both shifted position and their hands brushed each other's; Lana pulled her arm back as if she'd experienced an electric shock.

They looked at each other and Flora felt her forehead burn, her throat go shockingly dry.

"So, what's your deal?" Lana asked, as if she'd been thinking it through and couldn't hold it in any longer. She sat back on her heels and cleared her throat. "It sounds like you have a really nice parent. And what, you can't play computer games anymore? So what? You're just gonna run away?"

"I'm not, ahh, running away from home," Flora stuttered, kneeling and then standing up, patting her sides. "What, no. No, definitely not running away." She felt her face become a positive beacon in the dim light; a huge red orb that would distract ships at sea.

Lana zipped the last of the hammocks into a bag, her hands steady, and Flora wondered why her own hands were shaking so badly.

"Running away and protecting yourself are two very different things, to be fair," Lana said, as if to herself. She cleared her throat. "So, why are you here?"

"Why would me being here mean that I'm suddenly running away?" Flora countered with a question of her own. She'd briefly joined the Debate Club at school, before deciding that she hated public speaking. In the few sessions that she'd been involved in, she'd learned a valuable lesson; when she couldn't answer a question, she should ask a question.

"All of us are running away from something," Lana drawled. "Much as we try not to admit it, or to pretend that we're actually running *towards* something."

She dragged the bag of hammocks to the staircase and then lifted it atop a pile.

"What's Ritchie running away from?" Flora asked, feeling oddly desperate and not liking the distance that Lana had put between them, as if she'd said something wrong. She reached out to one of the towering wooden poles that were dotted through the room. The wood felt as if it had been ravaged by savage beasts.

"As if I'd tell," said Lana, flashing Flora a look.

She hates me.

"So, you're all runaways? A group of runaways who are working on a boat?" asked Flora, trying to summarise the situation. Knowledge meant power. The more she could understand, the more she felt in control of the situation. The situation meaning the very real and bizarre place in which she now found herself; in the depths of an old pirate ship, discussing running away with the seventeen-year-old captain of a ship, when she should have been at school.

Lana didn't answer, she just rummaged around in the hammock cupboard, setting them neatly atop each other.

"Apart from Tane, right? Isn't he mega-rich?"

Lana looked at her.

"How do you know that?"

"Ritchie told me. He's Tane Nuku, as in Esmerelda Nuku. He must be dirt rich."

The sun broke out from the clouds, causing dust motes to swirl in the new light from the cannon holes. Lana's eyes were intensely blue. Flora had never seen anything like them.

"Look, if you want the middle-England life, this ain't it," Lana finally said, her voice low.

"What?"

Lana moved again then, picking up a hammock from where it had fallen off the pile. It felt, to Flora, as if a spell had been broken.

"The middle-England life. The Hula Hoops in the afternoon, sixty-inch television, saving up for a ten grand car to park in the generic driveway, orange brick, neat pavements and chicken tikka on a Saturday, lottery tickets and alarm clocks, pretend your cat's a pedigree, annual holiday to Costa del Sol, ironing your underwear, complaining about your neighbours, complaining about litter, complaining about traffic, organise your spice rack, read the Sunday papers, sit in your comfort zone, middle-England kind of life. This ain't it."

A gust of wind whistled through the nearest cannon

hole.

"Right." Flora swallowed, processing the lengthy description and wondering whether it was racist. "How do you know so much about England?"

"We've got a fair amount of you guys onboard."

"Let me guess, the wild ones?" Flora tried to make her tone sound jokey, but came off as bitter. It made sense, then, that Lana only hired the people who shirked 'middle-England life'. "Is that where you come from? Middle-America life?"

"Ha, no." Lana let out a short, bitter laugh. "My family were a fois gras on a Saturday, arguments on a Sunday, cars in the garage so the plebeians don't steal them, summers in Bora Bora, maids ironing the Gucci thongs, tight lips and thin hips special kind of unbearable."

"Oh, so you're rich?" Flora asked, wondering what fois gras was and why anyone would buy a Gucci thong.

"It's all relative, isn't it?" Lana shrugged, hooking the end of a hammock. She didn't do anything with it, just fiddled with the loop. "Compared to Tane, we were peasants."

"Did you already know Tane then?" Flora still wasn't sure how this medley of crew members had congregated, although it had become clear that Tane could easily afford to buy the boat.

"Yeah, course. We grew up together, he's the closest thing to family I've got. And same for him." Lana wound the hammock loop around her index finger. She should have been shutting the door on the neat pile, but she was staring at nothing, distracted.

"What's wrong with his family?" Flora asked, thinking that they couldn't have a whole lot of worries, what with them being at least millionaires and probably billionaires, who probably also had nice cars in the garage and designer thongs. What could possibly be wrong in a family like that?

"I think that's enough chat for today." Lana dropped the loop and closed the door, causing the stairs to shake. She pulled a packet of spices from her pocket and proceeded to roll a pinch into a paper case.

Is she annoyed?

It was hard to tell. Lana's forehead remained expressionless, her skin as smooth as an ice sculpture. Her lips were full and plump, irate and stunning.

"So, what's your tattoo of?" Flora asked, trying to turn the conversation around and show Lana that she was a genuine, interested person. Lana flicked her gaze to her shoulder and tugged her vest down slightly so that the inky bow of a ship was no longer visible.

The wood shook under Flora's fingers.

"I need to talk to the guys," Lana said, her voice all shades of lazy disdain. Without waiting for a response from Flora she yelled "McLarty, Richie, top deck," and strode up the stairs.

Flora watched her leave and felt as if a tiny part of her had been amputated. Perhaps an ear, or her little finger.

△△△

It was only because of how still she was standing and how empty the room had become that she was able to overhear snatches of their conversation. Lana had been joined by Ritchie and a morose voice that she didn't recognise, which must have belonged to 'McLarty'. They stood above her, their shoes shaking the boards of the ceiling.

"I'm not sure this is gonna work," Lana said.

"Aww come on, I like her. She's cute. And gullible." That was Ritchie.

"Trust me, Lana," the morose voice said. He sounded sad and urgent. It was an odd combination.

"It's a careful balance here," Lana muttered.

"One we have to protect," the morose guy said. "You know Tane wouldn't be able to make this call."

"Quiet, McLarty. Tane's made decisions that you

wouldn't understand in your wildest nightmares." A pause. Lana sighed. "Sorry guys, I just don't see it."

"I like her," Ritchie repeated. "She's cute."

"Yeah look, she's hot, alright," Lana said, and Flora felt her face burn. "And anyone would like her. She's vanilla ice cream." Flora felt her throat pulsate as if she were being strangled. "We don't have room for that here. We need extraordinary."

"She got into the elephant enclosure," McLarty said.

Flora felt her heart slam into her ribs.

How does he know about that?

"I think you're making a mistake," McLarty said. "I, for one, don't want to be tracked down and killed in my sleep. We need her. She's good."

"And she's hot," Ritchie said, repeating Lana's own word. Flora felt the fire from her face spread through the rest of her body.

"We don't need someone hot for Poseidon." McLarty snorted.

"What's Poseidon?" Ritchie asked, quick as a whip.

"McLarty..." Lana's voice was a warning. She ignored Ritchie. "You're lucky you're good, or you'd be out on your arse. Remember that."

"Noted." He sounded sarcastic.

"Poseidon?" Ritchie repeated, confused.

"Drop it," Lana said, and Flora could tell that her word was final.

"Fine. I had to have all that chat though," Ritchie grumbled. "Such a waste of time."

"It was McLarty's idiot idea," Lana said, flatly.

There was a scramble of ropes. The wind howled through the cannon holes.

"...seen too much?" someone was asking.

"She's seen nothing. Who's she gonna tell? The National School Board?" That was Ritchie. He snickered again. It sounded like the tines of two forks rubbing together.

We don't have room for vanilla ice cream here.

Flora didn't wait to hear anymore. She couldn't bear the thought of Lana thinking such things about her; she stormed up the stairs, ready for battle.

CHAPTER SEVEN
EPHEMERAL

She had been assigned a hammock. There were eighteen people on the boat including Flora, she'd been told, but Lana and Tane had their own rooms.

The hammock needed hanging, just five short hours after she'd rolled up the thing. After her argument, she'd been able to sit on the deck and watch the afternoon roll across the harbour.

I'll give you 'middle England life'.

Lana had looked admiring when Flora had thundered from below deck. As if she had passed. Never mind the fact that Flora had looked at all three of them with utter angst; by the end of her tirade – "You've cast massive aspersions on someone you've met for five minutes and I'm sick of it" – they were all smiling. As if they were impressed.

She would only stay one night. Give Albert the run of her bedroom.

△△△

The sea tasted different at night. Microscopic beads of salt and H20 and perhaps even grit and sand bonded into globules that pelted the side of the ship and freckled her face through gaps in the wood.

It sounded different as well. During the daytime there

had been seagulls to break up the creaks of the boat, creating a friendly – if not slightly annoying – harmony. The light had settled the swell so that an ethereal heaven-like ambience had soaked into her earlier, the kind of noise that sucks out echoes and flattens shrieks.

But now, there was nothing to dampen the noise. It felt raw, fresh, the sound of ropes on wood, of sea slapping against the sides, of iron bolts creaking in their clutches, ratlines writhing in the wind. The sea spray sounded like hell wreaking fury against the side of the boats, whispering along the flat smooth plastic of the yachts and the small sailboats, screaming within the sails.

Lana had lent her a scratchy wool jumper and she'd found a pile of other clothes in the lost-and-found. The clothes in there were all very jazzy. She stretched out her legs, which were clad in silver leggings. Under the jumper she was wearing her usual bra, the underwire missing from the right cup, and a soft band t-shirt, whose name she'd already forgotten.

The crew had called out welcomes to her, as if they'd known she would be there. A few of the crewmates were topless and she noticed that they all had the same tattoo; a small ship that looked exactly like Poukai.

"Alright, Brock?" a lanky boy with blonde curls waved at her.

"Hey," a girl with a green bangle pushed up her arm smiled, as she folded clothes into a dry sack.

"Don't act like you already know Brock," Ritchie said to the blonde boy, punching him on the arm. They both guffawed and Ritchie jumped into his hammock.

"Hello, I'm Frances," a portly boy with a smart shirt told her, grabbing her fingers. She muttered a greeting and shook his hand, feeling anxious. He seemed to have assigned himself great importance, and gave off the vibe of a Prime Minister.

They were getting ready for bed, padding in and out of the room in various half-dressed states, some with toothbrushes sticking out of their mouths, talking to each other and spraying toothpaste out onto the dark wood floor. The whole room was rocking gently, and the light of the lanterns was in continuous movement, creating long lines of shadows that jumped back and forth.

McLarty, who Flora had met earlier when she accosted the group on the deck, lay in a hammock and wrote furiously in a notebook, his black hair falling into his eyes.

A few people were eating in their hammocks. A girl with large glasses was eating a bright yellow fruit while attempting to read her book in the dim light. Another boy was licking the chocolate from the inside of a small cardboard box, which presumably had been a box of chocolates shortly beforehand.

Having established her bed for the night, she found a new toothbrush from a cupboard by the toilets and nabbed some toothpaste from a tube that was being passed around.

Toothpaste firmly on, she escaped to the toilets. Inside a cubicle, she let out a huge sigh and sat down on the toilet seat, looking at the back of the blank door, letting her mind take a break. What was she doing? Why was she spending the night on board? Could she really dip her toe into this life and then leave again in the morning?

She had to. She would wake up early and head home.

Behind the door, she could hear someone calling out to someone else and then a resounding laugh in response, and chatter as two of the crew stood in the corridor discussing something they'd seen in town that day, and then Frances trying to restore order in the large hammock room.

The day coursed through Flora's head until the adrenaline beat a tune in her arms. She closed her eyes and relived it. Meeting Ritchie in the park. Seeing Poukai. Skipping school. And meeting Lana, a young female captain with captivating eyes and a terrible soul. Her hands burned from hanging hammocks; the most physical labour she'd done in a while.

Where am I?

She pulled out her phone and searched for 'Poukai'. One

result:

> The Poukai, to this day, is the only ship in existence to have its pirate history – and treasure – confirmed. The ship – and its captain – reigned in the 17th and 18th centuries and continued until The Poukai went missing (believed to have sunk) in the mid-1800s, taking with it tens of thousands of coins that the captain was believed to have stashed. Now, there is no knowing where the shipwreck lies, somewhere in the vast ocean.

Flora felt a shiver work its way down her back, as if she were still standing on the jetty, the water dark and cold around them.

Believed to have sank.

She searched for 'Esmerelda Nuku', after 'Tane Nuku' turned up no results. A recent article topped the list:

> No news in search for Nuku-Halliday as 6-month mark approaches
>
> There has been no progress in the hunt for missing Axer Nuku-Halliday, husband of Karina Nuku, the world-renowned artist Esmerelda Nuku's great-granddaughter. Nuku-Halliday was last seen setting sail from Salcombe in the family's 2018 Azimut 72 Flybridge; a 4-bedroom, 72-foot motor yacht that cost the family £3m.
>
> Nuku-Halliday, described by wife of three-years Karina as an experienced sailor and captain, is thought to have taken the boat out alone, under mysterious circumstances.
>
> "He didn't tell us where he was going, or why he thought he could handle it on his own. We always have staff man it, you see," Karina explained in a press conference, shortly after reporting her husband missing.
>
> Karina went on to explain that she indicated to him that the winds were bad and the seas rough, but he insisted on taking the boat out.
>
> The Azimut was found drifting in the open ocean near Pico

Island in the Azores, a month after he first set sail in April 2022. Nuku-Halliday was no longer onboard, but the accompanying speedboat was missing, a sign that Nuku-Halliday might have set off for dry land.

"There are several little islands within a 20-mile radius that he could have ended up at," said a spokesperson for the family, directly disagreeing with the Portuguese authorities, who searched every inch of the Portuguese-owned land as part of a three-month search.

Although now presumed dead, Karina Nuku insists that Nuku-Halliday is a strong sailor and that her Medium is certain that he is still alive. At her behest, an army of well-to-do yacht owners and their unfortunate staff are still conducting a manhunt around the vast ocean off Albufeira, while even the UK police have conceded it a lost cause. There are rumours that a substantial prize has been offered for the safe return of Nuku-Halliday, but searches offer up no evidence to support this.

Although well-publicised, there is still no sighting of Halliday-Nuku and his smaller vessel, The Esmerelda, as the 6-month mark approaches. Is the Medium correct? Will the upper echelons of society succeed where the police weren't able to? Let's hope we find out.

Her screen flickered.

What if Tane was looking for him? What if that was the whole reason that he'd bought Poukai to begin with?

No, that didn't work. Ritchie had said that Lana had been fifteen when they got the boat, so two years ago. So, he must've already had it when his dad-slash-stepdad went missing at sea. What a coincidence.

Flora went back to her web browser and looked at the other articles. There were two articles that caught her eye, both posted on a website called ConspiracistsUnite.

Nuku-Halliday: missing or con-artist?

Although the disappearance of Axer Nuku-Halliday, new husband to Esmerelda Nuku's great-granddaughter, has had as much fanfare and publicity as Harold Holt, the missing Australian Prime Minister who famously disappeared at sea – after all, no one likes to discuss bad news – it's caught the attention of conspiracists everywhere.

So team, what do we know? That Axer Nuku-Halliday, formerly Alexander Halliday, was brought up in foster care and repeatedly thrown out of schools. By eighteen, he was living on the street, no qualifications to his name, no means of supporting himself. He got into gang crime (see New York Times reference below referring to the 'Jackeds', the gang who slaughtered a jewellery shop owner's entire family just to steal a miserable grand's worth of gold), drug abuse and gambling.

People went missing around them, bodies turned up unaccounted for, and still, Nuku-Halliday and his slippery gang seemed to get away with it every time. That might be when he started bare-knuckle fighting under the moniker Hulk Halliday.

So how did he manage to marry into one of the richest families in America? How did he manage to shirk his bad reputation of only a few years ago and become a respectable member of the US Golfing Society, an Ambassador for Children's Help US, a husband to a woman who is widely known to use a roster of Mediums to influence her actions?

Well, perhaps therein lies the answer. Karina Nuku, the wife who never adopted her husband's name, perhaps knew that something was afoot when Hulk Halliday wooed her with his tales of high society and bogus claims of knowing the US elite. All it would have taken was to pay off a few of Karina's Mediums and she would have been putty in his hands.

Certainly, Karina has had her fair share of suitors trying to woo her over the years; Gerard Butler himself claimed to have asked her on a date. But she stayed single, waiting for the one, or perhaps waiting until the spirits of the dead gave her a sign.

And then the Hulk came along.

Is he legit? Well, if an initial sourcing of his banking information is to be believed, he's managed to squander the entirety of the Nuku family fortune, to the tune of a cool $100m, in offshore investments, casinos and laundering through well-known tax evasion corporations.

The Nuku Foundation, started by Karina Nuku's famously conservative parents to fund underprivileged artistic talent, spent less than 10% of its annual revenue on charity work last year. 70% of the Foundation's income went into 'Owner and Administrative Costs'.

The money was followed, found and recorded missing, by members of ConspiracistsUnite.

Just one big transaction caused the forums to reach an easy conclusion; not long before he went missing, there was a multi-million-dollar pay-out to an untraceable offshore bank account. If that doesn't prove that Hulk Halliday's made off with what was left of the family's money, then what does?

He must be Tane's stepdad.
Flora found one final article:

> Scarface Jabez gets in on Nuku-Halliday Prize
>
> ConspiracistsUnite has been tipped off that well-known former bounty-hunter and hired killer Jabez Harben, also known as Scarface on account of the chunk of his face that a victim managed to gouge, is on the hunt for missing Axer Nuku-Halliday, following a reward for his return being released.
>
> The unknown sum is said to have been verbally promised by 'close friends' of Nuku-Halliday. It's no wonder that Scarface Jabez is on the hunt; renowned for the cruelty and torture of his target's friends and families, he is one of the most effective human trackers on the planet. Let's hope that Nuku-Halliday returns safely, before Jabez reaches any of his well-known and much-admired social circles.

Flora's legs tingled. *The man by the jetty.*

CHAPTER EIGHT
ERSTWHILE

Why wasn't there anything about Tane on the internet? Surely the news articles would drop a mention in there somewhere: "Oh, and Axer's stepson Tane is also missing." Or "His stepson Tane is living life on the high seas already." Or "Karina has now lost a son and a husband to the seas." Surely that would make a good story?

People go missing at sea all the time.

Flora couldn't sit there any longer. She made her way out of the toilet, spitting in the bowl as she went, and strode over to the staircase, ignoring the chaos and noise from the other shipmates. She flung open the trapdoor.

Lashings of black seawater rained over her; she slammed the hatch closed and ran to the same top-deck cabin that Ritchie had disappeared to earlier. She flung open the door in time to hear Lana complain: "Eccles still isn't back."

"That's not good," a boy replied. Flora tasted salt and night.

The two occupants of the cabin both looked up at Flora in unison. She was framed drastically in the doorway, a storm beating behind her. She slammed the door closed, accidentally dropping her phone in the process, and breathed in the fire, which crackled in a rusty black wood-burner. The smell of woodsmoke eased the stinging in her nostrils.

"Well, hey." The boy had his head cocked to one side, his expression curious.

This must be Tane.

He was of average build, tanned, his nose slightly large, Roman. His hair was light brown and pulled up into a bun, the rest straggling around his ears. His eyes were large, reflecting the flames of the fire, and his mouth, which was wide and full-lipped, was open in an enquiring smile. His hands were pushed into the pockets of his colourful woollen cardigan, the type that people wear to hippy festivals. He was wearing dark trousers and tattered white trainers that looked like the Balenciaga ones that Arlo trotted around in, only they were dirty, almost grey.

In fact, Flora thought, squinting to make him out in the dim room, he looked a bit like an 'After' version of Arlo, if Arlo had embarked on some Bear-Grylls style quest. Which was probably not the biggest complement in the world.

Tane slowly moved his head to stare at Flora's phone, which cast an unnatural white glow up into the corner of the room, onto a bookcase of leather-bound works which were held in place by thin rope.

"Why did you bring that thing with you?" he asked, and his voice was light-hearted and broad-brush neutral American.

"Err, hi, I'm Flora," she said, regaining her composure, feeling the motion of the sea again, the sound of the wind coming back to her. "I brought my phone so I can find my way home. It's not that easy from the jetty. But thank you for noticing."

She wasn't about to apologise for bringing a phone on board, and besides, she knew that women apologised way too easily; she'd read a magazine article about it. The article said that women should learn to say, 'thank you' instead of 'sorry'. Not 'Sorry I'm late for class', but 'Thank you for waiting for me'. In theory.

Tane didn't say anything, just stood staring at her phone for a minute, clearly thinking. When he'd come to some sort of conclusion, he abruptly stood up and his face changed entirely as he smiled.

"Hi, Flora," he said, pulling a hand from his pocket and holding it out. "I'm Tane. Everyone goes by their surnames here, but I'd rather be known as Tane."

Flora had to push Lana's sleeve back to free her hand. She shook his large, warm grasp and it was an odd moment of formality in an otherwise bizarre situation. His hand felt strong, the pads of his fingers thick, as if he were a builder or a carpenter.

Lana bent down and scooped up an empty wine glass, which she set on a hand-carved table in front of her, next to two others. She started to pour.

"Oh, I don't drink wine," Flora was quick to say.

"Really?" Tane asked. "What, any wine, even a light chardonnay?"

"Yes, even a light chardonnay," Flora replied, trying to resist rolling her eyes.

"Wow," he said, and it sounded perfect in his accent, as if Flora had been saying it wrong all these years. "Well, this ain't wine, at any rate. It's this berry thing that we make in Le Jardin. It's nice."

"Le Jardin?" Flora asked, as Tane sunk into the chair that he'd vacated. Her phone remained on the floor, the white light eventually falling to sleep.

"Yeah," he said, and there was a finality in his voice, as if that was the last he was going to say about that. "So, Brock," he leant back with his hands behind his head. *How does he know my surname?* "Why were you so hasty to come aboard our fine vessel?"

Only the back feet of his chair were on the floor.

He is a very visceral guy, Flora realised. Very physical in his movements. Not the kind of guy to hold anything back. Actually, an open book was refreshing; she found a lot of the people at her school were too closed off.

Myself included, she noted with hypocrisy.

But I'm not vanilla ice cream.

"I'm just… stopping by."

Plus, I have every intention of heading home first thing.

"Do you get the news here?" Flora asked. She was there to talk to them about Axer, to help Tane with his missing stepfather.

Tane brought the chair back down so that all four legs were placed firmly on the floor. He looked intently at her face for a moment, and then looked away, as if he'd read everything that he needed to know from her worried eyes.

"We pick up some news," he said, dismissive, the connection broken. Flora felt something inside her shrivel up. He reached out for his glass, but his eyes were looking towards the wood burner and he grasped at thin air for a moment, until he finally looked down and then picked it up for a swig.

"Well, I'm not sure if you've seen, but there's some news about your stepfather," Flora said, voice gentle, not knowing whether she should even say anything now. If he already knew, what was he doing hanging around Plymouth? And if he didn't know… well, if someone told her that her dad was missing, she could only imagine how she would react. She'd scream, howl, maybe punch them in the face. No, who was she kidding? She'd internalise it; she'd stay stock still and silent until she'd digested it in her mind, and then she'd be on her computer putting out messages everywhere, writing to news channels, using the wide-reaching span of the internet to help to find him.

Tane slowly swigged his drink and her thoughts whirled around her like their very own wind. He wouldn't look at her, and Lana was also ignoring her.

Great, thought Flora. *Two amazing, addictive new people and now neither of them will even look at me.*

"Skinner pretty much only drinks French wine." Tane looked at Lana.

Lana Skinner.

"When we were eleven my mom took us to France for Summer, and she got all obsessed with the people and the joie de vivre. And the fact that all the kids were drinking wine."

"Not all of them," Lana pointed out.

"Not all of them," Tane agreed, inclining his head towards her.

"Your mum took you both to France?" Flora asked.

"Yeah, that was before she met, well-"

"It was a while ago," Lana interrupted.

"Yeah, feels like another lifetime."

"Although not as good as this life," Lana said, examining the liquid in her goblet.

"No life is as good as this life," Tane agreed.

"The Poukai family trumps them all," Lana said, her voice tinged with bitterness, as if remembering another life, another family.

"Abso-bloody-lutely," said Tane. He also looked wistful, as if their new family had happened by requirement, rather than by choice.

"That's nice," Flora said, her voice coming out like lino spread across the floorboards. She cleared her throat. She hadn't meant to sound patronising, but she had.

"I think it's bedtime," Lana said, pointedly.

"Does Flora have a bed?"

"She can use the spare, since Lusty… fell overboard."

Flora felt her mouth fall open; she wanted to ask more about Lusty, but the pain of rejection had closed up her throat. Bedtime, just for her.

As she left the small cabin, which had two further doors going off of it – presumably bedrooms – she heard Lana speak again.

"As I said, Eccles isn't back yet, and McLarty said our target's on the move."

"How will Eccles get onboard?" Flora asked, turning, the thought suddenly hitting her. How would anyone climb aboard in such bad conditions?

"He'll bang the code onto the sternpost," Tane said, looking at Flora with interest.

CHAPTER NINE
FUGACIOUS

It felt nigh on impossible to get to sleep that night, with the rope from the hammock digging into her back and the sway of the ship causing her to rock around. The wind was so close that it felt like it was inside the ship, whipping through her hair, pulling her body in all directions. She yanked her blankets tighter around her, locking herself in musty smelling wool.

A few people started to snore, and she thought of Lana upstairs in her own bedroom, not having to listen to any of this noise. Why on earth had Lana been granted captain status? Clearly, she was more capable than anyone on board, but it was Tane's boat. Had it been a democratic process? Had they voted for her?

Tane didn't seem like the type to lead. He seemed like the class clown, the kind of guy who would drive Lana up the wall. Maybe he had, in the beginning, when Poukai first set sail.

Maybe, maybe, maybe.

Only one thing is certain, Flora thought, as her leg clamped over a fold of blanket and she found an odd, but comfortable, sleeping position. *They both know about the missing stepdad.* That had been obvious at her mention of the news, at them moving the conversation straight on. And, if they knew that he was missing, they clearly didn't care, because if they cared then they would've wanted to find out everything that Flora knew.

How strange, she thought, as the sound of the waves started to become more relaxing. She remembered the murderous look in Lana's eyes, as if she would kill the guy given half the chance.

Flora was confused, but there was always tomorrow. Tomorrow she would find out more.

And with that, her breathing slowed and she finally relaxed, down into the ropes of the hammock, the hollow belly of Poukai, which writhed in a sea of eels.

△△△

The next day, Flora woke up to commotion and yelling and whooping from up above. She had been having a weird dream where McLarty took her to an island which turned out to be a real-life replica of Pictopia, and then Axer Nuku-Halliday had shown up in the form of an eagle to try and kill them. Waking up, her heart was thudding, and she was, for once, grateful for all the noise.

Lana called instructions and Frances's voice swam in and out of her earholes. Gulls screeched. The noise of the waves had changed. They were more sporadic and dramatic, lurching the boat in great, even seizures.

Flora sat up, momentarily feeling dizzy, spots appearing in front of her eyes. She'd eaten as much last night as she could – a very healthy bowl of lettuce leaves, chopped carrots and tinned sardines with a great slab of bread and some tonic water, handed to her by Frances – but she hadn't had as much water as she knew she needed.

Despite the dehydration, Flora staggered to her feet and gripped the wooden railing. She licked her lips and the fresh sprinkle of leaked seawater on her skin burned.

She wiped her stinging eyes with the back of her hand and looked out of a cannon hole. A great growth of wilderness was looming towards her, a green boil on the ocean's surface, the dot atop a division symbol. There was still salt in her eyes and tanned sands flickered like a flame in her vision, diving into blackness as she was forced to blink hard.

It's tomorrow. I overslept and now we're on the open sea.

The thought hit her like a lead weight. No one else was in the sleeping quarters; empty hammocks swung forlornly and she could hear people yelling and stomping around above board.

Her dad must be panicking. She quickly retrieved her phone and saw that she had only one missed call from him. Odd. Without stopping to think about the fact that the boat was moving, that it looked a lot more tropical than Plymouth outside, she could only think of her dad.

He picked up on the first ring.

"Dad, I'm so so-"

"Sorry Flo, can we talk later? I'm so-" he yawned. "You know. Where are you, dya stay at Jens?"

"Err, no." Flora felt the cogs of her mind whirr. What had she got herself into? "I've got…" Outside, a gull screamed. "I got a train to stay with Mum. She err, told me to come stay, and I can do school online like during Covid."

"You're with your mum?" he asked, and he sounded slightly more alert.

"Yeah, it's nice to spend some time together, now I'm basically an adult and all," Flora said, trying to stress the point that she was about to turn seventeen and so her dad shouldn't worry about where she was and perhaps report her missing or something like that.

"It is nice," he agreed, out of the blue. "And it's so noisy here. And school are happy?"

"School are happy," she confirmed, knowing that her dad didn't really have a clue about these things.

"Have a great time then, sweetheart. Bye." And her dad hung up the phone.

Flora didn't waste time thinking about how easy it had

been to come up with an excuse; she wanted to know where Poukai had taken them. She was up on the deck in a matter of seconds, hurling through the trapdoor to join the cacophony of motion on the rest of the ship.

Her fury and confusion were put on pause as the view hit her.

An island spread out either side of them until they were the dot of the division symbol and the island was the line. Sprawls of greenery rose high into the air, where it was replaced by rock, great orange- and sand-coloured beasts rising craggily towards the sky. Beyond those were hills; pure green waves, rising up to their own peaks, as if the land had once been part of the sea and had solidified into shades of emerald and butter yellow.

The waves crashed against the outer rocks and the trees, forming a great white mist which sparkled in the daylight.

Poukai was being steered around the side of the island and after a short while, Flora saw why. An opening, only about three times the width of Poukai, was visible, and they were headed directly towards it.

"Where are we?" Flora yelled to a boy who was hanging above her, pulling on ropes with one hand, making loud whooping noises. He had one hand wrapped up in bandages, but that wasn't stopping him from swinging wildly from a ladder of ropes, his legs hooked securely in the maze of strings, as if he'd been caught by a giant squid.

"Home," he yelled back, grinning brightly, his red hair turning bright yellow in the sunlight.

"And where is home?" she yelled back, feeling her face peel into a grin of its own. The excitement was infectious, even if she had been kidnapped.

"Officially, we might be in the Azores," he called. "Or most definitely in Macaronesia. We're most likely at the edge of the African tectonic plate, but close enough to French Guiana to cause enough political rift that we get away with it. Officially, it's a national park and so no one's allowed to set foot on the island, but also officially, no one actually owns it," he explained. "And it's not on the map, so who knows? We call it Taniwha."

"Taniwha," Flora repeated, liking the sound of the word on her tongue. "Why?"

"Apparently, they hide in the ocean," the boy said, climbing down the rope using his one good hand, until he was stood right next to Flora. He smiled towards Taniwha, letting out a sound that was half sigh, half euphoria.

"How come you don't get seen by planes?" Flora asked, seeing a streak of white high up in the sky.

"They're never close enough; to them it's just another dark pinprick on the ocean. There are thousands of them. I doubt even the army knows we're here. Or Elon Musk."

Flora smirked.

"I'm Flora, by the way."

"Eccles," the boy replied, not proffering a hand, as Frances had done, but shooting her a grin, "and I doubt we'll call you that. What's your surname?"

"Brock," Flora said, his name ringing a bell, the truth dawning on her.

This is Eccles, the boy who got back late. And his hand is bandaged. What happened?

Could she really ask?

"Great, Brock it is."

"Why do you not use first names?" Flora asked, buying herself time, wondering whether to broach the subject of his injury. What happened to him? Was it the scar-faced man?

"I dunno," Eccles replied, looking genuinely confused, as if he'd never thought to question it before. He scratched his head with his bandage. "I know that we try and keep this secret thing going on. Tane doesn't want us being tracked or getting to know anyone on the mainland, so maybe he thinks it's safer to use surnames."

"Surely surnames are more recognisable?"

"I dunno, they're all pretty standard surnames on

board. Tane's is the most unusual, so he gets us to call him by his first name. Besides, no one's as good at spying as I am; I doubt anyone would figure anything out."

"Tane Nuku," Flora said, absentmindedly. Tane Nuku, who's stepfather was missing. Perhaps they should be spending their time trying to find him, or his mother's money, rather than jaunting off to Portuguese islands. Was Eccles trying to find him, perhaps, when he injured himself? It was worth trying to do some light digging. "Good at spying, are you?" she asked, catching up with him too late.

"They call me The Oracle," he said, grinning. "I always know what's going on. Always in the right place at the right time."

"Who calls you that?" Flora tried not to laugh.

"Well, no one yet, but you could be the first," he said, sticking his chest out, clearly glad to have made Flora laugh.

There was a long moment of amicable silence.

"I read that Tane's stepdad is missing." Flora tried to sound nonchalant. She desperately wanted to ask someone about Axer.

"Yeah, I heard that too." Eccles scratched his cheek. He darted a glance towards Flora before looking out again, towards the crocodile-coloured island on the sparkling ocean. "Went missing in his little boat, The Emerald or something."

"The Esmerelda. Does Tane talk about it?"

"No," Eccles snorted. "Tane wouldn't talk to me about it."

He glanced down at his bandaged hand.

"What do you mean?"

"Oh," Eccles looked a bit unsure. "I mean, I'd like it if he did. He knows that he could talk to any of us about anything. But he can keep himself to himself."

Above them, a gull shrieked.

"He's got guts though; I'll give him that."

"How come?" Flora asked.

"I mean, stealing money from your parents to buy a ship

and then taking off without a word to anyone. He just does what he wants, you know?"

The sea spray suddenly whipped up and slapped against Flora's face: a wall of ice-cold salt and squirming weeds.

"Oh... right." Flora coughed and spluttered and stored the information for later, when she could digest it properly. Her nostrils were filled with the fleshy brute of wet seaweed; when she breathed in, it burned her throat.

"Eccles," Lana called, her voice brusque, cutting through the churn of the waves. "Go and check everything's tied down, won't you?"

"Err, alright," Eccles yelled back, clearly confused. Lana caught Flora's eye and indicated for her to join her by the wheel.

Flora climbed up to stand by Lana, feeling adrenaline course through her arms. The chill of the sea spray had disappeared; she felt as if the water were hissing from her hot skin and turning into steam.

They both stood and watched the approaching island for a long moment. Flora wanted to ask about Eccles, about what the bandage was hiding, but she didn't want to ruin the mood.

And besides, Eccles looked as healthy as anything, apart from his hand. Clearly, he was fine.

"So New Girl, what do you think?"

I think you've kidnapped me and you should take me home, immediately.

The thought of demanding to be taken home filled Flora with a strange dread. She should feel scared; she should call the police and organise a helicopter to rescue her. She should push Lana overboard and take control of the wheel, spinning them right back around to Plymouth. She should call the other girl out for conning her into spending 'just one night'.

Flora licked her bottom lip, tasting crusty salt.

"It's beautiful."

I don't want to go home. Not just yet. I'll work something out tomorrow, once I've talked to Lana, seen where they all live.

"Indeed, there are much worse islands to find yourself on."

"Oh really?"

"Of course," Lana said, snorting a laugh. "Have you ever heard of Devil's Island?"

"Devil's Island? No."

"It was an old prison island, like a penal colony where they sent criminals or people who did things wrong. It was a harsh place. Something like 75% of people on the island died, and they used to put people in solitary confinement until they went crazy."

"That sounds awful."

Ok, so Lana killed the conversation.

"I dunno. Some people deserve it."

A sudden hush drowned out the noise of the waves; they were getting close to the island.

CHAPTER TEN
GAMBOL

Poukai passed majestically through the parting in the rock. Glorious turquoise sea lay in front of them, clear enough to see fish darting below its glassy surface, flashes of orange and yellow that swilled in formation. Other bird noise interrupted the gulls, filling the air with exotic squawks and slow 'brr' sounds.

As they passed between two towering formations, Flora noticed patterns and carvings, huge wooden pillars that had been erected and then painted in an array of vivid colours. Giant eagles with rectangle wings, square jellyfish, a roster of ships in all shapes and sizes. Flora could have examined them forever, but Poukai didn't slow, and they were soon past the murals.

They had arrived into a huge round lagoon; a circle where sand met vivid blue ocean, where a cacophony of trees and shrubbery and enormous, colourful fruits leaned down the mountainside towards them. Gigantic, feathered leaves swayed in the breeze. Vast faces of rock shot up into the air like pointed fingers, littered with tree roots and branches and towering trunks.

The landscape was every shade of green imaginable, and yellow, and rusty copper, and fuchsia. The smell of tropical fruits washed towards the boat on the back of the ocean breeze. Heat rose from the flat rock surfaces, distorting the air so that it glittered.

The whole island sparkled with an electric current under the gaze of the sun: moving, swaying, alive.

Nirvana.

"Don't get me wrong," Eccles said, seeking Flora out again, as if he'd forgotten something. She'd left Lana to steer and now stood at the bow. She couldn't stop staring at the lagoon, the island, the wild colours that moved in the breeze like flags. Actually, there *were* flags. Colourful flags in all colours, from all countries, some patterned, some plain, hung from the trees nearby, tattered and flowing and proud. "I'm super grateful that he's taken me on. We all are. I've been stuck in homes and foster care since I was two. This is beyond my, like, craziest dreams. I was just saying, maybe he doesn't care that much about the stepdad, you know?"

Poukai slid slowly onwards, gliding through the lagoon under Lana's careful gaze.

"It's ok, I'm not going to tell him," Flora promised, unable to take her eyes off of the array of flowers that were appearing. Purples and pinks and yellows adorned the bushes and the trees, flashing like a storm of bright parrots. She could smell the trees, a verdant, fresh scent travelling along on the sea air, tinged with pine and rosemary and orange. "Does anyone live here?"

"Apart from us? Nah. Sometimes there's the occasional tourist boat, but they wouldn't dare moor up, it's too hard to navigate the gap. Plus, we're a million miles from anywhere and the sea's too unpredictable. If you're here when a storm hits, you're stuck."

Flora felt a shiver travel down her spine, as if a drop of seawater had made it into her jumper. She shuddered, imagining being stuck in a storm, trying to find shelter in all of that wilderness.

There must be caves, she thought, casting an eye around at the mass of craggy rock, rising from the foliage. *Plus, they must live here somewhere...*

Poukai passed a string of incongruous jet skis, tied to

one another and then to the trunk of a thick tree. The plastic looked harsh against the greenery. A solar panel peeked out of the bushes nearby.

"Plus, they'd have to watch out for the dinosaurs," Eccles said, and Flora looked at him.

"What?"

"Ha! I'm only joking, you should see your face." He walked off laughing, rubbing his bandage subconsciously.

To be fair, Flora thought, looking around at the rising greenery, the backdrop of marbled stone, the grey rings of cloud in the distance, *it does look Jurassic. Exactly like the kind of place where you might accidentally discover dinosaurs.*

Who knew what might be lurking behind all of that undergrowth?

△△△

"Tane sent me to get your phone," said a voice. Flora looked up to see a girl with red hair standing over her, fixing her with a blank stare.

"Who are you?" Flora asked, thinking the other girl very rude. At least everyone else had made the effort of introductions before launching into their requests.

"Hive," the girl said, not asking Flora for her name. "I need your phone."

"My phone, why?"

Flora had been asked to bring a bag of toilet rolls to shore with them, but the rolls were all stored in a foot-high cupboard in the bathroom, the one where she'd found a toothbrush. Only, the toilet rolls were right at the back of the cupboard. She was lying fully down on the floor, two hands reaching into the darkness, and she'd still only managed to retrieve five rolls, while also jostling around in very questionable stains.

"No phones on board, no phones on Taniwha. Phones

track you using GPS from your operator's network, and you can easily be found." The girl recited this as if reading it straight from a mobile phone guide, with no emotion whatsoever.

"I can just turn it off."

"No dice, Tane wants to destroy it. Location tracking can be really dangerous, one government even used it to find out who was at an anti-government protest so that they could arrest them afterwards."

"Well, no one's going to arrest me."

"Enemies might do worse than arrest you."

"What enemies?" Flora wished that she wasn't splayed on the filthy floor.

"You'd be surprised," Hive said, grimness breaking up her monotonous tone.

"Hive, leave her alone," came a voice, and Flora saw McLarty standing in the doorway, arms folded, leaning against the frame.

"It's a direct instruction from Tane," Hive replied, seeming like she had absolutely no qualms with continuing the fight with both of them.

"I can scramble the tracking," McLarty said, as if he was tired of having this argument.

"Tane doesn't think that that's an effective and accurate way of dealing with trackable electronics," Hive recited.

"Well, you can tell Tane that if my methods aren't *effective and accurate*, then he can find someone else to track his ridiculous family," McLarty replied, unfolding his arms, sticking his hands in his pockets and stalking off.

Flora watched him leave, propping herself up on her elbows and only realising after a moment that her mouth had fallen open.

"What did he mean, tracking Tane's family?" Flora asked, but Hive looked as impenetrable as a prison officer.

"Are you going to give me your phone?"

"No."

"Ok then, I will have to let Tane know."

"Fine," Flora said, turning back to the toilet roll cupboard and the depths that lay within. *Honestly, this place is worse than school*, she grumbled internally, setting herself flat on her front again so that she could delve her hands into the darkness.

△△△

Despite the inelegant start to her visit, Flora's breath was taken away when she made it back up on deck, a string sack of toilet rolls secured around her shoulder. She'd forgotten quite where she was; her mind had been full of dank and dirty cupboards.

Tropical paradise stretched out in front of her, a mass of tangled jungle and smooth beach, craggy rocks and swooping, vibrant birds.

It reminded her of the setting of *Pigeon Point Hurldown*, a game she'd played a few years ago that was set in Trinidad and Tobago. Just like the game, there were swaying brown palm trees and golden retriever sands and gentle waves washing the shoreline. Unlike the game, there weren't zombies hurtling towards her.

They were anchored up in the circular bay, the prow of the ship just touching the white sand ahead. A huge volleyball court had been built from logs and rope. Plush beanbags littered the sand. Old fishing nets were strung over branches that shadowed the sand, oscillating in the breeze.

The crew were coming and going, leaving a mass of footprints, carrying sacks and bottles and boxes and other cargo up from the ship's hold towards a path that had been forged through the palm trees. Just as someone disappeared, someone else appeared, pushing foliage out of the way, sweat streaming down their forehead, energy fizzing through the air.

Glad to be contributing something to the mass migration of everything on the ship, Flora carefully climbed down the ladder and dropped into the shallows. Warm water instantly flooded into her trainers, and she waded to the beach feeling annoyed that she hadn't first checked how close the boat was to the shore.

"You've gotta take your shoes off first," Eccles called, cackling with laughter as he hauled a carton of clanking glass bottles up onto his shoulder with his good hand. His bandaged hand stayed by his side.

"Yeah, thanks," Flora retorted sarcastically, dragging her sodden feet up the sand and following the path that that was laid out in front of her, in the form of darkened footprints.

"Don't worry, most of our shoes go into the trees for the birds. They can nest in them, see." Sure enough, Flora noticed that everyone else had shed their shoes and were walking around barefoot, seemingly oblivious to the twigs and stones and shells underfoot.

A few of them, including Ritchie, had huge bruises on the insides of their feet, and she wondered what they'd been doing. Flora looked down at her feet. Her trainers were cheap ones from a bargain bin, but they were the only shoes that she had with her and she didn't love the idea of birds nesting in them.

I'll try and dry them out.

With that sorted, Flora took the first opportunity to look at her surroundings from the ground.

The air was different on the island. Stiller, warmer, as if they'd broken into a different world. The trilling sounds of jungle birds seemed to occupy a higher level of air, as if the atmosphere was split into strata. The lagoon was calmer than the open sea, and Flora had the sense of being in a dream.

"So, this is your first time here," Eccles said, indicating that she should follow him. She fell in line next to him, his glass bottles clinking with each step. "Excited?"

"I'm not staying for long," Flora clarified, her shoes sinking into the white sand. She was still wearing the silver leggings, which she'd hiked up to her kneecaps, and the band t-shirt, but she'd left the scratchy jumper on Poukai. "I need to try and get back to Plymouth at some point, or my dad'll get worried."

Probably an understatement. Really, I should use this opportunity to steal the ship and sail back home. But that is, really, a lot of trouble.

"Your dad?" Eccles asked, confusion and squawking birds filling the air. "Why'd you leave then?"

Flora pushed a branch out of the way and continued further into the dense jungle, the sandy path giving way to matted earth. She passed several other crew members heading the other way, giving her nods and calls of "Alright?"

I didn't 'leave'. I was kidnapped.

"Nice to have you here, Flora," murmured a girl with silky black hair.

"Good job on the loo rolls," someone else said as they passed. "Did the rats not get you?"

"Rats?" Flora asked, as their back departed.

"Yeah, did no one tell you? There are rats in the toilet roll cupboard. Usually nick a few of the rolls, use them for food and bedding, you know."

"What if I'd been bitten?" Flora asked, aghast, temporarily stopping in her tracks before realising how heavy Eccles's load must be and carrying on walking, the toilet rolls bobbing on her back.

"It happens," Eccles replied. "No cases of rabies yet though."

"Great." Flora's voice was flat with sarcasm.

"Brock," a voice said, and Tane appeared ahead of her, his baggy, bright harem pants all muddy. He wiped sweat back from his forehead into a red bandana that held his hair on end. "Let's catch up later, yeah?"

"Ok," she replied, feeling as if the head teacher had just asked her to come to his office. She continued walking, kicking up a sullen storm on the path, and as she passed him, she didn't make eye contact. He smelled like musk and sweat.

When they'd walked past hearing distance, Eccles

hissed from behind her: "Why does he want to talk to *you*?"

"Probably because I won't give up my phone," Flora replied, furious with herself for just agreeing to go and talk to him. Why should she feel obliged to effectively go to his office to be yelled at? She'd done nothing wrong, and if he wanted to control his crew members then fine, but he wasn't going to control her.

"You really should, you know," Eccles said, huffing with the effort of carrying the bottles. She could hear his pace slowing behind her, but she was too incensed to slow down, until she remembered his hand.

"Can I help at all?" she asked, stopping, trying to control her annoyance and remember her manners.

"Nah, all good. I've still got a few working fingers." Eccles grinned weakly, using his good hand to hike the bag back onto his shoulder. His forehead was dripping sweat onto his t-shirt.

"Alright, well let me know if you do need anything," Flora said, wondering whether she should just yank the whole bag off him. "I know that you're injured, so…"

"Yeah, but I'll be alright soon. Hive will reset them." Eccles followed his words with a shrug. He started walking again and strode past Flora, as if possessed by a new lease of life.

She followed, shuddering at the word 'reset'. Nothing good, medically, came with the word 'reset'.

The pathway ended at a smooth, nondescript rock face. Flora followed Eccles along an overgrown trail that cut through the forest to the left of the rock, her wet shoes rubbing.

Eccles waited patiently for her as she navigated the brambles, unused to such wilderness.

"Where now?" she asked, feeling a thorn tear into her ankle.

"What's wrong?"

"Nothing."

"If you're annoyed about your phone then you seriously need to question why you need it so much."

Eccles carried on walking, taking a right and slipping between two trees into a tangle of ferns and shade. She followed, stepping over a gnarled tree trunk that had wound into a fist in the middle of the jungle floor. Croaking noises surrounded them, and the clicking of insects, and the odd squawk from birds that seemed far too close but never appeared.

"I don't need my phone," Flora huffed, eventually, about three minutes after his original statement, as she negotiated around a tangle of red berries. "It's the principle, that's all. Who says that Tane gets to decide everything that we do?"

"It's his boat," Eccles called over his shoulder. "He's a good guy, you know. He just wants us all to stay safe. Best not to go up against him."

"Oh, I wouldn't dare," Flora said, sarcastically. Although actually, she wouldn't dare, because she had no interest in running the camp, and no resources to maintain things like the boat and the jet skis and solar panels and what looked like a waterpark protruding through the trees.

"Fair. Lusty tried and that didn't go down well either."

Flora remembered Lusty's name. Didn't he fall overboard?

"Well, I don't like this dictatorship. I think we should stage a mass protest," Flora huffed, starting to really dislike Tane the more that she thought about him. Her ankle was definitely bleeding.

Everyone's running around like headless chickens, carrying all this stuff and risking getting bitten by rats so that he can have toilet roll, and what's Tane doing? Rolling around in the mud, by the looks of it. And throwing mutineers overboard. Not ideal.

"And protest what? Having our phones back? I think he's already chucked them in the sea," Eccles said, his voice reserved. It was clear that no matter how much he might not agree with Tane, he respected him.

The noise of the forest died down.

"He chucked your phone in the sea? Well, that's good for the environment. Not." Flora was glad for any additional excuse to hate Tane. Now he was littering the sea with electronics, just so that his crew members couldn't use the internet. It was like a dictatorship, this small society that she'd stumbled into, and she realised that they needed saving.

Bloody branches.

Bloody island.

"I don't know that he actually threw them in the sea, it's just a rumour." Eccles slowed his pace.

"He probably did. It sounds like the kind of thing that he'd do."

"Know him well, do you?" Eccles asked, and she could tell that he was smiling, even though all that she could see were the auburn curls at the back of his skull.

"Does anyone?"

"Lana does, I guess."

"Yes, of course, Lana," Flora wheezed, angry with the captain now, too. Angry that someone as smart and savvy as Lana could let Tane get away with it, could sit by and let him control her crew.

"You don't like Lana now either?" Eccles said, and this time he did laugh, a high-pitched giggle that was incongruous against the stillness of the jungle. It had been a while since they'd passed anyone, and Flora supposed that everything had now been collected and was on its way behind them.

"How far have we got left?"

"We're basically there. This is a short cut, but no one takes it because it's likely that you'll break a leg."

"Great," Flora replied sarcastically, blowing her hair out of her face.

CHAPTER ELEVEN
INGLENOOK

Finally, they stepped out of the dense jungle and into a vast clearing. Flora set the toilet rolls onto the crusted, terracotta earth and looked around.
Six identical huts were lined up at the opposite side of a clearing, looking like something out of a storybook. Shrubs and canes and all manner of natural objects were propped outside of each of the huts, holding them stable, marking out pathways between them, twining up the wood so that the houses almost formed part of the forest.

Flags and painted signs and totem poles and fishing nets and colourful ropes distinguished between home and tree, art and nature. In the centre of the vast clearing sat a circle of logs, clearly intended as seats, with a mess of charcoal in the centre, over which a rusty metal pot swung from a tripod.

Nearby, a wooden bowl was tied into a bamboo contraption, with tea towels waving in the light breeze. Someone had pressed bright glass into the floor around the campfire and the washing up area.

To her left - but set far back - was a larger shack with two doors, onto which the words *Privy Shack* had been roughly painted in dripping white paint.

To the right of the clearing a huge tepee had been erected, it's walls made of hessian and sacks and patterned fabrics, all sewn together. A make-shift chimney topped the array of exotic colours, out of which a gentle trickle of stream was already climbing.

The crew were hurrying around, carrying wood - which was dumped onto the charcoal pit in the floor - eking water out of a huge water butt, lighting lanterns, which swung shadows into the early evening air. They were chatting and laughing and throwing things at one another, and Flora felt a bit like being on a school playground. Only, she had no friends.

"The Privy Shack's over there," Eccles said, nodding his head towards the shed, "and you'll need to put the loo rolls in the plastic box, so they survive. I'm gonna go deliver these to The Kitch."

With effort, he heaved the bag back on his shoulder and started wandering towards the tepee, where the spindle of smoke was rising up into a hazy dusk sky.

Flora meandered in the direction that he'd indicated, passing near the huts as she went. Six wooden shacks, built in the same shape as the safari tents that she'd seen on nature documentaries, with the dim light of lanterns swinging between the panes of wood as if they were chasing her.

The Privy Shack had a small queue of people waiting outside.

"Hey, Flora," a girl grinned, smiling as if they were already best friends. Flora gave a shy smile back, and then Frances, the boy with the Prime Minister vibe and smart shirt, yelled her name.

"I'm here," she replied, swinging the bag from her shoulder and setting it down on the floor. It was fairly light, and she was glad that she'd been given toilet roll duty, in the end, rather than bottles of water or sacks of flour.

"Great, I'll take a few and the rest go over there." Frances nodded towards a bizarre looking box, which was made from all sorts of different plastic items – water bottles, frisbees, an oar, pens, all tied together with crisp packets and plastic bags. Flora supposed that this must have all washed up on Taniwha's shores and been collected by the crew. It was some ingenious craftsmanship that held it all together and made the innards waterproof, and she was quietly impressed as she opened it up and deposited the toilet roll inside.

"Who made this?" she asked Frances, as the toilet queue moved along.

"Tane," he replied. "He's pretty big on keeping the place clean and recycling whatever can be recycled."

"Right," Flora replied, not liking this response at all. She was annoyed at Tane – he was a controlling dictator. She didn't want to think of him saving the turtles.

Frances filed off to use the toilet and Flora once again felt a bit lost. She turned back towards the camp and could see that they had a full fire roaring now, spitting and hissing up towards the emerging stars. Someone was playing a guitar and she could smell spices from The Kitch tent oozing across in the evening breeze.

I am so far from home right now.

Everyone was talking to someone, whether they were gathered around the fire or sat in their huts or singing with the guitar. Everyone had someone and Flora had never felt so alone. Even when it was just her and Jen in the school café, she never felt alone. Even on the odd occasion that Jen was off sick, and it really was the odd occasion because Jen was never ill, she would go and join the quiet table who liked to read, and she'd get some homework done.

But there seemed no place for her here. She couldn't spot Eccles or McLarty. Frances was in the bathroom and would no doubt be back to bossing everyone around shortly. Hive wasn't an option; she didn't seem like particularly friendly company. Flora wasn't in the mood to find Lana or Tane, and she didn't have any energy to strike up conversation with a new group.

As her mind basked in the loneliness and the growing smell of cumin, her feet moved seemingly of their own accord, towards a rugged, narrow pathway that she'd spotted against a towering rock near the Privy Shack. She slipped away from the hubbub of noise and light and smells and felt her damp feet clutch at spiky rocks and loose stones, making her way up the narrow path to nowhere.

△△△

As she ascended what turned out to be the rocky side of a hill, motion-activated lights kept going off. They lit up various bright rockpools and man-made hot tubs, which were producing billows of hot steam, only visible under the bright blue and purple lights that appeared with each step that Flora took.

Illuminations appeared at the side of the path and each pool that she walked past lit up, inviting her to jump in. She realised that they were all connected by streams and slides, creating a huge waterfall of pools which dotted all the way down the hillside and back to camp. The walkway became a mass of stars, twinkling in mellow amber and tawny gold. Solar panels glinted from the surrounding trees, reflecting the stars.

Flora trailed a hand against the rockface as she went, pushing her body until she had to pause for breath. She looked to her right and her heart jumped into her throat.

She was above the trees. The moon was out now, a huge, full moon that turned the rippling lagoon into a bright barcode. Vying for attention, Poukai swayed, sails billowing gently, a majestic silhouette. She saw that one of the windows was lit with a blue light, far down into the bow of the ship. It looked like a computer light. It couldn't be the light from a mobile phone; there was no way that she'd see that from way up here.

Is there a computer on board?

A noise peeled into the night, a vast bird which swooped from somewhere behind her and caused her to jump. Without really knowing why, and sure that it was the wrong decision, she carried on up the path. Perhaps there was something at the top.

What are you expecting, a McDonalds? she asked herself, wryly. Although, knowing Tane as little as she did, nothing would surprise her...

Her hand trailed against the rock as she went, and it started to keep her warm as her limbs adjusted to the higher altitude. *What a time to not wear a jumper*, she thought, remembering the heat of the sun on the boat.

She scrambled up a boulder, trying to remember where the footholds were so that she'd be able to get down again later. *I'm not reliant on the adventures of others*, she thought defiantly, *I make my own adventure.*

What's gotten into me? was her next thought. She was usually pretty amiable. Shy. Loud only to her gaming friends, and they mainly consisted of Stu from Bolton, who she'd never actually met.

Why am I so angry today?

The conversation that she'd had with her dad that morning floated back to her. Not only had he not cared that she'd gone, but he hadn't seemed particularly worried that she was about to get a train to visit her estranged mother. Normally, he would insist on going with her. He knew what her mum could be like. He wouldn't want to risk Flora going alone and finding out that substances had been consumed, vicious words were about to pounce.

All of these toxic thoughts, which ran through her body like a special kind of poison, instantly vanished as she reached the top.

It quite literally took her breath away.

"Whoa," she said out loud, into the night. The view was astounding. Below her, a string of pearly blue pools were illuminated in the lush forest, creating a serene azure pattern through the trees.

The moonlight painted her a picture of a ring-shaped

island with a huge lagoon in its centre. The ring only had one gap; the one they'd sailed through earlier. Thousands upon thousands of trees thicky swathed the land, silver in the light, reflected in the edges of the lagoon.

She had an absurd urge to howl like a wolf, which she quashed. They might hear her down in camp and either be worried that they were about to get mauled by a wolf or get even more worried that they'd invited her to stay with them.

Instead, she let out a single whistle, and felt a delicious shiver run down her body as it reverberated purely in the clear air. She'd never inhaled air like it: so clean, so free from the throes of traffic and takeaways and badly laid tarmac.

Flora sat down on a jut of rock, which looked out over the whole island and beyond. The sea turned from silver to deathly black in the distance, merging into the sky and becoming constellations. Orion's belt seemed to span the width of Taniwha.

She felt free. She felt as if she ruled the world. Her chest inflated.

A voice made her jump.

"Brock, what are you doing up here?"

CHAPTER TWELVE
INCIPIENT

It was Tane, of course. *Who else would be mad enough to follow me up here?*

There was no chance that Frances would dare to make the trek in the dark. Hive was too sensible as well. Lana was too disinterested. Eccles and Ritchie, too young.

So, it was Tane that had trailed her, and she felt oddly flattered.

There aren't many people who would have made that trek at night, let alone to follow someone that they barely know.

She couldn't make out his facial expression in the moonlight, but his heavy brow looked either concerned or annoyed. Either way, he strode up to her and looked out, his gaze catching on Poukai and staying there for a moment, like a father looking at his new-born baby in the hospital.

"What are you doing up here?" he asked, eventually, ripping his eyes away from Poukai and turning his full attention to Flora.

"Why, have you come to take my mobile?" she asked, her petulant voice sounding jarring in the serene setting. She immediately regretted sounding so harsh. *What's wrong with me?*

"You need to destroy that, immediately," he said, as if he were playing a part in a film. "Seriously Brock, I'm not joking. There are people that would track me down and shoot me without a second's thought. You don't know who can find you on those things."

I didn't even want to be here and now I'm being made to feel like the villain!

Tane started pacing, his feet grinding into the rock, the noise echoing out into the still air. Flora sat shivering, staring at the moonlight on the water, wondering who on earth would want to shoot Tane. His stepfather perhaps? That could be one reason that the guy had gone missing; he was trying to track down Tane. But how far would he realistically have travelled in The Esmerelda? Not all the way to Taniwha, of that Flora was sure.

"Who wants you dead?" she asked, eventually, showing interest despite herself. She didn't want to ask him questions, she didn't want to show interest in this guy who was trying to control her phone usage. It sounded like coercive control, something else that she'd read about in a magazine.

Tane sighed, and the energy seemed to leave him in one fell swoop. He sank down next to Flora and sat, legs straight out in front of him, leaning back onto his hands.

"It's a long story, Brock. But I can't risk it, you see? Let me try this from another angle," he said, and once again Flora felt as if she were with Mrs White. "Why do you want your phone so bad?"

She stared out into the quiet evening. Cicadas seemed to be starting up an orchestra nearby, croaking out slowly into the night. Somewhere, an owl cooed. The smell of bonfire crept through the air. It tasted delicious.

"My dad. I need to stay in touch with him. I didn't even want to be here, I was going to walk home this morning. I've been kidnapped… I obviously need my phone." Flora was unsure whether this accurately summed up the situation. She obviously couldn't just go 'off grid'. Her dad would worry, he'd report her missing and before they knew it, her tracked phone would be the least of their troubles. No doubt there was CCTV at Plymouth harbour; they'd just pull that, find Poukai and send out a search. She was a sixteen-year-old schoolgirl. They would take that seriously.

It would be so easy, as well. I could call Dad right now and ask him to report me missing, to find me. It would be so easy...

"I see," Tane said, his voice gentler now, his energy somehow stiller. His legs lay flat on the ground. "Yes, we can't have him worrying. I get that. How about this; we concoct a realistic plan for why you're not home, then we work on getting you back to him asap?" He said 'asap' as if it were two words: a sap. He sounded disappointed.

Flora bit her lip, feeling her anxiety start up. She didn't know how to respond. She didn't know whether to continue with the story about her mum, maybe give her dad another call to really hit the story home. Or whether to tell him the truth. Or maybe not to say anything at all. Would he even notice?

And did she really want to go back home *a sap*? Her phone still had battery, and Jen hadn't missed her. In fact, the last picture she'd seen of Jen, when she'd popped to the toilet earlier and had opened up social media, had been her with Arlo's gang. Her school hadn't contacted her, although presumably they'd tried to get hold of her dad, who probably wouldn't have answered the phone. She didn't legally have to go to school; she could pretend to have an apprenticeship; she doubted the school would check.

What am I going back for?

There was the small matter of her nearly completing Lost Grace, which was, to be fair, a huge achievement. She didn't know anyone apart from TheEagle who'd made it that far, and she held a real chance of being one of the first people, and perhaps the first female gamer, to finish it. She'd heard of other gamers being invited to gaming conferences, being asked to represent brands, sometimes even being paid to play. Could she achieve all of that if she finished Lost Grace?

But then, why would she search for a virtual adventure when she was, quite literally, in the middle of a real one?

It was becoming a bit of a minefield and she did

something that she hadn't done in a while, raising her hand and biting her nails. Immediately, Tane put his hand out and gently pushed hers away from her mouth, as if he'd done it a million times.

"What do you think of that tree over there?" he asked, nodding his head towards the battered silhouette of a tree that was hanging right over the edge of the cliff. Despite its precarious position, its roots weren't giving way to the breeze; it looked as sturdy as any other tree.

"It's alright," Flora said, unsure where Tane was going with this. "It's a tree."

He smiled.

"The strongest tree on the island isn't that huge oak you can see over there, the one protected by hundreds of other trees. The oak that never even feels a storm. It's this one here, the one that has to stand on its own every day, who has to face the storms and the scorching sun, has to struggle for existence, all alone, every day.

But it stays standing."

Flora felt the sticky taste of bonfires coat her throat until she couldn't swallow. She blinked and looked at the tattered tree, worn but holding strong.

"Why... why are you telling me this?" she asked, but already her brain was thinking about all of those times when she felt that there was no one to catch her, when she felt as if she had to keep swimming or she'd drown.

"It just makes me think of you, that's all."

Flora blinked and felt tears trail thinly down her cheeks. Tane looked at her for a long minute.

"What is with you, Brock?" he asked, and his voice was soft.

"What do you mean?" She didn't dare to turn her head towards him. Her heart had started thrumming in her ears. She breathed in, and as she did a name burst into her mind, like brilliant sunshine. Lana.

Why am I thinking about Lana?

"You're this gamer; you like computer games and you can be all quiet and seem really introverted. And then suddenly you're yelling at Lana and scaling this mountain without a second's thought. And who knows what's out here, snakes, bats, anything… You can be really brave, really wild."

His breath created clouds of steam in the air and Flora watched as the steam dissipated and the air became inky black once more.

"So, just because I'm female I can't be like, shy and feminine, *and* a warrior?" she eventually asked, losing some of the momentum in the time it had taken her to reply. She meant it to sound condescending, but instead it sounded like a genuine question.

"It makes no difference to me what gender you are," Tane said, and Flora turned her head then, to look even further away from him. "I just want to get my mind around you. You're unusual."

"You mean, I'm not just some spoilt, rich kid?" she asked, stinging from his sentence – it makes no difference to me what gender you are – even though she really had no right to assume anything.

Get a grip, she told herself. She'd never had a crush before, and she was starting to wonder whether she might be developing two at once. *Are crushes like buses? None come for ages and then they all arrive at once?*

Well, there was Arlo. Could she even call that a crush though? He was like an annoying younger brother whose social media profile she looked at a little too much.

"Ha. Hell hath no fury like a woman scorned," Tane replied. She laughed, despite herself, liking the idea that she had wrought some form of hell upon him.

Does that make me sadistic? Perhaps.

"I'm freezing," Flora said.

"You want my jacket?" he asked, immediately slipping it off without waiting for a reply. "Why'd you come up here without a jacket?"

"I left my jumper on the boat."

"Jumper," he repeated, mimicking her English accent and laughing. "I like that. Look, you have my jacket and I've got something that'll warm up the cockles."

"The what?" she asked, accepting the heavy jacket. She slipped it on and felt as if she were in a warm cocoon. A heavy, warm cocoon. What was it made from, sheepskin and candle wax? She sunk her arms into the sleeves and had to pull them back to release her hands.

"Warm the cockles of someone's heart," he replied, reaching into the pocket of the jacket that he'd given her and pulling out a small glass bottle. She felt his hand against her side, and it felt oddly intimate. She had to remind herself to breathe.

"What's that?" she asked, referring both to the odd turn of phrase that he'd uttered and the strange dark liquid jostling about in the hand-sized bottle.

"Some kind of broad bean fermented thing from Le Jardin. Frances invented it, I have no idea what's in it."

"Is it alcoholic?"

"You know what, I don't think so," he replied, laughing into the open world. His breath created a fog. "I know it warms you up."

"Is it nice?" Flora asked, watching him take a swig and feeling oddly excited. She pulled up her legs and wrapped the coat around her knees.

"Not really. You want some?"

"Ok," she said, as if he'd convinced her, as if she weren't both parched and poised for more new things.

He handed her the bottle and it was the type where the stopper dangled from the neck like a chicken head. She positioned it out of the way and then took a deep swig, far deeper than she would have if she'd stopped to consider the thick liquid inside.

"Gah," she said, feeling the liquid clack and click in her throat, burning the roof of her mouth. It was a million times stronger than anything she'd ever tried and had a yeasty, fermented edge that stung. "What the hell is in that?"

"Language, Brock," he said, bemused.

"Hell? Hell isn't swearing."

"It's not something you want to discuss under a full moon either," he replied.

Hell hath no fury…

Silence followed for one beat, two beats, and then he made a ghoulish noise and pounced at her, resulting in her sloshing the horrible liquid all over his coat and him falling back on the ground laughing. "Ah, I'm just messing with you."

She lay back too so that they were both flat on the ground, looking at the thousands of stars spread out above them. She'd never seen a night's sky like it. In Plymouth she could see some stars at night, but they were mostly shrouded by grey fog and telephone cables. Here, it was if a ball were happening above them, or a candle-lit dinner party for thousands, or a concert was going on, millions of lighters held up and swaying in the air.

"What's your middle name?" Tane asked.

"What, why?"

"Just interested."

"What's yours?"

"I don't have one."

"Really?" Flora asked, propping herself up slightly so she could look at him in surprise. If she was honest with herself, she wasn't particularly surprised, in that it wasn't that interesting. But it was good to have an excuse to look at him.

"Yeah, they landed me with Tane and left it at that." He grinned. He looked up at her and there was a moment when her tongue felt like it had lurched itself down her throat. She felt her face grow red. His mouth slowly twisted into a sideways grin. His eyes flicked away from hers and down to her lips, just for a second.

Pull yourself together.

"Wow." Flora swallowed, trying to remember how to

speak. She lay back down to rearrange her mouth, which had opened just enough that hot air was making guilty clouds between them.

"Promise you won't laugh?" she said, swallowing again to generate some saliva.

"I never promise not to laugh," he said, and she could hear that he was still grinning.

"Ok, well I have two…"

"And they are?"

"Ophelia Jaimeson."

"Ophelia Jaimeson? So, you're Flora Ophelia Jaimeson Brock?" He repeated it quietly to himself, as if committing it to memory. "That sounds mighty grand."

"It's really not."

"Where'd the names come from?"

"Well, err, Ophelia because my dad thought it was all poetic."

"Nice. And Jaimeson?"

"And Jaimeson because it's my mum's favourite drink."

"Oh, lovely," Tane said, and he sounded momentarily annoyed. A cloud passed the moon and then they were bathed in silver and bone once more. Flora felt the atmosphere change.

Why is he annoyed?

"Anyway," he said after a moment, and she felt his mind move on. He bent his knee and brought it down to the side, where it landed on her leg. He didn't move it away. "I don't know what to do, Brock." His voice had become more serious, and quiet, as if the stars were listening to them. She felt her heartbeat whirr, but not in the usual, anxious way.

"About what?" she asked, her voice quiet too, eyes taking in the sky, finally warmed through in the midst of his heavy jacket.

"Lana," he replied, and her heart instantly stopped humming and some of the stars withdrew from the sky, and that one star was really just an aeroplane pretending.

Fraud.

"Lana?"

"Right."

"What about her?"

"It's complicated." He sighed. A stream clouded from his mouth and pierced the blackness. Flora shivered. "I just feel like you'll find it all out soon anyway, Brock. You aren't the type to just believe, are you? You seem like you need to know stuff. Like McLarty."

"Right," Flora replied, a little flatly. She didn't particularly like being compared to McLarty, as if they were their own weird little investigative duo. And she also didn't want Tane thinking of her as a female version of the creepy guy with droopy black hair and morose attitude.

Tane took a rattling breath in and then let it out again.

"My stepdad… he's not a great man. I know you know that he's missing."

There was a silence into which Flora didn't speak. She lay still, flat, waiting. Her emotions felt like they were rearranging themselves every second.

"He was a diabolical husband. Is a diabolical husband, I guess. Married into the family for money. My great-great-grandmother was this famous artist, you see. She was really good."

Flora thought that an understatement, but let it slide.

"He made sure there wasn't a pre-nup – one of those things where they sometimes tie up the family money – so he had access to it all. He gambled, he drank, he charmed the arse off anyone who met him. Even Karina was fooled for a long time, even her Mediums and her crystals and her shaman didn't warn her about him. I tried to tell her to end it."

"And she didn't?" Flora kept her voice as low as possible, not wanting to interrupt his flow.

"She didn't. And boy, he hated it when he found out. Tried to get rid of me."

"Get rid of you?"

"Yeah, we live in Colorado, and he drove me to this bear spot, left me there without a phone or food or anything, assuming I'd get eaten. He couldn't actively kill me, you see. Too obvious. But if they find my mauled carcass, half eaten by bears, well. He's a happy boy."

"What?" Flora asked, turning onto her side and propping her head on her palm so that she could look at him. He carried on watching the sky, his eyes shining.

"Yeah, it was pretty mad. Lucky that I'm good with nature, I just get it. I feel like the forest is my home. Well, when I'm not on the sea, that is. Anyway, he failed, and I didn't get eaten and I think that must've bummed him out."

"Well, yes," Flora said, nodding at his latest understatement.

"Ok, and then, what's worse is... well, part two of this story I guess," he took a deep breath in, and Flora watched as his chest rose and deflated.

"I'm a mistake. Never knew my dad, apparently he was some musician who happened to be playing as a support act at a Guns N' Roses gig she went to. She couldn't tell anyone that she was pregnant, her family aren't like that. She had me in secret and sort-of leased me out to this old couple, like an adoption.

She got away with it, they never found out, but it means that I'm basically this secret lovechild. Now she's made it in society with Hulk Halliday and she's going to dinner parties and feeling as successful as her family line would've wanted her to be... Well, she's not so interested in what I've got to say about the guy."

"But Lana said that your surname's Nuku? How have the media not found out?"

"That's nice of Lana. That's not my official surname. I guess it should be, I'm the Nuku bloodline, but the adopting couple gave me their surname, so that's what's on my passport and everywhere. They're both dead now. It feels weird. I don't really use a family name, not really. Mum always told everyone I was her nephew. 'I'm just taking my nephew and his girlfriend on a wine tasting tour,'" he mimicked her voice, "and the paps can be really harsh, you know, even picking on what my mom's wearing when she goes out."

His last sentence seemed erratic at the end of the admission that his own mother denied his existence. But that's what love did, Flora supposed. Allowed you to forgive where it probably wasn't deserved, just so you could maintain some semblance of normality. Thinking about what Tane had been through and the fact that he was still indignant about the paparazzi harassing his mother... Flora felt her chest ache.

"That must've been hard," she replied, softly. Silence followed, giving her time to process everything that he was saying. She lay back down, feeling the lumps and bumps of the rock beneath her.

Tane was a secret; that's why she hadn't seen anything about him in any of the articles. And this Hulk Halliday guy sounded like bad news.

"I just think he'll be mega pissed off with me now." Tane sighed.

"You think he'd try and kill you again?"

"Oh no, probably not. No, I don't know if he was ever really serious about that." For some reason Flora felt a sudden, deep sorrow for him, as if he was trying too hard to kid himself. "No, I think he'd want to find me to get me back home. Karina's probably worried. I'm not sure she's bought that I'm at boarding school, although she's usually so out of it that it's not like she'd check. She meditates. A lot."

"A pretend school is your cover story?"

"That's all of our cover stories. We have a brochure and everything. Taniwha Academy. Although 90% of the kids here come from homes that won't miss them. We're quite specific about that. But still, we have an academy. Ha." He let out a bitter laugh. "You want to enrol?"

"Ha," Flora replied.

She felt the back of his hand against hers. His finger

moved a millimetre towards her. She felt as if she couldn't breathe. Her finger burned. She moved hers back, just a tiny bit, just enough to know that he'd felt it, and then she remembered the beginning of the conversation.

"Why are you worried about Lana?"

He pulled his finger away.

"I think she's keeping stuff from me. I don't know what. She's just acting really weird, like even right now, I don't know where she is. I thought she'd maybe come up here."

"Oh," Flora replied, digesting this. "So that's why you came up here? To find Lana?" She hated herself for feeling disappointed.

"Yeah, I thought I saw her heading this way."

"Well, I'm not sure what I can do. Maybe if she had her phone on her, we could try and track her down," Flora joked. Neither of them laughed.

"You want some more of Frances's famous broad bean bonanza?" Tane asked suddenly, sitting up and scooping up the bottle, which was nearly empty thanks to Flora's ability to scare easily.

"Definitely not," Flora replied, feeling odd being the only one lying down. She sat up, pulling the hefty coat with her. She was once again hit by the beauty of the view: the moonlight on the sea, the swaying mass of silver trees, the occasional black swoop of a bird across the fingers of light from the moon. "Why are bats scary?"

"What?"

"Earlier, you said there might be snakes or bats up here. What's wrong with bats?"

"You know they have rabies, right?"

"Bats do?"

"Sure, some of them do."

"Right."

"Right, indeed. Any more questions?"

"Yes. What's Colorado like?"

"Epic. And also, not really home. I've got New Zealand

blood, I was born in Colorado, I went to English junior boarding school. Who knows where I belong, hey? I've always dreamed about going to the Norwegian Fjords. I just feel like that's where I belong. What about you?"

"What do you mean?"

"Where are your parents from? And you?"

"One hundred percent boring old British, I'm afraid," Flora sighed. She wished she had something more interesting to say. Her pale skin and messy blonde hair were fairly nondescript.

"Sounds bloody brilliant," Tane teased, enjoying his fake British accent again. "Let's go eat."

He stood up in one swift movement, shaking his legs out as if they'd gone numb, popping the top back onto the bottle. That energy was back again, the one that Flora had noticed before. It felt as if he were plugged into a huge socket which hummed all through his body.

Perhaps he's also an anxious person, Flora wondered, staggering to her feet under the sheepskin.

"Are you always so full of energy?" she grumbled, trying to shrug the jacket back around her shoulders with difficulty.

"Sure am," he said, laughing, and then strode over to the edge of the cliff in front of them, where he was framed by Poukai to his left and the dark mass of forest to his right. In front of them, the oscillations of light from the hot tubs and whirlpools shone out into the night.

"What is this place?" Flora asked, joining him and looking down at the various fluorescent pools of water and light.

"It's like, part waterpark, part bathing river," Tane said, shrugging as if it were no big deal. "In fact, there's a waterfall that's a quicker way down. If you'd dare?"

"Dare what? Jump?"

"Why not? I thought you were Flora Brock, nighttime ninja." With that, Tane let out a piercing wolf cry into the night. He repeated it three times, and after the third time various cries came back to them.

As she let out a short gust of laughter – *this place is insane* - Flora felt adventure rise up in her veins. She pushed her hair away from her face, catching the scent of Tane's musky jacket on her sleeve. "Who was that?"

"First, you need to take off my jacket," Tane said, ignoring her question. He reached out and helped her to take it off, his hand brushing her ear. She tried to ignore the spark of butterflies that lurched up her oesophagus.

"You want me to jump, in my clothes?"

"You'd better believe it," he replied, and he walked towards the edge of the jutting rock and looked around, as if waiting for something.

Flora took a few shaky steps forward and noticed that far, far below her was a waterfall, illuminated in the night with a radiating green light; a waterfall that towered and thundered and crashed into a huge pool that was way, way down below them.

She looked out at the moonlight on the sea, the shape of Poukai oscillating next to the beach, the swooping of barely visible birds across the horizon.

The wolf cry came back to them again, this time closer, and without warning a huge burst of light spilled below their feet. The light cleared and Flora could see a ring of flames circling the pool at the bottom of the waterfall, roaring and flickering and billowing into the night.

"Wow," Flora said, feeling as if she was speaking for both of them, not quite believing her eyes as they took in the fire, the water, the hundred-foot drop.

"Welcome to paradise, Flora Brock," Tane said, grinning wolfishly at her before grabbing her hand and flinging them both over the edge.

Flora barely registered his words, his hand, his fingers between hers, as she plummeted alongside him, down towards the water, the fire, the unknown far, far below.

CHAPTER THIRTEEN
INURE

McLarty crouched by the campfire, feeding it decapitated branches that splintered and spluttered to life within the heat. Flora found it strange that they would trust the pyromaniac to make the fire. *But then, he's probably the best at it.*

He leant forward and set fire to another branch, watching with rapture as the flames turned from orange to green and back again.

It must have been past 10 pm, but Flora noticed that no one had even eaten yet. They were clearly holding odd hours, the rules thrown out of the metaphorical window.

Her hair was starting to dry, her adrenaline was settling down, and she was dithering. Tane had all but disappeared after helping her out of the pool, and Ritchie, who had been sporting some form of body paint, had led her back to the safety of the camp.

Apart from McLarty, everyone else was scattered around: sat near the fire, using the fallen tree trunks for seats: wandering around with stacks of wood hugged to their bodies: buzzing between their hut and The Kitch. Mostly, they were clearly too busy to chat, or paired off already in deep conversation.

Giving up on her half-hearted desire to talk to someone new, Flora decided to sit next to McLarty, who had managed to rid a flimsy branch of all leaves and was now driving it into the ground with force.

"What're you up to?" she asked. He looked astonished, as if it were rare that anyone would talk to him, let alone voluntarily come to sit with him.

"Hey," he said, dropping the wood immediately and digging his hands into his pockets. Flora pretended not to see the stick that had been driven with some force into the soil. She noticed three teens with dyed lime green hair and colourful eye make-up slouching at the side of the circle, chewing what looked like short sticks.

"Who are they?" Flora asked.

"The Harleys," McLarty replied, little interest in his already monotonous voice. "They're not much use to be honest. They come from Norway, don't speak that much English. They're great at gutting fish though."

"What?"

"Their dad was some kind of fish trawler Captain," he replied, rolling his eyes at Flora. "They also enjoy pulling the guts out of the things. They're pretty gothic."

"Right," said Flora, thinking that that was rich coming from McLarty, with his pale skin and jet-black hair, wearing his skinny black jeans and a permanent look of mourning. What was his deal? She felt as if he was the hardest to read on the island, even though Lana was fiery and Tane was almost too cheerful; McLarty was baleful and soulful and almost hopeless, in a way that felt lost, even to himself.

Flora liked to spend time pondering other people. She supposed it was like how therapists supposedly needed therapy more than anyone. It was easier to look outwards.

When her and Jen had been eleven, they'd started secondary school. A psychologist had been there on their first day to make sure they were ingratiated suitably into this new, scary land. She had taught them the value of labelling their emotions and making sure they asked themselves "Why?", if they were angry or sad or lonely. She'd said that by asking yourself the simple question "Why?" a few times, you usually got to the real issue.

That evening, Flora had been having a sleepover at Jen's house and they'd wormed their way under Jen's duvet and played 'Therapy'.

"I'm really mad at my mum," Jen had said.

"Ok, why?" Flora replied.

"Because she said I could get the Danger Zone upgrade if I got to Grade 3 on the piano and now that I have, she's said that I have to get to Grade 4."

"Ok, and why is that annoying?"

"Because I hate piano and I don't want to get to Grade 4."

"Ok, and why do you hate piano?"

"Because Mr Arsey, the piano teacher, always stands too close and his breath stinks and I hate him."

"Ok," Flora had replied, feeling out of her depth. "And why don't you tell your mum that?"

"I guess..." Jen had replied, pondering in a way that was unusually deep for her, "...because when I do well at stuff, they pay me attention. If I stop piano, I stop being interesting, and they don't care about computer games, so it's the only way to make them happy."

"There you go," Flora had replied, wisely. To her mind, she'd solved all of Jen's problems, although in the following days, weeks, years, she wished she'd told Jen to just put her parent-related ego aside and quit piano. Life was too short to put up with uncomfortable situations, as easy as that was for Flora to say when she wasn't stuck in that small room smelling that guys' breath to make her parents love her.

"Ok, your turn," Jen had said.

"That's ok, let's do ghost stories. Remember the one with the drip, drip, drip coming from the ceiling?" Flora replied, and the conversation had quickly been steered into another direction.

Because what could she say? That she was secretly furious with Jen for not appreciating what she had? Because she wished that her mum was around and making her go to after-school clubs and learn instruments? That she would cut off her own arm to have parents like Jen's? That every day she had to work on her internal anger at the unfairness of the universe, and that actually, this 'Therapy' game scared the spleen out of her because she didn't want to have to face that anger.

Gaming had become her therapy. And then Jen had told her that gaming wasn't cool anymore, that she would never be accepted in school if she carried on in her world of escapism.

Flora felt as if she'd been physically attacked.

"You still have your phone?" McLarty asked, breaking Flora out of her mental prison.

"Yeah." Flora sighed, although that did remind her that she hadn't turned it off since her last text to her dad. She surreptitiously pulled it out of her pocket and switched it off, the glare making a brief flash in the dimming light. Less than 5% battery left.

Turning it off is a good compromise, she thought. She wasn't going to hand it in, but she could at least make sure that they weren't being tracked.

Although, privately, she thought them all a bit too dramatic on that front. Sure, Tane's mum was probably hoping that he'd still turn up at home, and maybe Lana's parents missed her passive-aggressive browbeating, but as for the rest of them... well, she wasn't expecting the CIA to turn up any day now.

And besides, despite probably breaking some sort of truancy laws, they weren't really breaking the law. They weren't trafficking drugs or harbouring fugitives (apart from McLarty's pyromaniac ways) or even really doing that much with this power that they'd been afforded. They had a boat and a globe.

"I'm not sure it's even worth turning it off, but on the off chance that the FBI are tracking my dad's old iPhone then I suppose I can play ball," Flora said, and she felt McLarty both smile and look surprised.

"You're funny," he said, and it was her turn to be surprised. No one had ever called her funny before. Smart, yes. Nerdy, yes. Sometimes even pretty, when she bothered to slug on eyeliner, which was rarely because she always got some on her eyeball. But never funny.

Well, Lana called me hot, she remembered. That had been the only good thing to come out of her eavesdropping on the boat.

Was that only yesterday? It feels like a million years ago.

"Thanks," she said, unsure of what to say and wishing she was holding something so that her hands didn't feel so useless. She leaned forward and pulled the stick out of the ground. Ahead of them, the fire crackled and sparked, sending neon orange fireflies up into the sky.

"They can track your phone, even when it's off."

"Oh, right," Flora said, uninterested. "I thought you could scramble the tracking?"

"I just said that to get Hive off your case. People don't like waiting for the toilet roll."

"Oh. Thanks. So, what should I do with my phone?"

"Destroy it," he said, without a moment's hesitation. "The other side aren't as good as us, yet. But they will be, and when they are it'll only take them a moment to realise that there's one wayward signal this far from the Azores."

"*The other side?*" she asked, trying not to smile but feeling the edge of her lip twist up anyway. They really were in their own dramatic little world, weren't they?

"The acquaintances of Axer Nuku-Halliday," McLarty replied, his face screwing up as if those acquaintances were bees in his mouth. He was sitting slumped over with his weedy legs stretched out in front of him, his back curved as if protecting him from the wind. Flora sat up a bit straighter.

"And they're trying to find him?" Flora prompted.

"Yes," McLarty replied, tearing his eyes away from the fire to look at her. His dark irises were two full stops in the firelight.

"Right. Does Tane know?"

"No," McLarty muttered, rolling his eyes. "Bless little Tane, he has no idea. Lana runs the joint. He lives in his own mad little world."

"I'm not sure…" Flora started to say, but her words ran out. She wanted to defend Tane, but the look on McLarty's face was so sour that she didn't dare. And besides, there were bigger things than that right now.

This Axer Nuku-Halliday was presumably furious at Tane for using the family money to buy a ship. He didn't see Tane as a real member of the family and had tried to track him down and potentially take the ship back. Or feed Tane to the bears.

What a delightful man, Flora thought, sarcastic even in her own head.

"So, you understand now, why you can't have your phone?" he asked, still staring at her in an unrelenting way. She looked back at him, and his lack of blinking made her nervous.

She cleared her throat to reply, but she was saved by a jubilant voice, one of her new favourite voices, rising from behind the ashes.

CHAPTER FOURTEEN
LILT

"Good evening, Poukers," Tane yelled, and the whole circle immediately broke into a chorus of whoops and whistles. The campmates jumped around, some on the logs, some stamping their feet so that a refrain of leaves flew into the air and cascaded around them like confetti. Leaves caught fire in mid-air and lit up the shadows. The smell of flames was all-consuming.

In a nearby tree, a boy wearing a fishnet bodysuit swung by his legs, waving a smoking charcoal stick.

"Poukers unite," he cheered, repeating the slogan over and over.

"Poukers?" Flora muttered, smiling despite herself. The cheering was infectious.

McLarty treated himself to a rare smile in return. He liked that Flora was taking the mickey out of Tane, she could tell.

Flora noticed that most of the others had now filed in, steaming metal mugs and half-filled goblets in hand. Some were topless, Poukai tattoos on show, and others had mad fancy-dress style items on: top hats and feather boas and fur coats and necklaces with medallions that reflected the fire.

There were chunky rings and silk scarves and ripped trousers and red boots: painted faces and slopping gauntlets and even a sword, which a girl with black hair was wielding towards the sky. The atmosphere was so thick that Flora could almost see it; a flurry of firework bursts, like brilliant colourful arms framing everyone.

The group of gothic teenagers, the Harleys, were painting each other's hair with a dark red liquid. Eccles wore a velvet cape. Ritchie had painted his whole body in neon triangles.

Everyone was focused on Tane, ecstatic, war cries and whoops piercing the air. It was a world away from the quiet crew that she'd met in the underbelly of the boat in England. It was as if their real personalities had been here, waiting to explode, all along.

"Where did those clothes come from?" Flora stared at the flamboyant, punkish, wild attire.

"Tane's parents. His dad toured with Guns N' Roses and his mum worked in the theatre," McLarty replied, his tone bordering on sarcastic. "I've told them they look ridiculous."

Tane jumped up on a log and Flora could only see him when the flames changed direction. He was wearing a fur deerstalker hat which gave the impression of a huge animal directing an orchestra. The crew, with their wild clothes and devil-may-care attitudes, reminded Flora of Arlo's gang back at school. She was finally sat with them.

"Ride or die," Eccles yelled, his voice so loud that startled birds flapped in the trees, feathered silhouettes in a fiery sky.

"Zip it please," Tane said, waving his hand to indicate that he wanted to move on. "So, I say again, good evening Poukers. Great sailing today; it got pretty wild out there, but, as usual, we ruled the sea."

More whooping. Someone whistled manically. Eccles sat silently this time, admonished.

"Thank you all for doing an incredible job on our trip to England. We hit Penzance, we hit Fowey and we hit Plymouth, and we made some real-life experiences!"

"Real life sucks," someone yelled.

"Never again," someone else called. Several people

clinked goblets.

"We were able to buy eggs, Cheddar cheese, hundreds of scones, all sorts of fantastic food items to keep our bellies filled for a little while longer. We picked up our campmates who had to spend Summer with their families-"

"Boring," someone interrupted.

"-and most importantly, we got Bell to his grandmother just in time."

Everyone looked towards Bell, the tall blonde boy, who was staring at Tane with shining eyes.

"Our condolences," Tane said, and Bell's face suddenly dissolved into tears. He ran off towards the Privy Shack and Ritchie ran after him.

"Calm down, calm down," Tane called to the crowd, who had started talking loudly, jabbering away about hospitals and death. "In other news, Frances is no doubt concocting all sorts from Le Jardin, our one-of-a-kind hydroponic gardening system. Frances, what do we have on the go right now?"

Flora watched as Frances stood up, his shiny face reflecting the flames.

"Well, it's rather good news all round," he announced, clearing his throat as if he were delivering a speech in the House of Lords. "We've been able to harvest the last of the summer fruits, which has given us enough to make about fifty jars of jam. It's pear season right now, so the pear trees are all going to need to be picked soon. I'll assign jobs for that in a week or so, unless anyone wants to volunteer. We're also still seeing reams of orange peppers growing, which we'll be able to make into soup or chutneys."

"Chutney?" Flora whispered to McLarty, raising her eyebrows. Wasn't that something that old people ate?

"It keeps for like, years," he whispered back, rolling his own eyes in return. He seemed in a better mood than he had all day. "We do a load of prep for winter; everyone gets upset when there are no fresh figs in January. And don't even get me started on the goats milk soap."

"Oh, I won't," Flora said, smiling.

"Brock, everything ok?" Tane called. Flora whipped her head towards the front. Tane's face looked tight, his fur bonnet tilted to one side.

"Yes, sorry," she mumbled.

"Fantastic. Well, thank you Frances, that all sounds really positive."

"It is, and can I just remind everyone that The Kitch isn't to be raided out of hours. We'll sort you three meals a day, but if you want anything else then you'll have to forage for it. I noticed already earlier that there was some-"

"Does anyone know what the shipping forecast is for tomorrow?" Lana interrupted, loudly. Flora hadn't noticed her arrive, but she felt something inside her spark to life. At home, their gas oven took several tries to make it take; when she was younger and trying to cook for herself, she'd often filled the kitchen with the sharp tang of gas. Soon after, when she was seven or eight, she learned that it was safer to just eat toast.

There was a brief murmur of chatter, during which Tane shot Lana a look of consternation, as if she had broken the sacred rules of decorum. Frances's own demeanour moved to annoyance and then to confidence again.

"Yes, Northwest winds of around 12 miles-per-hour, very good visibility," Frances said, adjusting his shirt collar.

"Thanks Frances." Tane had a note of apology in his voice. Frances sat down, adjusting his shirt further. "And Hive, how are the nets?"

Hive stood up and cleared her throat, swishing her straight red hair over her shoulder and adjusting her glasses.

"It's been a good fortnight for fish, I can report. It was a real success to come back to; we've caught a few white marlins and even a swordfish."

A rumble of appreciation went up around the group.

"No more hammerheads?" Tane asked, letting off a whistle of a laugh.

"No," Hive replied flatly, then took her seat again.

"Well, thank goodness for that," Tane said, and the circle grumbled with laughter. "In other business, you'll notice that we have a visitor with us. Brock?"

All heads instantly turned towards Flora. She felt the fire burn her face. She stumbled to her feet and Tane stared at her through the moving flames, which refused to give her a break.

"Err, hi everyone," Flora said, raising a limp hand in a wave. There was a long and awkward pause while everyone waited for her to say something else.

"Brock is a total ninja," Tane said, saving her from her embarrassment. A rumble of appreciative laughter rose up from the rest of them. "Earlier, she strode right up to the lookout point, on her own, in the dark." He put emphasis on the word 'dark' and there was a greater rumble and a ripple of chatter.

"The computer girl," someone whispered to someone else.

"Well, I wouldn't call myself a ninja," Flora said, noticing that there was now a silence into which she was expected to speak. "I'm a gamer, back home. I play all sorts, Adventure, Action, Puzzles, Stealth, Real-time Strategy, whatever I can get my hands on. So, in a weird way, that sort of prepares me for things like this."

"For scaling a mountain?" someone called.

"Yep, well I played this game, *Wreck of Atlanta-*"

"You didn't?" McLarty interrupted. His face had broken into another smile. "That game was so rubbish."

"Not if you killed the pirates and took the ship," she replied, smiling at how corny the game felt now.

"Yeah, and then what, you just had to sail off into the sunset," he replied, laughing, straightening up so that he was no longer slumped.

"Anyway," Tane interjected, his tone hardening slightly, "yes, Brock is a ninja, but unfortunately, she's not sticking around. She wants to head back to Plymouth, her hometown, where her family await."

"What?" someone in the circle asked.

"Preposterous," spluttered Frances.

"Oh, so you're going back?" McLarty asked. He didn't actually sound annoyed by it; his voice almost sounded relieved.

"Why would you want to leave?" someone asked, incredulous.

Flora stared at Tane through the flames. His eyes reflected the fire back at her. Why had he told everyone? Was this really the right time? People were looking at her, people were asking questions, the mood had changed. She had known that she was on borrowed time, but she didn't want *them* to know that. To think that she didn't feel that this life was good enough for her.

Despite her annoyance at Tane, she felt flattered that so many people seemed to mind whether she was there or not; she'd hardly been a particularly useful guest since arriving. She had brought the toilet roll, she supposed. Quite a crucial item.

"Unless," said Tane, and the group immediately fell silent, "we can convince her to stay." His mouth broke into a wicked grin, his teeth gripping his bottom lip and taunting her behind the flicker of fireflies and sooty smoke. He raised his eyebrow at her, as if challenging her to say something in response, but her lips had fallen into an unwanted smile. She bit her bottom lip, mirroring him.

"Hurrah," said Frances, and someone else whooped, and immediately the mood was back to normal, and the smell of food wafted across the camp and, somewhere, two birds had a loud conversation. Flora sat down.

"Anyway, I think that concludes all of our business. Does anyone have anything else?"

"Yes," said Lana, and she stood up from where she had been sat near Tane. She was clutching a steaming mug of tea. "As you all know, we are keeping our whereabouts a secret from the rest of the world. We cannot afford to have slip ups and we can't afford to be seen. What does this mean? Well firstly, whoever thought it wise to make the fire so big tonight, sort your lives out. We can't be building these towering great fires that can be seen from outer space."

There was a mumble and a few people directed apologies towards the floor.

"You can't see this from outer space," Flora muttered to McLarty.

"She's exaggerating for effect," he replied, smirking.

"Secondly, McLarty's found signal on the radar, on our island. There appears to be a mobile phone here, shouting our location for the world to see."

Lana stopped striding around the circle and stopped, staring at Flora. Her face was completely blank, her eyes unblinking. If there had been anything between them before, it seemed to no longer exist. Flora could be a complete stranger.

Flora struggled to breathe; she felt faces all turning to look at her, and she glanced towards McLarty for an answer. He wasn't making eye contact and his back had slumped into an even deeper arc than before, as if he were trying to disappear.

He knew she had her phone; they'd talked about it. If he was going to report it back to Lana, why didn't he just tell her? What was this mad situation where she couldn't even have her mobile phone without the whole lot of them going off on one?

"I need my phone," Flora said, flatly, and she heard Hive say, "I told you so," to Frances.

"We don't allow phones," Lana replied, walking to Flora and holding her hand out.

"It's fine, Lana," Tane suddenly said from across the circle. "She gave it to me earlier. I've destroyed it. The signal should be gone now."

Lana turned slowly to face Tane, her eyes searching out the truth, or otherwise, in his face, and Flora felt McLarty stare at her. He'd seen her phone, just a moment ago. He would know that Tane was lying for her, and what did that mean?

She had no idea.

"Thanks for that though Lana, a valuable reminder to us all. And now, time for food and music. Eccles, you got your guitar ready for us?" Tane said, hopping down from the log, his feet causing a flurry of leaves to rise up.

"Sure do," Eccles replied with glee, proffering a battered, expensive-looking instrument.

Frances, Hive and about five of the others all stood up and started filing off towards The Kitch, and Lana strode towards one of the huts. Flora was about to walk over to Tane and ask what was going on, but he immediately swung around and started following Lana.

"Wait," she heard him call, before they both disappeared into the darkness.

Flora fiddled with a knotted strand of hair.

Eccles started playing the guitar and, despite an overwhelming urge to follow Tane and Lana, Flora had no idea what she would say. *"What the hell are you guys talking about?"*

Instead, she sank down next to McLarty and tried to resume conversation, despite her hands shaking. He'd turned her in. But could she afford to lose her only friend? Tane seemed annoyed at her, and Lana was acting as if she didn't exist. If they were going off to have a private conversation, and everyone else was busy, then she needed McLarty.

And, if she was really honest with herself, she didn't care about what McLarty had or hadn't done. The point was that Tane had covered for her. Why?

"So," Flora said. McLarty remained silent. "You didn't like *Wreck of Atlanta*?" She nibbled at her nail. This time, no one stopped her. Her chest felt like it had caught fire, ignited by a wayward spark from the roaring monster in front of them.

Did Lana know that Tane was lying for me?

"What the hell was that?" McLarty snapped, pushing his hair back from his forehead. It looked like he'd been deciding between being amicable and calling her out and had fallen on the side of the latter. "Why was Tane saying he'd taken it off you? Do you have two phones, or was he just lying?"

"Ah. It's really hard for me to..." Flora said, trailing off. She couldn't say that Tane was lying for her, for some unknown reason, as clearly, he meant something around here. But she also couldn't say that she had two phones, because who had two phones? Drug dealers and people having affairs, most likely. She didn't think he'd believe that she was either of those. Perhaps she should offer him some Class A broad bean syrup.

"It's hard for you to know if you have two phones?" he asked, sarcasm dripping off of his tongue, his hand reaching up to push his hair back again but finding that it was already out of his face.

"No, it's not that, it's just..." Flora trailed off, wishing that she'd gone with her first instinct of walking away.

"One rule for you, another rule for everyone else?" he asked, his voice low now, the bitchy tone of some of the people in Arlo's gang back at school.

"Why are you so upset, you must have at least your phone if you're doing all this tracking?"

"I don't," he said immediately, the words falling off his lips. She raised her eyebrows and a pained look flashed across his face. She knew that he couldn't say anything else without tying himself up in lies.

"Well then. I'll keep your secret if you keep mine," Flora said, voice prim, standing up without really meaning to, and then walking off, because she couldn't very well stay standing over him like that.

Her feet took her in the direction of Lana's hut.

CHAPTER FIFTEEN
LASSITUDE

"I really don't care," Lana insisted. The walls of the huts were wooden and not remotely soundproof; Flora stood at the back of the hut and could hear them as if she were in the room. The only downside was that she was stood close to a thick tangle of jungle, and with the night rising as if from the floor her imagination was running riot. Surely there couldn't be lions or tigers on an island like this, but what about baboons? Vicious iguanas? Snakes? Probably not rabid bats, hopefully.

"What is with you at the moment?" Tane asked, his voice high and frustrated. "You're being a pain in the ass. I know you better than anyone – I know something's bothering you."

"Nothing's... bothering me," Lana said, and even from outside, Flora could tell that she was lying.

"Because if there's a problem, you need to tell me. This camp's not going to work... we can't run this camp if we're not talking to each other. Is it about Axer?"

"No," Lana said, quickly.

"Because you don't need to worry about him, ok? He's probably drowned. And if he is alive, he'd never find us out here, we're in the middle of absolute nowhere."

"Mmm," Lana mumbled. One of them tapped the wall; the sound beat impatiently through the wood by Flora's ear.

"You need to cheer up. Have you forgotten why

we're here? The whole reason that we fled. Why we risked everything?"

"You risked everything," Lana replied. She didn't sound like she was being unkind, only tired. "I didn't have anything to risk. I rode along on your gamble, and God, I appreciate it so much. But how long can we keep this up? It's tiring. I don't understand why you keep making us trek around the planet when we have everything we need here. But then, at the same time, I'd go crazy if I was here all the time. We all would." There was a long pause during which Flora barely dared to breathe. "I get that I'm not making sense, but maybe I'm just fed up, you know?"

"Listen to me," Tane said, and his voice was lower, and Flora felt something burning in her chest. A part of her wanted to stride around to the door and open it, but she focused on her breathing. In for four, out for eight. "It's when we want to give up that we *have* to go on. We knew it was never going to be easy, right?"

"Well, yes."

"But it's better than the alternative."

"Without a doubt."

There was a long pause and it drove Flora crazy that she couldn't see what was happening inside. What were they doing? Staring at each other? Kissing?! She hadn't picked up a romantic spark between the pair of them, but she wasn't exactly known for her ability to understand romance. The person she usually confessed her innermost thoughts to was Stu from Bolton, and that's only because it was relatively effortless and anonymous.

"Can't we just drop anyone that has to go home for summer?" Lana asked. Flora could tell that it wasn't the first time that she'd asked that question, by the way that she already sounded resigned to a negative answer. "They aren't really living the life, just treating this place like boarding school. And I really, really hate risking going back to the mainland. If I could teach someone else to drive Poukai…"

"That's not an option," Tane said, dismissively. "I don't trust anyone else to get us out in an emergency."

Flora felt her face burn with indignation, although she knew she really had no right to let it. Of course, Tane didn't trust her to drive his ship. He'd really only just met her. And she couldn't drive a ship.

"The reason we go back to the mainland is more than just picking up the summer folk," Tane said, and he started tapping the wall again. "Number one, like you said, our people need community. The two things that make life worth living are value and community. We have our value here, right? We have it nailed. I am one hundred percent behind this cause. But what about community? We have a great family here, but we can't live in isolation. If we never talk to anyone outside our family, then we never learn anything new, we become worse people. That's how all sorts of bad things start up in the world, when we start to think that our opinions are the only opinions. We need community, and we need it outside of our backyard. We need new recruits. Fresh blood."

"You mean we'll all start to become pyromaniacs and exotic dancers?" Lana asked, and Flora could tell that she was cracking a rare smile.

"Just imagine," Tane replied, and his voice rose, and he let out a guffaw that made Flora jump. "Pyromaniacs and exotic dancers," he repeated.

"And what about the new girl?" Lana asked, and Tane immediately stopped laughing and Flora felt her body turn to ice. Lana must mean her; there was no other new girl that she knew of. If there had been, Tane would have introduced them around the firepit.

There was a long, silent second. Flora panicked that she might have temporarily gone deaf, and she'd miss his answer, but then he replied, his voice deliberately slow.

"What about her?"

"I know she still has her phone. It's written all over her face. Why'd you lie for her?" Lana sounded absolutely and unreasonably furious.

"Ah," Tane said, and Flora thought she heard relief written in that one syllable. Although, how much can you really tell from one short syllable? Perhaps she'd been hoping that he was relieved, that Lana wasn't asking anything more.

"Ah? You better not be falling for this kid, Tane."

"Why, because you like her?"

"Ha." Lana made a strangled noise that was hard to interpret. Then: "This camp is the most important thing to me."

Flora felt her shoelace start to seriously itch the top of her foot, to the point where it was almost painful. Her eyes prickled. She used the heel of one damp trainer to itch the top of the other foot. She nearly kicked the wood and bit her lip to stop from gasping.

"Look, Skinner. Brock, she…"

Flora wished her heart would stop beating so loudly. She leaned against the hut and turned her face so that her ear was pressed right up against the wood, splinters be damned.

"…she's got family, you know? A real one. A dad who misses her. Who's here, who's alive, who wants to talk to his daughter. We can't even imagine what that's like. Who am I to take that away from her? What if he calls and she doesn't answer because we've taken her phone? I couldn't live with that."

There was a silence that was so deep that when a rat scurried out of the trees and towards Flora, she shrieked louder than she meant to, and the small creature quickly veered off course and scattered away into the distance. But the damage was done.

"Who's that?" Lana asked.

Footsteps strode to the door of the hut.

Her heart in her throat, Flora dived for a stick that was pointing out of the foliage and tugged, her hands burning, until it came loose in her grip. The movement caused the tree to shake, and leaves and debris rained down upon her, along with hyperactive insects that scuttled down her neck.

She spun around at the exact moment that they arrived at the back of the hut, Tane's eyebrows up, Lana's eyes murderous. If Lana was surprised that it was Flora, she didn't show it.

"Brock?" Tane asked, stunned.

"What are you doing out here?" Lana hissed, shooting a glance at Tane that clearly said, 'our recruitment process isn't thorough enough'.

"I was just collecting wood," Flora panted, holding up the piece of wood, pushing a strand of leaves out of her face.

"You're collecting wood?" Tane looked down at the flimsy branch in Flora's hand and suddenly, without wanting to, whether from nerves or something else, Flora burst out laughing. Imagine! She had a whole forest to forage from and she'd managed to pick up one flimsy branch and had struggled to dismantle even that.

She was laughing at her own cover story and blowing it in the process. It had a positive effect to some extent though; Tane started laughing too, in a way that told her that he found her totally bizarre but couldn't miss a good opportunity to laugh. He walked forward and held his hand out for the stick, and as Flora handed it to him, she brushed his skin and it was warm and soft and she felt instantly breathless, as if someone was wringing her lungs.

"Great find, Brock," Tane said, examining the stick, his laughing coming for real now, rumbling up from his belly and exploding in a guttural guffaw.

Lana didn't so much as twitch a single facial muscle. She was looking between Flora and the stick, her hands twitching with a rage that couldn't be contained.

"This is no place for eavesdroppers," she said. "I'm getting a peppermint tea." She turned on her heel and stomped off towards The Kitch, her thick boots grinding into the earth as she went.

Flora watched her go, feeling the smile on her face melt

into nothingness. She turned her attention back to Tane.

"I'm sorry," she said.

"It's ok," he replied, his smile also dissolving, his eyes looking at a bug on her arm. He brushed it off and her heart hummed. "If you did hear, then I meant what I said. You're very lucky. But Lana's right, it's not cool to go listening at other people's huts. Please don't tell me that that's who you are?"

"Of course not," she replied, feeling her face burn. She was blatantly lying. Clearly, she *was* that kind of person. "I just... I just don't know everything about what's going on yet. I still don't really get it all. I mean, why you're all here?

It's a great adventure and I get that you're all escaping from stuff, but I still don't really understand the bigger picture. I was hoping that you guys might explain something. And I wasn't planning on eavesdropping, I hate that, and I hate standing by the jungle in the dark waiting to get eaten by iguanas, so it definitely won't happen again."

Someone howled by the fire in the centre of the camp.

"Eaten by iguanas?" Tane asked, looking mildly impressed at the suggestion. "Now there's a new one. I don't think we've had anyone get eaten by an iguana yet, but I'll keep my eye on you, just in case."

"Please do," she replied, smiling for a moment before feeling instantly mortified and breaking eye contact to look down at the ground, where her shoe was shuffling a pile of brown debris.

"Hey," he said, and she looked up again. He had moved an inch closer to her and she could barely breathe; the green smell of the forest, the smoke from the fire, the sound of Lana's feet crunching away from them, it all felt at once deafening and insignificant. "It's great to have you here. Really." His voice was quiet now and she couldn't break eye contact away from his own deep brown gaze, which reflected the forest, her face, a hopeless kind of anguish. "Please do think about staying."

The moon started to beat down on the leaves around them, casting the world in a whitewashed glow.

"I will," she replied, the words falling heavily off her lips.

"Good," he muttered, and his warm breath was close enough to prickle her skin. Her stomach churned. She felt her hands flicker, as if they had magical powers, as if she could summon him without needing to move.

Before she could succumb to the will of her electric veins, Tane turned and strode back towards camp, dragging the stick along the side of the wooden hut, creating a juddering melody that left Flora feeling even more confused when it finished.

CHAPTER SIXTEEN
MELLIFLUOUS

"Flora, it's already 6.30 am," a voice said primly, right in her face. She opened her eyes and was met with two large, glaring orbs. Hive moved backwards and her glasses focused into view.

"So?" Flora croaked, throat dry, trying to remember where she was.

"Well, if you're going to help with kitchen duty then you'd better get up."

Hive straightened up to standing and strode out of the open hut door. Frances was already gone and a morning chill swept through the small room.

Last night, it had been agreed that she would share a hut with Frances and Hive, who had two spare beds, since no one else seemed to want to share with them.

"They're great," Tane had told her enthusiastically, as they waited in line to brush their teeth by the Privy Shack. "You'll love bunking with them."

"Really?" Flora asked, already dreading the intense organisation that was bound to come from sharing with such uptight campmates.

"Trust me, there's a reason we recruited them," Tane said, his voice so low that only Flora could hear it. "Hive's gonna be a doctor, she's been studying medical science since she was like, six years old. In April, she gave me stiches in my leg, and I didn't even feel it, and last year when Chan broke her arm, Hive strapped it up and got her on her way again."

"She broke her arm, and you didn't go back to the mainland?" Flora asked, flatly.

"Didn't need to, Brock." Tane grinned. Flora couldn't help but send a reluctant grin back. "Hive's got a whole jungle at her disposal. Strapped her up with some Madagascan Periwinkle and a bunch of yarn."

Someone in the Privy Shack loudly spat a glob of toothpaste against a bowl.

"And what about Frances? What's his superpower?" Flora asked. The queue shuffled on. People were glancing at her and Tane talking so closely, trying to listen in. It felt as if she were having an illicit moment with a celebrity.

"Oh, they're just best friends. Hive wouldn't come without him, and we lucked out that they're both from the same foster family, so it's just one story." Tane shrugged and grinned again at Flora, seemingly unaware of the people watching and whispering.

That's why Frances is always so keen to be part of things. He's afraid of being thrown out; he has no superpower.

"Right." Flora tapped her toothbrush against her hand.

As she brushed her teeth, her mind had dreaded the upcoming prospect of sleeping in a bed near the homemade medicine marvel.

Bed had been a misleading term, she soon realised, when she'd carried her meagre things in search of the refuge. She was to sleep on a padded futon on the floor, with a thick, scratchy blanket and one oppressed pillow to see her through.

Aside from the lacklustre bedding, their hut was at least homely and clean, with a few pictures of pressed flowers nailed to the walls and neat boxes with signs on for 'Shoes', 'Toiletries' and 'Clean Towels'. A set of tartan fabrics had been hung to act as curtains, which didn't seem to meet in the middle but gave the place a kitsch feel.

Flora suspected that theirs was the only hut with this level of neatness; she imagined that some of the others must look like an explosion of clothes and snacks.

Next to each of their beds were a few small items; "memorables," Frances had called them. "Everyone has a few from back home," he'd explained. "It makes us feel connected to the mainland, which is sometimes rather nice. But also, for most of us, the memorables remind us why we left."

"What are your memorables?" Flora asked, looking at the odd assortment of items on his bedside table. A tiny felt mouse, a shining Pokemon card and what looked like a military pin sat facing his bed.

"We don't explain our memorables," Frances said, pompously, before puffing up his pillow. Flora had shot a look over at Hive's memorables: a stethoscope charm that looked like it should be on a bracelet, a tiny calculator, a tattered photograph of a lady with red hair, a small bottle of perfume.

Flora wished that she had brought something from home.

Now that Hive had woken her up, the smell of the morning started climbing over her bedding; the scent of new shrubbery, the distinct brine of the sea, a waft of coffee. Flora inhaled deeply from under her woollen blanket. It was the most comforting, relaxing smell.

She took her phone out from under her pillow and turned it on. Only 4% battery left. No messages. She checked that she had signal, and that the internet was still working from this far off place, but there it was: 4G. She had signal on a desert island and yet not a single person had made it worth the battle to keep her phone.

'How's it all going?', she messaged her dad. Then she turned her phone back off, slid it into her pillowcase and reached up to stretch her back.

"Flora?" Hive yelled from somewhere in the distance.

"Coming," Flora yelled back. "For goodness' sake," she then muttered, throwing back the covers and heaving herself up off the futon. Breakfast duty it was.

△△△

There was something magical about the campsite in the morning. As Flora wandered towards The Kitch she inhaled deeply: fresh dew, salty air, something that smelled similar to rosemary, the first tendrils of sunlight creeping through the trees. The sense of quiet calmed her and she felt an urge to walk down through the foliage to the ocean, to watch the morning waves break along the shoreline.

Birds were waking up, chattering morning song from various branches, and she could hear crickets hiding in the crevices, rubbing their legs together, one long stream of clicking.

There was a slight wind and it rustled through the canopy, sending a spray of pollen twirling towards the ground. The leaves underfoot were turning autumnal, and her bare feet crunched on rusty oranges and deep auburns. Around the edges of the camp, grasses rustled softly in the breeze.

Flora could hear snoring coming from a few of the huts and the sound made her smile. She wondered who it was, especially that one almighty snore coming from the hut closest to The Kitch. It sounded like a baby elephant was trapped inside.

For the first time, she was glad that she was sharing with Hive and Frances, even if it did seem to automatically enrol her for early starts.

Near to The Kitch, there was a number carved into a tree. Flora strained to read it, but when the roughly carved figures made themselves clear it read: 09.06.22. Was that when Tane had arrived on the island?

"You alright?" a voice asked, and it was Bell, the tall boy with a baby face. He sauntered over in swim shorts, drying his straggly blonde hair with a t-shirt. Under his other arm was a short red surfboard.

"What's the date for? 9th June 2022?"

"Nah, it's the American date format. 6th September 2022. That's when Tane started a new term, walked out the door to go to school and never looked back. Changed his life for a new term on the seas, two years ago now." Bell set his surfboard down against the tree.

"He's been out here for that long?"

"Yeah, man."

"How long have you guys all been here?"

"About the same, I guess. Like, a load of us are the OG's. Lana was the first, obviously. Then McLarty joined and managed to recruit a load of stowaways from like, the dark web or something. Then there's, like, referrals, you know. Our little gang – me, Easton, Eccles, Ritchie and Chan – have been bests since the beginning. We barely lose anyone, as well."

"Apart from Lusty?"

"Yeah," Bell said, his face becoming a perfect picture of grief. "Yeah, RIP Lusty. He was a great kid. One of the best. So weird to think that he went to school with Lana and Tane, you'd think he was like, totally not like that."

"Right," Flora said, trying to remember what she'd been told about Lusty. "He fell overboard, right?"

"What? No, of course not. He wasn't an idiot, man. He was a bright kid. One of my closest mates here, after Eccles and Ritchie. Good friends with Tane too, they were like brothers before... But yeah, they got him, in the end. The Hulk and his guys. RIP Lusty."

Flora stared at Bell for a long moment, but he didn't seem to notice. She felt a chill go through her that had nothing to do with the morning air.

"What?" she whispered, but he was distracted with noises from The Kitch, and he didn't hear her. He tilted his head to the side and shook it, as if he had water in his ears.

"Are you ok?" Flora asked, wondering whether he was having a stroke.

"Yeah, great. Cold seas this morning, man."

"You've been out surfing?"

"Yeah, I go every morning. Best way to crack the dawn. When you don't get hit by a jelly, that is."

"A jellyfish?" Flora asked. She struggled to understand Bell and his surfer-dude lingo.

"Yeah, couple of jellies out there today, but managed to avoid them."

"Oh, well done." Flora had literally no idea what else to say.

Thankfully, Bell didn't seem like the kind of guy to crave proper conversation, and he wandered off, still shaking his head like a golden retriever. Flora watched him go and tried to put two and two together and make four. But her mind was putting up a blocker and she couldn't process it. On some level, she knew why; she was falling in love with Taniwha.

She didn't want to think about anything that might compromise that.

△△△

The Kitch sounded like it was abuzz with activity, but when Flora let herself in through the door flap, there were only three people inside: Hive, Frances and a girl that she hadn't yet talked to.

The tent was much bigger than it appeared from the outside. A metal table ran down the centre, covered in chopping boards and tubs and huge jars of sauce. A large bottle filled with deep brown liquid had 'agave syrup' written on a label around its neck. Other jars contained homemade blueberry jam, marmalade and passata. The spine of a foreboding fish sat along a chopping board.

Around the long table there were various other stations: a sink area, a chest freezer, a towering fridge.

It had the fusty smell of every outdoor shop that Flora had been in – which admittedly wasn't many – of tents and pegs and damp canvas and the great outdoors, mixed with brine and fermented fruit.

"How on earth did you get those here?" Flora asked, walking over to the freezer. *That thing must weigh a tonne.*

"That was one of our more impressive feats," Frances replied, pausing in his examination of a tray of yellow peppers. "It took six of us, but we managed it."

"And how do you get electricity?" Flora asked, as she pulled the freezer open, half expecting to see nothing inside. She was met with a great chill and pile upon pile of frozen food: brown paper packets, fish fillets, punnets of green beans.

"Solar," Hive replied, "but please don't keep it open."

"Sorry." Flora closed it so quickly that the noise reverberated around the tent, and she swung around, mortified, to apologise to a glowering Hive. She caught the eye of the unknown girl, who smiled at her with a grin that said 'We've all been there.'

"I'm Hope," the girl said, raising the knife in her hand to wave. Her other hand was holding a half-chopped celery stick in place.

"Flora. So, you've kept your first name as well?"

"Nah, that's my surname. I'm Jacinda Hope, just lucked out, I guess, that it sounds like a first name. It's not too embarrassing." She shot a meaningful look in Frances's direction and for the first time Flora realised how unusual it was that he was keeping his first name, when everyone else went by their family name.

"What's your surname, Frances?" Flora asked.

"Hoare," he said, matter-of-factly. "Which is a perfectly good, Anglo-Saxon surname. However, the group felt that I should keep to my assigned non-familial nomenclature."

"Because everyone was walking around the campsite yelling 'Hoare'. It's your fault for being so in demand." Hope winked at Flora and recommenced chopping. She must have been about sixteen too. Her dreadlocked hair was tied back behind her head, and she had a lone green bangle pushed up her arm. Flora liked her instantly.

"Should I be asking you all to call me Brock?" Flora asked, not wanting to be the only one for whom the rules didn't apply. *Well, there's always Tane and Lana,* she remembered.

Although, did it look like she was trying to join the same rank as them, without first earning her stripes?

"No, you can be Flora unless you decide to officially join us and do the initiation ceremony," Hive said. "If you become one of us, then we'll call you Brock." As she said it, she seemed to involuntarily glance at her own shoulder, where the bow of a boat could be seen poking out of her sleeve.

"Right," Flora replied, feeling slightly put out, even though she had no right to be. She couldn't be upset that they didn't see her as 'one of them'; she'd made it quite clear that she was heading back to the mainland at some point.

Is it bad that I want to stay a bit longer?

"Now, Flora, you're on chopping duty," Hive said, walking over to her with a huge knife that reflected everything in its blade. "We've got two trays of tomatoes and fifteen garlic bulbs that need chopping. Hope will do the onions when the celery's all finished. I'll cook up the pasta sauce ready for the jars, and Frances is in charge of breakfast."

"I'm perfectly fine to sort the morning meal," Frances confirmed.

"Cool." Flora cast a glance at the huge AGA-style oven that they'd managed to get in the tent. On one of the rings, a coffee percolator was simmering gently, releasing an earthy smelling steam into the room.

Delicious.

△△△

The next hour passed in a whirlwind of chopping tomatoes, trying to stop the onions from making her cry, and having a laugh with Hope. It turned out that Hope had been on Taniwha for a year. She didn't say why she'd left home, but Flora got the impression that she'd been having family troubles. She ran away and that's when she'd seen Poukai, anchored at her local bay, Port of Tyne. She had a strong accent and a wicked laugh and regaled Flora with stories of her ten brothers and sisters, who Flora could tell she missed badly.

"I don't think they wanted me on board at first, but when I told them about cooking for ten kids, they pretty much kidnapped me," Hope said, flashing her pearly teeth.

Hope finished chopping all of the onions before Flora had made any real progress with the tomatoes, and so the garlic-chopping was handed over.

"I'm going to smell mint today," Hope commented.

By the time their chopping duties were complete, a few additional people had wandered into the tent to join them. They started to all pitch in on creating breakfast from the barbeque butterbeans that Frances had cooked; he flapped around overseeing the activities. Hope sawed hunks of bread to toast directly over the fire, skewering them on thin reeds of bamboo.

"Chan, get the paprika, would you?" Hive yelled to a girl with silky black hair, who was milling around waiting for someone to ask her to do something.

"Flora, you're still here," exclaimed Eccles, as he walked through the door wearing a punk rock t-shirt and nursing his bandaged hand. "Glad you didn't sneak off in the night."

"I was tempted, but I dunno how I'd fare trying to sail Poukai on my own."

"I think you'd be fine," Hope assured, patting Flora's arm. "You know what a mainsail is right?"

"And how to rig ratlines?" Eccles asked.

"And you know how to steer, right?"

"And how to read a compass?"

"Ok, ok, I get it." Flora threw a tea towel at Eccles, who deftly caught it. "I would be hopeless out there. I'd probably steer us into some slip stream towards Australia."

"Are you basing your entire sea knowledge on the plot of Finding Nemo?" Hope asked.

"Yes, yes I am."

"Fine, well in that case watch out for Bruce."

"And Australia would be the least of your worries," Frances interrupted, waltzing over to them with a stack of tin plates. "You could find yourself stranded in the middle of the ocean and disappear forever." The group fell silent.

"I'm just saying," Frances hastily amended, "that you probably shouldn't steal the ship."

"Who's going to steal my ship?" Tane strode into the tent, wide-eyed and clean, his freshly washed, wet hair flopping around his face. Flora looked away, towards the plate stack that Frances was holding. She realised that he was waiting for one of them to take it off of him.

She proffered her arms as Lana mooched into the tent too, looking around for something to eat. She had a half-empty mug of peppermint tea in her hand, and the smell arrived with her.

"Flora," Frances replied breezily. "She was threatening to sneak off in the middle of the night and steal Poukai."

"Really, Brock?" Tane asked, and she could feel that his gaze was both humorous and concerned. Hadn't she just promised him hours ago that she would think about staying?

"It was a joke," Flora muttered, taking the plates from Frances and then stooping over with the weight of them. "I was saying that I couldn't possibly handle Poukai on my own."

"Hey, I don't believe that for a second," Tane said, and she could feel him move forward, as if to help her with the plates, and then think better of it. Instead, Hope put her hands halfway down the stack and lifted the top half into her arms. "If I had to put a wager on it, I'd say that you're more of a pirate than all of us."

"What?" Flora asked, looking up at him, but he was smiling again, and she couldn't tell if he was joking, which surely he must have been.

"I think you're pretty pirate," Lana said, shooting Flora a quick grin. Hope was watching the exchange and she looked at Flora with wide eyes.

"Yo ho ho, it's a pirate's life for me," Lana started singing, and Flora raised her eyebrows. Lana was smiling and holding an apple, from which she took a huge bite. She was in a good mood. "We don't sing enough," she said, and Flora nearly giggled, it was such an unusual thing for Lana to say.

"Well, maybe we don't know the words?" Hope suggested, looking at Lana pointedly, her face looking a little redder than before.

"You'll have to remind us," Flora said, a wicked smile growing on her face.

"Oh, I can do better than that," Lana replied. It seemed as if she'd forgiven Flora for the eavesdropping; she was looking at her with shining eyes. "I know the jig."

"There's a jig?"

"I have got to see this," Tane said loudly, whooping, and Flora felt something like a sudden dart of jealousy pierce her heart, which she quickly shrugged off. Lana smiling and being cheerful was a vast improvement; she wasn't about to upset the balance.

"I'll show you sometime Flora, if you're lucky," Lana said, before walking off singing loudly: "Yo ho ho and a bottle of rum to fill my tum!"

"What the hell?" Flora heard Hope mutter, but it was too late to ask her about it, as more people started joining in with the sea song and then they were all off, setting down plates, ladling beans, carrying great wobbling piles of sliced bread off to the campfire.

Someone yelled for Flora to bring ketchup and she retrieved the huge jar of homemade sauce, which was bigger than her head, and set off to the campfire, the sound of sea shanties still echoing around the tent behind her.

CHAPTER SEVENTEEN
REDOLENT

B reakfast was chaos.
"Lennox has two more bits of toast than me and now there's no bread left!"

"My beans have started sprouting, are you sure they're actually edible?"

"That's not fair, Ritchie, you've got way more beans than me and I'm eight months older than you. Just because you helped Hive put up her curtains, it's favouritism and it's not democratic."

"Why are we acting like this is a democracy, it's a dual dictatorship! No, sorry, I'm only joking…"

"Actually, Frances and I were discussing the extent to which we actually pose as a socialist society. He made the rather fascinating point that we favour a technocratic-driven approach, assuming, of course, that we classify Lana as an expert in sailing and Tane as an expert in environmental solutions."

"Way to kill the buzz, Hive."

"I'm no sailing expert," Lana said, laying on the floor and looking up at the sky. She seemed like a totally different person today. "In fact, I wish I'd never learnt."

"Hey, Flora, watch me burp the alphabet backwards!"

"I'm good, Eccles," Flora replied, the buzz of chatter and

the odd piece of food flying past her. Lana was staring at the sky in her own little world, and Flora found it disconcerting. Lana's trademark white vest had a smudge of marinara sauce across it.

A French boy and girl were talking rapidly in their mother tongue. Their names were Gasquet and DeCalbiac, Ritchie had told her. Gasquet was always on clothes duty; DeCalbiac was some sort of maths and coding genius.

Tane finished eating and took his plate back towards The Kitch, stopping on the way to check that one of the camp radios was secure. There were various radios nailed to boards around the camp; in theory, they linked to Poukai's ship radio, but they looked rarely used. Satisfied that everything was as it should be, Tane continued to the kitchen tent, disappearing behind a colourful teal flap.

Flora looked down. She felt as if she had a beacon that only picked up the location of Tane and Lana. She was getting exhausted listening to it, and looking up every time one of them moved, feeling like a planet orbiting around a double sun.

She was suddenly hit on the top of the head by a flying butterbean. She flinched, too late, and wiped the offending sauce from her brow.

"Is it like this every day?" she asked Hope, who sat next to her and had hoovered up her food in about ten seconds flat. That's when it had become clear that Hope really did have a lot of siblings.

"Pretty much." Hope beamed at the noisy semblance around them. "It's not that different to my old home, you know. Lots of food and mess and burping. Not quite as many real arguments."

I've never experienced anything like it.

Flora watched as Hive and Frances continued a conversation about socialism. Eccles stood in front of a group of his friends showing them his burping accomplishments. The two French-speakers were weighing up who'd been given the most beans. McLarty sat silently, a sharp knife in his hand, whittling a stick into something jagged, and Tane had reappeared from The Kitch only to head in the direction of the beach and Poukai.

Flora felt something glow in her chest. She didn't have siblings – apart from Albert – and her house was mostly silent in the mornings. She felt as if she were part of something. She wanted to interrupt Frances, to tell him about the errs of technocratic-driven societies, and to tell Eccles that his burping was indistinguishable, but she didn't dare. For now, it was enough to glow on the sidelines.

"I'm gonna shower," McLarty said, standing up. "There's usually a queue, unless you go at mealtimes."

"Great. Enjoy." Flora scooped a forkful of beans into her mouth. She hadn't realised how hungry she was. She'd also seen the showers earlier that day, and the word 'shower' was clearly a loose descriptor. It was pretty much a big water butt that had been hoisted up into a tree. The water was cold, and the shower curtain was a mismatched flap of badly sewn-together clothing. Flora wasn't jumping at the chance to try it.

Besides, she thought, as she wolfed down food, *my hair is a nightmare in a normal shower scenario, let alone here.*

Her thick, blonde tumble of curls and tangles took a special conditioner and comb to manage. It was her mum's hair exactly, although her mum had rolled hers into dreadlocks, and there was often a heart-stopping moment when she caught sight of herself in a shop window or a reflective surface and she thought it was her mother.

Flora hated that she looked so much like her mum.

"That was SO FUN," someone was saying. They were all talking about this time that they'd moored up in Norway and it had been so cold that they'd nearly frozen to death while they slept. It had been really funny, apparently.

And here we go on all of the stories about times that I wasn't there...

When Flora was annoyed, she found that everyone

around her started speaking too loudly and she didn't have room to breathe in the space that was left. She would crave being alone, totally alone, the kind of alone where even the sudden caw of a bird would pierce her lungs like a broken stalactite.

She was thinking about getting up and leaving, when someone else seemed to read her mind.

Lana jumped to her feet and wandered over to The Kitch, moving quickly, as if she didn't want to draw attention to herself. If Flora wasn't already highly attuned to the older girl's movements, then she wouldn't have noticed Lana skulk off.

Flora watched the flap of the tent as it swung behind Lana, the chaos carrying on around her: food being thrown, laughter carrying on the smells from the campfire, the sound of forks scraping the last morsels from tin plates, everyone talking about their top Poukai moments.

After a few minutes, Lana appeared again. By her side, her hand clutched a thick chain with a lock on one end. Flora narrowed her eyes, checking that she was seeing it correctly. *Where on earth did that come from?*

Instead of walking towards the campfire, Lana set off in the direction of the toilets, her face downtrodden, her bare feet moving as if she were trying to run without being too conspicuous. Her ankles were laden with colourful anklets and they seemed to flash as she hurried towards the Privy Shack.

That's weird, thought Flora. What was there to chain up in that strange toilet that needed physically emptying? Perhaps Lana had some DIY to do; perhaps she was making something from wood and chains?

Instead of going into the Privy Shack, Lana took an immediate right turn, heading off around the side of the Shack into a densely packed tangle of trees. Flora lost sight of her.

"That was bizarre," she said, only realising that she'd said it out loud a moment too late. She didn't want to cause any more friction with Lana. Not after last night's eavesdropping.

"What was?" Chan asked. She was sat near to Flora and Hope and seemed interested in anything macabre. Despite not being particularly friendly, she oozed a coolness that Flora wished she also possessed.

"Just this... orange bird. It flew into the forest."

"Oh." Chan turned back to her food.

"Really?" Hope asked. "I wonder what it was. My dad's a bit of an ornithologist, he would absolutely love it here. McLarty pointed out an Azores Bullfinch the other day, which apparently is super rare. Bit small for my liking though, I'm looking out for an eagle."

"That would be cool," Flora replied, watching the spot where Lana had disappeared. Why would she need a padlock? Perhaps she was creating some sort of animal pen for the goats.

"Err, Hope," Flora said, feeling her nerves whip up a storm in her chest. "You know... err, Lana?"

"Yeah," Hope said, her voice carefully casual, as if she knew what Flora was about to ask.

"Is she like... single, or... What's her deal, I guess? Does she ever, like, date anyone?"

"Ha." Hope let out a blunt laugh. She paused and Flora saw her swallow. "She's one of the main people in this camp, you know. If you started anything, then I don't think people would like it. Everyone's quite... consistent here."

She seemed to be putting more emphasis on her words than was strictly necessary, and Flora searched desperately for the double meaning.

"Do you know if... if, she'd be looking for a boyfriend, or like, not? If it *was* something... consistent?" Flora struggled to find the right words.

"I think that she *wouldn't* be looking for a boyfriend," Hope said, slowly, thinking it through. "But I still think that you'd be wise to remember what I said about consistency. Trust me, people here hate change. Everyone's desperate for this life to work."

"I get it," Flora replied, her heart hammering in her chest.

Yes, *consistency*; she understood. But most importantly, Lana didn't seem interested in getting a *boyfriend*. It was this thought, above everything, that made Flora suddenly feel a lot more cheerful than she'd felt in a while. She looked around and really appreciated, for the first time, just how beautiful their camp was: trails of sunshine dappled the ground: fronds of fishing nets with jewelled buoys trailed from the trees: huge gnarly shells, gigantic primordial looking things that must have washed up on the beach, and Bell's wooden surfboards, decorated the camp. Bohemian paradise, in harmony with the cheerful calls from the campmates as they set about the morning's duties.

Someone whipped Flora's plate out of her hand, and as she re-entered the present moment, she realised that Hope had left.

"Thank you," she called after Lennox, who was stalking to the washing-up area with a stack of dirty pots, including her plate.

Flora flashed a final look towards the Privy Shack, waiting for Lana to appear, waiting for something to happen. The wind picked up around her ankles.

Why was Lana taking a *chain* into the forest?

△△△

Their hut smelt of her school's wood workshop and fresh flowers. Flora decided that she'd make the effort to neaten her bed every day, and as she picked up her pillow, she remembered her phone inside and that she'd texted her father.

She turned it on and waited for the reassuring vibration in her hand that connected her back to the world. The *real world*, as the Poukers had put it.

Straight away, a notification heralded from the top of

the screen. Her dad had replied. Her heart spluttered and split in half.

CHAPTER EIGHTEEN
PYRRHIC

'Not good, Abbie in hospital, complication. Tried calling you.'

Without a second of hesitation, she called him, and there was one trilling ring in her ear before absolute silence. Her phone had finally died. She stared at the black screen, seeing her horrified face reflected back at her.

Abbie was in hospital. What did 'complication' mean? Was she going to die? How was her dad? And her brother? Her dad must be distraught, he must need someone to lean on, and Flora was out here worrying about goat pens. She ran out of her hut with her phone proffered in front of her, tears streaming down her face already, running to find someone, anyone, who might have a way to contact the mainland.

McLarty was at the campfire, dousing it in a bucket of seawater, carefully keeping his legs and black trainers out of the way of the froth. He looked up as she approached, his face moving from distaste to worry in a flash.

"What's happened?"

"It's my Dad, well no, it's my step mum, she's just had a baby and I texted Dad to see how he was and he said there's a complication and I tried to call him back and my phone died and I don't know whether Abbie's going to be ok or is it a complication with the baby? And he needs me, and I can't call him, do you know if there's anywhere that I can-"

Before she'd finished talking, McLarty had thrown down the bucket, grabbed her hand and was pulling her towards the pathway that would lead them down to the beach. She used her free hand to slot her phone into her borrowed hoodie pocket and then wiped tears and snot off of her face. They both ran on, his fingers tight around her own.

His fierce clench hurt, but she didn't say anything, because it looked like he was going to help her. Maybe he kept a secret mobile phone under a rock on the beach. Or had wired something up in one of the trees. Flora's mind was swinging around, possibilities coming to her as farfetched as him having a cliffside lair with a helipad and a direct link to MI5.

McLarty's trainers crunched the leaves as they ducked under thick arms of foliage, avoiding patches of swamp and swooping lianas. Flora's bare feet were no match, but she ignored the stinging in the fleshy parts of her toes. Eventually, he had to let go of Flora's hand to navigate a fallen tree, and she clutched her fingers to her chest, feeling as if her bones were bruised.

They broke out onto the beach, where small tumbling waves chased each other to the shore under brilliant sunshine. After the depths of the jungle, it felt to Flora as if she'd been reborn, but she didn't dare stop.

McLarty hurried ahead and she was glad of his urgency as she tripped behind him, falling over her own feet on the sand, trying not to think about her dad at the hospital all alone, perhaps rocking the baby while Abbie was in the depths of surgery. Or – God forbid – had the worst happened, and he was at home, howling, unable to even look at Albert?

Stop thinking about it, Flora instructed herself, as she felt fresh tears spill over and fly down her face.

They headed towards Poukai, which was anchored up in the shallows, pulling against its ropes as if it longed to be back on the open sea. *McLarty must keep his phone on the boat*, Flora realised. It didn't make for ease of retrieval, but it certainly had the element of secrecy. If he'd been sneaking off to make phone calls from Poukai, then she certainly hadn't noticed.

They climbed aboard Poukai, using the ladder that McLarty had picked up from the beach, and Flora scaled the rungs quickly, swinging herself over the ledge and onto the deck. Despite her desperation to retrieve McLarty's phone, she automatically inhaled deeply, relishing the smell of the boat, all sun kissed wood and cracked rope. She felt different onboard now, as if she could easily scale the side of it, even steer it. Power was roaring through her, power and adrenaline that threatened to reign in the anchor, slash the ropes and take the boat back to England, with or without McLarty.

While she was scheming, McLarty leant down and unlocked the huge trapdoor which led down to the sleeping quarters. He heaved it open.

"Come on," he urged, and she followed. They descended the stairs into the cavernous, empty room, where lonely hammock hooks glinted from the ceiling. The sound of the sea felt close underfoot, swaying and sloshing against the wooden shell of the ship.

As they arrived in the middle of the room, McLarty spun around, and Flora nearly walked into him. She took a step backwards.

"Look," McLarty said, and his face was shadowed, "you can't tell anyone about this, ok?"

"Of course, I won't tell anyone. Promise."

A vague voice in the back of her mind reminded her that she didn't promise, she never promised, ever since her mum had promised to stay in the city that her dad lived in, and her dad had promised to love her mum for the rest of his life. Flora had long ago decided that promises meant nothing, and she should steer well clear of them.

But this was different, and McLarty had nodded as if the word were the secret to unlocking his trust, and so she went along with it.

"So?" Flora asked, impatient for him to stride over to his secret cubby hole and retrieve what was no doubt a state-of-the-art new phone (because he seemed like the type).

McLarty walked out of the room at the other side, the door that led to the toilets, and after a second of confusion, Flora followed. He walked past the door to the loos and stood at another door, which looked like a bog-standard cupboard. He slid back a thin piece of wood on the door to reveal a coded lock. It was a shiny metal panel with a digital display and a small metal knob.

He swiftly typed in the code: 131118.

"13th of November?" Flora asked, without meaning to. She didn't care, really. She was just on edge, picking on the first thing that might distract her.

"The date of the fire," McLarty muttered. He cast a dark look back at Flora's tear-stained face and then ducked down into the newly unlocked cupboard.

Flora followed him, not stopping to appreciate the fact that the cupboard looked so normal, not like it led to a secret lair at all, and the staircase behind the door was steep and winding and must have taken an age to build. There was light emanating from the bottom of the stairs: blue light, green light, even spots of red light, as if they were descending into a spaceship.

"Welcome to The Den," she heard McLarty say, his voice flattened by the close proximity of the reinforced walls.

△△△

Flora descended and the room was revealed. Computer screens, monitors, wires, keyboards. A huge radar emitted a ghoulish green light across the ceiling. A tiny box-window barely encouraged any daylight. There were empty coffee cups and screwed up balls of paper and stubs of old pencils scattered around, looking as if they'd been there forever, but they must have only been a few days old or they would've fallen on the floor during the last voyage. Flora imagined this room turned into an absolute whirlwind when Poukai was on the move.

In the corner, DeCalbiac hunched in front of two monitors, wearing headphones.

McLarty tapped digits into a huge screen. "DeCalbiac is a genius, but best left alone. What's your dad's number?" He typed '+44'.

Flora recited her dad's number, hoping that she was right. She held her breath as the screen started ringing. *He never answers a call from an unknown number.*

Her and McLarty stared at each other, eyes wide, until finally the voice that she loved most in the world answered.

"Hello? Is that the hospital?"

"Dad, it's me," Flora burst out, rushing forward and causing chaos to all of the empty cups in the process. McLarty ducked out of the way and started to tidy up, trying to be as quiet as possible.

"Flora, what number is this?"

"I'm on my friend's phone. Are you ok?"

"Oh, I thought it might be the doctor," her dad said, sounding like his usual jovial self. "A friend, eh?" he asked. "Not another gamer I hope?"

Flora shot a look towards McLarty, who was pretending not to listen.

"No. But seriously, what's going on? Is Abbie ok? Your message said she was in hospital?"

"Yes, she was," her dad said, a huge sigh following his words. "She had a ruptured cyst. Lots of blood, it was horrendous. I took her in and they've sorted her out and she's back home now. It's all ok, she'll be right as rain in a few days. I'm just waiting on a call to tell us if we need to come back in at all." He sounded tired.

"What about the baby?" Flora asked.

"Albie is absolutely fine. Flourishing, in fact. Hungry little thing, Abbie's already sore from breastfeeding."

"Right," Flora said. She had no idea how to comment on

this, so she swiftly moved back a level. "But seriously, are you ok? I'm going to come home as soon as possible."

"No, don't be silly." Her dad yawned. "You have fun with your mum. It's about time you two spent some time together. Honestly, we're fine here. Abbie's sleeping and me and Albie are about to watch last night's recorded Leeds game. You enjoy yourself.

So, who's this new friend of yours, anything romantic I should know about? Because I've got their phone number, you know."

"No Dad, nothing like that." Flora finally grinned and allowed relief to wash over her. He was alright, Abbie was alright, and the baby was a greedy guts. "He's another gamer type I'm afraid, so I know you wouldn't approve anyway, even if it was like that."

"Too right," her dad replied, and she could hear him opening a bottle of beer. "No more gamers, thank you very much. Speaking of which, some guy called Stu from Bolton called the house phone. Said you haven't been online in a while and he was worried. I told him that you've got yourself a life and hung up."

"Dad!"

"What? I can't have these gaming types calling up the house, Flo. Hacking the landline, probably. Selling our number to buy virtual hamburgers or something."

"They don't do that," Flora said, rolling her eyes and hoping that McLarty would notice and smile, but he was still studiously ignoring her, sweeping piles of papers into a recycling bin.

"Anyway Flo, it's kick off time. You have a good day."

"Should I be worried that you're drinking beer first thing in the morning?" Flora asked, then kicked herself. Was it early morning back home? What was the time difference?

"Don't worry, it's decaf. Or alcohol free, whatever they're calling it. Just the thing to drink with my Weetabix. Catch you later." He hung up the phone.

Flora rubbed her shoulder and felt a knotted muscle slowly relax. She breathed in deeply: stale coffee, the ever-present aroma of Poukai. Rather than missing home even more, hearing her dad sound so involved in his new life made her feel more relaxed about being away. Perhaps she could stay a little bit longer.

"Well, that's a relief," she said, when her heartbeat had returned to normal and McLarty had finished clearing all of the sides until the room resembled more of a working office environment. "So, what is this place? Your secret lair?"

She looked around anew, taking the time to soak in every part of The Den now that she didn't have Abbie to worry about. Abbie was ok. Flora could afford to travel on her curiosities for a few more days at least.

Most of the room's contents were a solid battleship grey. A radar indicated a range of moving dots, creeping slowly along the screen together in a V-formation, the circles slowly throbbing as they moved. The computers were all gently whirring, green lights showing as 'On', but the attached monitors were off. Flora felt an urge to flick all the monitors on, to see what McLarty had been looking at.

'LUSTY 60°25'19.6"N 0°43'43.1"W' was written on a scrap of paper and sellotaped to a metal notice board.

"Wait, isn't that the person who fell overboard?" she asked, pretending that she barely knew about it. In truth, she hadn't forgotten for one minute that Bell had said that Lusty, a member of their crew, had been killed by Tane's stepdad.

"What do you mean?" McLarty asked, but his eyes darted towards the noticeboard without even realising that that was where Flora was looking.

"Lusty, I remember Tane and Lana saying that he'd fallen overboard."

"Ha." McLarty let out a short bark of a laugh and wiped his mouth with the back of his hand. "He didn't fall overboard. He fell for the reward."

"What reward?"

"The reward that Tane's stepdad put on information about Tane's whereabouts. It's a pretty good reward, you'd be tempted initially. But he's an odd guy and I could never do that to Tane, no matter how annoying he can be."

McLarty raised one of his long arms and stroked his other arm subconsciously, his gaze moving to one of the monitors in the corner.

"Wait, wait, wait. So, this kid told Tane's stepdad where to find him?"

"He tried to. He had a secret phone on the island, texted to arrange a call, but our monitors instantly flagged it. We'd already found the phone and mirrored it, so we could see if he did anything." McLarty looked vaguely impressed with himself, but his eyes were still on the other monitor.

Have they mirrored my phone?

"Ok, and then you talked to him?"

"No, then we set off on our next trip. Then I told Lana and then we left him on a beach somewhere. Well, *there* to be exact." He nodded at the coordinates.

"You just abandoned him on a beach somewhere?"

"Yeah. Lana didn't like that one bit."

"What did she want?"

"Execute him. Kill him and push him overboard. It would've been way more secure; now he could still be alive somewhere. And he knows we're near the Azores."

"What?" Flora asked, trying to get her head around all of this information. Someone called Lusty had tried to sell Tane's location to his evil stepfather; Lana had actually wanted them to *kill* a boy. "How come no one here cared about that? Bell said he was like, one of his best friends?"

"Yeah, they have a little gang, that lot. Bell, Eccles, Ritchie, Chan and Easton. Lusty was sort of their leader. He had a lot of influence over them," McLarty said darkly, lingering on the word 'influence'. "They called themselves the DOT Party: Democracy on Taniwha. Had a flag and everything, which Lusty put outside his rubbish little clubhouse.

Bell's pretty stupid, so he didn't really realise what was going on, and Easton's always too busy practising with the... practising, so mainly it was just Lusty trying to get them all together to plot taking over the island. It was really idiotic. I mean, we have enough of a job to stick together and keep this place a secret as it is, let alone splitting off and making side groups.

Well, apart from our operation of course, but that's top, top secret."

There was a silence following his words, as Flora tried to remember her original question. He seemed to be thinking the same thing.

"Oh, and you asked why no one cared that we abandoned him. Obviously, we didn't tell them. We told everyone he was captured and killed. Helped with our whole agenda of making sure no one does anything stupid."

Stupid? Like fraternising with one of the camp bosses, perhaps?

"Still," Flora said, swallowing before she carried on. "How could Lana be ok with killing someone?"

That doesn't compute with the Lana that I know.

"Lana would kill to keep this life," McLarty shrugged. "They all would. Yes, Lana pretends to hate us, to hate the trekking around all over the place. But she'd do anything to keep it, because the alternative is going back to her hellish family. You know her mum chucked her out at eight-years-old because she got her hair cut short?"

"What?"

"Yeah, just chucked her out, locked the door. Lana ended up sleeping in a barn for a week and nearly froze to death; it was Colorado, you know. In the end, she was found by a farmer who took her to the owner of the land. And that's the first time she met Tane's family."

"Wow," Flora said, for want of anything better to say. *Doesn't it just show,* she thought to herself, *that you can have all the money in the world and still have a hellish childhood?*

"Tane said he'd never seen anything so bedraggled." McLarty let out a bitter snort. "Said she looked as if she'd been in the barn for a year. She'd missed school for a week and nearly got kicked out. He said she ate like there was no tomorrow, devouring everything in their kitchen. They were instant friends."

"That's horrendous, she must have been starving," Flora commented. It was deeper than that though, wasn't it? She doubted Lana worried much now about sleeping rough for a week, but it must have been a childhood filled with betrayal, anxiety, abandonment.

"Of course, they had to get out of Tane's house sharpish. In the end," McLarty muttered, his voice mysterious and closed. Flora knew that he wouldn't elaborate.

"It must have been a nightmare for them both," she commented. From what she did know – that Tane's stepdad was a well-known borderline psychopath who milled around the richest parts of American society – it already sounded ripe for disaster. And that was before Tane stole the money.

"Meh, family," McLarty said, his voice filled with distaste. He was waiting for the nearest monitor to spring to life.

"You don't like your own family?"

A look flickered across McLarty's face. The monitor finally displayed his home screen, and he opened an existing tab and started typing lines of Python code into the dark and stuttering programme. Flora leant in closely and saw that he was typing in 'Update' instructions for image recognition, utilising saved photographs on the computer and some sort of Portuguese CCTV system. He pressed Ctrl, Alt and N on the keyboard and the code started to run.

"You're pretty intuitive, you know," Flora said, changing tack. She couldn't be bothered to watch the code run; she was feeling the aftereffects of adrenaline running down her arms. She wanted to hear more about Lana. "I can't believe you've managed to gauge so much from talking to Lana. She always seems like such a closed book."

"Ha, she didn't tell me," McLarty said then, his voice edging on bitter. He watched as hundreds of lines of code started writing themselves. "It's in her emails."

He closed the programme and switched on the monitor that he'd been looking at earlier. The home page for Pictopia flashed up on the screen, beckoning them to log in.

CHAPTER NINETEEN
SERENDIPITY

"What?" Flora cried, instantly forgetting McLarty's admission that he'd read Lana's emails. "What are you doing on Pictopia, there's no way you Pict?"

He looked at her with a sheepish grin and she remembered what he'd said before, about Flora making it to the elephant enclosure.

"'Course I Pict." McLarty grabbed two chairs and set them closely together in front of the monitor. "Can I get you a drink or anything? We have some elderflower cordial upstairs. It's not too bad actually."

"Yeah, ok." Flora nodded, sitting in one of the chairs. "Oh wait, I'm supposed to be on toilet duty today. I can't stay long."

"It's fine, what are they gonna do?" McLarty pushed the sweaty hair back from his forehead. "I doubt Tane would ever have a go at *you*."

"What do you mean?" Flora asked, too quickly, feeling the back of her feet kick the chair.

"What do you think?" he asked. He let out an accidental sigh and then turned and loped up the stairs, his long, wiry legs taking them two at a time.

What do I think? Flora asked herself, but she didn't dare to think on the question in any real way. She leant back in her chair and looked at the post-it note declaring Lusty's

whereabouts to the world.
They just abandoned him.
He was about to sell out Tane.
There was a reward out there for Tane's whereabouts.
Were they all on the run?
The Den was really a who's who of enemies. Tracking the abandoned ex-crew members, the vengeful stepdad, his band of reward-hunters. Flora wondered how much the reward was. A thousand pounds? A hundred thousand pounds? How much was Tane worth?

It's how much Poukai and all the stuff on the island is worth, Flora supposed.

How much does a boat like Poukai cost? How much had Tane spent on pimping up the island, adding in the cascading hot tubs, the sleeping huts, the offshore water park, the professional standard marine volleyball courts?

I mean, there's nothing too fancy. He could have a helipad on this thing, but I suppose that anything here would have had to be brought and built by the crew. Realistically, they aren't going to be able to build a helipad.

A leaflet that had been stuck to the board sung of the benefits of marine conservation. Another piece of paper waved tide times at her, although it didn't say for where. Above both was a register of crew members, with allergies marked. *How incredibly organised.*

Lana – no allergies
Tane – bee stings
Eccles – apple skin, almonds
Frances – no allergies
Hive – no allergies
McLarty – no allergies
Bell - shellfish
Gasquet – dairy
Lennox – no allergies
Ritchie – no allergies

Easton – no allergies
Chan – hay fever
The Harleys – no allergies
DeCalbiac – no allergies
Hope – no allergies

Lusty's name had been crossed through. He had no allergies.

Flora wasn't on the list. Seeing it laid out in black-and-white stung.

You can't have it both ways, she told herself. *You can't aim to get back to the mainland and still want to be part of the family here.*

How long would her dad believe that she was staying with her mum? And wasn't he at all worried about her; her mum had been known to go through all sorts of 'episodes'?

He's tired with the baby, Flora supposed. *Tired and half-delirious.*

Flora realised that if she leant forward and logged into Pictopia then she could potentially be chatting to Stu from Bolton as if no time had passed. He'd ask her how school was, and she'd ask him how many takeaways he'd had that day.

But is that *real* friendship? Would Stu from Bolton have revealed his secret technology lair to help her call her dad? Would he have lied about taking her phone, just so that she could keep hold of it? Would he have offered to teach her to dance?

Well, to be fair, Stu had called the house phone. That must count for something. She may not know whether Stu from Bolton was a real person or perhaps a sophisticated AI robot developed by the nerds at Pictopia, but he obviously cared.

Although, the fact that a gamer that she'd never met had been so worried that she hadn't been in Pictopia that he managed to track down her home telephone number surely spelled out that she spent too much time gaming?

She clicked the button to login and automatically the

suggested username popped up on the screen.

TheEagle.

She was about to log in as TheEagle.

The gamer that Flora had been following so obsessively back home.

The gamer that she'd been watching live on her bus journeys, trying to emulate. The way that TheEagle seemed to be able to defeat anything in their path with zero effort.

The gamer that she'd met in the dark web, talked to in the chat room under the elephant enclosure, who had dismissed her as quickly as he'd met her.

TheEagle was McLarty. Flora felt her stomach flip.

Footsteps. Her heart pounded in her ears. McLarty reappeared. His gaze flicked between her and the screen.

"What's wrong?"

Pull yourself together, fan girl.

"Oh, I was just thinking of Stu from Bolton calling my house. Thinking that that probably means that I game too much, you know?" She swallowed. She didn't want to admit that she'd heard of him, that she followed him obsessively back home. She gazed up at him in a new way, still unable to believe it.

This guy, the one with stooped shoulders and nervous disposition, who constantly moved his hair, this was TheEagle, one of the most powerful gamers in Pictopia. Didn't Stu tell her that he'd talked to TheEagle about Flora? That he'd told TheEagle about her 'broken' home life? That he was always looking for people to help?

McLarty had talked to her in the chat room under the elephant enclosure. He knew who she was. He'd found her.

Was it a co-incidence that she bumped into Ritchie that day in Marks & Spencer? Or was TheEagle coming for her? How much had he already looked into her life? How much of her life had he already hacked before conveniently enlisting her on this ship?

Flora's head was spinning. Her stomach threatened to

heave.

"I've talked to Stu," McLarty said, oblivious to Flora's churning mind, the way that she was staring at him.

Who are you?

"Nice guy," McLarty said.

Why me?

CHAPTER TWENTY
WHEREWITHAL

"Yeah, level 2." McLarty set down the drinks and yanked his chair under him with his foot. "He'd spent fifteen hours trying to get past General Boggle so I showed him how. He was clearly drunk, said he was in the middle of a divorce and Picting was all he had left. A bit sad, but you know, a nice guy."

Flora's shoulders tightened. Stu from Bolton was getting a divorce? This was the first that she'd heard of it. He'd been drinking and upset. He'd spent fifteen hours trying to get past the General, who guarded the Cadaverous Tiger. It was all too much to take in. Stu from Bolton was, in many ways, her closest confidante. Why hadn't he mentioned anything to her? He must have talked to McLarty for what, five minutes?

Stu from Bolton had been the person that she talked to the most back home, in the *real world*. And she hadn't even known this huge thing about him. McLarty might have lied, might have pretended to have no idea who she was... but at least someone wanted her.

Suddenly, she lost all impetus to lean forward and login and talk to Stu. She picked up her mug and took a swig as McLarty started up the game. His fingers moved rapidly across the keyboard, like spiders. His veins were oddly blue.

"McLarty?" Flora asked, as the new Lost Grace level of Pictopia appeared on the screen and McLarty's avatar, a figure with blazing eyes and an eagle across his cloak, sprang into action. Flora felt her mind break into fragments, replaced with nothingness.

Do I know anything about anything in this world?

"Mmm?"

"What's the initiation ceremony? To become part of the group?"

CHAPTER TWENTY-ONE
SURREPTITIOUS

Flora's back hurt. She'd forgotten how much physical commitment it took to game, whether playing or just watching. Five hours had passed, and her fingers twitched as she stored every manoeuvre that McLarty made.

He made it seem so simple. He spoke in a low, fast voice to anyone he met. Their replies came in surround sound, bouncing around the walls of the cabin so that Flora could feel involved, but at least half of them were automated AI bots, designed to make it look like someone else was ahead in the game. Non-Player Characters: too cheerful, too enigmatic, their voices rising with inflection.

The game designers couldn't have McLarty relaxing and logging out for a break; they needed him there, addicted, playing. They tried to sell him skins and designer shoes. They tried to lure him into a virtual bar, where he could buy a virtual beer and play pool against robots. It was easy to see the problem, when you weren't playing.

DeCalbiac shot glances in their direction every so often, rolling her eyes.

"I can't believe you do that rubbish too, Flora," she said with derision, but she gave Flora a friendly smile as she said it. She got up at one point and went for a swim, returning with salty, wet hair, and Flora was glad that the other girl didn't lock herself up *all* day.

McLarty was almost through with Lost Grace and Flora

had no doubt that he'd be one of the first. She'd never seen anyone play as fluidly, as single-mindedly, as in-sync with the game and the developers. She'd found herself lost in the world of Pictopia for great stretches at a time, bounding around giants, darting into neglected prisons, storing up energy, before being brought back to earth by the surround sound voice of a middle-aged Texan woman asking them how to shoot the giant pigeon.

Inside the game, the trees were vibrant, the sea was lifelike, the detail on McLarty's avatar made it look almost like a real person in a cloak. Apart from a few quick toilet breaks, they'd made excellent progress in this uncannily realistic world, and Flora was filled with an immense sense of satisfaction, marred by the anxiety from her twitching thumbs.

That came crashing down when she heard footsteps descending the stairs rapidly.

Tane's face shone, sweat causing his hair to stick up on end. For a moment, he just looked at them, chest heaving as if he'd ran a great distance, eyes wild.

"Where the hell have you been?" he asked, his eyes settling back into wide almonds as he exhaled.

"What does it look like?" McLarty asked, his voice sullen, eyes on the screen. After a moment, when it became clear that Tane wasn't just passing by, he paused the game. Both him and Flora twisted slightly in their seats, faces raised towards Tane, like flowers that have finally been introduced to sunshine.

"You've both missed duties. And look, I'm not a teacher, I'm not gonna run around telling you what to do. But Brock, it's your first week here, I don't really understand why you're running off to game already? And McLarty, why is Brock even down here?"

"Her dad called," McLarty grunted.

"What? About what, is he ok?" Tane asked, immediately alert, eyes finding Flora's. She appreciated for a quick moment that he didn't care about her having her phone on, because that's the only way that she could have known that her dad called, and she felt a rush of feeling.

"Absolutely fine," she assured him, liking the fact that he had been so worried about her whereabouts. He'd clearly been out looking for her, if his dishevelled appearance was anything to go by. "It was a complication, but they're all great now."

"Right," Tane said, holding her gaze for a second too long. Flora's face burned. He took a deep breath in and let it out loudly, his gaze moving towards the radar. "Any news?"

"Nothing," DeCalbiac replied, seeming eager to take part in any conversation with Tane. She'd taken her headphones off the moment that he'd arrived.

"You keep me updated, yeah?"

"Always do," McLarty muttered.

"Look, McLarty, this is sooner than I would have wanted," Tane said, and he was trying to convey something with his eyes that Flora didn't understand.

"I know, but now she's down here…"

"It's just… I want her to like life on the island, you know. Not just think we're… using her." Tane flashed an apologetic glance in Flora's direction.

"Are you guys talking about me?" Flora asked. Tane immediately looked guilty, as if she had cracked some secret code that she couldn't possibly have understood. "What are you going on about: sooner than you would've wanted?"

"We might need some help." McLarty sighed. "DeCalbiac and I can't handle it all ourselves, there's so much to do and so much that we don't know. I saw how good you were at gaming, and your grades in IT, well, you're top 1% in the country. So Tane told me to find you, to get you to be part of our Operation. Operation Poseidon we call it, and we've got a small team here who're working to battle enemies and keep our location a secret. But yeah, I don't want you thinking that we just wanted you here for that. Tane was just thinking…it was his idea, all of this."

McLarty trailed off following a glare from Tane that could burn a hole in the wall. DeCalbiac was looking at Flora with her teeth clenched, her eyes wide.

Flora barely noticed. Her eyes were glued to Tane's face, which had drained of colour, which was looking at her with a helpless sort of pleading, his hands hanging uselessly by his sides. She stared at Tane, the Tane that needed her help with computing, who had brought her onto the island to work in their computer lab, who had deliberately sat and talked to her because he wanted her to enjoy the island so that she would stay working here. The guy who'd stopped her biting her nails and brushed an insect off of her arm and told her that she should think about staying.

Who had manipulated her and pulled on her emotions as if they were toys to be played with.

Flora's eyes filled with hot, angry tears, and she looked down so that her hair swung in front of her face. Heat, as hot as fire, flew through her body, burning her heart, turning it to embers.

"Well, I guess I'll leave you guys to it," Tane said, breathing out, loudly, as if he couldn't handle the tension in the room. His statement seemed to be a question, as if inviting someone, anyone, to say something, to break the choking awkwardness. He wanted to be saved.

"What the hell, Tane?" Flora muttered, and her voice sounded exactly like Lana's, and she blinked away the tears and looked up with the heat of a thousand suns. Tane flinched. His mouth dropped open, but no words came out.

"You don't have to," McLarty offered. "We can just take you home, that's fine."

Both Tane and Flora looked at him. He turned back to the computer and instantly resumed playing. His avatar was about to swing from a cliff and Flora distractedly watched as McLarty scaled down it, grabbing a purple catmint on the way and storing the energy.

"I'm absolutely fine on my own," McLarty said, as if he were talking to himself. Flora didn't dare move in case she smashed something, such was her rage. "He's the one who thought I needed help."

"It's a big job." Tane's voice was low, pleading. He wasn't talking to McLarty. "Look, we're just keeping tabs on my stepfather, ok? He's an arse. Understatement. I just want to make sure that he doesn't try and find me. I mean, he's missing, right, so he's probably drowned at sea, but I don't know. It's just a case of checking in on the family, reading a few emails, accessing some smart home features…"

McLarty carried on playing, as if he could read Flora's mind, as if he knew that she couldn't breathe and she needed something to distract her.

Tane was just using her. He'd conned her.

"We're calling it Operation Poseidon, and I think you could be a really great part of the Operation…"

Flora felt her face burn, but she didn't move her gaze from the screen. She wouldn't give Tane the satisfaction of thinking that she found anything he said remotely interesting.

"Well, then, I'll… I'll leave you guys to it," Tane said, finally, his voice even quieter than before.

Flora's heart pulsed in her throat. DeCalbiac was looking at her as if she were crazy. Footsteps ascended the stairs. A moment later, a door clicked shut.

CHAPTER TWENTY-TWO
PLUVIOPHILE

"I was thinking," McLarty said, when Flora's heart had stopped racing, when her face had lost its flush, "that we could do something about your evil step mum."

He'd progressed further into Lost Grace and was trying to juggle three tortoises, apparently for fun. Flora had to assume that there was some other reason for torturing the poor, virtual creatures.

"Evil step mum?"

"Yeah, this Abbie. It sounds like you've landed yourself a bad one there?"

"No, not at all. She's really nice; she's the only reason there's food in the house."

"Mmm, I get it." Suddenly, the tortoises burst and turned into warrior armour, cladding themselves over McLarty's avatar. "Wanna spy on her?"

"What do you mean?" Flora asked, but McLarty was already tapping away until a phone book appeared on his screen.

"Is this her, Abs and then a heart?"

"What's that?"

"Your dads phone book," McLarty said, trying not to sound impressed with himself, forcing nonchalance.

"Err, then yes, I guess that's her."

"Cool, let's see what she's got... Texts, can't get into

them... Ah, she's a fan of the new Asian instant messaging site, Zip. Lovely. Let's see what we can find in there."

Around them computer monitors whirred, radars beeped. It had the same stuffy atmosphere as her maths classroom, but adrenaline was still coursing through Flora, and she welcomed the everyday sounds of beeping and clicking. Sometimes, on the island, she felt as if she were breathing different air in a new world, which wasn't always pleasant. She found herself craving normal things to anchor her.

Hacking into Abbie's phone would be a welcome distraction. Flora pretended to herself that she wanted him to stop, that it wasn't ethical. But she said nothing.

"Who is Zoe?"

"Abbie's sister," Flora replied, seeing hundreds of messages suddenly load up on his screen. He scrolled through the last few, which were from several days ago.

"Zoe broke her toe, something about a TV show, natural remedies, blah blah blah," McLarty muttered, scrolling upwards. "Oh, this looks interesting. Abbie's annoyed that your dad spent all night in the casino again."

"What?" Flora asked, sitting up straight and straining towards the screen, where black and white text spelled out the problems of her father's marriage. "Dad doesn't gamble."

Flora grabbed the mouse off McLarty and read.

Abbie: Andy spent all night at casino again. Lost everything again. Foodbank for us AGAIN!

Zoe: You've gotta get him help Abs. Can't keep going on like this. How will he help with baby if he's out all night?

Abbie: I know but I can't stop him, can I? He always comes back with f-ing McDonalds too. At least F at her mums, can't be bothered with more drama.

Zoe: You're a SAINT, Abs. Honest to G. No one else would put up with it.

Abbie: I know, just gotta look after my little A. And my big A, when he's not being an idiot.

Zoe: An idiot that you love tho.

Abbie: True.

"I've got to go." Flora's tongue felt heavy, furry. Her vision was blurred. *I can't breathe.*

"Why, what's wrong?" McLarty asked, as if they weren't looking at the same thing. "Are you still upset about Tane using you?"

Flora staggered to her feet and hurried up the stairs, slamming the door behind her. McLarty didn't try and follow. Ahead of her was the entrance to the hammock room, to her left, the toilets. The smell of damp wood penetrated the air. She needed space. She needed the outdoors. She made it onto the deck.

Flora yanked off her hoodie, abandoning it on the planks, and then ran and jumped off the back of Poukai. For a second, her innards all swooped upwards, freefalling, freedom, breathless, weightless… and then cold water, gushing up her nostrils. Deep blue, bubbles. She broke the surface.

Coughing, Flora blinked. The water looked like pure molten glass. She breathed and the air bit at her throat. Tears mingled with the seawater on her cheeks.

Her dad was gambling? He wasn't working nights? As angry and confused as she felt, she couldn't help but take a second to appreciate where she was. She had been met by blinding sunshine and the kind of powdered sand beaches that Pictopia would never be able to accurately portray. Betrayal coursed through her, but it was met with the most astonishing view; her head whirled, and she breathed in deeply, feeling the smell of the sea inflate her, breathing out the musty smell of old coffee cups and computer dust.

Her dad was a gambler.

Tane was nice to her so that she'd work for him.

Flora floated on her back and looked up at the sky, where lazy trails of cloud puffed across pure blue, where bright flashes of unusual birds flew past, heading out to sea. Her arms were half goosebumps, half sunshine. A bird chirruped; the sound echoed off a nearby rock face.

She felt the stress of back home, of the 'real world', melt and sink into the seabed. It was a problem for another time. For another place. She couldn't worry about it now; she couldn't do anything. She felt helpless. She felt as if the island might drive her mad.

I am utterly unable to control anything from here.

She could control herself, that was all. She could control her legs, which kicked at the water to keep her afloat. She could control her mouth, which spat seawater down her chin.

As she tried to make up her mind about what to do, an exotic bird swooped out of the forest, a streak of red, blue and yellow that trilled as it flew. It plummeted down, its long tail feathers straightening, before hovering for a moment and regarding Flora. It let out an almighty squawk and then sped into the distance, to the east side of the island, far beyond the camp. Finally, it disappeared.

Adventure it is, Flora decided, taking the bird as a sign.

△△△

She had followed the bird east, the opposite side to the Privy Shack and Le Jardin. Someone had told her that the full eastern coastline was cliffs; the sea battered the island from that direction, which is why the area around the camp was calm. She'd picked the wrong side to explore, she quickly realised. Dense jungle and the smell of dried animal scat filled her nostrils. Her wet clothes clung to her body as she walked, steaming in the brief glimpses of sunshine. Her hands grew tired of moving branches, and she wished she had water.

Even a stream would be good for her right about now; she'd happily get on all fours and lap at some cool river water.

Eventually, she came across a rough pathway that seemed to be hacked through the trees. Whether manmade or a natural coincidence, she was happy for the breather and the ability to walk without having her hands in front of her.

She followed the pathway, keeping the low rumble of the sea on her right, the sound of bullfinches and croaking frogs steady in her ears. She heard scurrying in the bushes, but every time she turned there was nothing there. Vibrant flowers peaked from the undergrowth; a bright purple frog hopped in her path, forcing her to take a step sideways in case it was poisonous; the smell of freshly grown shoots and damp bogs hit her at different points. She passed a branch coated in huge ants, almost an inch long, which she ducked under.

Ramshackle paths spiralled in all directions; the jungle had borne a natural labyrinth. Her knees were scratched and bleeding, but she finally stumbled into a dusty clearing. Ahead of her, the blue lagoon peeked through the trees.

I've literally done one big loop.

A huge sheet of tarpaulin had been wrenched up and attached to the trees to make an open tent, with only a ceiling and two sides. In front of the canopy, a path dipped down out of sight, presumably heading steeply down to the beach.

As she progressed, wooden statues unveiled themselves: heraldic beasts, totem poles, a cascading wooden wave. There were trinkets and small pieces of mirror set into bamboo, glinting sea glass and swirls of fishing net. The low canopy made it feel like a cave, and the smell of dried incense sticks, set below a fragmentary mirror, brought to mind spells and curses.

Propped against a fallen log, under the sturdy tarpaulin, were three paintings of the sea. A tryptic. Flora wondered how much these original Esmerelda Nuku paintings would be worth. A few million each, at least. They mutilated the sea into a whisper of diamond and dragons. Flora smiled. A private showing at the world's most tropical art gallery.

A mural leant against a thick tree trunk, depicting a woman with an air of sadness staring up at a night's sky. She bore a strong resemblance to Tane.

Also under the canopy squatted a makeshift kitchen, strung-together with bamboo and fresh green shoots. A rusty black kettle sat atop a pile of charcoal, next to a basket of logs and a wooden bucket of water.

The murmurous forest intertwined with the sound of wind and waves, which Flora soon realised was rain hitting the canopy. It fell in great drops around her shelter, the air becoming instantly humid and sweet smelling. The croaking thrum of hundreds of frogs rose up from the forest as one, and she stood and watched the jungle come alive under the pitter-patter of warm raindrops.

May as well make some tea, she figured, not wanting to brave the forest again in the rain. Under the watchful eye of a carved phoenix, she set about arranging logs in the small firepit, using a match to strike a flame and setting the kettle, which already had water inside, onto a ceramic tile, which was being used as a hob.

The kettle whistled and the noise startled a deer, which streaked past the entrance to the canopy, its knobbly, spindled legs navigating the ground with ease. It was in love, no doubt, with life on Taniwha; scared and excited at the same time. Flora listened to its footsteps as it skittered away, feeling a sudden warmth, a feeling akin to bliss. Even though she was alone, she had never felt less lonely. The forest hummed around her. Taniwha fizzed with life, injecting her breath with a type of addictive drug, the name of which she pressed across the inside of her mind. Nature.

Flora made tea using fresh mint leaves that were growing near the logs, inhaling the cleansing bite, and then sunk into a smooth wooden chair by the entrance of the canopy. It was only her and the universe, and for the first time in a while, she found she could think clearly. She watched the rain as it cascaded the length of long, sultry leaves, pooling in golden rivulets on the floor, reflecting the autumn leaves towards the stormy sky.

It reminded her of English countryside, of the Forest of Dean or the thickets of Cornwall, rain on a Summer Sunday, hopeful fresh green buds, collecting bugs in jamjars. She created a Snail Olympics one year; another year she caught butterflies and looked up their latin names.

Does Tane sit here to think? To decide what to do about his stepfather, about the camp? To decide who to recruit next, and how they might be useful? To decide who to sit with and watch the stars, to have pretend conversations with, all the while knowing that you're only trying to keep them happy so they'll work for you?

It's not worth trusting anyone. Just look at dad.

Even if Flora's dad *was* into gambling and had an addiction, it didn't change him as a father, she reasoned. He probably felt shamed into silence. She remembered reading about Axer Nuku-Halliday, how he'd got himself into debt, how he was desperately chasing the money so that he could repay his creditors. *Another proud man, but at least Dad hasn't got a bounty on my head.*

She remembered how Lusty had fallen for the money, how Lana wanted him killed. That was a different problem altogether. She was furious with Tane; she felt as if she had, for all intents and purposes, been kidnapped. It was one thing when she'd stayed somewhat willingly, thinking that she was joining them on their adventure as an equal, excited to be part of a huge group of friends, all living together on an island so stunning that she couldn't have made it up in her wildest dreams.

But it was another thing knowing that they'd conned her into joining. That they didn't want her as an equal; they wanted her as a worker, as a lookout.

Ritchie must have tracked her down. And then he'd borrowed her phone, she remembered. He must have added the same tracking software that they had on Lusty's phone, probably mirrored her own, watched as she spent evenings scrolling through Arlo and Natalia's social media feeds: desperate, sad, alone.

She burned with shame. Had they thought her a loser, a social media stalker, with her 'broken' home life and her sickening longing for Balenciaga shoes, for the beanie hat in M&S, for something *nice?*

When Flora's eyes decided to cry, she instinctively stuck out her tongue to taste the sadness.

It was a lot to take on. And then there was McLarty's statement that she didn't *have* to stay, that they could take her home. She wasn't ready for that; no matter how angry she was at Tane, she wasn't ready to detach herself from this world. She already felt so bonded to the island that it would cause physical grief.

It's not just the island. It's who I can be here. It's not having to constantly worry about Jen, exams, and now my dad... It's waking up to the sunny campsite, hearing people snoring, bickering over food, requesting to join Planet Belonging. It's the air *here.*

Before long, the stars started to wake. They sparkled and flirted across the sky, overtaken by aeroplanes filled with well-dressed individuals heading to far flung destinations. The thought of being packed into an aeroplane, surrounded by fuggy breath and normal humans, made Flora shudder.

She wiped her face and then stood up to wash her mug, or at the very least to swill it out. She noticed a plaque on the workbench. It had been half engraved with ornate flowers and barely-there letters.

What does it say?

She moved a white-handled tool and brushed away the sawdust.

Flora.

CHAPTER TWENTY-THREE
ELIXIR

Flora was used to not being missed and so, when she finally arrived back at the campsite, the consternation of not only McLarty and Hope, but also Lana, was disconcerting.

"Babe, you can't just run off," were Hope's welcoming words, accompanied by a sympathetic smile, as if Flora had tried to escape the island and failed.

"Are you ok?" McLarty asked. He was sat on a log. Flora nodded, wondering if they all really cared about where she was, or whether they were just pretending.

"Where were you?" Lana asked, and there was a strange expression in her eyes. Flora licked her lips, tasted saltwater.

"I wasn't trying to run off." Flora looked down at her filthy feet. Around her, the crew were preparing for a rainy night inside the huts: carrying plates to their rooms, scurrying to avoid the last stray drops from a rumbling, hungry sky. The rain had paused but was due to start up again, or so their resident meteorologist, one of the Harley siblings, had informed everyone.

The most startling of all of the skills in the camp was Bell's skill, which turned out to be horticulture, surprising only because Bell didn't seem like the type.

"It's like, art meets science, you know?" he'd told Flora, as she watched him examine a bucket of gnarled courgettes and innocent baby pumpkins.

"Good, because you won't get very far. Try and stick around camp," Lana said, the odd expression dropped. Flora nodded again, feeling the hot ground reject the rain, tasting the droplets as they soared back up.

"Trust me, I've been there," Hope murmured. "I once got as far as Sunset Beach, past the Privy Shack. Ended up kipping on the sand and finding out why everyone calls it that; it's beautiful at night, but right far away."

"How long ago was that?" Lana asked, her voice sharp. Flora accidentally looked at her lips and then looked away, trying not to imagine kissing them.

"Err, ages ago. Like, a year ago."

"Good." Lana strode off to help with the Privy Shack. There had been a leak and Frances was stood outside, clutching damp toilet rolls and loudly panicking.

"Still, better than going the other way, to the east of the island. No man's land, that. Just you and miles of wild jungle." Hope shuddered.

That was the direction Flora had taken to get to Tane's carpentry tent. She breathed out slowly into the damp air, realising just how lucky she'd been. She could still be wandering through the wilderness, looking to the candlelit skies for a sign.

"Nightmare," Flora said, still slightly distracted by Lana, who was being told, in woeful detail, how exactly the leak occurred.

"Anyway, let's go to your hut. I'll bring the food, you go and nab a bottle of the bean stuff, would you? Frances keeps it in a cubby in the back of the tree outside The Kitch." Hope pushed her bangle up her arm.

"That stuff is disgusting."

"I know, but after a few sips you don't notice. Lennox had a whole bottle to himself once, swears that he saw a bear strolling through camp. Listen," Hope lowered her voice and looked, "Tane told me that you know about Operation Poseidon. We've got a meeting tomorrow night, midnight, in

Tane's treehouse."

"But…" Flora started to say, feeling a million thoughts spring to mind: she didn't really know what Operation Poseidon was, still, and she was annoyed at Tane, and she wasn't sure that she should be going to a secret meeting if she wasn't committed to joining them, and also… she felt betrayed.

If Hope noticed any of these thoughts on Flora's face then she didn't respond, merely saying "I know, how cool is it that he has a treehouse!", and then sidling off to steal food. Flora was left standing alone, feeling the prickling of dusk in her extremities.

"Are you Flora Brock?" a voice muttered. She started, but it was only one of the Harley siblings, the youngest, whose spiked hair and wide eyes resembled a surprised hedgehog. They were clasping a steaming cup of something that smelt like vomit. It made Flora, in her still-damp clothes, swallow on impulse.

"Yeah. How come?"

"I overheard that you want to be initiated."

"Well, I was just asking about it. I don't know whether it's like a long-term, like, being one of you, or…"

"You're already one of us," the random Harley sibling told her.

"Oh right," Flora said, feeling her chest glow, even though she'd never met this person before. She'd never been told such a thing, and here it had been gifted from the most random of sources. "But doesn't it hurt?"

"Don't worry," the person with the spiked hair told her. "We'll get extra bean juice."

△△△

"There is no way you've kissed Harry Styles," Hope blasted out, her laughter ricocheting off the low ceiling, meeting the low rumble of thunder outside. Raindrops the size of marbles fell on the roof of the hut and the sole window was steamed up so that it had become useless, serving only as an indication of the sun setting.

It was two hours later, and Flora's hut was packed to bursting. She was slowly drying, having recently sprinted from one of the huts nearby, getting lashed with rain in the process.

She sat on Frances's bed, pushed against the wooden wall by Hope. Next to Hope sat Lennox, his hand casually resting on Hope's leg every so often, causing her to blush a deep shade of crimson that she clearly thought no one would notice. Next to Lennox sat Frances, who had at first been chagrined about so many people on his bed, but after a few swigs of bean juice had started to talk loudly, to anyone who would listen, about the merits of jellyfish.

Hive sat on her bed facing them, next to Eccles and Tane, who was sat with one leg out in front of him and the other bent so that his bare foot met his trousered inner knee. He was at a complete diagonal to Flora; she sat at the top of Frances's bed and he sat at the foot of Hives', and yet their eyes constantly caught, as if they were sat across from one another. She was furious with him, and yet she couldn't stop accidentally looking. At one point she was sure that he mouthed the word 'sorry', but she wouldn't look directly at him to find out.

She was too busy trying not to smile, anyway; it felt like having a sleepover with a group of friends. She worried about talking, in case she said something wrong, in case they thought her weird.

I shouldn't mention gaming, that's for sure. Just look how McLarty hasn't been invited.

The three Harley siblings sat on Flora's futon, joining in the conversation every so often, but mostly tattooing each other without putting any ink in the gun.

In the background, a solar powered radio played French

pop songs, interrupted sporadically by static and low-voiced crackling, which was drowned out at any rate by the loud voices on the beds.

"I did, actually," Hive said, indignant, sipping her metal mug of steaming liquid. "My mum took me to his concert, and we met outside the toilets. He was nice."

"No way," Hope cried, and Eccles guffawed so loudly that he nearly fell off the bed. "Why was Harry Styles outside the public loos? Surely, he's got his own toilet?"

"Well, I don't know. Maybe his toilet was broken."

"Watermelon Sugar," Lennox sang in his Irish twang, his mighty eyebrows raised. He was drinking a goblet of rum; Tane had brought a bottle of Ron Zacapa Centenario XO rum, which both he and Lennox were drinking, because "Lennox is eighteen, legal drinking age in Portugal, our nearest landmass, and I'm eighteen soon."

Flora had pointed out to Lennox that she would be eighteen next year, which was basically the same thing, to which Lennox had given her a flagon with a tiny amount of rum circling the bottom. She'd tried it and it caused her to cough and splutter, and Tane had asked her if she was ok. She'd ignored him.

"Watermelon Sugar…" Lennox sang.

"…High," Eccles continued, as always the loudest voice. They all fell about laughing, Lennox purposefully leaning on Hope. She batted him away with a deep blush in her cheeks.

"There is no way that Harry Styles was just lurking outside the public toilets waiting for a snog," Hope said, causing a round of laughter. "Sorry mate."

"Well, I wish I hadn't told you all." Hive sniffed and there was a lull while everyone tried to work out whether she was actually offended.

"If you believe you kissed Harry Styles, then who are we to object?" Flora said kindly, but Hive sniffed at her hot drink and didn't make eye contact.

"True," Tane said, joining the conversation eagerly. "I

mean, what is reality? If Hive believes something, that's her reality. How can we have a reality on the situation if we weren't there?"

"Reality can't only be formed by being somewhere," Flora said, pushing Hope so that she could sit back up and causing Hope to fall onto Lennox in the process, something he didn't look too unhappy about.

"You can actually make noodles out of them," Frances told the Harleys, who were blatantly ignoring him. No one cared about jellyfish.

"If a tree falls in the forest," said Tane, reaching out for the bottle of bean juice that was being passed around. He took a swig and then leaned forward to hand it to Flora. She took it without looking directly at him, feeling that she had no choice. A tiny part of her felt a smidgen of the old joy.

"If a tree falls in the forest and no one's there to hear it, then it still fell," Flora said.

"I'm surprised at that," Tane said, as Flora burnt her throat with one swig. "Isn't a second reality your bag? Isn't that what gaming essentially is, taking yourself to an alternate reality for a while?"

"Well, yes," Flora said, trying to sound careful and considered. "But you'd have to be an idiot to think that you were actually living the game. You need toilet breaks, for one."

"Good point," Tane said, smiling at the floor.

"It's the classic solipsist debate," Frances said suddenly, giving up on entertaining the Harleys with the errs of cooking with jellyfish. "What is reality? Is it merely in our own heads? Is there such a thing?"

"I really like your hair," one of the Harley siblings called to Flora, leaning forward so that her gloomy voice could be heard amongst the chatter.

"Thanks," Flora replied, brightly. She had barely heard the Harleys talk since they'd arrived in the hut alongside her. "I like yours."

"Can I dye it?" the girl asked, her eyeliner-framed

eyeballs looking keenly at Flora.

"Err, how?"

"Just a few streaks. Like, a dark red. It would look so good on you."

"Ok, maybe," Flora replied, still trying to look friendly and pleasant despite the odd turn that the conversation had taken. Tane was trying not to laugh.

"My reality is that we need Frances to make nicer drinks," Eccles shouted, taking another swig of the flask and then spitting out the whole mouthful with a loud: "gahhh!"

"It's time for you to go to bed." Hive's voice was firm, her eyeballs wide and appalled. A thin trail of green spots lay soaking into her duvet.

"Yeah, we could do," replied Eccles, "but that would be boring."

"I know..." Frances stood up and wavered slightly. "Let's go skinny dipping!" He raised his metal goblet in a toast.

"Alright," said Lennox straight away, standing up and pulling Hope up by the hand, his face displaying such an eager smile that Flora found it almost entirely off-putting. Thankfully, he wasn't looking at her.

"Let's go down to the sea," Hope said cautiously, "but maybe not skinny dip."

"I'm in," Tane said, standing up and looking towards the misted window. "I love a swim in the rain."

"Can I swim already?" Flora asked the Harleys.

"Just try not to get your shoulder too wet," they advised, in unison.

CHAPTER TWENTY
CYNOSURE

The sea was still warm until she reached her breastbone, and then her feet found the cold silt that lay further within the lagoon. It felt as if her toes had been plunged into ice, and she willed the hot blood from the rest of her body to travel south, quickly.

At night, Taniwha's lagoon was ethereal, lit only by moonlight and stars, the thick jungle a sprawling mass around them. Wisps of textured cloud moved slowly through the sky, evolving into different shapes, of dragons and vipers, mushrooms and arrows.

Owls and crickets created a chorus, filling in the space left by the French radio station, their tune carried on a breeze that was colder than the daytime gusts.

Flora was starting to feel a little funny from the drink. Behind her, the trees were talking, but she didn't strain to hear what they were saying. Above her, a cloud formed the shape of a pen, and then a seahorse.

On her shoulder, cling film shone up at the sky, reflecting the moon. They didn't all know yet. They didn't know what she'd done. She wanted one person to see it first.

"Fair play," a voice called from the shore. Flora smiled. Dolphins started diving around her, splashing her body. It felt refreshing and it took her a moment to wonder why she hadn't seen dolphins here before. She wondered that for a long time, staring at the moonlight on the water, before Tane's face swam in front of her.

"Did you see the dolphins?" she asked him, her voice sounding far away.

"Dolphins?" he asked. He seemed delighted, but perhaps that was because someone else was laughing. "I don't think there are dolphins out here, Brock. Maybe out of the lagoon, but I haven't seen any come in here. Frances, how much of that stuff did she have?"

"Jellyfish," Frances cried from the shore, and as Flora turned, she saw him raise his hands high into the air, as if the moon were a giant jellyfish. Maybe it was.

"Brock, are you ok?" Tane asked. He didn't reach out to her, maybe because she was wearing her underwear. She felt as if she were wrapped in a cool blanket, being nursed by the gently rocking water, dressed in moving, shifting black waves.

"I'm perfect," she said, and she meant it. *I have never felt so light*, she thought. Or maybe she said. She felt as if she were drifting up towards the moon.

"Ok, I'm in," a voice screeched, and it sounded a lot like Hope, but it was followed by a stream of dolphin clicks.

They all left. Flora heard them howling through the forest, back to camp, to undertake some mad dare that Lennox had just made for them.

They were alone, Flora and Tane, in the vast expanse of the lagoon, of the universe. The night was still, the stars hung like a theatre set. The rain was on pause. A shooting star, or more likely a plane, streaked across the sky, and the movement took Flora's breath away.

"This is my favourite moment," she said, smiling at Tane, his face the only thing visible in a sea of rippling navy. The sharp features of his nose, the line of his top lip, the stubble that clung to his skin, all of it in various shades of grey. The moment hung, still, for a long moment.

"Why did you engrave my name on a plaque?" she whispered.

"What?" he asked, suddenly, voice sharp. His voice was

like the loud crack of a whip, and she immediately regretted asking.

"I found it in your carpentry workshop. A wooden plaque with Flora on."

"Ah, right," he said, and he looked away from her. "I was just practising with letters. They're harder than you think, you know."

"Right," Flora said, the cold pressing against her lungs.

"And..." he breathed in, ran a hand through his hair and looked back at Flora, "...and obviously there was only one name I wanted to practise with."

She took a sharp breath in. His eyes were alive, dancing, reflecting the waves.

"Why?" she whispered, needing him to say it, needing to hear those words that would make everything different, that would tell her that she was right, it wasn't all about Operation Poseidon, it meant more to him.

He opened his mouth to respond, but no sound came out. He just looked at her, his eyes holding something between confusion and pain, his breath ragged. Flora couldn't stand it for a moment longer, she felt as if she were about to burst; her heart had started physically slamming her organs so hard that she had to do something, anything.

She stepped forwards, until they were inches apart, and very gently leant in and put her lips against his.

Cold, smooth, harder than she was expecting. Everything fired through her brain, and nothing did. Nights on Pictopia. The school bus. The smell of Marks and Spencer. Jen's bedroom. Oxygen.

Oxygen and sea, and the smell of fire. The smell of Tane's carpentry tent. That plaque: *Flora*. There was only one name that he wanted to practise with. Passion and lust and excitement coursed through her whole body.

But he didn't kiss her back.

Flora pulled her face away and took a step backwards, towards the shore, her eyes searching his face, wondering whether she'd misread everything.

"I can't," he said, and he made a noise of anguish, like *Ugghhh*, into the night. "I just feel like it's not the responsible thing to do."

"What do you mean?"

"Are you of sound mind?" Tane asked, looking at Flora with an expression of torment and lust, his eyes black and alight, his lips parted. He raised a hand to push his hair back and his skin, ivory under the moonlight, stretched across a toned bicep. She shuddered. The cold silt slid over her toes.

"Are you joking?" Her voice stuttered; she'd started shaking from the cold, from the moment, from the effort of not crying. He looked down at her for another moment; her wet hair cascading around her, her shivering jaw, her eyes, which were filling with tears. And then he pulled her towards him by the waist, his hands firm on her skin, his lips hard against hers, hungry, wild, absolute, crushing her to his body, running his hand up her back and tangling his fingers in her hair.

She felt as if she were leaving her body, watching from above, while at the same time being terribly and deliciously present, her heart skipping in loops around them, his breath hot against hers, his strong arms holding her in place, heating her through, steadying her.

They were lost in one another, the only two people in the world, heart-to-heart. Nothing else mattered. Their heartbeats hammered together as one.

Tane pulled away first.

He looked around quickly, as if to see who might be watching. When it became clear that no one was, he relaxed, letting go of Flora.

"No," he said, his voice low and husky. He seemed to be talking to himself; he shook his head as if he had water in his ears. "Not like this."

His voice was almost lost in the hush of the ocean, and the waves shone brilliantly under the moonlight until Flora could barely keep her eyes open. She felt tired all of a sudden; completely exhausted. Trees hummed around them; cicadas shivered out a mournful bale. The world was subdued. The jellyfish moon disappeared behind clouds, and Tane turned into a chalky statue.

"Not like what?" Flora muttered, her body suddenly cold and empty. He wasn't looking at her; he was still staring at the shore as if searching for someone. She wished that he would dip his head down again and kiss her. But he remained resolute, frozen, as if he were suddenly rendered in marble.

"If this is going to happen," he said, and his voice was barely a rusty croak, "and believe me, I really want it to happen, then I'll be damned if it happens after a night on that homemade moonshine. And..."

"And what?"

"I don't know if it even can. Happen, I mean. It wouldn't work for the camp. For Lana, for Frances, for all of them."

Flora felt her heart drop down into the silt, where it was enveloped and sealed off.

"Who cares about the stupid camp?" she asked. The wind started to prick at her eyeballs, trying to wash away her words. She moved backwards.

"Ah, you don't get it yet. You don't feel it, but you will," Tane replied, looking at her sadly, as if he was a million years old. The waves picked up around them. Flora felt seaweed move around her feet, as if the seabed had come alive, as if hands were reaching up to stroke her bare skin, to tell her that Taniwha wasn't merely a lump of rock in a thrashing sea. It was an island of magic.

"Did you know that the Portuguese believe that all of these islands are mountain peaks from the submerged continent of Atlantis?" Tane asked, looking towards the raw sand, which dragged at the mouth of the ocean.

"Arabian caravels tried to move onto these islands and they were driven back by dangerous seas; they couldn't manage it, even though they thought it paradise. The islands between here and the Azores had habits of actually *disappearing* and then reappearing; the island next to S. Miguel hid from view soon after it was mapped.

The nearest islands believe in fairies, that there are actually fairies living in the wooded slopes of Monte Brasil, and the fisherfolk who visit the Ilheos de Cabras on the Bay of Angra watch as their kids leave for America, to become what my mom would've wanted, even as their bays, their land, is spun by fairies.

Visit the boiling springs, visit the craggy east side of our island, wait until you see a spouting geyser or the distant smoke from a flaming volcano and then you'll see it. We're on enchanted ground. It's not just about protecting our hearts."

Flora felt a confusion so deep that it made her heart ache. And still, all she could think was: *Lana lives on enchanted ground.* She wanted the other girl to show her the boiling springs and the geysers and the far-off glimpse of the world's rage.

"You understand, right?" he asked, and his eyes were the saddest things that she'd ever seen, so sad that she wanted to forget where she ended and he began so that she could swallow his pain.

"Understand that you're so worried about what people would think that this thing between us can't happen?" she muttered, digging her toes into the grasping fingers of the seabed.

"Yes," Tane said, perhaps mistakenly. "Because everyone... because Lana-"

"Yeah, I understand," Flora interrupted.

She understood what he really meant; he couldn't risk his friendship with Lana. They were blood brothers, entwined together forever, the backbone and the skull of the camp, the fossil and the rock underfoot. The river water and the sea water, converged together so that they physically couldn't be filtered apart, so that no one could taste where one ended and the other started.

It wasn't love as she understood it. She had never known a love like it.

Tane looked away again, his brow furrowed. Flora felt another shiver bolt through her from the cold water.

"I should go to bed," she said, her voice calm, mature. She wasn't going to waste time with Tane anymore; he'd already let her down once, and now this. It was an emotional rollercoaster that Flora just didn't need to be on.

She looked around, trying to still her breathing to match her new resolution, to remember how it was so that she could move forwards into the new.

This calm, white world would never be the same, because that magic could never be recreated, only added to in a different situation, like a brand-new painting that still held the beating heart of the original scene, but the picture would be slightly different. That was the moment and it happened, and it could never happen again, not the same, because that was the curse of time, of not moving backwards. She forced herself to press on, to let Taniwha into her pores, into the cavity in her chest.

"I like you, Brock," Tane said. He fell onto his back and floated on the black surface, easily undulating with the seawater. Flora turned towards the shore. She felt goosebumps on the soles of her feet, where her skin met the silt and sand. Poukai remained quiet, silenced by fairies who were giving her a moment.

Tane drifted forward until his hand was on her back. She reached out and the fingers of his other hand slipped between hers. She felt the seabed clutch her heart tightly between ever-moving digits. Tane and Flora held each other all the way up to the shore, where he turned away to pull on a pair of shorts and wait for her to get dressed.

Friendship handholding. A final goodbye.

She imagined him saying the word "Sorry". Or perhaps he did say it; perhaps it travelled to her on the breeze, which felt warmer from the land.

She didn't reply, either way. She couldn't find her clothes and she put on a t-shirt instead, which smelt overwhelmingly of Tane, of musk and sweat. She looked around further and found her leggings by the tree, an immense tiredness growing within her.

Finally, she arrived back to Tane, and with the beautiful sadness of an inevitable ending, they wandered into the jungle, arriving at the campsite all too quickly, smelling like moonlight and secrets, passion and all of that which could never be.

CHAPTER TWENTY-FIVE
PHOSPHENES

As Flora lay in bed, her shoulder stinging, firing off pain receptors in parts of her skull that she didn't know existed, she had something akin to an epiphany. Perhaps it was the moonshine.

Lana and Tane are the beating heart of this life. This life that everyone relies on. Lana and Tane are the only thing. They both like me. They both know that the other likes me. No one is willing to break the camp up over one silly, gaming, nerdy, frightened, thoughtless, broken, broken girl.

She decided that it was definitely the moonshine.

She waited until the adrenaline stopped filtering through the ceiling before she closed her eyes.

△△△

"Be quiet," her mum was saying, her eyes filled with rage. Her hands pushed Flora roughly onto the floor and then pulled her back up. She twisted to the side and her bedding tried to strangle her. Only it wasn't her mum, it was Mrs White, and she was screaming at her for fraternising with boys.

You'd love Tane, Flora tried to say, but she couldn't breathe well enough to get the words out. *Would* Mrs White love Tane? Possibly not. Possibly she'd think that was an entitled, obnoxious, rich kid. That would be her first impression. If she got to know him, if she really spent time with him, she'd see that the money didn't make any difference to his whirlwind of a mind.

If he had been born poor, he'd likely still be living up in the Colorado mountains, sleeping between trees in a roughly plaited hammock, talking to the bears, attracting people to him like the Pied Piper.

She wanted to explain that, only Mrs White was still strangling her. Flora couldn't swallow; her throat was burning; her face wanted to burst; her lungs felt as if they might explode. Someone put a pillow over Flora's face, pressed down. It felt like two pairs of hands now; she'd sprouted additional arms, and they were pressing down until she found herself somewhere between nightmare and consciousness, where her eyelids were pressing a hellish red into her skull.

Suddenly, all pressure let off.

"Leave Tane alone." The words were hissed into her ear. Everything was dark. The pillow was still over her face. Mrs White just wanted to warn her, not to actually kill her. The door closed.

In the silence, Mrs White went to sit in the corner. She stared at Flora with malevolent eyes. The lack of oxygen sent Flora spiralling back down, down towards the world that lay between granite and fire.

CHAPTER TWENTY-SIX
AURORA

I *haven't done anything*, she thought. It was late morning. The pillow wasn't on Flora's face anymore, but the words were still in her ears, as fresh as if they were being played on repeat.

"Anything about what? If you want to skip breakfast, see if I care, but I know you'll regret it later if you don't eat." It was Hope, who was sat on Flora's feet, her own voice groggy.

"Agh," Flora cried, feeling headachy and sick. Her neck hurt. "I've got a cold. Maybe the flu." Her voice came out as a rasp. She could feel her arms shaking.

"You haven't got a cold," Hope teased, laying down on Flora's futon. "You're feeling the aftereffects of some seriously rancid broad beans. Frances should be ashamed of himself."

"What's going on?" Flora asked, trying to collect her thoughts. Had that all been a dream, or had someone really tried to strangle her? Had someone actually told her to stay away from Tane?

Because it wasn't true, her first thought: *I haven't done anything*. She *had* done something. She'd kissed him, out there in the ocean. Her chest burned. Her mind couldn't grasp a solid thought. If someone had tried to strangle her then they'd picked a time when she couldn't tell reality from the broad bean after-effects. *Am I imagining it? Was it all a nightmare?*

Hope was nattering away and laughing, something about Hive and Frances being in a huff that no one was ready for kitchen duty. Flora felt her mouth peel into a dehydrated smile. It reminded her of how she and Jen used to lie awake in the same bed, swapping stories. There was something immensely soothing about lying in bed next to a friend.

What happened last night?

"I love your new hair," Hope said, and that was enough to get Flora to sit upright. "It looks really good." Flora scrambled out of bed and ran to the small rusty mirror that was tacked onto the back of the door.

"What the…" Her hair, her blonde mass of scrambled curls and matted tendrils, had streaks throughout, starting as a frame around her face. The streaks were a dark burgundy, almost a pink in some areas, and a deep blood-red in others.

It almost distracted from the crimson bruising that sat either side of her neck, hiding in the shadows.

Flora looked at her neck. *Did the Harleys strangle me, when they snuck in to dye my hair? Who did this? Why would they warn me against Tane?*

Don't tell Hope. She'll only worry. But surely, she'd be on my side? You can't let her know that you're breaking up camp. You're causing problems. If she knows, if everyone finds out, then they'll take you home. You'll be evicted, just like Lusty was.

"Please tell me this isn't dyed with blood?" Flora asked, coughing a laugh, running her hand through the crimson and pulling it forwards to hide her neck. It was the first time that she'd been grateful for her thick mass of hair.

"Oh my God, mate, I doubt it," Hope said, cackling. "They use some kind of henna thing. It's organic."

How come she hasn't noticed the bruising?

"Oh, well that's ok then," Flora said, rolling her eyes. Her heart was thrumming. She secretly did her finger touching routine: one, two, three, four, one, two, three, four.

"It just looks more dramatic because you're blonde. I'm sure they've done it to loads of us, but you can't see it as much on brunettes. In fact, I remember Bell having it done last year. It grew out, don't worry."

So, someone did try to kill me.

"Ugh," Flora said, trying to sort her feelings, which kept falling through her mental sieve and then churning up again. She felt dehydrated and hungry and couldn't hold on to any real thoughts. "Let's find breakfast."

"In a minute," Hope said, looking up at Flora from her own bed. Hope's eyes were full of mischief. "First, I want you to tell me everything."

No.

"Everything about what?" Flora's heart lurched into her throat. How much did Hope see last night? Had the others really left to go back to the camp, or had they been on the beach? She couldn't remember now.

And had Tane really kissed her, or was that her imagination? She remembered kissing him, forcing herself on him. That made her cringe. Mrs White would consider that assault. The thought of having to face him today, of seeing him at breakfast...

Maybe I should let them take me back to England.

"You and Tane! He's clearly absolutely obsessed with you. You know, he never usually hangs out with us? And last night, you were literally all he was looking at."

Flora felt a shard of her heart break off and poke her in the throat. Her neck ached. She started plaiting a few strands of her hair. She pulled too hard. Her scalp burned; a hair came loose.

"I'm sure he wasn't." Flora rolled her eyes, hoping it looked nonchalant. She looked back at the mirror. This time, someone else looked out from behind the rusty smears. Smiling lips. Scared eyes.

"You're wearing his t-shirt," Hope said flatly, looking down at Flora's chest, where the Colorado Eagle spread its wings. Wings that beat just a few inches from the bruises.

Freedom meets hell.

"Oh, right." Flora felt her ears engage and pull the skin back from her face in an involuntary grimace. That was true, at least. No matter what might or might not be able to happen, and no matter who was warning her, she took a glimmer of pleasure from wearing his t-shirt.

When did I start caring what people think?
When they started trying to murder me.

The t-shirt smelled like Tane and she sniffed her shoulder, inhaling his musky scent. Her new tattoo prickled and burned. Her body felt very present.

"But I thought that you and Lana were like, into each other?" Hope asked, lowering her voice as they heard someone walk past the hut. Flora felt her face burn. Hope sounded accusatory.

The idea that she liked both sexes was still new to Flora, and she hadn't yet solidified this element of her personality. If, indeed, it needed solidifying. It didn't feel like something that needed a brand, which required a change in how she acted or how she explained herself; instead, it felt fluid and exciting and just right. As if her personality and her breath had merged into one, finally, and she was free to live, to love, to fill in the gaps that were previously pervading as anxiety and loneliness and feeling like an outsider.

And it helps that Hope is treating this all as totally normal.

"I know, I know," Flora said. She set herself down onto the bed gingerly, taking care not to touch her shoulder to anything. She lay back and they looked up at the roughly hewn wooden ceiling. "It's hard. I like them both, you know. And then I think, does Lana even like me? Is there any point in wasting time there? And Tane..."

She couldn't finish the sentence. She couldn't say it. *Tane doesn't want anything to happen between us because he's so worried about what the camp will think.*

After being strangled in her sleep, and having seen the marks around her neck, she couldn't blame him. His tribe were more loyal than perhaps even *he* could imagine.

"Who do you like more?" Hope asked, her voice unusually tight.

Who cares? I can't have either. Never mind the fact that someone clearly wanted to send me a message this morning; Tane doesn't want it to happen either.

"I genuinely don't know."

What if she *did* have the choice? When Flora thought about Lana, it felt electric and exciting and addictive. Lana had the most beautiful face, and those lips… she was intelligent and witty and strong, captivating and smart. Flora felt desperately that she wanted Lana's approval. But, at the same time, she was hard and sullen and defensive. Whereas Tane… well, Tane was the complete opposite; excitable and positive and adventurous. Like a puppy on steroids. Flora didn't particularly crave his approval, insofar as he pretty much seemed to like everything that anyone did. And everyone liked him, give or take a few of Lusty's old pals.

She remembered last night. His hands against her hips. The way that his face, usually so relaxed and cheerful, was serious, lined with pain. And suddenly, in her memory, his face was replaced with Arlo's, the boy from school. Because they did look similar, however much she tried to avoid thinking about it. Hadn't that been her first impression of Tane; that he looked like an 'after version' of Arlo going on some mountaineering adventure?

Arlo had been desired by everyone at their school. The students, the teachers, even Flora's best friend, Jen. And she'd felt slightly smug, even to the point of arrogance, that he'd seemed to like Flora. He'd been flirting with her since the day they met; he didn't shun her the way that everyone else in school seemed to, but instead found her exotic, interesting, exciting. He liked that she was passionate about gaming; he loved that she didn't seem interested in him.

And so, she'd inevitably felt like she should fancy him back. Why wouldn't she; didn't society demand that a good looking, well-off (because his family were 'millionaires', Flora remembered, with a wry internal smile) boy should be the perfect choice for her?

But was it ever what she really wanted? If she was honest with herself, didn't Natalia, Arlo's ex-girlfriend, elicit more of a thrill in Flora? Wasn't it Natalia whose hair she looked at, longing to stroke it, who's lips she'd watched, longing to kiss them? Only, that wasn't what society expected. Arlo was the safe choice, the easy choice. It was easy to convince her brain that it was Arlo she was looking at when she scrolled through his social media pages, and not glimpses of Natalia. That it was Arlo she would stare at in that picture of their group on the beach, and not Natalia in the baby pink bikini.

Flora felt something inside her piece together, something that she'd long since pushed down where it might never be discovered. She felt her insides twinge.

"Oh," she said out loud, and it was only the use of her vocal chords that brought her thoughts back into her body, which brought her crashing back down to reality. Her neck hurt, and the memory of being strangled, still biting and fresh, made her queasy.

Who the hell did it? Chan?

Her lungs and heart seemed to be rejecting her body, stuttering in rebellious collaboration. She couldn't deal with it all, not while Hope was there, having a normal conversation about normal things. She would have to think about it later.

"Oh, what problems you have," Hope sighed, but she was being sarcastic. "Two gorgeous people both love you and you can't decide between them."

"Ha, they do not both love me," Flora said, not wanting to tell Hope about last night, about Tane, about the mess that she'd inadvertently got herself into.

'It wouldn't work for the camp.' Who cares if it works for the camp or not?! If Tane really likes me, if he's serious about giving us a go, then why would he care?

Or maybe I'm not good enough for him, she thought, savagely, trying to piece together the confusion. It wasn't enough to know that, perhaps, Tane wasn't the one for her; she still felt betrayed, she wanted him to want her.

That was basic human psychology; she felt rejected, no matter whether she might have later rejected him. *He's, like, a zillionaire, and I'm from an estate in England where we can't even afford to pay for school meals. Of course he thinks I'm below him; of course, his mum probably wouldn't approve, if he ever dared to take me home. He probably wants someone well-off, someone like Lana.*

All of the bitter things that she'd been thinking about Tane poured through her veins like a toxic substance, until she was on her feet, stomping over to sit on Hive's bed, where Hive's memorables sat in a ray of sunshine. The air in the hut was stifling.

Liking either of their camp's leaders was not a good idea for Flora. She didn't fit into that world, no matter whether they were on Taniwha or not; the truth was that they had a different upbringing, a different life, which left an imprint, no matter whether the person tried to run away and start a money-free life on an island or not.

'Running away and protecting yourself are two very different things,' Lana had once told her.

"Ugh," Flora said, out loud, laying back on Hive's bed. Why couldn't she just like Frances, or Hive, or even Hope?

But that wasn't how love worked; it provoked your heart with something much deeper and more inconvenient than logic.

"It would be good to know where Lana stands, to be fair," Flora muttered. Hope had left her in silence the whole time that she'd been thinking; perhaps she realised that Flora was going through some rocky internal discoveries and didn't want to get in the way.

Did Lana feel the same way as Tane? Was she willing to forsake her own happiness for the sake of the camp? Or did she consider 'the balance' of the camp more important than her own personal happiness? And if so, why on earth were there so many martyrs? Where were the supposed rebels that she'd been expecting after meeting Ritchie, with his Slash-style earring?

They heard a noise outside the hut, something like a rat scurrying across wet leaves.

"What's that?"

"Just a bird, probs," Hope remarked. Flora turned her head and saw that Hope was still staring up at the ceiling. "Anyway, for me, I don't know if that stuff will come so easy."

"Err, excuse me," Flora replied, propping herself up on her elbows. "You and Lennox are literally all over each other! You're like the celebrity couple of camp."

"Oh, shut up."

"I'm serious, you guys are made for each other."

"Well, yeah, I think he's really cute. But is he a bit..."

"What?"

"Enthusiastic? He's not my usual type."

Flora guffawed then, great belly laughs that were half a result of Hope's description of Lennox and half a distillation of all of the nervous tension. She accidentally snorted and then Hope started laughing too and they both rolled around, giddy with excitement and hopelessness.

"The other thing is," Hope said, lowering her voice, "that he isn't in the Operation. I mean, Tane doesn't seem to really trust him, and I know that he was a big fan of Lusty. We're like, different political parties, basically. I just don't know how well that could go, even if it did go. Tane and Lana might not like it, you know?" Something about her voice sounded oddly hopeful, as if she wanted to cause some drama in the camp.

"I'm sure they wouldn't care," Flora said, genuinely thinking this to be the case.

"Ha." Hope sounded as if she'd been stung. "Yeah, who knows what they really want?"

Flora lay still and felt her freshly inked shoulder start to burn. She felt tears in her eyes. Only some of them were from the laughter.

"'Oh, new girl, I love you so much'," Hope suddenly cackled, imitating Lana, her voice tinged with something that sounded like envy. *She wishes Lennox would be honest about how much he likes her.*

"Oh, back to me now, is it?"

"Yes. Let's get clear," Hope said, coughing so that the edge to her voice disappeared and her normal tone resumed. "You're gonna figure out who you prefer, Lana or Tane. Sort out this whole power-hungry lover in you."

"There is not a *power-hungry lover* in me!" Flora objected, appalled.

"Oh purr-lease, why do I get the impression that only the camp leaders would be your type?"

"That's not..." Flora started to say, but the words were already being chewed over in her mind.

"It's true and you know it. There are loads of eligible people here: Eccles, Ritchie, Bell – I mean, he's gorgeous – maybe even Hive, or definitely Chan – she's stunning. But you've gone straight for the two who're off limits. You're the kind of person who would fall in love with the boss, if you worked for a company, or your teacher, probably. Authority turns you on, admit it."

Hope cackled with laughter, the guttural sound rebounding off of the wooden ceiling.

"I absolutely deny it," Flora said, although she wasn't sure.

"I think you just like someone else to be in control," Hope said, the laughter dying in her throat. "Maybe it's because you never had control growing up?"

She'd told Hope about her parents, of course she had. How her mum was basically non-existent, for all intents and purposes, and how her dad, as cheerful as he was, had missed all of the basic events. She hadn't had a birthday present in three years.

"I don't like this conversation anymore," Flora said, her voice flat. She felt like Hope was using that information, her most private information, to make huge sweeping judgements on her romantic tastes, and it grated. But at least she'd been distracted from the strangulation.

For now.

CHAPTER TWENTY-SEVEN
SANGUINE

Breakfast was muesli from the depths of their hollowed-out store cupboard. Apparently Frances, who was one-half of the duo who were supposed to be cooking breakfast, was sat on the beach feeling sick, and Hive was helping him through it.

Flora shook a pile of oats into her bowl, the raisins falling like dead flies. Her head ached. Not wanting to draw attention to her neck, which would perhaps lead to her having to explain her midnight visitor, which might then further lead to everyone finding out what happened with Tane – and no matter what she tried to tell herself, she did today feel a crippling embarrassment that he had rejected her so thoroughly, in favour of his beloved camp – she'd surreptitiously pinned her thick mass of frizzy hair so that it met under her chin.

For the most part this went unnoticed – everyone was used to the body odour, messy hair and dirty clothes that came from living on a desert island – but Gasquet did seem somewhat horrified when he saw her.

"Chan," he called, his voice wavering. "Do you have some serum or something for our friend here? We can't let her look like this."

Chan turned to see what Gasquet was referring to. When she saw Flora, pored over her muesli, she gave such a deep look of loathing that Flora nearly flinched.

"No," the other girl said shortly, turning back to her outspread fingers, onto which she was carefully drawing intricate swirls with henna ink. Gasquet looked surprised as well. He turned to Flora, as if to ask what Chan's glare had been about, but Flora's face was so blank with shock that he quickly realised that he shouldn't ask.

"Ok, then," he said, falsifying a sort of brightness, and he waltzed off towards his hut, leaving a stunned Flora wondering what on earth she had done to upset Chan.

"Brock?" Tane called from the entrance to The Kitch, where he stood looking at a list of duties on a huge board of bark which had been balanced against a tree. He'd called with such hesitance that she was sure that he would rather be talking to anyone else.

She watched blankly as he opened his mouth to talk, closed it again, and then swapped his resistance for the resoluteness of a leader who knows that normal life must continue.

"You're on restroom duty. Go find Bell, he'll tell you what to do. You'd usually do it alone but I've taken Bell off lookout duty just for today, so someone can show you the ropes."

"Great," Flora called back, hoping that her sarcasm didn't get lost in the wind. Tane flashed her a quick grin that was steeped in sadness, and then disappeared into the kitchen. *And breathe.* Flora wandered over to examine the splayed bark, which stretched out like a dried corpse.

Down the left-hand side were carved a list of duties. People's names were then adorned in white paint on big, glossy leaves that had been pinned to the corresponding duty for the day. As days changed, Flora supposed that Tane moved the leaves to ensure that everyone got a fair mix.

The duties were: Clothes, Goats, Kitch, Washing-Up, Bathroom, Fishing, Jardin, Lookout, Poukai, Spin. Flora's name was on a leaf next to 'Bathroom', pinned with Bell. As Tane had alluded to, there was no name against 'Lookout'.

Gasquet and Chan's names were on 'Clothes' duty, Lana's name was next to 'Goats', Hive and Frances were on 'Kitch', Lennox and Ritchie were on 'Washing-Up', the Harleys were on 'Fishing', Hope, Eccles and Tane were on 'Jardin', McLarty and DeCalbiac were on 'Poukai' duty, and there was a single name next to the mysterious 'Spin': Easton.

Flora wondered what 'Spin' meant; she vaguely remembered that it was the name for cycling classes, but doubted that they had any reason to introduce cycling. That was another question for another day.

The prospect of a whole day of being on toilet duty was not an exciting one, especially when some of the other duties, like cleaning clothes or working in the gardens, sounded more appealing. Flora would be emptying and cleaning the old sloshing pots that housed eighteen people's bowels throughout the day. Delightful. 'Compost toilets' is how Hive had described them, but Flora hardly saw anything composting about them. They seemed to be giant buckets with seats on.

"Why do we need to do actual work on a billionaire's island?" she grumbled, out loud. *Why not just hire people?*

Tane's imagined reply came straight away: *individual commitment to a group effort builds a civilization.*

Flora rolled her eyes, wishing that she didn't already know him so well.

△△△

Before she embarked on finding Bell, Flora walked back to her hut for her toothbrush. The hut was empty, the dent still in Hive's bedding where Flora had lain earlier. She sat back on Hive's bed and looked at her memorables for a long time, waiting for her mind to stop churning and her neck to stop aching.

△△△

By the time the evening arrived, alongside the promise of her first Operation Poseidon meeting in a treehouse that she had yet to spot, she was glad of the distraction. Cleaning toilets had been as disgusting as she had feared; the smell was atrocious, and the huge pots sloshed and swayed as if possessed. She'd struggled to get them to the composting system *with* Bell's help; she had no idea how she was going to do it without him.

Then Bell had tried to engage her in a game of Jungleball, which she didn't fully understand and didn't have the mental capacity to learn.

"So, we play with a giddyfruit, the giddy ball we call it-" he'd said, proffering a fruit that looked like a huge kiwi with star anise set into the sides. Flora had taken it off him and been surprised by its weight; it felt as though it had a huge, solid pip inside. The outside skin was covered in short fur, but it felt as thick as leather and impossible to pierce.

"Why's it called a giddyfruit?" she asked.

"Oh, we call it that 'cos if you eat it then it makes you feel like, really giddy," he explained, looking quite confused himself. Bell often looked confused. "So anyway, you can just use your feet and your, err, elbows, but you can't use your hands, and you can only use the inside of your foot too. So you, err, kick the ball, or you can elbow it up, but you won't have enough strength in your arms, and you have to get it to balance on the log, but like, the goalkeepers are up in the trees and they're gonna try and stop you."

"Right," Flora said, feeling queasy. Flashbacks of last night kept attacking her mind: Tane in the moonlight, her moving in for a kiss and him not returning it, their intense moment of passion followed by his admission that nothing could happen, and then her being strangled in her sleep – her thinking that it was a dream, only the bruises proved otherwise...

"The scoring system is really simple; you get a point for getting it above the log – or at least I think you do; I'll need to check with Frances – and you lose five points if the goalkeeper manages to bat it away. I know, weird, but there was a lot of arguments and... anyway... then if you get it to stay on the log, it's twenty points. Then, the rest of the points are based on where it lands if it doesn't stay on the log, but twenty is the most points you can get. See here, in the markings..."

He proceeded to explain the markings on the floor, which Flora could barely distinguish. She was in no mood to learn how to play Jungleball, and so when Eccles and Ritchie appeared, showing obvious enthusiasm about practising the game with Bell, she relinquished her position under the swaying log, having only tried to kick the giddy ball once and nearly breaking her foot in the process.

That explains why some of them have huge bruises on their feet, she thought, grimly.

△△△

The Operation Poseidon meeting was due to start at midnight. Flora wasn't yet sure who was in on the Operation and so she didn't dare mention it or even look at anyone in the wrong way. She felt sure that whoever was part of the secret group knew that she was joining them tonight, and was probably watching her, waiting to see if she was trustworthy, waiting to see if she would mess up.

She wouldn't give them the satisfaction; exhausted as she was, she maintained a look of quiet dignity all evening. There was so much going on that Flora also didn't have time to make huge personal discoveries; her love life would have to take a backseat, at least for tonight.

If she didn't help with Poseidon, then there was a chance that Axer Nuku-Halliday would discover the camp and put a stop to them all living there. That would mean no more seeing Tane or Lana, and potentially losing her new self, her stronger self, the person that she was discovering on Taniwha.

Her heart stung at the thought. Which meant that, basically, she'd already decided that she had to be part of the Operation, if only so that she could buy herself more time to weigh up her options. But she wasn't going to tell the secret group that, not right away.

"So, what's the deal tonight?" she eventually whispered to McLarty, after he'd helped himself to homely, steaming stew. "Obviously, I'm not sure that I'm joining this Operation thingy, but I'll come to the meeting."

He turned his baleful gaze towards her; he had started taking small, sharp bites of his plateful. The stew consisted mainly of mahi-mahi, but there were also kidney beans, yellow peppers, sweet potatoes, carrots and the odd surprising bay leaf.

"I'll give you the co-ordinates later," he muttered, once he'd swallowed.

"Co-ordinates?" She'd said it a little too loudly; the Harley's broke from their conversation to look at her. "Sorry," she muttered to McLarty, whose eyes looked as if they might burn a hole in her face. He'd been a bit off with her all day. She thought that maybe he felt left out because he hadn't been invited to the hut party the evening before. Or perhaps he just didn't want her to be part of the Operation.

He's probably territorial about his Den, Flora thought. *The idea of another IT bod coming in and challenging him can't be that endearing.*

They'd had a lot of fun in Pictopia together. Perhaps he didn't want to mix work and play; he wanted someone he could work with who wouldn't distract him with questions about giants and blue mines.

"Look, just follow Hope later, ok?" he muttered, so quietly that she could barely hear him and was forced to lean forward so that her head was just a few inches away from his.

"Ok, will do," she muttered back, looking around to make sure that no one else had heard her this time. The Harley's had gone back to their conversation; everyone else was either helping themselves to more stew from the vat over the fire or dropping their plates at the washing-up stand.

Tane had been watching her, she saw with a jolt, but he looked away so quickly, and was so deep in conversation with Eccles when she looked, that she wondered whether it had been a trick of the light. Lana was sat on her own, tying fishing knots and eating her stew at the same time, pausing between loops of rope to inhale another mouthful of fish. Her fingers were fast and adept and she whizzed through three different knots before she noticed that Flora was watching her.

Lana's eyes flicked up lazily, resting on Flora's face with a cool kind of indifference which seemed to have more meaning brewing below the surface. Flora wondered if she didn't look a bit… hurt.

In the end, Flora looked away first.

CHAPTER TWENTY-EIGHT
DEMESNE

Flora couldn't guarantee that Hive and Frances were part of Operation Poseidon, and so it was with relief when, as she was lying in bed trying to come up with excuses for why she might need to leave the hut, Hive swung her feet onto the well-swept floor.

"Come on, guys," she said a little too loudly, flicking on a torch. *Isn't it supposed to be a secret mission? What if someone else hears?* Even then, though, there were snores emanating from a hut nearby, and a stillness from outside that acted as an atmospheric clock.

Flora got up and yanked on her pair of gauche lamé leggings, but Frances took longer, having fallen asleep in the thirty minutes since they'd been back.

"Ugh," he muttered, disgruntled, falling out of bed and causing a crash that made Hive's announcement earlier sound positively mouselike.

"Quiet, Frances," she admonished, tapping him on the back of the head as if he were a naughty animal.

"Bugger off, would you," he grumbled, wiping his eyes. Flora suppressed a smile, turning towards the door.

Five minutes later, they trod quietly across the cold earth, away from the camp, towards the goats' pens and dense forest. Flora's heart had started to thrum as they stepped past the other huts, trying to stay quiet, pausing every time one of them stepped on a twig or caused a pile of leaves to rustle.

Frances had brought the torch, but there was no need; the sky was awash with stars and moonlight, not a cloud in sight.

"-and I suppose we'll be expected to get up at 6 o'clock to start breakfast," Frances grumbled, as they picked their way over branches. Flora was becoming more adept at feeling the way with her bare feet now; she felt as if her soles were starting to read the ground and move accordingly. Before long, she suspected that she might even be able to navigate the campsite under a hidden moon, relying solely on the pulse of the earth, which beat a rhythm below her.

Or perhaps she'd just had one too many broad bean moonshines, she thought, as she nearly tripped over a sinister-looking root in the darkness.

Eventually, having narrowly avoided the Bovidae Bedroom and inhaled all manner of dung scents in the process, they happened upon little pinpricks of light in the trees. They started off just one or two, like fireflies, but soon, as they traversed through dense forest, the lights grew in number, crowding together in the trees, little swaying stars that pulsed a deep and smoky glow into the thickets of foliage.

They stumbled on, the lights eventually becoming an all-encompassing arch around them, lighting up a well-trodden pathway, creating a magical harmony against the backdrop of humming crickets and night birds.

"I've only been here once before." Frances sounded nervous. "I can't remember how... oh." The archway arrived at a dead end, a huge tree trunk that was at least 20m in circumference. The tree ascended high up into the night, beyond the faux fireflies.

"I think we just tap," Hive said, her voice higher than Flora had ever heard it. Something about the jungle at night was making both Hive and Frances nervous. On the contrary, Flora found the jungle more magical at night: the stillness, the moonlight, the feeling that she was the only person in the world awake.

Perhaps they'd witnessed more than she had on the

island, though. And besides, Flora had stopped loving the night-time quite so much after last night, with Tane, when perhaps she'd found things a little *too* magical, when perhaps she'd got a little *too* carried away...

Frances rapped on the tree trunk smartly, and then held his knuckles with his other hand. The sound of his knocking had been hollow, and a few seconds later a loosely hewn door appeared from the rough bark of the tree. It was on a long and complicated lever, which forced the door away from the tree and towards them for a second, before rising upwards.

Inside, a foot above ground level, was a large metal disk, around one meter wide. Frances shot a hesitant look at Hive, who stepped forward first and staggered up onto the disk, righting herself as she did so. The disk seemed to sway slightly, and she held onto the wall. The hollowed tube seemed to be an extention of the tree, rather than part of it.

"Come on," she said, briskly.

Frances and then Flora followed, both wavering as their feet stepped onto the odd disk, both holding onto the walls for support. Finally, they all stood closely together in the bowels of the tree, looking through the empty bark doorway at the swaying arch of pinprick lights outside, waiting for something to happen.

"So, is there supposed to be-" Flora started to say, but before she could finish her sentence, the bark door suddenly snapped back into place, plunging them all into a deeper darkness than she had ever known, and then the floor moved, ascending so quickly that Flora had to snatch her hand away from the wall, her heart plummeting into her feet, the speed rocketing through her body.

Both Frances and Hive grabbed her for support; hands gripped her arms, surprisingly tight, almost like they'd gripped onto her before, clamping down as they went up, up, up, causing Flora's throat to constrict, her memory to trigger, causing her to grab the hand on her arm and throw it off, perhaps too violently, because the person next to her nearly fell over and then –

They arrived, spilling out of the lift onto a shaggy rug. Warmth. The smell of firewood. Flickering light.

"What the hell, Flora?" Hive's nostrils flared as she hopped up from the floor, looking at Flora with unadulterated anger. "You could've killed me."

"Sorry," Flora gasped from the floor, still feeling the memory of being strangled pulse through her, causing her to choke. She hadn't realised that she was so affected by it, but of course she was; she couldn't push something like that to the back of her mind for long. The minute that it was dark, the minute that she'd felt Hive's grip on her arm, it had all come back.

Hive looked away, nostrils still flared, patting her clothes down as if the journey had made her filthy. Frances staggered to his feet, groaning out noises of dizziness, and Flora followed suit, careful to straighten up slowly to avoid fainting.

She looked around and, as was becoming increasingly common in her new life, gasped in wonder.

They'd fallen into a sanctuary. White shaggy rugs were lain across rustic floorboards. A huge window demonstrated the stars and the moonlight and Taniwha's black lagoon and the ever-present Poukai, bobbing away gently. There were two wood burners, crackling merrily, casting a shifting, comfortable glow over the large room. In one corner of the vast treehouse a single futon lay on the floor, draped in blankets and sheepskin throws; in another corner, a small kitchen set-up showed a few ceramic mugs, a large jug, various glasses, a plate, a bowl and a handful of cutlery all stowed in a handmade unit of sorts, created from gnarled sticks and patterned beechwood.

A rocking chair took pride of place in front of the window, next to which stood an impressive golden globe and a stack of books. A radio completed the atmosphere of a serene spa, or perhaps a forest library, filling the air with harpsicords and flutes.

Tane was nowhere to be seen, although looking around more closely, Flora noticed something that looked suspiciously like a door hidden next to the edge of the huge window.

"It's quite something, isn't it?" Frances asked. Even Hive had let her nostrils deflate and her shoulders slump.

"Where's Tane?" Flora wondered aloud.

"Oof," someone said from behind them, as they dropped onto the rug. The sound juddered through the wooden floorboards and vibrated through Flora's body.

"McLarty?" she asked the heap on the carpet, as a curtain of black hair looked up at them all, showing only pursed lips.

"Who else?" He pushed his wiry frame up so that he was sitting, took stock of his body, and then staggered to standing, wiping his shoulder-length hair out of his face. "The others are behind me."

The door opened again and out lurched Hope, Lana and DeCalbiac, who all managed to step out without falling over. Why none of them had wanted to travel with McLarty and had chosen instead to squeeze together, Flora didn't know.

"Hey Flo," Hope said, brightly, sauntering past her and throwing herself into the rocking chair. DeCalbiac shot Flora a shy grin which Flora immediately returned; it was nice to see the other girl without a screen pressed to the end of her nose.

"Alright," Lana nodded, but it wasn't clear who she was greeting, and so everyone muttered a non-committal response.

"Who built this place?" Flora asked.

"That would be me," Tane said, as he pushed the secret doorway open – Flora had been right – and stood in a power-stance, a fire silhouetting him from behind, "and Lusty."

"Lusty?"

"Yep, he was a strong kid," Tane said, dismissively. "The biggest feat was getting this pane of glass up here, it weighs an absolute tonne. Took an age."

"And you had a bit of help," Frances said crossly, wiping his sweating forehead. Flora wondered why he was so sweaty, but then noticed that he'd been stood very close to one of the wood burners. He seemed to realise this at the same time and hopped backwards, nearly tripping over one of the shaggy rugs.

"Apologies, Frances." Tane nodded, waving his hand as if to move the moment on. "Anyway, I've got smores on the go outside and I've set up some floor cushions. Please come."

They all followed him outside, onto a wide balcony that had been affixed to another tree, two towering brother giants holding a firepit in their joined hands. The flames crackled delightedly within the centre of the balcony, around which they all sat. An owl hooted nearby; the moonlight rustled in the moving leaves.

"This is so surreal," DeCalbiac whispered to Flora, who wondered whether the other girl had spent much time in the camp, or exploring Taniwha. She probably hadn't; from choice, or otherwise, she seemed to spend all her time in that stuffy little den.

I'd go mad.

"Welcome, everyone, to a meeting concerning Operation Poseidon," Tane said, gravely. He was standing, his whole body reflecting the flames. The heat was such that Flora's eyes had started smarting; she blinked and looked away until they felt normal again.

"As you all know, this is a top-secret meeting," Lana drawled from her position on the highest beanbag. "I don't expect to hear that anyone's been talking about it; security is our top priority on the island." She looked around at them all, her gaze landing for just a second too long on Hope. Flora wondered why, and then remembered that Hope was seeing Lennox, who clearly wasn't in the secret club. "As we all know, Easton is working on a top-secret project for us, but he's still just a little too close to Lusty's lot. For that reason, we thought it wise not to initiate him into this group, not just yet.

The aim of these meetings, which you all know, but for Flora's benefit-" her eyes finally, reluctantly, made their way to Flora's face, where the same look that she'd had by the fire earlier hid behind her irises, "is because Axer Nuku-Halliday is tracking us down. Tane took what was rightfully his – as much of his inheritance as he could get his hands on, given that Axer had spent so much of it-"

"Tosser," Frances interrupted, savagely, causing Lana's mouth to flicker with the ghost of a smile.

"Quite," she agreed. "Anyway, he threatens to find us and destroy all of this. He will not hesitate to kill each and every one of us. He would happily burn down Taniwha and take Poukai, which is where the real money is, of course, but not before he tortures each of us to find out where Tane's keeping the rest of the money."

Looks of alarm cast themselves around the circle.

"But we don't know where Tane keeps the money," Frances said, looking between Tane and Lana.

"Obviously," McLarty said, drawing the word out and rolling his eyes.

"Alright, there's no need to-" Frances started to say, puffing his chest up, but Lana interrupted:

"My point is," she said, "that this isn't just some silly little treehouse club. This is a meeting to discuss how we avoid torture, murder and the loss of everything that we all know as home.

So, what's the agenda then? First up, it would be good to hear from Frances how the island defences are coming along. I know that we have Bell on lookout duty, but I wouldn't trust that boy to tell a ship from a turtle, so that's hardly fool proof. Then it would be great to hear from the IT crew; DeCalbiac, how are we getting on with tracking him down? Finally, it would be helpful for Tane to give us a bit more insight into what he's like, just so that if he ever does find us, we know how to... deal with him, better.

Happy?" she asked, leaning forward and picking up a

ceramic mug, which was filled with some sort of peppermint drink which filled the air with toothpaste smells.

"Certainly," Frances replied, staggering to his feet. Tane, realising that his part was done, at least for a while, sank down onto the pillow beneath him, crossed his legs and looked up, his eyes ancient and sad.

CHAPTER TWENTY-NINE
IMPENDENT

The hours progressed and the fire waned, turning into a silken, moving mix of fluorescent lines across charcoal, emanating a deep and powerful heat that warmed their faces and made their eyes water. Flora knew that her hair would smell like bonfires for a long time, but she was too intrigued about the looks that Lana was shooting her to dwell on that.

Frances had given the group a long and detailed laydown of the various security measures that he was ensuring were in place, supported in his descriptions by Hive, who focused him and sped him up in equal measure.

"Yes, we've got the Harley's fishing in an area off the east of the island that enables a full one-eighty view, making up for the limited eastern view from Bell's lookout point, and they're well-practised in what to do in the case of an emergency…"

And on he went, explaining how he'd concocted a story of fisher people seeking rare catches on enemy territory that had the Harley's suitably riled, before going on to explain how he was working with Easton on the top secret weaponry unit, but of course, he couldn't tell the group much about that, and he was looking into Poukai's very own defences and the feasibility of getting the one remaining cannon back up-and-running.

In the meantime, Flora felt someone watching her, and every time that she looked away from Frances, she was proven right; Lana was looking at her with her impassive face and plump lips and wide eyes, which showed firelight and starlight, hurt and anger.

Every time that Flora noticed Lana looking and looked back, the older girl looked away, so that Flora was forced to focus back on Frances until the next time that she felt herself being watched.

Only, on one occasion, Lana didn't look away. She held Flora's gaze and, determined that she wouldn't be the first to look away this time, Flora continued to look back. Their gazes locked into each other's across the spluttering fire, as Frances droned on about cannonballs and the difficulty of procuring gunpowder, and Flora felt her heart start to judder like a jackhammer, she felt her lips part, just slightly, she felt as though Lana were looking deep into her soul, she felt something like molten lead flood through her stomach, her legs, she was just about to say something, forgetting that anyone else was there, when Lana interrupted Frances:

"That doesn't make any sense," she said. She was still looking at Flora, and a small line had appeared between her eyebrows; it was as if she was saying that what she found on Flora's face didn't make any sense. Flora's insides were still melted, pounding through her body, but her ribs seemed to freeze in place, her tongue clamping to the roof of her mouth. She gazed at Lana, willing the older girl to indicate that they should go back inside the treehouse and talk, just talk, or sit on the balcony, the two of them together, watching the stars, talking for hours into the night, for Lana to explain what didn't make sense so that Flora could make everything alright.

An image flashed through her mind of Lana's head in her lap, Flora stroking the hair off her face, tracing those perfect lips with one finger, and it caused her chest to shudder even more violently until she was sure that she might have a heart attack.

"That gunpowder is hard to procure?" Frances asked, surprised that someone had interrupted, and, in fact, seemingly surprised that anyone else was even there. He'd been so deep into his security monologue that he looked to have forgotten that he wasn't at the forefront of the UK Government, giving a speech in the House of Lords. "It is surprising, isn't it, only it's not the first time in gunpowder's history, actually; it was first invented for medicinal purposes by the Taoists, long before we ever used it for warfare-"

"Frances," Hive snapped, and Frances stuttered for a moment, looked around, and then continued on his original torrent.

Lana didn't look at Flora again after that, instead fixing her brooding eyes on the smouldering fire. Flora felt her heartbeat settle, but there was still a lump in her throat that she couldn't make disappear, no matter how many times she swallowed.

It was bad enough that she was sat directly across from Lana, making it harder than ever not to look at that beautiful face, that strong, lithe body... but to add insult to injury, Tane was sat right next to Lana, studiously ignoring Flora, but emanating all sorts of emotions himself, none of which related to Frances's tales of drones and tracking devices. Tane had wilted; he seemed downtrodden, browbeaten, exhausted.

Flora thought she knew a bit of what he was feeling; she herself felt exhausted, not helped by the fact that Frances must have been talking for an hour.

By the time that DeCalbiac stood up to talk, the smores were all finished, and everyone had started to drink some of Lana's weird peppermint liquid, for lack of anything else to consume.

"I'll keep this short," DeCalbiac said, shooting a glance at Frances. She was met with a rumble of approval, most heartily from McLarty, who had yawned the entire time that Frances was speaking. "We have seen a few horrible things going on that we can quite firmly link back to Nuku-Halliday." She picked up what looked like a foot-long silver pole, pressed a button, and caused a hologramlike screen to spring to life from the length of the pole, hovering in mid-air.

Flora gasped.

The semi-transparent image that DeCalbiac was projecting showed a woman who had been tied-up, her throat slit. Dried blood crusted her neck and the light blue dress that she was wearing. Her face was blank of expression, her eyes closed. The image flickered in the darkness, burning itself into all of their retinas.

"What the..." whispered Flora, looking at the image and then everyone sat around the fire. McLarty and Lana hadn't looked up; clearly, they'd seen the picture before.

"Who is it?" Hope choked out. So far, Hope had been silent, just listening and occasionally yawning, but now she looked alert, terrified.

"Lusty's mother. We think that when Lusty went missing after promising Nuku-Halliday information on Tane's whereabouts, Axer thought that he'd backed out. He thought, mistakenly, that Lusty might have informed his mother about where we are, and so went on to torture and eventually kill her, hoping to get useful information."

"How can we be sure that she didn't give him any?" Tane asked, seeming more worried about her giving away information than the fact that she had been brutally murdered. Flora shot him a look of pure disgust.

"We can't, but we do know that this was two weeks ago and since then, there's been another victim. It doesn't appear likely that he would have done this if he'd got his answer..." DeCalbiac said, tapping buttons on the side of the metal pole and waiting for another image to appear. "However, there's no telling whether it was actually Axer, or someone after the reward."

For one long, heart-stopping moment, Flora imagined them flashing up an image of her father, mutilated, bled to death, and felt her whole body convulse, as if she might actually be sick. Suddenly, the fact that she'd fought so hard to keep her phone, the fact that she'd been so resistant to their over-the-top security measures, made her feel like a small child; shame trickled through her, replacing the stupid, selfish worries that she'd had. *How could I have been so petulant?*

A new image flashed up and someone gasped. Lana. She obviously hadn't seen this picture before.

It was a dog, a sandy coloured dog with a large, lolling tongue and eyes that must have once sparkled.

"Freddy," Lana croaked.

"This happened yesterday," DeCalbiac said, quietly, closing the image. "I'm so sorry, Lana."

"Why... why just kill the dog?" Hope asked, swallowing, as if she'd seen quite enough. "Why not kill Lana's mum, if they're happy to kill Lusty's?"

Lana shot Hope a look of deep loathing, and Flora could only imagine just how attached Lana had been to Freddy. Hope's insensitivity rang around the balcony.

"We think," DeCalbiac said carefully, shooting a look at McLarty, "that Lusty's mum was an easy target; she lives alone in a one-storey; it wouldn't have taken much to get to her, and it's certainly easier to hide than trying to waltz into Lana's family's heavily protected mansion. Plus, this sends more of a message to us; with Lusty's mother, he wanted information, but with this, he wants to send a warning. Perhaps next time, it would..." she didn't finish the sentence, instead glancing hopelessly at McLarty.

"How did Lusty afford to go to your school if he grew up in a tiny bungalow?" Hope asked Lana, clearly completely oblivious to the other girl's pain, and once again demonstrating a complete lack of tact.

"He won a scholarship," Tane said, his voice as steely and cold as Flora had ever heard it. He put his hand on Lana's knee, and Flora saw Hope flinch as if she'd been hit. Flora clasped her elbows and looked away from the group, out towards the treetops.

"Anyway, the point is," Tane said, standing up, "and thank you – DeCalbiac – your skills on Poukai are absolutely integral to the success of this Operation," he nodded her a look of thanks, to which McLarty positively seethed, "but, we must only take this as another sign that this Operation is absolutely essential to the survival of our camp. Every single campmate relies on the group assembled here to find Axer before he finds us."

A silence fell over the treehouse that had nothing to do with the fallen winds, the depths of night that had crept across the island. Tane's words rang out into the night air, as crystal clear as the constellations of stars overhead.

"In terms of providing any more insight into Axer's behaviour," Tane said, clearly struggling to say his stepfather's name, "then I do not wish to give you all any more nightmares than you'll have already. I'll only say this.

He is a scared man. Yes," he said, for Frances had accidentally let out a snort of scorn, "that's right. I'm not saying that what he's doing is right, and I'm not saying that if we do find him I won't... you know, but it's important to remember that he has issues, as well. He's a gambling addict, for starters," Tane said, and he cleared his throat, just as McLarty shot a look at Flora that was probably supposed to go unnoticed. Flora felt her face burn and it had nothing to do with the fire; she ignored him and stared, instead, at the shrivelled form of Lana, who had her eyes closed.

"He owes some bad men a lot of money," Tane continued, steeling himself even more, as if telling this story caused him more pain than anyone.

"Yes, he spent a hell of a lot of my grandparent's money and has caused Mom a lot of sleepless nights, but he's also petrified for his life right now. He wouldn't be... he wouldn't be tracking us down if he didn't think it was the key to saving his own bacon, and that's what makes him the most dangerous of all.

Because he's a proud, proud man. And proud men are the most susceptible to violence, the least likely to listen to reason, and the first to start a war."

His final words rang out into the deep, fragrant sky. Overhead, a colony of bats wavered.

"I think that's everything for tonight," Tane said, wearily. "Any questions?"

"Yes," Hive said, as if she'd been patiently waiting for the meeting to finish before she could ask. "In terms of our visuals, the circumference by which we can actually see what's going on, aren't we sort of sitting ducks? It's all very well to say that we'll keep a lookout for ships and things," she shot Frances a grim look of apology, "but shouldn't we be trying to find his whereabouts long before he actually gets to the island?"

"What do you suggest?" DeCalbiac asked coolly, her face reddening in the glow from the fire.

"Well, CCTV in the nearest harbours, perhaps?" Hive said, as if she'd been waiting for this question. "CCTV anywhere, in fact. Location tracking: can we establish any further details about his mobile devices? I mean, I'm no expert, but surely if we can hack into police databases to get these... awful images... then we can get into some CCTV feeds?"

A silence followed her words, during which McLarty looked as if he'd taken a bite of something disgusting. Eventually, when everyone was looking at him, he spoke.

"Thanks for your ideas, Hive. We'll certainly... investigate."

"Great." Tane was still standing, but his voice sounded carefully controlled.

Perhaps they do need help, Flora thought.

"On that note then, let's call it a night, but keep in touch – if anything happens then we'll assemble here, ok? Keep this group and this Operation a secret, and if anyone starts asking questions, come up with a suitable lie that we can all use, ok?"

"Ok," a few people muttered, thinking – Flora was sure, because she was thinking the same – that this instruction sounded a bit vague.

They stumbled to their feet, one by one, and under the blanket of absolute night, smelling like firewood, they made their way back to camp.

CHAPTER THIRTY
CLANDESTINE

The next day passed in a blur of feeling tired. Flora still felt ashamed about the fuss that she'd kicked up about her phone. The image of Lusty's innocent mother, bled to death, eyes closed, had haunted her all night.

And was Lana ok? Last night, the image of Freddy… well, Flora had hoped to grab Lana on the way out, but the older girl had hurried off first, descending on her own and disappearing before anyone else arrived on the forest floor.

When Lana wasn't at breakfast the next morning, Flora felt a painful ache in her side. As she ate eggs on toast, served by a very tired Frances and Hope, she pondered, once again, her feelings towards Lana. They extended past a fierce protectiveness for her grief. It felt so much stronger than that to Flora.

How much was she a product of society's expectations: who was she really, when you stripped away everything she *should* do, everything that was easy and safe? Was Lana upset that Flora had kissed Tane; did she somehow know? Is that why she'd glared all evening? Was Lana trying to communicate something?

Flora had been put on goat duty and as she milked away, angling the teats towards a wooden bucket and mostly missing, her mind whirred. She'd been left to it; only one person was usually on goat duty.

She felt a strange affinity with the animals as they

gambolled and tried to nuzzle her clothes. It was weird to have goats on the island. It was weird for Flora to be on the island. They were making the best of things; they had the most amazing play zone and they all seemed to get on well, but they probably had complicated feelings about the matter. Maybe they had goat families back home; maybe they just wanted to be left alone for a while.

Am I really comparing myself to goats? I need to pull myself together. I need to talk to Lana.

△△△

Getting time with Lana proved incredibly hard, but Flora's chance arrived a few days later. In the meantime, the bruises on her neck had started healing, and she hadn't had any more nighttime visitors. Frances and Hive had made her feel somewhat safe, even if they were sometimes too honest for their own good.

She hadn't mentioned the strangulation to anyone, but it had grown and grown in her mind until it was a monster that needed to be tackled. She didn't like to think about it; the fact that anyone could hurt her, that it was definitely someone on the island and therefore someone who saw her every day, who pretended to be friendly with her every day, caused an anxiety within her that she hadn't felt since she'd arrived on Taniwha.

But she knew it had to be tackled. Monsters would grow and grow if you let them; just look at Jen's phobia of pianos; now she couldn't even listen to the instrument. Flora wouldn't let her monster win, and so she resolved to continue investigating, while also helping to track down Axer and find out how Lana really felt.

It was a lot to think about. The safety element was addressed one evening, while Flora, Hive and Frances all lay in bed, the room dark around them.

"Guys, does anyone ever get injured here?"

"What do you mean?" Hive had immediately asked, her voice suspicious.

"Like, does anyone ever get hurt? I guess, I mean, do you guys ever fight between each other, like internal camp fighting?"

"Not since Lusty," Frances had replied, his voice as official as always. "He tried to attack Tane, to vie for leader of the camp. Of course, it was preposterous. Tane bought Poukai, for starters. He funds everything; Lusty didn't have a penny to his name. And besides that, no one would have listened to Lusty. Everyone is very fond of Tane. I think we were all relieved when Lusty went, to be honest. If he'd stayed, someone probably would've ended him."

"Ended him?"

"Killed him," Hive said, matter-of-factly. "But a lot of people hated him from the day he arrived, so you can't feel sorry for him. He called us all 'dirty'. He said that anyone under fifteen should dress as servants and serve the elders. He tried to create a new camp on the other side of the island."

"He was a lunatic," Frances confirmed.

"I thought he went to school with Lana and Tane," Flora said, trying to remember something that Bell had said. "So how come he didn't arrive with them?"

"He had a good family back home," Frances sighed, his voice sad. "Tane was very reluctant to get him in the beginning. However, Lusty was a clever chap, actually managed to track us down, if you'd believe it."

"He tracked you down?" Flora asked, horrified.

"Well, yes," Hive said. "But you have to remember that he knew both Tane and Lana very well. No doubt Tane was talking for ages about commandeering a pirate ship and finding a paradise island. It wouldn't have taken forever to find us if you knew Tane."

"Marvellous tracking, it was," Frances said, his regard at odds with Flora's horrified expression, which only their ceiling could see.

"But still, that's not great, is it?"

There was a long silence, during which Flora felt both much better and much worse. At least she hadn't tried to do any of the awful things that Lusty had done. The worst that had happened is that she had kissed Tane; she hadn't tried to create any hierarchies or build a new camp. If Lusty had managed to survive without being murdered, then surely that boded well for Flora?

On the other hand, it was surely more alarming for Operation Poseidon if a teenage boy was able to track them down so easily?

"Him leaving still feels quite fresh," Hive said, suddenly. "I think that we've all had a taste of how bad it could be. When Lusty was setting up the other camp, people started talking about going home. There was a rumour that Tane was going to close Taniwha down entirely and drop us all where we came from. It was a scary time."

"We still maintained the schedule," Frances pointed out.

"Yes, we did," Hive said, and it sounded somewhat sarcastic. Flora smiled, despite herself.

"But I think that now people would... well, everyone's even more keen for it to work. Everyone had to start thinking about going home, about what that would mean. For those of us who don't have... who would have to go back into care, well. And then some of the others have terrible families, families who try and send them abroad to marry strangers, families who hurt them... well, it was a hard time. I think there's a lot of relief in the camp, now that things are back to normal."

Flora felt her eyebrows shoot up. The pictures that DeCalbiac had showed them certainly weren't *normal*.

"Does that answer your question, Brock?" Frances asked.

"Yes, thank you." Flora felt ever-so-slightly better, if only for the fact that they would have told her if someone in the camp was going around threatening and injuring everyone. Clearly, whoever had tried to strangle her wasn't a serial offender. Perhaps it was just a warning that had been taken too far.

Feeling better about the strangulation, although still on the lookout for anyone acting oddly towards her, Flora was able to turn her attention towards her growing feelings for Lana. It felt like, having accepted that she'd never really liked Arlo, she had unleashed her wild, true feelings. Unbidden thoughts that involved her and Lana in a steamy embrace in the lagoon, rather than her and Tane, kept jolting into her mind at inopportune moments and distracting her; she'd broken a plate and nearly slopped one of the toilet buckets everywhere.

Tane had since removed her from bathroom duty, so the lapse had actually worked in her favour.

Nevertheless, she needed to find out how Lana felt, which surely couldn't annoy her attacker. They had only told her to stay away from Tane, right? Her getting close to Lana didn't threaten the 'balance of the camp', surely? And Tane hadn't been around as much as usual, so she hadn't had to face much awkwardness.

The morning after the secret meeting, he had been nowhere to be found. She later overheard that he had volunteered for lookout duty; sitting up at the lookout point and watching for any potential approaching boats. It was a fool's errand; there were never any boats, aside from cruise ships fifty miles away, and so they usually sent the least useful campmates up there.

"Tane's decided to take it upon himself for a few days," Frances had said. Had Flora been imagining it or had he followed up the sentence with a prolonged, meaningful look into Flora's eyes?

No, she must have been imagining things.

"Perhaps he's injured," Hope had suggested.

"Doubt it," Ritchie called. He'd been walking past and

had overheard. "He's probably trying to avoid the toilets; have you guys smelt them recently? I don't even want to know what's going on there."

Flora had blushed a deep red. Perhaps she'd sped up her duties slightly by not emptying every single one of the vats...

She hadn't wanted to dwell on Tane's new interest in his pointless lookout job. The fact was, he was rarely in camp. Even when he was, he maintained a distance from Flora. She wasn't sure if it was on purpose, or it just happened that way, but she was glad. Her face burned every time she thought of him having to politely inform her that it just couldn't happen between them.

Her chance to talk to Lana occurred, happily, on a day when she finally woke up not feeling exhausted, having caught up with the camp's sleep schedule.

The thought of having a proper conversation with Lana gave Flora an overwhelming feeling of excitement and anxiety. She knew that the two were close bedfellows. She would find out how Lana was feeling, so that she could manage her own feelings.

After enquiring with Frances, she found out that Lana was tending to the goats.

"Goat duty, and don't be noisy up there," Frances had muttered. "Since Gasquet had his freak out after one small goat bite, they've been a bit on edge."

"Noted."

Lana often missed breakfast, seeming to use The Kitch at other random times, so it wasn't surprising that she'd gone straight to her day's duty.

When Flora arrived at the goat pen, which was actually a huge, interconnected maze of pens and play areas, she found Lana in the Bovidae Bedroom, a cave in the rock that was filled with moss and golden light, the room name carved into a piece of driftwood.

"It's important for the goats to feel that they're having a good time," Hive had advised her, when Flora first learnt of the giant complex for their four-legged friends.

"Right," Flora had agreed, amused.

There she is.

Lana was on the floor, leaning against a rock. She looked relaxed, tranquil, her forehead smooth. She was stroking one of the goats along its full brown-and-white flank. Flora paused by the entrance of the cave and watched her for a long moment, her heartbeat in her throat. Was she really about to do this? About to open up a conversation that she had no way of knowing would be successful?

May as well get this situationship cleared up.

"Hey," Flora eventually said, her voice soft. Lana and two goats looked up. The goat that was being stroked let out a baleful 'brrr', before immediately ducking back down to nibble at Lana's fingers.

"Oh, hey," Lana said, raising her non-goat hand to push her hair back. Lines reappeared on her forehead. Her eyes became guarded. "What's happened?"

"Nothing's happened."

Lana cleared her throat and pushed her hair back again. She shook her other hand free of a few bits of straw, watching as the goat bent down and attempted to lick it from the muddy floor.

Flora stood alone in the open mouth of the cave.

"I wanted to show you something," she said, when Lana didn't look back up at her.

"Ok." Lana's voice was tight, controlled. She remained watching the goats, as if it took great effort to do so. Waves of silence rolled off of her.

What's going on?

Flora couldn't think of anything else to do, and couldn't pull out now, so she awkwardly unbuttoned her shirt until it was halfway open, and then shrugged it off her shoulder.

Lana looked up. Proudly stabbed over Flora's shoulder was a majestic, three-inch-wide replica of Poukai. It was the same design as Lana's. More intricate than the tattoos that inched across everyone else's collarbones, detailed in swoops and swirls and a sincere love for the boat.

Even now, as Lana sat on the floor, her white vest askew, the same sail was evidenced from her protruding skin: the same mast pointed towards her ear. The same detailed threads indicated ratlines spun in spirals.

"What's that?" Lana whispered, although she knew. Her face was a mixture of horror and surprise, her eyes flicking through emotions without looking away from Flora's shoulder.

"I got the tattoo," Flora said, softly, feeling desperation curl into her words. "I want… I want to stay."

She'd taken the cling film off now and her shoulder shone with the Vaseline that the Harley's had given her.

"Why?" The question was sharp. Flora pulled her top back over her shoulder, wincing.

"I thought you'd like it."

"You thought I'd like it if you copied my exact design?" Lana asked. Her voice was low and hurt. "Be original, Flora."

"What's wrong?" Flora's hands were shaking.

"It's weird," Lana said, all sorts of dismissive. The goats wandered away from her, as if they could sense the tension. "A bit fan girl."

Flora felt her eyeballs prickle. It was the pain from her shoulder; it ached into her soul. "Sorry."

"Right," Lana replied, her low American drawl coming out harsh and flat. She pulled her knees up towards her body and looped her arms around them. Flora could tell that she was itching to smoke; she must not have her supplies on her. "So, I hear congratulations are in order."

"Why?" Flora asked, too quickly, feeling sweat trickle down her spine. She rubbed her palms against her sides. Black blobs clouded in the corners of her vision.

"You and Tane. Seen in the sea. Hardly the most private place for a, what do you call it, snog, is it?"

"I-," Flora started, but her brain had filled with the

sweat from her scalp. She didn't finish the sentence. She thought she might faint.

"I think it's really cute," Lana said, brushing off her legs and standing up. Flora could tell that Lana had never used the word 'cute' seriously in her entire life. "If you want to date Tane, go for it."

She was still looking at her chequered trousers, as if the remnants of hay were ruining them, and Flora felt a wave of nausea rising through her body.

"Look, if you like Tane…" Flora said. She didn't know why she said it. The words came out and it was already too late to stop them. Lana flicked her head up and gave her a look of pure fire.

"What?" She snapped, her tongue spitting a short fury, her shoulders roving upwards, her fingers involuntarily twitching into fists. "Are you kidding me?"

"No, I…" Flora said, once again pathetically tailoring off.

"You're on another planet," Lana proclaimed, hell turned sour, spit hitting the ground, bits of the sky falling on Flora's head, scalp, neck, pricking her all over.

She remained frozen in place long after Lana's footsteps had ground into silence.

CHAPTER THIRTY-ONE
SUPINE

Life on paradise island, when the two leaders were both ignoring you, was hard. Fact.

Flora had been overlooking the others, she knew that. Although she'd physically spent time washing up with Hope, flicking each other with suds, and discussing the Autumn/ Winter fashion line with Gasquet (she had no idea what he was talking about, but apparently 'metalcore' was 'in'), and sitting with McLarty, hacking into shipping data (they still weren't able to locate 'The Esmerelda'; the boat was too small and unconnected), she was mentally never quite there.

She was reliving two of the most excruciating moments of her life.

Tane's face, dripping with woe.

Lana's face, spitting out fire.

And her, a pathetic idiot with a ship tattoo for the rest of her life.

She had gone from being single to staying single, and yet she felt as if she'd lost everything in the middle.

Lana had quickly made a new friend. Chan was usually on clothes duty with Gasquet. She had a shining curtain of black hair which she brushed almost constantly. She never smiled, but her lips, which were often defined with dark lipliner, also rarely moved. She was silent and beautiful and

Lana's new BFF.

Lana sat next to Chan by the campfire, made sarcastic jokes to her during downtime and requested Chan work with her when they had three buckets of orange peppers to chop. Chan, clearly flattered to get attention from the second most important person in camp, and the most important person on Poukai, ditched Gasquet and clothes duty in a heartbeat.

"Looks like Lana and Chan are a bit close, hey?" Lennox said to Hope and Flora one afternoon, when they were lying on the beach trying to sunbathe. *Trying*, because the others were playing volleyball in the sea and the cheering was distracting. Easton and Bell were on jet skis in the lagoon, churning up the water with whirring motors.

"Who?" Flora asked, reddening. She already knew it; she wasn't blind. But the fact that someone else had noticed it too made it more real, somehow. Her heart thudded behind her closed eyelids.

"There's no way that Lana likes her," Hope declared.

Hope was in a hard position, Flora knew. She understood everything; that Flora had thrown herself at Tane, that she'd copied Lana's ink, that she'd made a fool of herself. Hope couldn't very well act as if there was no possibility of Lana moving on, of her meeting someone else. But she also couldn't be a bad friend; she had to set Flora up for reality while also staying on her team.

Deftly, Hope changed the subject to her preferred types of cheese, and Lennox was immediately distracted by describing exactly how he ate a brie sandwich.

Flora was left to die slowly on the sand in peace.

△△△

Despite a low-level feeling of worry and loneliness, Flora knew that she was physically looking better than ever. Her skin became tanned, and she actually had abs from laughing so much, even if that laughter was mostly to cover her pain. Her hair, which had always been wild and unruly, suited her new look.

"Surfer girl chic," Gasquet told her, approvingly.

She'd been working with him more often. Clothes duty was her favourite, because she liked seeing the swirls of fabric in the great wooden barrels. She had to climb into the barrel and stamp on the fabrics, which billowed around her and soaked her through. Band t-shirts and silk scarves and leather trousers and fishnet tights: they all went in.

Gasquet would fold the dried clothes in a perfectionist manner, and she would tease him about it; *you know they're only gonna get filthy again tomorrow?*

It was fun. It was messy, and she abhorred having to scrub dirty underwear, but it had an element of satisfaction that she didn't feel when she was bent over yanking weeds from the crumbling earth in Le Jardin.

The campmates who usually worked in Le Jardin were keen for Flora to help there as well. She'd played a few farm-based games before and understood a surprising amount about hydroponic watering systems and efficiency. She redesigned how the machines worked so that they could water most of the plants in half of the time.

She'd also hunted out huge leaves to hang over their bedroom window to block out the remaining light from Hive's pretty-but-useless curtains, creating a riot of requests for her to hang the same in everyone else's huts.

She had agreed and been given a standing ovation by the campfire. Nearly everyone had whooped - any excuse to scream and shout – and Flora had filled with pride. She ignored Lana, who was busy muttering to Chan, and Tane, who was whittling an axe handle.

She wondered what had happened to the plaque he had been making. *It's probably been put on the campfire,* she thought, sourly.

Apart from the ongoing disdain from Lana and Tane,

Flora was growing used to Taniwha life. No one had tried to strangle her again, which she considered a positive. Probably because she was staying away from Tane, as instructed, although it was more to do with the fact that he was avoiding her than anything else.

Every morning, after waking up to the reassuring smell of the wooden hut and the scuffled sounds of Hive and Frances getting ready for the day, she stretched out and took it all in. Her own comfy bed, the sounds of nature outside, the beams of sunlight that filtered in through sporadic gaps in the wood. The smells of breakfast wafting across the camp, the sounds of her new friends starting up conversation by the campfire.

Having a purpose, whether that be taking on the role of clothes duty or supporting McLarty with endless online tracking, made her feel valued.

Often in the morning, she thought about her dad. How much he would love it on Taniwha. How she wished she could send him her location and have him turn up to enjoy adventurous island life. He'd get on well with the crew; he'd be like a nutty older brother to everyone. He'd come up with ideas; he was 'innovative'.

He would brainstorm better ways to distil the seawater to produce drinking water, better ways to keep the mosquitos at bay without making lemon water, improved methods of fishing so that they didn't end up throwing a load of jellyfish back (although, to be fair, Frances had made some jellyfish ceviche a few nights ago that had been generally enjoyed).

Her dad would probably love Tane. He would probably not understand Lana.

Sometimes, when she couldn't sleep and the jungle noise was too much, Flora's mind would drift to imagining taking each of them home to meet her dad and Abbie. She would imagine Lana, her fiery eyes and heavy eyebrows taking up space on their ratty old sofa, and her dad trying to make conversation. Trying to make Lana laugh. Lana would just roll her eyes.

And then Tane. Tane wouldn't be sat on the sofa. He'd probably be stood on it, waving something from the kitchen that he found insane, like their frog-shaped spatula. Her dad would be rendered speechless, in that version of events.

Stop being such a loser. As if either of them will ever meet your dad.

She was making the most of her days on the island as if she were at a summer camp.

If she was honest with herself, the thought of stepping back into her old life filled her with a certain amount of dread. The idea of sitting in maths class, dust swilling around her in tendrils, trying not to fall asleep. Of nappies and wiping up brown and yellow sludge every day. Of waking up, going to school, getting home, firing up Pictopia and then going to sleep, every single day.

She'd lost most of her desire to finish Pictopia. It was just a game – just a bunch of pixels manipulating her emotions. When she stood on the beach on Taniwha and watched the sun setting, dying the sky all shades of orange and pink, she felt as if she couldn't believe her own eyes. Escapism lost its appeal when you had no desire to escape.

Her hair still had shades of burgundy buttered across it.

"Err, my hair?" Flora had said to the relevant Harley one morning, when she'd managed to get her on her own. The girl looked blankly at Flora for a long moment, like a lemur who had come across a human.

"Why did you dye it in my sleep?" Flora tried again, waiting for the girl to come up with an explanation. She didn't believe, in her heart, that any of the Harleys had tried to strangle her; they didn't seem to care what went on with the other campmates.

"I think you look cute," she said, her voice timid. "Not like, romantically... Obviously," her eyes grew wild as she backpaddled. "Don't tell Lana I said it looked cute, I just meant... you know, it suits you."

"Right," Flora said, completely stumped for a response.

Lana wouldn't care if you called me an absolute effing hottie.

To be fair, she had had a lot of complements on the new look. First there was Gasquet, who had loudly complemented her at least three times, and then Lennox, who clearly wanted to be nice to Flora to make Hope like him. Then a few of the others, including Ritchie, had complemented her, and she started to genuinely like her new hair.

Then there was Hive: "I'm not sure it looks very natural."

Flora let any annoyance at that comment go; the new, more dramatic look certainly wasn't Hive's style.

Flora had overheard the same Harley girl ask Tane if he could pick up more ink the next time he went back to the mainland for medical supplies.

"I used up the last of it on Flora," the girl had said, quiet and squirrel-like. She had glanced furtively in Flora's direction, forcing Tane to do the same. Tane's eyes had met Flora's across the camp circle, and he'd looked momentarily lost for words. They stared at each other for a second too long, or so it felt to Flora, and then McLarty leant over to tell Flora something about solar panels and the moment was broken.

She had turned back to McLarty and realised that someone had been watching the whole interaction. Lana sat near her, her fingers intertwined with Chan's, her eyes glaring at Flora: dark, complicated.

"I can't believe how small they are," Flora replied pointedly to McLarty, referring to the solar panels on board Poukai, which powered their computer lair. She had looked away from Lana with a burning face and McLarty had seemed delighted to get her full attention, for once.

"I can't believe how full on they are already," Flora said to Hope, one evening, as they tucked into banana and cacao pudding.

"Who?"

"Those two," Flora muttered, flashing her eyes towards Lana and Chan.

"They're only holding hands," Hope said, cautiously. "A lot of people just do that with their friends. In fact, in India men always hold hands with their male friends. It probably doesn't mean anything."

"Total garbage," Flora said. She said it loudly and Hope hid her surprise well. Lana seemed to hear, and the corner of her lip curled up into a smile, which Flora ignored.

She was set into her routine. Wake up, breakfast, be given her tasks for the day, usually from Hive or Frances, work for a few hours and then enjoy the afternoon with Hope or Gasquet or whoever was free.

If Lana wanted to hold hands with Chan and Tane wanted to ignore her, then she was still doing just fine. Tonight, they would finish eating by the campfire, and someone would tell a ridiculous story, and she would laugh, and there would be no phones or technology or risk of finding out that Jen still thought she was a loser. Flora would go to bed full and exhausted and sleep like a baby.

△△△

"What's wrong?" McLarty asked. It was mid-morning and they were holed up in The Den, using live satellites to search the surrounding seas. They were scanning from far too high; they might spot the odd cruise ship or mega yacht, but there was no way that they would be able to find a smaller vessel. They both knew this, and the atmosphere had been flat for the last hour.

"Nothing," Flora said, although she knew that her voice gave her away. She coughed.

In the corner, DeCalbiac was tapping away on her keyboard, running rows of code that would allow her to keep track of Tane's mum in her smart house. It also enabled her to see any messages that she might have sent via their voice-activated messaging system.

DeCalbiac sat looking gloomy and tense; it didn't look

like there was any new news.

"I don't believe that for a second," McLarty said, wryly. "You look like you want to kill someone. Aren't you enjoying life in paradise?"

Flora looked around them and laughed. Crumpled up paper plates sat next to stained coffee mugs and half-eaten tubes of sweets. The smell of damp wood penetrated the air in The Den until it was almost suffocating. The computers created a nasal buzzing.

"Can you call this paradise?"

"Hey, it's a great set-up."

"I know," Flora sighed. "And I do love life on the island. It's just..."

"Just what?"

"Nothing," she said. How could she explain to McLarty? She couldn't tell him that she was jealous of Chan. That she regretted almost everything that she'd said to Lana since she first set foot on the ship. That, if she had her time again, she would have done everything differently.

"Lana and Chan are looking a bit close, aren't they?" McLarty suddenly said. Flora looked across at him.

"What do you mean?" Her heartbeat started accelerating.

"It's not great for the camp," he said, as if she hadn't spoken. "Chan should mind herself. Lana's a big deal around here, and people don't like change."

"What's the worst that could happen?" Flora asked, the words falling clumsily off of her tongue. There it was again: *people won't like the camp balance being upset.*

"The worst? Someone gets between Lana and Tane. They aren't friends any more. Tane starts to change his mind about life on the island; he takes his money and his ship and leaves. You think we could afford to live here without him?"

"But you have Le Jardin," Flora muttered desperately. "You're self-sufficient, why would you still need Tane?"

"Ha, you think the world of jet skis and water parks and

pirate ships comes for free? You think that this is it? Every month the island gets better, and it gets better because Tane can afford it. Who knows how amazing it could be a year from now? If we can get rid of Axer, that is," McLarty finished, directing his attention back to the screen in front of him.

A long silence followed his words. DeCalbiac's headphones pulsed a small tune into the air.

"Oh," McLarty said suddenly, sitting upright in his chair.

"What?" Flora asked, whipping her head to look at his screen.

"DeCalbiac," McLarty snapped. "Have you seen the CCTV from Santa Cruz das Flores harbour?"

"Merde," DeCalbiac whispered, looking at his screen. "Let me check the harbour register." She turned back to her computer and started typing away.

"What's going on?" Flora asked.

"Yesterday, eighteen hundred hours," McLarty said, flicking through CCTV images so quickly that Flora couldn't focus on one single image. Renderings of the sea, boats, white sails, flickered in two dimensions.

"Yes, found them," DeCalbaic said, her voice low and urgent. "American Buoy, checked in yesterday. One night only."

"Why haven't we seen it on the satellites?"

"Is it him?" Flora asked urgently, imagining Axer's slicked hair and dead eyes arriving on a nearby island.

"No," DeCalbiac replied, clearly feeling sorry for Flora and how out of the loop she was. "His boat is called The Esmerelda. This boat belongs to Jabez Harben."

"Scarface." Flora thought back to the article that she'd read in a different time in a different world. Scarface, who could track down anyone. Scarface, who she'd seen at the jetty in Plymouth.

"I thought we threw him off when we left England," McLarty muttered angrily, flicking through the images on his screen even faster now, a frenzy of masts and static sailors flying backwards and forwards.

"We did," DeCalbiac blustered. "I moved his tracking device myself; put it on another boat. He must have figured it out."

"Well, that's not exactly hard," McLarty whispered, viciously. "All it would take is for him to look up at the boat they were following. Poukai doesn't look like any other boat out there, it would have been obvious. It was a stupid idea."

"Fine," DeCalbiac fumed, standing up and throwing her headphones down onto the desk. Her forehead was shining with sweat. "Next time, you can sort it out. I risked my life moving that device, and if you want to whine about it now then you can die for all I care."

With that, she stormed up the stairs, slamming the closet door behind her. McLarty hadn't moved from his picture scanning. It was as if he hadn't heard her, as if he didn't care. Flora felt panic eating at her throat

"McLarty," she said, and she could barely breathe.

"What?" he asked, his voice flat. His eyes were black and shining.

"If that Harben, Scarface, is nearly here, then what about Axer? If they find us, then surely *he'll* find us?"

"Don't worry," McLarty said, his voice softening, as if he'd only just realised that Flora was scared. "I won't let that happen. We're better than them. We just need to find them first. Leave it to me, ok?"

He went back to his screen and his typing, taking a snapshot of one of the boats and zooming in, watching as a man in a black hooded jumper walked from the boat. He zoomed in on the man, and the same pair of sunglasses that Flora had seen in the shadows of Plymouth Harbour flashed out at them.

"Time to play," McLarty muttered to himself, firing up a second monitor and opening the data of a real-time satellite. "You who dare to threaten Taniwha…"

He continued to mutter to himself, getting darker and

more threatening in tone, while Flora sat watching, feeling more and more claustrophobic. In the end, she got up and left, knowing that she wasn't helping, knowing that he didn't want her there anyway. As she climbed the stairs, he didn't look up.

CHAPTER THIRTY-TWO
CLINOMANIA

Flora arrived back at the camp feeling shaken. The man with the scarred face was nearby. Taniwha was under threat. They were about to be discovered. And if Scarface found them, what about Axer? A cold-blooded murderer, a man filled with pride that thwarted his empathy, a man who would torture an innocent woman, kill a beautiful canine.

Frances was the first to find her, which was typical. He bustled up to her with his keen eyes and busybody air and said that he was looking for someone to fulfil an urgent job.

"Err, sure, what can I do?" Flora asked, her mind flitting between a million different things. She didn't want to help Frances, yet what else could she do? If she went to her hut, then Hive would probably find her anyway and get her helping out in the kitchen. She didn't want to walk up to the lookout point; she was too distracted; she would probably fall off the cliff and die. She couldn't tell anyone; all hell would break loose.

It was a cooler day than previous ones and the sky threatened to drizzle. The sea seemed to infiltrate the air around them, clinging to her skin.

"You see those boxes over there?" Frances asked, nodding his head towards some boxes that were propped outside one of the sleeping huts. Without waiting for a reply, he continued, "when we went to England, to your town actually, Eccles used a stolen passport to rent a car for the day and then drove it over to the dump."

Flora barely had time to raise her eyebrows. *Never mind the fact that Eccles looks about five years' old.*

"They found a whole box of rather ornate pottery. Bowls and plates, you know the type of thing. I was thinking that you could smash it up and then use it to mark out the main pathways. The path to the Privy Shack, and the beach, and to Le Jardin, and wherever else you think might be useful. The soil seems quite damp today, so just push the pieces in facing upwards. If you need any help breaking the china, then grab Lana. She has a toolbox under her bed."

"Right," Flora said, trying to understand what exactly was being asked. And also why, specifically, Frances had asked her? Had she come across as some artistic maverick? Perhaps it was her strong gaming fingers. *Damn them.*

Frances strolled off before Flora had time to think of any questions, and when she focused further, she found that she didn't have any anyway. It wasn't the nicest of jobs, but it wasn't exactly difficult, and she'd rather make a mosaic than empty the bogs or attempt to think about how they could prevent certain death.

The scarred man is at the nearest harbour.

Which wasn't close to Taniwha, she reminded herself. Even though he'd found their general area, there was no guarantee that he'd find the island. She had to trust McLarty.

And she wasn't going to bother Lana. She was probably busy with Chan. She was also nowhere to be seen, or felt, given that Flora was often unconsciously aware of her whereabouts, which also saved her the trouble of really thinking about it. Her signal wasn't picking up Lana; she couldn't be near the camp.

Flora found a pointed rock and retrieved the china.

△△△

Smashing up the beautiful, ornate pottery actually turned out to be pretty cathartic. She took each pot out in turn, put it on one of the seating logs around the campfire and whacked it. It wasn't very graceful, and she was sure that she looked a bit zany to anyone who was looking, but it did the job (albeit with tiny white shards of china spitting everywhere) and with only a few cuts to her hands and arms, which she'd stopped noticing anyway. Her muscles had already become leaner, the pads on her fingers harder.

Health and safety wasn't the top priority on Taniwha, and, to be honest, Flora was glad. Doing this kind of organic and messy craft was something that appealed to her massively, and she knew that if she was still in Art class then she'd have to wear gloves and goggles and probably a whole hazmat suit.

Mosaic pieces made, it was time to create the pathways.

Pushing the china into the dirt turned out to be a whole other matter. The crust of the earth was hard and gritty, not the damp putty that she was sure Frances had been imagining. In the end, she took to stomping on the pretty blue-and-white designs to get them to set into the ground, making an ornate Hansel-and-Grettel trail into the forest, towards the beach.

For the first hour, it went smoothly, the pieces making a beautiful path through the dense trees. Ferns fluttered against her skin as she worked, filling her nostrils with verdant greenery. The action distracted her mind from the impending danger; she could almost forget that Axer's hired bounty hunter had made it to the Azores.

As the afternoon grew weary, bugs started growing in number and birds started cawing overhead. The thickness of the jungle pressed her from all sides.

Adventure is overrated, Flora thought, as she wiped yet another bug from her leg and swept her mass of salty, matted hair away from her face. She wished she had a hair tie, having already tried to use a length of dead leaf.

Deep along the pathway, it had grown cooler. Every so often, Flora would come to a clearing, where trails of lame sunlight would stroke the floor and birds would cry out from overhead, looking for the small animals that scurried through the undergrowth.

Outside of the dappled clearings, she was absorbed into shadows and hushed whispers, the wind rustling through the trees, the leaves crunching underfoot, the sound of birds swooping through the branches. A melody of cicadas started up, as lianas swayed in the growing breeze.

Flora continued building her path until she reached a clearing of wild, tropical flowers. Huge pink trumpet-like flowers with bright orange stems dipped and swayed, dainty berries lined thick, verdant stalks, a cacophony of daisy-like flowers created a carpet either side of her pottery.

"Beautiful," Flora whistled, watching as dusk's pollen rose from the scene. It looked like a watercolour painting, like the type of dappled glen that would line the walls of libraries and manor houses throughout England.

"Hey."

It was a husky, calm voice, and it appeared from the path behind her. Flora felt something warm stir inside her chest.

"Lana?" Flora turned. She had felt alone, completely alone, in this beautiful, surreal part of the forest. Birds cawed gently overhead, while huge crimson butterflies swooped between flowers. "What's going on?"

Lana just smiled and walked closer, looking around at the clearing as she walked. She was wearing her usual clothes; plain vest and trousers lined with pockets. Her bright, blonde cropped hair had grown out slightly, and she'd flipped it over to one side. *It suits her.*

"It's beautiful, hey?" Flora said, her own voice quiet now, as if there was a spell on the clearing. Above them, a bird whistled and another one chirped back. The trees seemed to hum.

"Yeah, it's a great time of day," Lana replied. She sounded nervous. She looked down at the ground, shuffling her feet. Flora felt as if she couldn't talk for a moment; Lana was so close that she could smell her: her shampoo, the sweet smell of sweat on her skin.

"Oh, wow," Flora said, without thinking, as a huge frog with a speckled back hopped past their feet.

"Iberian green frog," Lana muttered. They both watched as the frog dived into a patch of thick grass. "Have you been ok?"

"Fine," Flora said, surprised. Her hands were covered in mud and her face was coated in sweat, but otherwise, there was no reason for Lana to ask.

Unless she's heard about Scarface? In which case, why does she care what I think?

"We love having you here," Lana said, her voice low again. "I just talked to McLarty, tried to help him with... well, it's all getting serious, and I thought that if I don't do anything now... if I don't say anything..." Lana's voice cracked. She looked up at the same time that Flora did, and they locked eyes, and an electric shock pounded through Flora's whole body.

With that one look, she knew what Lana was going to say, and what was going to happen next, and all of the million feelings of frustration and wondering and tension and being hyper aware of her every movement came to the surface, and before she could help it, she threw down the piece of pottery onto the hard soil.

She grabbed the older girl by the shoulders and pushed her against the tree trunk next to them. And then they kissed. Flora tasted the sweet cushion of the other girl's lips, the warm slip of her tongue, the feel of Lana's hands against her back, her hair, the heat of their bodies pressed together, Lana's mouth against her neck, her collarbone.

"Oh God," Lana groaned, and whether it was out of passion or pain or guilt or something else, Flora didn't care, pushing her lips against Lana's again, tasting her hot breath.

Flora loosened Lana's t-shirt and kissed along her collarbone, until the full scale of Lana's tattoo was revealed; a huge, detailed version of Poukai, complete with hull and mast and detailed ratlines and the powerful, fierce personality of the boat, sinking deep down onto Lana's breast, covering her whole shoulder blade.

"Yours is better," Flora whispered, her voice husky, and without meaning to, and without knowing why, she felt tears prick her eyes. She looked at the tattoo and fully realised everything that it meant. What it signified. How wrong Flora had been to copy her, because Flora wasn't running, Flora didn't need to signify that same feeling of freedom.

"I'm sorry," Flora whispered, as Lana hungrily found Flora's lips again, and Flora felt their tongues dance together, light and nimble and passionate and deep. One of Lana's hands was spread along Flora's neck, the other pulling her lower back closer, so their heaving bodies were pressed together, their heat magnified by a thousand.

This is everything I've ever wanted. And I can't do it.

"I'm sorry," Flora repeated, pulling herself away from Lana, from the beauty and pain in front of her. She looked down to blink away the tears, feeling all of the emotions under the sun clog in her throat until she could barely swallow.

"I thought that this is what you wanted," Lana whispered. She sounded as if she wanted to cry as well.

"I do, it's just…" *I don't know my own mind.*

Flora took a quick, deep breath in, looked up at Lana's pained eyes for a long moment and then hurried back down the path, back towards camp, away from the perfect clearing and everything that it meant.

CHAPTER THIRTY-THREE
LOQUACIOUS

She told them all that she was sick. She stayed in bed all evening and lay flat on her back, looking up at the wooden ceiling. The one that she looked at often, the one that criss-crossed over and over a hundred times, the one that presented confusion over and over again, but tied together to make something safe.

Hope came to see her, but Flora wasn't ready to tell her what had happened.

"You look terrible," Hope said, honestly.

"Thanks," Flora grumbled. It wasn't even an act anymore; she felt all jumbled up inside as if she'd eaten too much food, even though her stomach was grumbling. She felt as if she couldn't breathe, but also as if she wanted nothing more than to be back by the campfire, having fun with everyone.

"So, what's happened?" Hope prompted, not seeming to believe that Flora was ill.

"Nothing," Flora lied.

She knew that she needed to decide what she wanted before she could go and socialise. She couldn't lead anyone on; it wasn't fair.

The problem was that she wasn't sure what she wanted; she was only sure of what she didn't want, which was the everyday lifestyle once described by Lana. The chicken tikka on a Saturday, lottery tickets and alarm clocks, middle-

England kind of life.

Flora didn't want that. She wanted adventure, excitement, the feeling of being outside her comfort zone, the feeling of falling in love, the feeling of being in love, the feeling of constantly wanting to vomit while also wanting to fall into the sea and watch the stars and think 'How lucky am I?'

She wanted to feel Lana's body pressed against hers, she wanted to taste her again, she wanted Lana's hands on her back, telling her that everything would be alright.

But also, Tane. She hated that she was thinking of Tane when so much had happened with Lana. Flora and Lana had crossed a line; they'd taken things to a whole new level. It wasn't just the passion by the tree trunk, it was the ongoing tension, the way that they tried to avoid looking each other in the eyes, but when they did, they couldn't stop. It was the way that Flora was certain that everyone knew what was going on just by the sheer force of electricity that surged between them whenever they were in the same place, but also the feeling of having a secret, the breath-stealing moments in which they had something to hide.

Every time that Lana had been holding hands and cuddling Chan, she had been acutely aware of Flora too. Flora knew that by the fact that she would overhear things that Flora said to the others, she would smile when Flora made a joke nearby, she would move slightly when Flora stood up.

It wasn't just me.

But Tane. Well. Tane was the type that you would spend the day with. He was positive and talkative and optimistic. He would be the type to take you on a trek and hack down the trees in your path, to get you to try new foods and live outside your comfort zone, to learn foreign languages and play games and laugh with. Flora had spent a lot more time laughing with Tane than she had with Lana. She had spent a lot more time imagining herself in bed with Lana than she had with Tane.

And now she lay in the bed that she'd made, listening to the rest of the world having fun in the camp outside, while the sun dimmed and eventually bathed her hut in a cool charcoal grey, through which she blinked numbness.

△△△

She had a dream that the door kept opening, that Hive and Frances weren't in their beds. She heard leaves rustling and a branch crack, but she kept her eyes squeezed closed, willing the dream world to stop feeling so real, afraid of feeling a pair of hands around her neck.

Another crack from a branch and then she fell back to sleep.

△△△

"Dude, you cannot still be sick," Hope said, laying over Flora's legs. She'd had an amazing chat with Lennox last night, during which they'd basically both admitted that they loved each other, and Hope was bored with Flora's mystery illness. "I think I could see him for the short term, you know?"

"Yeah, you guys are great together," Flora mumbled. She had slept terribly, a night punctuated with Lana running after her through a forest, and Tane meeting her on a secret beach, and her dad telling her that she'd failed all of her exams. In the end, she'd lain awake since dawn, listening as the forest woke up around them.

"I know, but like, what's the next step? Are we supposed to get, like, a cabin together?"

"Woah," Flora said, suddenly engaging with what Hope was saying. "Don't be insane. It's way too soon to think about living together. Like, have you even kissed?"

"Err," Hope replied, looking sheepishly towards the door.

"What," Flora said, crying out in a mixture of admiration and jealousy that everything was so easy for Hope, that she loved Lennox, and he loved her.

"I know, it was on the beach last night. A bit like you and Tane, but we weren't in the sea," Hope admitted, biting her lip and smiling.

"What do you mean, me and Tane?"

"Oh babe, we saw you, obvs. You and Tane were getting it on in the sea, but don't worry, I know you were just caught up in the moment. It didn't mean anything, otherwise you'd still be getting together now, right. And, clearly, you're not interested in Tane anymore, which is really for the best."

"Right," Flora said, a sinking feeling pushing her down into the futon. How many people saw them? Had they really been that obvious?

"Don't be annoyed. I'm just so... like, confused, I just don't know what to do."

"Isn't it simple?" Flora snapped. "You like Lennox, he likes you. That's it."

"Mmmm."

Flora made her excuses to escape and have a shower.

She washed her hair and her face and spent extra time lathering the goats milk suds on her skin until she felt gleaming, soft, and ready to take on the day.

△△△

She had missed breakfast.

"You missed a really questionable omelette," the lemur-like Harley whispered to her.

"I don't even know if that was real meat," DeCalbiac said, loudly. "It tasted like a chicken that's been dead for ten years."

I should really check in with McLarty.

She'd been neglecting the real news of the moment; the fact that Jabez was close enough to smell on the wind. The only consolation that she afforded herself was how driven McLarty ked when she left him. *It's easy to convince myself that he   ll in hand.*

She checked with Frances whether McLarty had requested her on Poukai duty, but he hadn't. In fact, he'd told Frances to keep everyone away from the ship. Flora was happy to oblige. It was too big a task, and she didn't know what she was doing. She was far more comfortable doing the more mindless tasks.

Instead of coding, Frances dully informed her that she was on clothes duty again, this time with both Gasquet and Chan.

Chan? Great.

It was interesting that Chan was back on clothes duty; she'd shirked it pretty much every day since she started seeing Lana.

Are they not seeing each other anymore?

Flora felt guilt lurch through her body. She couldn't imagine anything worse than having to spend the morning with Chan, and yet... she wanted to know what was going on between her and Lana.

Gasquet and Chan were both fashionistas. They had their bandanas tied around their heads when Flora arrived, turning rags into haute couture. They shared the same blue eyeliner, which Flora secretly wanted to try but didn't dare ask about, and they spent the first hour of their duties regaling each other with their favourite moments from America's Next Top Model.

Flora was quiet while the other two whiled away the task, discussing which of the Carteles – a famous family who had a show tracking their every move – they found the most annoying. Flora was able to slip into the background of the conversation, scrubbing the clothes until they were clean and smelling fresh, battering them against a huge rock so that the wrinkles would disappear, hanging them neatly in rows to dry.

She relished the distraction, moving through the methodological movements of cleaning dirty clothing without having to think too much, barely skimming the surface of her pool of thoughts, which took on several big topics, such as:

1. Did she prefer Tane or Lana? If she was with Lana then she would officially be in a queer relationship, which would be her first, but she felt like that wasn't a big deal anymore, not like it had been for her parents. There were loads of queer people at her school, and her dad would be fine with it.
2. What would happen when one of them ultimately found out about the other one? They were best friends, and Flora was essentially coming between them. She worried that either they would end up hating each other, or they would both end up hating Flora.
3. How soon did she need to decide? She had kissed them both, which essentially made her a harlot, a word that her dad would have used to describe someone who would play around back in the day. While it was fair enough that she should weigh up her options, she knew that she was also playing with people's feelings at the same time, and that the former shouldn't butcher the latter too much. What was the time frame on this type of thing? Could she make out with them both again, just to make sure, or did it get more complicated every time something happened?
4. Which kiss did she prefer? She could barely remember kissing Tane, although she remembered the salty taste of his lips, the way that she felt as if she was having an out-of-body experience. Then yesterday with Lana, it had felt rugged, real, as if her body was about to explode. Which one was better?

And then her final thought: did any of the above even

matter? While she was spending hours thinking about them, were either of them even thinking about her? Was Lana even interested anymore? *Why did I leave?*

She felt furious with herself, and she took it out on various items of clothing, battering them against the rocks until sleeves started sprouting frayed threads. *I can't believe I left Lana in the clearing.*

Her heart often felt as if it had acted in a way that was out of tune with her head. But this was something else altogether: she liked Lana; she knew that. So, what on earth was her heart trying to say? *Or was it my head, trying to protect me?*

Lana was hardly a solid choice. She was famously angry. She had, for all intents and purposes, a girlfriend, for goodness' sake. Chan.

"Hey, Chan, I don't think we've had much chance to speak," Flora said, grabbing the bull by the horns in a moment of quiet. Gasquet had popped to the Privy Shack, which was a good twenty-minute walk from their makeshift laundrette.

"Don't talk to me," Chan hissed. Her thick hair had fallen around her face. For a moment, Flora wondered whether she'd imagined it.

"Err, sorry, I didn't quite-"

"I said, don't talk to me," Chan interrupted, looking up at Flora with such venom in her eyes that Flora took a step back and nearly dropped the silk scarf that she was holding.

"Ok," Flora said, slowly, trying to process the other girl's reaction.

"What's... like, what's wrong?"

"What's wrong? How about the fact that you stole my girlfriend? *You?* What the hell does she see in you?" Chan said, her jaw holding so much tension that spit was flying out with each word. She stared at Flora with wide, furious eyes. Flora felt her mouth drop open, but she had no words.

Lana told her that she was leaving her... for me?

"I'm not... I'm not seeing Lana, Chan," Flora said,

eventually, breaking the silence, causing Chan to look down at the jumper that she was wringing out.

"Liar."

"It's true, I swear."

"Well, that's what Lana told me. She kicked me out of her bed two nights ago, told me that she'd fallen for someone else. I questioned her, obviously, and it became clear that this mystery girl was... *is*, you."

Flora felt the hot mist of jealousy rise up within her. They were in bed together?

"Well, we're not an item, so you don't need to worry," Flora said, marvelling at her ability to speak actual words when she felt as if her whole body was on fire. She examined the silk scarf in detail, trying to stop tears welling up, trying to prevent her body from spontaneously combusting. *Lana said she's fallen for me?*

"Well, I hope you two are very happy together. But I warn you, people won't like it. You're a newbie, you've barely been here five minutes, and you think you can be with Lana? You're in way over your head. People didn't like me being with her, and I'm, well... you know, here for keeps."

"What do you mean people didn't like you being with her?" Flora asked, quickly.

Chan didn't reply, but her cheeks flushed.

"Did they... did people do things to you?" Flora asked, her voice low. Flashbacks of being strangled flicked through her mind. She could have died.

"It's... it was nothing," Chan said, quickly, her cheeks flaming.

"It's not nothing, Chan. We could-" Flora started to say, but they were interrupted by Gasquet, who appeared with a loud greeting and a proclamation that he refused to use the Privy Shack again due to the "poor hygiene".

Flora didn't get a chance to talk to Chan again, and when they finished with the day's clothes, Chan hurried off back to camp before she had a chance to corner her. *How strange. So, she was threatened too.*

CHAPTER THIRTY-FOUR
SANGUINOLENCY

Back at the camp, the campmates were tucking into lunch. The menu consisted of pulled jackfruit burgers with melted goats' cheese and sweet potato chips. Ritchie was on cooking duty and he had a taste for finer foods, or at least wasn't adept at spreading out the 'treat ingredients', which meant that everyone was happy except those in charge of stock taking.

"Ritchie, we were saving the goats cheese for a fondue night," Frances reproached, while Hive stood behind him shaking her head. They both looked a little off, but Flora couldn't put her finger on why. Their eyes were a little wider than usual; they were wearing clothes that they'd never worn before.

That's it. Frances always wears the same shirt, and he's not wearing it today.

Instead, he was wearing a tattered t-shirt with a band pasted across the front, which looked completely out of place on him. And Hive was wearing a vest top, something that she'd never worn before. *Maybe they're trying out a new look?*

"I bloody love goats' cheese," Hope said to Flora, as thick white strands fell down her chin. "We really don't make the most of the goats here, I swear we should be eating this every day."

"Mmm," Flora muttered back. She wasn't hungry. She'd eaten a handful of sweet potato chips, but she was sat tightly, her body seized up, waiting for Lana to arrive at the circle. She hadn't seen her since the jungle.

But she didn't arrive.

Instead, McLarty stomped into the circle and sat down next to Flora, grabbing her uneaten burger and taking a huge bite.

"I think they've found us," he said, his mouth full of dripping jackfruit, his eyes wild and unfocused.

"What? Where are they?" Flora asked, making to stand up but promptly sitting back down again. *Why is McLarty here then?*

She felt guilt shoot through her. She had been so caught up with the Lana situation that she'd relied on McLarty to sort out their villains while she sorted out her love life. She should have paid more attention. He looked terrible.

"I'm so sorry I haven't been helping," she whispered.

"I don't need you," he said straight away, rubbing his nose. It was dripping.

"Why do you think they've found Taniwha?"

"Dunno," he replied, wiping his mouth with the back of his black sleeve, blinking hard. There were deep circles under his eyes and his voice sounded croaky. "They just probably have. Probably. I think they must have done. I can't see them, can't hear them, can't find them anywhere. They must be nearby."

"McLarty, do you think you should get some sleep?" Flora asked gently, putting her hand on his arm. He looked down at her hand and it seemed to focus him. "Me and DeCalbiac can pick up the tracking. Just because they've made it to a harbour doesn't mean that they know where we are, right?"

"Probably not," he admitted, taking a final bite of the burger. He'd polished it off in five bites. "I just haven't been back to my hut, you know? There's too much to do. And Ritchie and Bell snore so loudly that I can't sleep there anyway, so I tried sleeping in The Den, but then I kept having ideas. I saw them leave the port yesterday, but I just can't find them, not on a satellite or anywhere. The boat's too small. I've tracked it back to his bank account, his address. He's a friend of Axer, that's not new news, and I found their email chain, but it's all in code and I don't know what he's saying.

But he's on his way, anyway. He might not know exactly where we are, and we don't know where he is, but they're on their way."

"Who's he with?" Flora asked, her voice low.

"There's just two of them. I don't know who the other guy is, but he's not Axer."

"Right," Flora said, grimly. She felt like a sitting duck. She looked around, as if Scarface and his right-hand man could stroll in from any direction. "How long would it take them to get here, if they did find us?"

"Probably a couple of days of searching," McLarty said. "Depending on conditions."

"How are conditions today?" Flora asked, thinking that that was quite an important point.

"Well, I don't know, *Flora*," McLarty said, suddenly angry. "Between trying to track them down and managing to hack into his private conversations, I wasn't able to spend a lot of time on the shipping forecast."

"Alright, sorry," Flora said, taken aback.

"Whatever. Just stay away from my Den. I've told Lana everything and she doesn't seem worried. In fact, she almost didn't care." McLarty breathed out, loudly. "DeCalbiac is handling the situation for an hour; I'm going to bed." He threw Flora's plate onto the floor and stormed off.

After a long moment, during which Hope let out a peal of laughter at a joke that Lennox had just told her, Flora picked up her plate. *They know where we are, and as of last night, they've come to find us.*

Flora didn't know what to do. She didn't have any resources, or any way of tracking them down that McLarty wouldn't already have tried. She was starting to feel like a fraud; McLarty was clearly much stronger than her at tracking. *They probably regret picking me up in the first place*, she thought, bitterly.

And then there was the fact that McLarty was now refusing to even listen to her. Flora was used to that.

When Frances asked for someone to help with retrieving the fishing nets, Flora volunteered. She didn't want to mooch around the camp, and she was also reluctant to go to The Den in case she touched something that she shouldn't. *Knowing me, I'd set off some sort of signal telling everyone our location.*

Instead, she joined the Harley siblings at the fishing nets. They retrieved a handful of squirming amberjack from slippery algae-adorned webs that had been lashed to stubborn rocks.

Flora was taught how to behead and gut the fish, and she pulled trails of crimson and puce from their long, fleshy bodies. *Oh, what a turn this paradise has taken.*

△△△

That evening, Flora felt exhausted. Her body ached from smashing clothes against the rocks all morning and lifting amberjack all afternoon. She sat next to Hope and listened to stories about Lennox and the crazy time that they'd had on jet skis all afternoon, while she kept watch for McLarty or any signs that their island had been discovered.

"We saw a Galapagos shark and everything, it was insane," Hope screeched, enthused and full of life. In comparison, Flora felt drained. She broke a dead stick into pieces, enjoying the destruction.

Why did Lana tell Chan that she was falling for me before finding out how I felt first? Did she just assume that I felt the same way? What a gamble.

Flora couldn't believe that Lana had called off her

relationship. It filled her with a beautiful and terrible breed of guilt. If she had the energy, she might even feel flattered. But she was far too tired for that.

She was so tired that when she got back to her hut and lit the oil lamp, ready to put her pyjamas on, she almost missed the blood-soaked paper parcel that sat on her pillow, saturating it in cherry red.

Almost.

"What the-" Flora said aloud.

Blood. The iron tang hit her.

She moved closer.

The smell of brine hit her next, and she threw herself backwards, looking around, breathing hard. The door was closed. Hive and Frances were in The Kitch; she couldn't see anyone out of the dim little window.

Her heart started beating up into her throat. She blinked. The dim light from the oil burner flickered on the package. Taking a deep breath, Flora reached out and picked it up. It was heavy and wet.

Open it, or throw it out the window?

She knew that she didn't have a choice. It was clearly a message. She couldn't ignore it. Flora unwrapped the crinkled paper. A string of fish guts fell out and landed on the floor, slapping the wood and writhing as if they were still alive. They settled and stopped moving, deceased, bleeding into the grain.

The paper had words written across it in crude, blue paint.

Stole a girlfriend. Kissed in forest. Watch your back new girl.

"Oh my God," Flora whispered, as fish blood dripped down her wrist.

A wave of nausea hit her, lurching acid up from her stomach. The smell from the fish gripped hold of everything.

New Girl. Lana's name for her. But Lana wouldn't do this, surely? Why would Lana refer to herself as being 'stolen'? *Chan. It must be. Don't be sick.*

Flora had told Chan earlier that her and Lana weren't an item, and Chan had seemed to believe her. Chan could hardly still think that Flora had stolen her girlfriend, and as for seeing them in the forest, well… that could be anyone. She looked around again, her eyes wild, her gaze roving over the wooden walls of the shack. Who was it?

On the floor, the guts seemed to laugh at her. *I can't sleep here.* The smell, the blood, the fish: it was all too much. Flora scooped the fish entrails up into the paper once again, feeling the slippery innards between her fingers, across her palm. *I can't leave this for the others.* She felt sick rise up her oesophagus. She squashed it down.

I won't let them get to me.

△△△

The clearing was quieter than usual, but as Flora strode up to the fire and dropped the package of innards onto the flames, she felt people watching her.

I won't let them get to me, she repeated to herself, striding onwards towards the newly mosaiced path, wiping her bloody hands on her legs, breathing in the safe and dangerous new smells of the forest.

CHAPTER THIRTY-FIVE
PROPINQUITY

Flora's first thought, as she woke up on the floor in The Den, warm from the server that she was pressed against, was Lana.

Where had Lana been when Flora was receiving threatening parcels of leftover guts, and having to put up with a furious Chan?

Yes, I left Lana in the forest. Yes, that wasn't cool. But still, it's not a reason to disappear.

She remembered thinking that Frances and Hive had left the hut in the middle of the night, the morning before talking to Chan. Had they gone to meet Lana? Had there been an Operation Poseidon meeting?

Flora stretched out, nearly hitting DeCalbiac, who had resumed her position in the corner, her headphones seeming to be a permanent part of her head.

"Morning." Flora yawned.

"It's not morning." DeCalbiac laughed, a short, non-humoured noise. "I can't find them. I keep looking, but I can't find them. I think they must be close."

"Close to the island? What makes you think that?" Flora asked, at once concerned and wondering what time it was. It was hard to tell in The Den; the light was always blue; the air was always stifling. A faint smell of urine had started to emanate from a plastic bin in the corner.

"They just must be," DeCalbiac replied, picking up a can of energy drink and taking a swig. It was 3 am, a nearby monitor informed Flora. *Funny, it feels like morning.*

The events of the night before, and, in fact, the whole day before, came flooding back to her. *Someone left fish guts on my pillow. The man with the scarred face is probably going to find the island. Lana is falling for me.*

She breathed out slowly and then clamoured to her feet.

"Can I, err, help at all?" she asked DeCalbiac, admiring the speed with which the other girl's fingers scuttled across the keyboard. *She'd be a good gamer.*

"No. Go," the girl instructed.

"Ok, give me a shout if you need anything," Flora replied, lamely.

What was DeCalbiac going to do; stand on the deck and shout across the forest until Flora turned up? It was an empty promise, but she felt slightly less guilty as she snuck away, feeling useless.

△△△

The forest air was thick with night. Croaks and soft caws and the sweeping motions of wings surrounded her. The moon whispered through the canopy, breaking onto the pathway, illuminating Flora's carefully lain mosaic tiles.

The camp was silent. Flora sat down by the dead campfire and looked at all of the sleeping huts, bathed white in the light, cast in dramatic shadows from the surrounding trees and cliffs. A mouse scurried across the ground. Flora felt her breathing slow; despite everything, Taniwha looked magical.

Minutes later, or perhaps hours, she heard a noise. A cry from far away, a shout, something that sounded like a scream. She jumped to her feet, wildly looking each way, trying to understand where the sound had flung itself from.

Everything was silent. *What was that? Did I imagine it?*

She stayed on her feet, rooted to the spot, waiting for more noise. Was someone in trouble? Who was out in the middle of the night?

The wind picked up and rustled through the trees, drowning out the opportunity to hear any other sounds.

Will you just be quiet, Flora thought, willing the wind to slow, the trees to stop moving. *Who's out here?*

Another rodent scurried across the camp, shuffling leaves and twigs out of its way, visible only as a movement of shadows and darkness against the silver ground.

Someone staggered from behind the Privy Shack. Flora looked around for a weapon. Picked up a stone.

"Lana?" she asked, as the figure groaned.

"Get Hive," Lana called. Her voice was slow, laboured, broken.

"Are you ok?" Flora asked, running to her, looking her up and down, trying to understand what was wrong, putting her hand on Lana's shoulder to steady them both.

Her arm. Her arm was in pain. Lana clutched it with her other hand, holding the wounded limb to her body.

"Get Hive," Lana barked, her voice harsh.

"Lana, I... I'm sorry," Flora said, knowing that it wasn't the time, but feeling as if she'd been physically stabbed by the lack of emotion in Lana's voice. "I'll get Hive, but please know, I'm really sorry. I regret... well, I regret everything."

She spun on her heel and ran to her hut, where she dived straight onto Hive.

"Hive, it's Lana, she needs you." Flora gushed the words out as if Hive wasn't asleep, as if the other girl would understand her blabbering voice, her broken words coming from her broken heart.

"I'm there," Hive replied, straight away, sitting up in bed, adorning her glasses and pushing Flora out of the way to get to standing. "Where is she?"

"Outside."

"Ok. You should go to bed." Hive headed straight for

the door without putting on shoes or yanking a jumper over her pyjamas. Seconds later, the door closed, and Hive had disappeared. Frances slept on.

What happened to Lana's arm?

Flora shivered. Fear streaked through her. Fear that had nothing to do with her own personal threats, and everything to do with Lana getting hurt. *Like hell am I going to bed.* Flora grabbed a hoodie and ran outside. There was no one there.

"Hive?" Flora called, quietly, looking around. "Lana?"

She ran to Lana's hut and tried to throw the door open, but it was locked shut. There was no light emanating from the window either; it was clearly empty.

"Guys?" Flora asked, her voice tight. She was met with silence. *Where the hell are they?*

CHAPTER THIRTY-SIX
BELEAGUER

"Hey, sleepy guts," Hope cooed, as she shook Flora.

"Where am I?" Flora muttered. Her mouth was so dry it felt as if her tongue was a dead September leaf.

"In the middle of the campsite, by the campfire. And everyone's arriving for breakfast." Hope laughed. A few other people joined in, and Flora opened her eyes. She was lying on the floor, on top of the dried leaves by the campfire logs. She'd fallen asleep on the ground. Her face stung where the morning sun had got to her skin before any sun cream had. Her throat felt heavy.

"Where's Lana?" Flora croaked, sitting up.

She'd waited. She'd sat waiting for Lana and Hive to reappear, for someone to explain what was going on. She must have fallen asleep.

"Probably in her hut, why?" Hope asked, looking closely at Flora. Her eyes were curious. "Flora, are you ok?"

"I'm fine," Flora said, pulling a twig out of her hair.

"I dunno mate, you look pretty bad," Hope said. Her eyes danced with amusement.

"You've gone proper Stig of the Dump," Lennox contributed.

"Who?" Ritchie asked, sauntering over with a plate of sausages. He sat down, noticed Flora and started laughing. One of the sausages rolled off of his plate and onto the floor. "Damn it," he said, picking it up.

"Oh now, you must've read Stig of the Dump when you were little?" Lennox asked.

"Yeah, my dad ran away, and my mum was, like... an escort who made me wait in the garden all night," Ritchie said, stuffing an entire sausage into his mouth. "They din't have a lorra time to read t'me."

"Maybe go and have a shower, yeah?" Hope whispered to Flora, nodding her head towards the Privy Shack.

"Yeah," Flora said, standing up, feeling as if she were in a daze. Around her, the world spun. "Yeah, I think I will. Can I just..." she started to say, reaching over and picking up Ritchie's water bottle. She lifted it to her dry lips and drank the whole bottle without pausing. "Gah," she said, wiping her mouth with the back of her dirty arm.

"You sure you're alright, Brock?" Ritchie looked up at her with a worried expression on his greasy lips.

"Yeah, you're not looking great," Lennox added.

Was it Ritchie who left guts on my pillow? Lennox?

"I'm going for a walk," Flora said, her eyes roving over the camp, seeing who else had arrived, who was there. No Lana. No Hive. Even Tane couldn't be seen.

"Mate, go and have a shower," Hope said from behind her. Flora stalked off towards the Privy Shack and, more specifically, the pathway that ran alongside it.

△△△

I'm useless, Flora thought, as she made her way along the unknown pathway. Lana had appeared with a broken arm and a face of pain, and she wanted Hive. They all had skills, and she wasn't adding anything.

Hive was a doctor; she'd stitched up Tane and fixed Chan's broken bones. Frances organised everyone. Lana and

Tane ran the place. Gasquet was fantastic with clothes; McLarty and DeCalbiac were expert hackers; Hope was a great chef; Ritchie and Eccles were surprisingly strong. Even Bell knew plants, and one of the Harleys was a meteorologist.

I'm literally useless. But I have information.

No one else knew about Scarface being close by; only her, McLarty, DeCalbiac and Lana. No one else knew about the impending danger, the way they were being hunted down. They were waiting gormlessly, just going about their daily lives with no idea of what was coming.

I saw him. I saw him and none of the others did.

She had knowledge that they didn't have. She knew what he looked like, knew the exact shape of his scar. Hive may be medically talented, but Flora liked to think that perhaps she was one of the resilient people on the island. She took things in her stride; she could handle things well. She felt tiredness pull at parts of her skull. She would explore the island and wait for the enemy to attack.

△△△

With no idea which direction to take, Flora ended up following the direction of a tropical bird, thinking that perhaps it was a sign. It was as good a gamble as any, and she knew that the direction was vaguely towards Sunset Beach, where Hope had confessed to waking up one morning after getting lost.

If Scarface does find the island, then he's unlikely to be able to make it into the lagoon. More likely, they'll moor up at a beach.

The sun was back to blazing. It simultaneously threatened to burn her skin in the sunny clearings and gave her shivers when she plunged once again into thick forest. She thought of DeCalbiac, sat in her stuffy little Den, the computers whirring while she tried to virtually find their enemies.

The sound of the sea broke through her thoughts. A few

strides later, she stumbled onto a stunning slice of icing sugar sand.

Palm trees created swaying shadows on the rim of the beach, where buttercup yellow met the jungle, divided by a tangle of roots and dried bark. The sand was hot; she had bare feet. Flora threw herself down in the shade, ignoring the many small bugs that instantly scuttled onto her legs. *What am I going to do now?*

Ahead of her, the ocean stretched on forever, not a boat or island to blemish its surface. She looked around at the rest of beach.

What?

She sat bolt upright. There, to her right, only a hundred feet away, were boats. Two boats of different sizes, washed up on the sand at the other end of the beach. Even from where she was sitting, she recognised the larger boat from McLarty's CCTV screenshot.

Scarface.

Flora was instantly on her feet.

As she crept towards the smaller of the two boats, the one she didn't recognise, the swirling, engraved text on the side of the craft swam into view, through the haze that rose up from the hot sand.

Flora traced her fingers over the letters, feeling slightly delirious.

The Esmerelda.

CHAPTER THIRTY-SEVEN
VESTIGIAL

Scarface's yacht smelled like sweat and danger. Heavy waves slapped the fiberglass; the boat pulsed with a manufactured heartbeat. Flora had scurried below board and discovered packets of food, stacks of cigarette cartons, a clanking box of bottles. There were two sweaty duvets making a bid for freedom, mashed into crisp packets and spilt beer and gritty cigarette butts.

The small windows let in a fuggy, yellow light, which turned the room into a mess of dirt and dust. Flora worked quickly, riffling through drawers, pockets, any cubby that she found. She needed to know more.

Who is Scarface? What does he want? Are there any weapons on board?

Her first instinct had been to go back and warn the camp, but she could still make it there ahead of Scarface and Axer. She knew where to go; they didn't. Sunset Beach was a good distance from camp; she would try and find a weapon and then return, waiting for them in the clearing.

But so far, no weapons. The only thing of interest that she found was a scrap of paper sellotaped to the wall of the cabin, which had co-ordinates and '1m' written on it. That was it.

She found a small wardrobe and started going through the clothes. Men's Size Large and Extra-Large rugged travel-shop clothing. One of the jackets had twenty pounds in the pocket. Another had an old lighter. Flora knelt down and found herself riffling through pairs of boots, her fingers feral, rooting through anything she found, raising things to her nose to check. *What am I looking for? I won't know until I've found it.*

Her hands stopped on something cold and hard. She pulled out the gun and stared at it for a long moment. The first gun that she'd ever seen in real life. It was smaller than she expected, and the black coating had been rubbed silver around the edges, as if it had been held often.

There was a noise from above. Footsteps climbing aboard.

Flora froze, feeling her chest swoop, and then stuffed the gun into the back of her waistband. She darted into the cupboard, closing the door behind her, holding a nail on the back. Her bare feet pressed into the pile of shoes, colours crept through the tiny gap.

Flora's heart was in her throat, her mouth, thrumming in her ears. Badoom, badoom, badoom. It matched the pace of the waves, which slapped and sloshed at the back of the cabin. In that moment, Flora felt at one with the sea, as if she had finally become part of the island. The sea was afraid.

Badoom, badoom, badoom.

Two sets of footsteps descended the ladder and landed with light thuds, just a meter away from where Flora hid in the tiny wardrobe. She heard her breath loudly in her ears, whooshing, in and out, in and out. She pressed her eye against the vivid slice of world that crept through the place where the door met its frame. She stifled a gasp.

In the centre of the cabin stood Frances and Hive, looking around with disgust.

"This place is absolutely filthy," Hive commented, her usually emotionless face screwed up, her freckles twisted into the lines. She was clutching her hands together, looking more distressed than Flora had ever seen her.

"Well, *they* were filthy," Frances replied, striding over to a wooden box that was filled with packets of dried foods.

"Here's the food that Lana promised us." He started rifling through the packets. "Dried macaroni cheese? I'm not sure that's going to go down well."

"I suppose it's good to have, in case of emergency," Hive replied, lifting up one of the grey duvets with two fingers, seeing that there was nothing underneath and then dropping it heavily. She wiped her hands on her corduroy trousers.

"Uggh," she said, suppressing a shiver. Inside the wardrobe, Flora was seconds from revealing herself. *These are my roommates, not the enemy*. But could she trust anyone?

For all she knew, Hive and Frances were on the side of Scarface and his accomplice. Otherwise, how did they know that the boat was here? What happened to Scarface? Flora felt her hot, fevered breath reflect off of the wardrobe door and burn her cheek.

"We need to use the smaller boat to drop their heads in the ocean. We can't do it here, we'll attract the sharks," Frances said, examining a packet of Super Noodles. Flora thought she must have misheard.

"And I suppose Lana wants *us* to do that?" Hive sighed, picking up a pair of binoculars and looking through them. How easy it would be for Hive to reach out and open the wardrobe.

"Naturally," replied Frances, shaking a handful of tinfoil-wrapped stock cubes from their square box. "No one else here has the guts to do it. I don't know why we don't get a few of them involved; it would have made the autopsy a lot easier."

"Stop calling it an autopsy," Hive said, voice flat. "You wouldn't call it that if it were an animal. It was a practical way to destroy evidence and get protein in our diets. And you can boil the bones for stock, so it's great for the winter."

"True," Frances replied. He looked around and then lowered his voice so much that Flora could barely hear him over the pounding of the ocean and the cries of seabirds. "It's lucky that Tane saw these two arrive. Having him on lookout duty has turned out to be incredibly useful."

"Taking him off lookout duty after the first boat arrived was also a nice touch," Hive said.

"Thank you. I knew he'd panic if he saw Axer arriving, and we can't have any erratic and hasty decisions being made."

Like eating two men? Flora felt her hands start to shake. Her fingers slipped against the rusty nail, but she managed to hang on.

"What's Lana done with the other one?"

"Who cares?" Hive replied. "He's not our responsibility. He arrived in the middle of the night; I never saw him, and these guys were dead by then. I had Lana's arm to attend to, and so we won't waste a single thought on him, ok?"

"Was it weird that neither of them had a-"

"Cut it out," Hive interrupted. "Do you need any help carrying food back to camp?"

Neither of them had what? A gun?

"No, but thank you for the offer," Frances said, begrudgingly, stuffing a handful of packets into the large pockets of his cargo shorts.

"Are you annoyed?" Hive asked suddenly, and Flora found it unusually astute of her to realise. She supposed that Hive and Frances were a lot closer than many of the other friendships.

"Not annoyed, just…" Frances trailed off, picking up another handful of food packets and rearranging them into some sort of order, "just guilty I suppose."

"Guilty?" Hive let out a snort of laughter. "You weren't saying that when we left Lusty to starve to death."

"Well, I kind of knew that he would be ok. I didn't have to sever his head from his still warm body. I didn't get covered in his blood," Frances said, and his voice was getting higher, verging on breaking. *That's why he's wearing a t-shirt.*

"And I'm pretty sure it wasn't me that came up with the idea of eating them."

France's usual demeanour slipped, and Flora could see the miserable and frightened boy underneath. For some reason, it calmed her.

"It's a practical way to dispose of evidence and ensure strong protein levels amongst the crew," Hive replied, as if she'd written this sentence down enough times to convince herself that it were true. "You know we struggle to get fresh meat, and Lana won't let me kill the goats." They were staring at each other, the tension palpable.

"Ok," Frances shrugged, eventually. He let out a long, loud breath.

"Now stop with all of this. Lana's our captain and it's not like she's moping around feeling guilty now, is it? Besides," Hive said, looking back down at the binoculars, "let it be a warning to anyone who tries to destroy our camp."

She suddenly looked up, flashed a quick smile of consternation at Frances and then made her way to the ladder. Flora watched as Hive deftly ascended into the world above. Frances stayed still for a long moment, staring at a wayward boot on the floor, his eyes reflecting the light from a window. Eventually, he took a deep breath in, let out a shuddering sigh and made his way up the ladder.

Flora heard their footsteps jump from the side of the boat, crunching onto the sand. And then nothing, except for the sounds of waves and birds, the slight creaking of the cabin. The smell of old leather started to reappear. She breathed in, breathed out. She became aware of the boat moving with every slap of the sea, creaking an inch either way, rocking her cupboard with each breath.

The smell of the shoes below her started to climb up her body until her nostrils could only taste the foreign scents of an unknown man's sweating toes. She accidentally breathed in through her mouth and then it became too much; she fell out of the cupboard hacking up spit and phlegm from the depths of her stomach.

CHAPTER THIRTY-EIGHT
PARADOX

Flora stayed on her knees, coughing spittle onto her hands, until her body felt exhausted. Long strings of saliva attached her to the carpet. Her right hand pressed cigarette ash and clammy sweat into a paste.

Away from her body, all was quiet, except for the constant voice of the sea, telling her to get up, to find strength.

Easy for you to say, she replied. *You didn't just find out that your cabinmates are murderers and the love of your life ordered them to do it.*

The smell of tanned cowhide followed her into the body of the boat and Flora felt an overwhelming urge to be outside, to feel land underneath her feet, to appeal to the mercy of Taniwha.

△△△

There were no signs of Hive or Frances on the beach. Flora could see their footprints imprinted into the sand, heading into the forest a different way from the direction that she'd arrived. She turned her head. Her fear was realised; her footprints were a clear trail along the white sand, from the craggy exit of the densest part of the forest all the way to the greying seafoam that regurgitated around the boats. *They must have seen, surely?*

Did they suspect that someone else was on the boat? If they *did* have suspicions then surely they would have searched the craft? It was too much to think about: her footprints, Hive and Francis's admission to murder, potential cannibalism. It was all too much, and Flora felt her mind close in around her, as if darkness was descending. A small crab scuttled across her foot; she cried out.

Fear, she thought. *That is this emotion, if I had to label it.* Fear that, once again, she didn't fully know the people that she was with. That she was stuck on an island with no method of escape, unless she suddenly learned how to drive a huge pirate ship. Knowing that the emotion was fear didn't help her. She was desperate to talk to someone, but who? Even her dad wouldn't be much use in this situation; he'd tell her to get the hell out of dodge.

I can't leave Taniwha now. There's still so much to learn, so much of the island to see.

Even though the walk back to camp was long, the gun pressing into the back of her waistband, time passed quicker than usual. Flora's mind was everywhere but the forest. Her feet stepped over branches and fallen trunks automatically, her head ducked under wreaths of spidered palms, her hands automatically swiped cobwebs and garlands of thorns out of the way. She moved on default, commanding the forest, crouching and ducking and pattering along fallen logs, her bare feet springing on moss and boggy earth.

Eventually, she arrived at Le Jardin, from which it would be a fairly short stumble downhill to camp.

"Hey," a voice called. Hope. She had been twisting sweet-smelling oranges from a top-heavy tree, the fruits adorned like the glinting lights of a circuit board, dropping them into a big basket. Seeing Flora, she dropped her latest pick and waved.

Flora raised a weak hand and waved back, scanning the rest of Le Jardin for any sign of Frances or Hive. There were three other crew members there, plucking yellow peppers from tall plants, breaking the spines of sticks to use as firewood and manoeuvring a large, noisy watering device over a rotating conveyer belt of tomato plants. None of the three were Frances or Hive.

A wayward thorn had dragged Flora's flesh, and she'd accidentally smeared blood over her cheek.

"What's up?" Hope asked, striding over to Flora and flashing a look at her cheek. "I hope someone's got a nail brush, because this stuff is never coming out." She held up her hand, showing her filthy nails. "They had me packing manure earlier, it was disgusting."

Flora stared at her blankly, lost for words, her mind on the last remaining survivor: Tane's stepdad. He must have been following Scarface's lead; he was following but was a day behind. *What's the point in McLarty and all of his tracking if it took Tane's rudimentary lookout to raise the alarm?* Although, he only raised the alarm on the two men. How did Lana know that Axer had arrived?

"The manure's from the goats," Hope clarified. "It's not my own."

"I didn't think it was your own," Flora said, and suddenly she was laughing hysterically, tears flying down her face as if they'd been waiting for a chance to escape, her hand on Hope's shoulder until Hope also started giggling and the pair of them clung to each other.

Hope also had tears running down her face and Flora wondered for a moment whether that was because of their manure conversation or whether Hope, like her, had been waiting for a chance to cry.

"Mate, you are hilarious," Hope said, when the pair had finally run out of laughter and the other garden workers had shot them confused grins.

"I missed toilet duty," Flora said, trying to remember whether she had a duty, or was that yesterday? The days were melting into one.

"Nah, I saw Tane doing them earlier," Hope replied,

picking a small stick up from the ground. She dug it under her thumb nail and dislodged some dirt. "Frances has given him a list as long as my arm, keep him busy."

"He's been emptying the toilets?"

"Yeah, they bloody stank," Hope made a face, as if she were about to vomit, and Flora let out another untoward laugh, which caught them both by surprise. "Is everything ok? You look a bit manic."

"Yes, absolutely fine," Flora said, casting her bloodshot gaze over Hope's shoulder towards the entrance to Le Jardin, wondering if she could maybe make a run for it. Get Poukai and sail back home. Would McLarty help her? She doubted it; even if he was willing to, he didn't seem like the kind of person who'd be much use at hauling the anchor or steering the ship.

"If we wanted to escape, do you think you'd be able to drive Poukai?" she asked.

"If we wanted to escape here?" Hope seemed bewildered. She paused her stick digging activities and examined Flora's face. "Homesick?"

"We're done now, Hope," a boy said, strolling up to them with a basket of yellow peppers under one arm. "And you must be the famous Brock?"

"Famous?" asked Flora, alarmed. She knew this boy: Easton. His flamed yellow and orange hair, dramatic against his dark skin, was stunning; she often wondered how he had created such a colour. He was usually on 'Spin' duty, whatever that was.

"I didn't mean anything by it. How are you finding it? Did I hear it that you're homesick?"

"Ah... something like that," Flora mumbled, her eyes roving around Le Jardin again, as if Frances might suddenly appear wielding a chainsaw.

"Don't worry, we've all been there. A couple of the guys here were crying for a week. You're handling it mighty fine, actually, all things considered. I didn't think you were gonna break."

"I haven't broken," Flora said, immediately scathing. How bad did she look?

"Ah come on, you're white as a sheet."

"She doesn't look that bad," Hope jumped in, giving the boy a scathing look of her own. Flora remembered Hope telling her that she looked manic earlier; she'd quickly changed her tune. "She's allowed to feel a bit homesick. And in answer to your question Flora: no, I don't think we could drive Poukai on our own."

"You want to take the boat?" the boy asked.

"It was theoretical," Flora said, eyes still holding some of their blaze. "Anyway, even if I did want to take the boat, what's it to you?"

"Nothing. I quite like the idea, if truth be told," he said, and his mouth flicked into a grin. "Although they'd kill you, you know that? Would you be prepared to fight?"

"No. I wasn't serious," Flora replied, as Easton let out a burst of laughter, turned and strolled towards the clearing at the end of the field. He didn't turn and so she shouted in his direction - "I wasn't serious!" - but he either didn't hear her or was ignoring her.

"Don't worry about him. He wanted to be a pilot growing up. Fancies himself behind some sort of heavy machinery, I reckon. He's a nice guy really though. He builds the hydroponics."

"I hope he doesn't seriously think that I'm going to steal Poukai," Flora said, but her voice was flat, and she already didn't care very much. What was he going to do? There were literal murderers around her; compared to that, stealing Poukai would be a drop in the ocean.

"You would be killed," Hope replied, mirroring his words and wandering back to her basket of lemons. "Want to grab a handle?"

"Sure." Flora made her way over to the other side of the basket and they picked it up, one of them on each handle. "Do you really think Tane would murder me?"

"Of course not," Hope snorted, her voice causing two birds to ricochet out of the tree above them. "He may be insane, but he's not gonna go around murdering everyone who tries to steal his ship. I wasn't talking about Tane."

"Right. Do people go around trying to steal his ship?"

"Well, they don't actually try, but everyone wants to, don't they? It's an old pirate's ship, for goodness' sake. I'd kill to have a ship like that. Call it The Jacinda and dominate the oceans."

"Well, why don't you?" Flora asked, picturing Jacinda Hope at the helm of her own ship. It was a suiting image. Hope fit the role of ship captain a lot more than Flora did. Flora felt that she'd be the skivvy: emptying the toilet, hanging the hammocks, generally following the others around. *Maybe the old me, anyway. The new me feels like I could kill a bear.*

She still had adrenaline bolting through her.

"Because I've got a good thing here," Hope replied, and Flora realised that there had been a long pause since she'd asked her question. "I didn't like it at home, you know. It wasn't a good place to be. My parents weren't good people, they made life hell for me and my siblings. I got out and I'm glad to be this person today. I know that it all made me, but I wouldn't risk having to go back there. No way."

"Don't you worry about your siblings?"

"You think I abandoned them? I didn't abandon them," Hope huffed, trying to get the basket under control. "I showed them the hole under the fence; it's not my fault if they don't climb under it, too. My older sister, she's twenty-four and hates living at home. The boys are all fine there. I have a younger brother who's four and he just calls me and his other sisters Stupid Girl and then punches us with his tiny fists, and they don't care that he's already like that. So yeah, I haven't done anything that they can't do."

"They can't all find a bonkers philanthropist with a massive ship and a secret island."

"That's true," Hope said, sniggering. "But

metaphorically, you know? Metaphorically, they can all get under that fence. Or over it. But past it, in whatever way they can."

"That's nice to think."

"It keeps me going. We all feel like that, here. That we've escaped into this new life, and we'd do anything to keep it."

"It is a good life," Flora said, but her words fell a little flat as she remembered Hive and Frances, and their admissions of murder and cannibalism. It *was* a good life. As long as you didn't know what was going on.

CHAPTER THIRTY-NINE
OBLIVION

They arrived back at camp, where normal life was humming from every corner. Eccles was building a huge campfire with long, gnarled sticks, a few people were arguing in the kitchen and several others were playing Jungleball.

Hope perked up. "Nice, let's drop this off and go play."

"I'm ok," Flora said, automatically, watching as Ritchie kicked the star-studded ball up into the air with the side of his foot. It ascended a log that had been suspended on two ropes high up in the air, but suddenly Chan appeared, dangling upside down from the same tree that the log was tied to, and she batted the ball away with her elbow, causing it to come plummeting back to earth with a smooth thwack.

"Yes Chan," Bell yelled, and he and Lennox cheered and stamped their feet. Nearby, Gasquet looked put out. Ritchie looked positively fuming.

Lana was stood between the two teams. She was clearly the referee, and, as the ball fell, she strode to check where it had landed within the white markings. She called out a number and Bell cheered again, yelling 'BOOMYA!' Lana rolled her eyes. Her arm had a fabric bandage around it, as if her wrist had been sprained.

In fact, she was gesturing with her injured arm to indicate the winning team. She looks fine. Relaxed. *What's going on?*

"You have to play, Flora," Hope said, disapprovingly. They reached The Kitch and lugged the huge basket through the flapping tent entrance.

"Who doesn't wanna play?" Tane asked. *Of course, he overheard. He always bloody overhears.*

"Flora," Hope said, shooting her a look that looked a little too annoyed to be playful.

"You don't wanna play, Brock?" Tane asked, and he was standing slightly taller than she'd ever seen. His voice was slightly deeper and his tone slightly more serious. *He seems like a different guy.*

"I... err, can't," Flora said. She hated that she could never make excuses on the island, because what else would she have to do? Unless she had a chore, which no one did in the late afternoon, then she would literally always be free.

"Fine, if you don't wanna make an effort to be part of camp," Hope said. She smiled, as if to show that she was joking, but it didn't meet her eyes, and then she shot a look at Tane, as if he should understand some deeper meaning behind her upset. *What's going on?*

With a final glance at them both, Hope dropped her side of the basket and exited through the colourful tent flap. They heard her yelling that she wanted to join the game.

"She was just hoping you'd even the teams," Tane said, laughing lightly. "It's always been them versus us. Lusty was a dab hand at Jungleball, he invented it, you know, so it's taken us a while to get our score up."

"Why didn't you just reset the score when Lusty... left?" Flora asked, wondering why anyone would carry on a game score for so long.

"It would've annoyed his little crew," Tane muttered, looking around to check that no one had suddenly appeared inside the tent. "There was a load of them who really liked him; they basically followed him. Lennox, Eccles, Ritchie, Bell, Chan, Gasquet, Easton," he listed them all, tapping his hand against a nearby worktop as he talked. "They all preferred

Lusty to me, thought that he'd be a more consistent leader, you know."

"I'm sure that's not true," Flora said, although she felt her face burning slightly, because she had had that exact thought before. Had she not wondered, on many occasions, why Lana wasn't the camp leader instead of Tane? Having an excitable, non-focused leader wasn't usually the best idea.

"Well, anyway, we still had more numbers in my court back then. That was before the Harley's crossed over; they've looked at me weirdly ever since Lusty left. I don't think they believed the story, you know? They've been hanging out with Lusty's crowd more; we didn't think that we could initiate them into Operation Poseidon without them telling everyone and creating uproar.

It's taken a while for them all to settle since Lusty left, you don't know how upset they all were. They were lost without their leader, Ritchie especially; he adored Lusty. They've finally come around to me being leader; if they knew that my crazy stepfather would literally murder everyone in their beds just to get to me, I think they'd lose confidence. Ignorance is bliss, as they say." He stopped drumming his fingers, his smile tight.

"But this was all your creation," she said, the words bursting out with indignance. "You bought the ship, you found the island, how could you not be leader?"

"Meh." Tane shrugged, though the tightness still didn't leave his eyes. "You've got it all now, haven't you? You don't need me anymore; they could've just finished me off and had a wild old time without me and Lana telling everyone what to do. It would've become savage."

Hearing him say 'me and Lana' so casually sent a cold shock through Flora's chest. Of course, they would have had to rid the camp of Lana if they wanted to rid it of Tane. Of course they came as a package; there was no way that Lana was going to sit around camp happily if Tane wasn't there.

"Any particular reason you don't want to play

Jungleball?" Tane asked, raising his voice slightly, clearly shrugging off the moment. He lifted his hand and ruffled his hair, which fell messily around his face, before pulling it up into a bun and fixing it in an elastic band. *Because I'm still reeling from the murder of two men. Because you know about their arrival. Because Axer is still here, somewhere.*

"Why is it such a big deal, a stupid game?" Her voice cracked. *Does Tane know about the double murders?*

"Hey, don't get upset," Tane said quickly. Telling Flora not to get upset opened something inside of her; she felt as if she were constantly on edge these days, always just a second away from crying or splitting open. For some reason that had almost nothing to do with Jungleball, tears broke in her eyes and started streaming down her face.

"Ugh, for goodness' sake," she said, rubbing them away. *I will not do this. I will not stand and cry like a baby in front of Tane. It's just all of it; murderers and cannibals and all the things that aren't right. I thought it was paradise. These people are monsters.*

"Let's go out," Tane said, firmly.

"I don't want to play." Flora sniffed, feeling like even more of a baby. *I can't tell Tane what I'm really crying about. Hive said that Tane doesn't know about Axer arriving. Does he know about them killing the men? Lana instructed the murders, not Tane. It's all so complicated.*

Flora looked at the huge chopping board nearby. Residues of burgundy were drying on the wood. Tears dripped into her mouth.

"I don't mean out there. I mean out to sea. I've built a canoe."

"You've built a canoe?" She asked, and the weirdness of this sentence paused her emotions for a second.

"I've built a canoe," Tane repeated, his mouth curling into a wicked smile.

"How funny," Flora said, sniffing, wiping her face. "You know what, maybe later."

She gave her face a final wipe, feeling strength bolster through her again. Sometimes she just needed a cry, a little overflow of emotions, to realise the strength that lay underneath.

"I've got something I need to do first," she told him, as cheers from the Jungleball players whirled around outside. *I need to find out where he is.*

CHAPTER FORTY
FORBEARANCE

The evening was starting to get cooler and her first port of call was her hut, to hide the gun under her futon. She'd been wearing a borrowed hoodie around her waist, and she pulled it on to protect her from the cool night air. *I need to know where Axer is. I need to know if Lana ordered his death as well.*

Hoodie on and gun hidden, she made her way round the back of The Kitch, where she came across a huge punnet of sliced peppers, a sack of cashew nuts and a whole box of paper-wrapped chocolate bars, all perched next to the jungle. She stuffed a handful of nuts and peppers into the front pocket of her hoodie, and then stashed three of the chocolate bars in her hood. She was just in time, because as soon as she stood upright again and looked around, Lana appeared.

"Flora, what are you doing here?" Lana asked, her voice genuinely surprised. Flora felt her face grow red. *You ordered the murders of two men.*

"Just trying to find someone to apologise to. I missed toilet duty earlier."

"You missed toilet duty? How come?"

"I was... err, with McLarty. We were doing a thing."

"Too much information," Lana said, laughing lightly and turning her attention to the box of chocolate bars. She had coloured around the ears. She picked up a handful and slid them into one of the pockets on her trousers.

"Listen, I'm really sorry-"

"I've got to sort something," Lana interrupted, deliberately not looking in Flora's direction. She rubbed her bandaged wrist. "Consider yourself absolved of your sins."

"Err, fine. Let's... let's talk later." Flora sidled straight into The Kitch without thinking twice, her face burning. *There are so many things that I want to say to Lana, I don't know where to start.*

Even though only Gasquet and the Harleys were inside The Kitch, it was havoc.

"Wine, where's the white wine?" Gasquet yelled, moving past people and pushing others out of the way. "We can't have spaghetti alla vongole without any wine!"

"God forbid," one of the Harleys muttered, and their siblings tittered, as they chopped parsley and whisked clams out of their shells. Bulb upon bulb of garlic was massacred, the sharp blade grating down onto the heavy, bloodstained chopping board.

△△△

As she dithered on the outskirts of the camp, deciding which way to go, Flora was distracted. She knew that she should be thinking about Hive and Frances and their admission earlier. She should be thinking about the poor men who'd lost their lives. The missing stepdad. Lana's weird behaviour. And Lana's outright psychotic choices, if Hive and Frances were to be believed.

But all she could think about was Tane inviting her on a canoe ride. Did he do that with everyone? Where was this canoe? And why was he still being nice to her?

Did he know about the men who'd come looking for him? Had he been involved? Did he come across as a charming philanthropist, but actually he was running a murder cult off of the coast of Portugal? How would Lana feel if Flora went on a boat ride with Tane?

Why can't life just be simple? If Lana had invited her on a boat ride then Flora knew that she would be out on the sea at that very moment, desperate to make amends. Instead, she was sneaking around the dark shadows in the corner of the camp. Bats had started to streak through the nights sky and she was reminded that they sometimes had rabies. She smiled at the memory, and then smiled at smiling about rabies. *Maybe I am going insane.*

The chocolate bars had had a good effect on her stomach, and she was comforted by the fact that the peppers had probably given her all of the vitamin C that she needed. It wasn't a sustainable diet, sure, but she was happy to skip the plateful of clams that everyone else would be wolfing down (everyone apart from Bell, presumably, on account of his shellfish allergy).

At the thought of them all eating, she had a sudden urge to join in with playing the game, to feel part of it. A feeling of loneliness washed over her and she leant against a tree.

Honestly, she thought, *I get annoyed when I'm with everyone, but I miss them when I'm on the outskirts.*

"Flora," a voice said. McLarty appeared from the undergrowth. He pushed branches and leaves out of the way, but they inevitably bent back and thwacked him in the face, so that he had marks on his skin and leaves in his hair when he finally sat down on the floor next to Flora with a loud 'huff'. She looked down at him for a moment, before sinking down to the ground herself.

"Alright?"

"Yes, fine." McLarty pulled a leaf from his hair. "How about you?"

"I'm good," Flora said. What was going on? How had McLarty seen her in the shadows?

"I'm glad to have, err, caught you," McLarty said, clearing his throat. A bird flew out of the forest behind them.

A few lone cicadas started making thrumming noises in the bushes.

"Well, there aren't many places I can go," Flora joked, eventually, when the pause had drawn on for too long. She could tell that he was looking at her, but she didn't want to turn her head and make eye contact. She didn't want the situation to turn into something that it probably wouldn't anyway, but if there was even the slightest chance that that was what he wanted then she wasn't about to encourage it. And besides, Lana was playing a game just fifty feet away from them. If she turned and saw them together, what would she think? *Probably nothing at all.*

"Ha, true," McLarty said, and his voice was laden with nerves. "It's great to find another gamer, you know. One that's so good. You could teach me a thing or two."

"Ha, unlikely," Flora said, starting to feel the suffocating grip of anxiety.

"I think we make a great team," McLarty said, his voice low. He was definitely leaning closer to her now. *Oh, for goodness' sake.*

"Why is The Esmerelda boat washed up on this island?" Flora asked, suddenly. Her loud voice killed the moment and she felt McLarty move backwards.

"What?"

"The Esmerelda. Axer Nuku-Halliday's boat. It's on this island, and I know that you must know that, because you were tracking him, right?"

McLarty was still reeling as if he'd been slapped, and it took him a moment to solidify his buttocks back in the sand and sit still. "That's a lie. I would've seen if his boat had turned up near the island. You're going crazy, Flora." There was a long, silent moment, during which Flora digested his words.

He'd called her crazy, yes. But more than that, he genuinely didn't seem to realise that Axer had found them. He could appear from the undergrowth at any moment, if Lana hadn't already ordered his execution.

"He's a monster, you know," McLarty said, his voice low. "For ages, he had Tane's mum locked up. Made us a video and everything – said if we gave him the money back then he'd free her. Tane nearly cracked. That's when Lana basically had to take over, for the sake of protecting us. There's a lot more at stake than just Tane being happy."

"What the hell?" Flora looked at him. His eyes were dark and watery, his cheeks red.

"Why do you care about Tane so much?" McLarty asked, laughing. It was a cruel laugh and it reverberated off of the trees.

"He had Tane's mum locked up?"

"Oh relax, it was only in their annex and they have like, fifteen TV's in there. And surround sound."

"How do you know?"

"Oh, I hacked their house. Everything's smart that can be. They were even looking at getting smart locks – I saw a quote come through to his email – but unfortunately they didn't or I could've let her out myself."

"What the hell," Flora repeated. "And the video?"

"Yeah, he sent Tane a video. Or rather, he found some computer geek who could hunt down Tane's old online activity and find his Pictopia movements. He managed to find the chat room under the elephant enclosure where Tane first met me."

"Tane was on Pictopia?" Flora asked, feeling her mouth drop open.

"Yeah, he used to be," McLarty shrugged, his voice filled with jubilation. She knew that he was loving dropping all of these bombshells about Tane. "Until The Hulk found him. That video was pretty full on; he was wearing a mask and everything."

"Can I see it?" Flora asked, unsure about why she wanted to see a video of Tane's stepdad threatening him, but also feeling oddly protective, as if she should deal with his bullies for him.

"Ha, no. It was available for 24 hours."

"You didn't save it?"

"Didn't need to. He made sure it didn't look or sound like him, and it was only when I hacked into the CCTV that I saw that he wasn't lying. He actually had kept her captive. Anyway, Lana said to tell Tane that it was fine, so I did. Then we kept an eye on the situation and whether he was going to kill her."

"What the actual hell?"

"Yeah, I kept close watch of his browsing, making sure he wasn't looking up methods of strangulation or something. Thankfully, all was alright. I mean, there was some pretty hardcore pornography in there, but Lana didn't say I needed to do anything about that, so…"

"So you just left Tane's mum trapped?"

"She had a whole annex!" McLarty exploded, standing up. "And she's totally dippy anyway. Probably didn't even notice. Lana said she spends more time talking to dead people than she ever has to anyone alive. She barely even realises that Tane's not there; she doesn't understand reality!"

Flora looked up at him, momentarily lost for words. Eventually, she struggled to her feet. His eyes lit up, as if she might take a step forward, but instead she raised one hand and slapped him, hard.

"That's for Tane," she said, stomping off into the jungle without a backwards glance. Just minutes later, she was ambushed.

CHAPTER FORTY-ONE
DISSEMBLE

"Get off me," Flora yelled, choking, as someone held her down and someone else tied a blindfold around her head. There were two of them, or at least two of them that she could hear scuffling around, and they were strong.

"Dude, relax," Hope's voice came into her ear, her lips too close. "You'll like this, I promise."

"Like what?" Flora asked, but she'd stopped struggling so much. She was on her back and branches were ripping holes in her arms. Someone was tying the blindfold tightly around her head.

"Is that ok?" It was Lennox.

"Perfect," Hope responded. They both moved their hands and Flora was left panting in the silence for a long moment.

"Should we strip her clothes off?" Lennox asked.

"What, why?" Flora said, suddenly feeling a chill rise up through her bleeding arms. Why would they strip her naked? Hope said it was a good surprise.

"We could take a picture, make sure you never do anything stupid," Hope threatened.

"How would that stop me doing something stupid?" Flora asked, her heartbeat in her throat. Her hands were tied together, but her feet were free, and she was sure that she could kick hard at anyone that tried to strip her.

"If you step out of line, we'd share the photo, obvs," Lennox replied. "A shame we don't have a phone. And that we didn't get one of you and Tane in the water. Lana would have liked that, wouldn't she?"

Hope laughed then, and the sound was everywhere. The cloth pressed hard against Flora's eyes until she could only see red. Tears were leaking out of her eyes, snot dribbling from her nostrils against her will. What were they doing? Why was no one coming near her? Was it just the two of them? The ground was cold and Flora smelt the sharp tang of fresh mud.

"Stay here," Hope instructed. Flora heard them both move away, and then there was silence. Birds started squawking, too close for comfort. It felt as if they were about to fly down and tear Flora apart. An evening chill crept over her. *Are they coming back?* Out of nowhere, a rock hit her shoulder.

"Oww," Flora cried, feeling the stabbing pain shoot up from her shoulder to her skull, throbbing along the right side of her body. It had hit her hard; she could tell that it was going to bruise. She brought her legs up into a protective curl, and tried to yank her hands apart. It was impossible; she was tightly bound.

"They're ready," a voice called from far away. Hope. A minute later, heavy footsteps crunched over the leaves.

"Right, let's get her up," Hope said, and Flora felt the two of them struggle as they heaved her to her feet. She wobbled, and Hope held her up.

"What's going on?" Flora asked, but she felt as if she'd been punched in the throat and the words were hard to understand. Was it still light outside? What if she tripped over a branch? Who threw a rock at her? They started moving.

"You know, we have a good life here, Lennox," Hope said, her voice light and airy.

"Indeed," Lennox replied, holding Flora's arm a little too hard.

"What would happen if we had to go back, I wonder?"

"Well, we'd be in trouble for faking a school, I suppose.

Plus, our parents might get arrested, or shunned from society. We'd fall behind in our classes and probably fail them. And even then, if we did pass, we'd have to get proper jobs, become lawyers and shop assistants and chefs. We'd have to sit and work for the same greasy-haired middle-aged man every day, burning ourselves out, never really living, growing old in the same worn-out office chair and eventually dying."

"Never having lived," Hope said.

"Miserable," Lennox added.

"How can you possibly know that it would be like that?" Flora asked, stumbling with every step, feeling branches hit her in the face.

"It's like that for all of them," Hive said, her voice knowing. "It's only us that's in the real world. That have a good thing to protect."

"To protect?" Flora asked, feeling the same chill in her arms as before, her hands drained of the last drops of blood as her circulation was cut off.

"We're here," Hope announced suddenly, her voice excited, and then Flora could hear other voices joining her, and laughing, and someone making the loud cry of a bird, and the spitting of a bonfire, and she could smell steaming food and hear a drum thrumming.

"Why is she all cut open?"

"What's with her hair?"

"I spent a lot of time on that hair," a Harley grumbled.

"She fell over," Lennox explained, and both sets of hands let her go. She stumbled and someone ripped off her blindfold, pulling out a handful of her hair in the process, and someone else cut the binds off of her wrists.

Light hit her. The light from the bonfire, the light reflecting in the tens of eyes that were staring at her eagerly, some nearby, some glancing from the treetops, and then she was lifted high up above everyone on the shoulders of two people, and Tane appeared from The Kitch with a platter of colourful fruit.

"Happy birthday," he cried, holding out the fruit platter and looking up at her like a child on Christmas morning.

"What the hell is going on?" Flora shrieked, something inside her still shaking, her wrists still smarting from the too-tight bindings. The noise immediately settled down and the two people upon whose shoulders she was resting set her back down on the floor.

"It's a birthday surprise," Tane said, his eager voice faltering slightly. "It wouldn't be a surprise if we waited until your actual birthday."

Axer is on the island, I've been attacked and Tane wants me to celebrate my birthday?!

Flora coughed and rubbed her wrists. She looked around. McLarty was sat on a log by the fire, glaring at her. Had he followed her, seen her laying on the floor? Had he watched as they'd ambushed her so violently, and then thrown a rock at her? *I did slap him.*

"Look, come and sit by the fire," Tane said, and he reached out and grabbed her arm. His touch made her flinch, and he looked concerned. "Are you ok?"

"She's fine," Hope said, grabbing Flora by the arm and frogmarching her to the fire. "She just got a bit spooked out, that's all."

"Maybe we shouldn't have sprung this on you," Tane said, following.

"Some people don't like surprise parties," Frances pointed out. He was wearing Tane's large fur hat which fell to one side. Behind him, Ritchie had his whole body covered in war paint.

"Can we just start the party already?" someone else whined. Gasquet. He was wearing a lavish gown of sequins.

"Flora, is that ok?" Tane asked, looking at her carefully. She couldn't begin to imagine what he was looking at. Snot and blood and tangled hair. She felt all of the eyes on her again, boring into her, holding a collective breath, waiting to see if she would be a buzzkill.

"Of course," she muttered, finally, when it was really the only option.

"Wahoo!" Tane cried, throwing the fruit platter onto the ground, where a mango rolled off into the shadow of a log. "Let's get this thing started."

"Ready boss?" someone called to him, and Tane agreed, and then fire sprung up from all around them, and the music started again, and someone carried a huge pitcher of iced orange cocktail from the kitchen, and someone brought out the powdered paint, and then the air was filled with clouds of loud orange and neon pink and astonishing yellow, a second fire of paints and powder and colour that meant that Flora could only see right in front of her, to the ruined mango that lay bruised and battered.

"Tan-i-wha, Tan-i-wha," someone chanted behind the paint barrier.

"Happy birthday," McLarty muttered, appearing and then disappearing again.

"Seventeen, is it?" Ritchie asked, all excited, taking a huge slurp of the orange drink and proffering his bamboo straw to Flora. She took a sip and then coughed, the liquid burning her oesophagus. *What's going on?*

"I can't wait to see what Tane's got her," she heard someone say, someone whose voice she didn't recognise, and that distracted her for a moment because she wondered what it meant and whether he was expecting to give her a birthday present.

Tane was nowhere to be found in the midst of the paint party, but then bongos started up and she heard him whooping from the same direction and calling out a heady mix of foreign words and chants. Around her, people crowed, screamed, whooped. Above her, she could hear people in the trees, drowning out the sounds of birds, or perhaps there were none.

"Too many firelighters," she heard someone shout nearby.

"... bad for the environment?"

"Actually, they're beeswax firelighters," she heard Hive say. She started to move towards the murderers voice, her hands outstretched, but more paint was thrown and then Hive was drowned out by other, closer voices, laughing and cackling about recovering a squirrel carcass. Cooking it for dinner. Someone was humming a low tune. A digeridoo was blown. Between the clouds of paint, great licks of fire towered up towards the sky.

Flora couldn't breathe. Her throat hurt, her eyes were blinded with powder, her ears were filled with howls and laughter and goads and squirrels.

And so she ran. First to The Kitch, which was abandoned, deserted. She grabbed the only knife that she could find; a streamlined filleting knife with a red plastic handle. She stashed it in her hoodie pocket. Felt it fall against her body.

And then her bare feet took her away. Away from the real world, as quickly as her bruised body could go.

CHAPTER FORTY-TWO
LABYRINTHINE

Her breath was ragged, her arms were bleeding, her hair was tangled in great clumps within the clutches of trees that she passed. Flora coughed and swatches of paint coloured her phlegm, globules of sunset colours smashing down onto the ground.

Behind her, chanting, shouting and bongos reverberated in the night air; howls pierced the sky like werewolves out for revenge. *Move, move, move, and don't look back.* Oxygen tore through her body.

She tried to retrace her steps up to the lookout point, but she knew that she would set off the lights in the hot tubs on the way up. She knew roughly that she was headed West, back towards the mosaic path that she'd made, towards the beach where the washed up boats of the murdered sailors were moored.

The darkness hummed as she arrived at a rockface with a swathe of thick trees above her; branches leant down from ledges on the mountain to clutch hands with the tall spindles on the firs around her. She put her fingers out to reach the rock and it beat along with her pulse: badoom, badoom, badoom.

The cold rock whirred with life. She knew where she was. Flora started to work her way towards Sunset Beach. The only idea she had was to get to the boats, and then either sleep on one, or escape. She'd had enough of the island.

Darkness crammed in around her until she could barely

breathe, the smells of thick bracken and gnarled beeches making her think of damp and mould and all things hairy. Her feet were tripping over themselves and the corpses of debris all around her; every so often she would land in something soft, with a squelch.

She continued to work her way around the rock face, feeling the cold ridges and grooves under her fingers, until her fingertips hit upon wood.

A door? Surely not.

She stood back, and in the moonlight the carved words on the roughly nailed-together door sunk into her bones.

Devil's Island.

△△△

It wasn't a fully-formed door, only two huge pork scratchings of bark nailed together with rusty nails that glowed dully in the moonlight. Flora could still hear the beatings of the party from far behind her. The light from the great fire created an orange glow that threatened the moon. She felt alone. She shivered.

She should carry on, try and find the beach and the boats. Or retrieve the gun from under her futon. Because if Hive would happily murder a group of sailors who had washed up on the beach, then she would almost certainly do terrible things to the girl who threatened their way of life. Their island family.

The old Flora would probably have gone to the beach, found the boat, curled up in the wardrobe amongst the stinking shoes of the dead sailors and waited to be found. But she wasn't that girl anymore. She pushed the bark door aside.

She was an adventurer, someone who liked to look behind closed doors, who relished adrenaline in the right circumstances. And besides, she thought, as slimy air hit her face, the door wasn't even locked. It could hardly have a dangerous creature inside.

Her breath clouded the darkness. Her heart reverberated in the artery of rock that she'd just entered. A thick roman candle and a box of matches sat just inside the doorway. Straight ahead, there was only darkness, as the cave dug its way into the mountain.

I should go. I should go to Sunset Beach, take a boat and sail to the Azores. From there, I could call dad and ask him to fly me home. He'd find the money, if he knew I was in trouble. I might even get a few days on the beach. Buy Vogue magazine and drink Diet Coke and pretend to be normal.

She lit the match. The flare caused a brief flash of light to illuminate the roughly hewn walls, the damp patches on the rocky ground. As she wandered into the tunnel, candle aloft, she filled her lungs with freezing, dank air. She started to shiver, and was glad for her hoodie.

Jumper, she remembered Tane saying in a silly British accent. Where was Tane now? Did he know that she was missing? Was he still playing the bongos, not a care in the world? Her footsteps sounded like echoing drips in the cave. Each step had a crunch and thunk, as small stones ground underfoot, the toes of her shoe slapping against the damp earth.

There was something up ahead; the candlelight light reflected off metal. She held the candle higher and walked forward, her steps slower now, her eyes struggling to make out whatever was. *It's a door. A proper door.*

It was the type of door that you might find in homeware stores all over England. Either side of the door, pieces of driftwood had been tied tightly together with barbed wire, filling in any gaps between the wood and the cave wall.

It was secured with a chain and a padlock. Flora felt something drip onto her scalp. *Lana was building this cell before Axer had even arrived.*

The damp air became cloying. Flora felt it stick to the roof of her mouth, pasting her tongue down, filling her gullet with mould and slime and fusty, clammy air. A locked semblance of a door in a hidden passageway into the mountain. Why would it need to be locked? Why did they call it Devil's Island?

She touched her thumb to her little finger. She should leave.

"Lana," a voice said. A man's voice in front of her, behind the door: weak, tired, stretched out, focused solely on getting the single word out, the single name that he could muster on a dead tongue, the single name that kept Flora's feet rooted to the spot. She heard the sound of a stone far behind her. She slowed her lungs. In the candlelight, her breath billowed and hung uselessly.

"Hello?" she finally whispered.

"Lana?" he repeated, his voice cracking on the second syllable. Flora heard something scurry behind her, perhaps a rat. The roof of the cave dripped into a pool on the floor. The sound was hollow.

"No, it's not… it's not Lana," Flora said, feeling the cold shudder through her, the light of the candle turning her blind to everything else. Everywhere she looked, bright white circles pinpricked the darkness.

"Help me," the voice said, and all of a sudden an eye was pressed to a gap in the driftwood, the iris large and manic, the white bloodshot and shining, the pupil dilated and hysterical. The voice grew stronger: "You have to let me out. Please, I'll do anything."

Flora opened her mouth to respond, but before she could think of anything to say, something heavy cracked against the back of her skull. The thud bolted down her spine and into her feet. The knife in her pocket clattered into the darkness. Everything disappeared.

CHAPTER FORTY-THREE
PENUMBRA

Choking, dampness, a blanket, shivers.
Flickers, drips, echoes, stone.
Hurt, numb,
Scared,
Alone.

CHAPTER FORTY-FOUR
AKIMBO

"I can hear the birds," Flora mumbled.

"Doubtful," a voice said. Hive. Flora opened her eyes. She was blindfolded, again. And her wrists were bound, for the second time that evening.

"Hive? Where am I?" Flora asked, feeling the coldness of the floor shudder through her. Someone had put a blanket over her, but it was itchy. "Why did you put a blanket on me?"

"We're not animals," Frances said. He sounded unnerved. Flora imagined that he didn't want to do this; he hadn't wanted to attack her any more than he'd wanted to kill Scarface and his colleague. *He wants to escape the island as badly as I do right now.*

"What's going on?" Flora asked. She sounded oddly calm, even though she was colder than she'd ever been before. "Did you hit me?"

"We certainly didn't. We just found you," Hive said, although Flora couldn't quite believe it.

"Are we still in the cave? Who was that locked inside?" Flora asked, feeling desperate for answers. The hard ground dug into her hipbone. She seemed to be in the cave entrance; she could see a faint white light.

"None of your concern," Hive said, primly.

"Axer. It was Axer Nuku-Halliday, wasn't it? You've got him trapped."

As if from far away, a voice called out. Axer. He sounded miles away; his voice echoed off of a low ceiling. Flora couldn't make out what he was saying.

"Shut up," Hive yelled. The calling stopped.

"How do you know that?" Frances asked, surprised.

"She was on the boat, Frances," Hive said, scathingly. "Didn't you see her footsteps?"

"No."

"If you knew I was on the boat, why didn't you say anything?"

"I thought it would do you good," Hive said, "to understand how far everyone is willing to go. We take instructions from Lana, but not everyone is so… manageable on the island. You'd do well to be a bit scared."

"So it was you? That strangled me? That left me fish guts all over my pillow, that threw that rock at me?" Flora asked, spluttering onto the floor, shivering with the cold. It felt as if she were lying on a block of ice.

"No," Hive said. "We're not monsters. We've certainly got no reason to hurt you; we've been informed that you're a highly skilled member of camp."

"Then who?"

"Hope and Lennox, obviously. With that little spy, Eccles, watching out for you. It's hugely distracting having these things going on in our own hut; I had a word with Hope after the strangling incident, but it clearly did nothing if your bloodstained pillow is anything to go by."

"You saw her strangling me and you did nothing?" Flora asked, aghast.

"It wasn't my place to interfere," Hive said, her voice flat.

"Why would she even try and strangle me?"

"It makes sense, actually," Frances muttered, slowly, as if he were catching up on the conversation. "Hope's always been the one most desperate to stay on the island. She never wants to go back to the mainland when we all go. I mean,

McLarty is also pretty desperate, but that's because he'd be arrested if he was taken back, whereas Hope... well, she'd do anything to keep this lifestyle."

"To never grow up," Hive added. There was a noise; footsteps splashing loudly.

"What in the name of a rotten giddyball is going on here?" Lana shouted, grabbing Flora's blindfold and ripping it from her face. Lana looked shocked, scared, as white as a sheet.

CHAPTER FORTY-FIVE
LIMERENCE

Flora caught up with Lana. She was heading towards the camp, taking great strides. They'd left Frances and Hive behind in the cave. Lana had screamed at them. Apparently they'd had no right to tie up Flora.

"What the hell just happened?" Flora shrieked now, grabbing Lana by the arm and spinning her round. Screaming the words had given her such a dose of relief that she screamed again, loudly, waiting for the sound to bounce off of the moon.

"Drop it, ok," Lana said gruffly, not making eye contact. Her face was swollen, red, her eyes large and shining and afraid.

"I will not *drop it*," Flora hissed, grabbing Lana by both arms. Her head panged. "I will not just drop it. They knocked me out and tied me up, and there's a man trapped in a cave who I assume is Tane's stepdad. Why the hell is he in there? Why was I put in there? What the actual, Lan?"

Maybe it was the fact that she used Tane's nickname, or maybe it was the anger in her voice, but Lana's resolve dissipated and her face crumbled. She reached her hands up to push tears away, but they fell thick and fast.

"I didn't know," Lana whispered, pushing her hair away from her face, using the back of her hand to wipe her nose. "I didn't know they did that to you. When McLarty told me, when I realised that you were in the same cave as that creep, I-"

"McLarty?" Flora asked, the word freezing in her mouth.

What the...?

"Yeah," Lana said, looking up towards the sky to try and stop her streaming eyes. "Of course. He's obsessed with the balance of the camp. He can't go home, can't risk getting arrested for all his stupid arson or whatever, so he didn't seem to have any problem with knocking you over the head and tying you up. He came to tell me that you'd found him."

"McLarty," Flora muttered, feeling the back of her head throb.

"I'm so sorry," Lana whispered. Her eyelashes were all stuck together; her mouth was red and swollen.

"I... I can't..." Flora said, feeling her physical body melt under Lana's gaze. *This girl has captured and locked up a man. She ordered the killing of two other men. She's not someone I should be involved with, should let into my life...It can't happen now; I can't ever forgive her.*

As their lips met, Flora felt tears silently slide down her face.

CHAPTER FORTY-SIX
SEMPITERNAL

Flora awoke with the sound of birds singing through the gaps in the eaves above. The scent of bracken filled the air around her. The bed was comfortable. It wasn't her own.

Waking up without Hive and Frances bumbling around was infinitely more pleasurable. She felt her face fall into a lazy smile. No more looking at Hive's huge white knickers. No more watching Frances shave into a bowl.

"We've missed breakfast," Flora murmured.

She felt as if she were somewhere else, somewhere luxurious. The Maldives, perhaps. It didn't make sense to her that just twenty meters away someone would be cooking breakfast. Just a few hundred meters away, they would be reeling in fishing nets.

"Mmm." Lana kissed her shoulder. The feel of Lana's lips on her skin made Flora shiver. She had forgotten about the pain in the back of her head. The pillow underneath her face lulled her into a world of comfort. This was her fate. This was everywhere that she wanted to be.

She could forget about the other world; the world outside. The place that they all called home, the place that was filled with liars and captors and murderers. Oddly, or perhaps not oddly, she felt more angry with Hope than anyone.

But Flora could forget about everything that she'd been through, even for a minute, as long as she had Lana. Flora clutched the other girl's hands tighter. It felt weird to hold someone else's hands within yours, as if you had a small bird between your fingers, soft and trusting. She never wanted to let go.

Lana had broken last night. She had cracked at the seams and all of her tension and trauma had come streaming out for Flora to catch.

She told Flora about her childhood. Lana's mum constantly threw her out of the house and bolted the doors. It was a choice between homelessness or staying with her best friend. She told Flora about that choice becoming harder the day that Tane's mum started dating Axer. About how he always looked at her in a funny way. About how Tane tried to avoid leaving her alone with Axer. About the final day that he took her out on his boat, with the promise that they were meeting Tane. About what he tried to do.

She managed to escape. She showered for three days, thinking of what might have happened.

When she told Tane, he promised her that she would never be put in that position again. He found a way to steal the money. He bought a boat. They ran.

"I owe Tane everything," Lana whispered. Tane had believed her from the first word. It was the purest form of love that Flora had ever witnessed, and it made her heart bleed. Not through jealously for Tane and Lana, and not even for Lana's deeply traumatic experience.

But for the fact that the family riches had been used to buy that ticket to freedom. That not everyone could afford that.

They talked for five long hours, whispering into the darkness. Flora asked Lana how she had managed to lock up Axer.

"Easy," Lana said, and she had sounded casual, although she had paused in tracing shapes on Flora's skin. "I saw him from the lookout and waited for him in the forest. Kicked him in the back of the shins to take him down and tied his wrists together with a dropper loop knot. He taught me that one, so I thought it was a nice touch."

"And your arm?" Flora asked, hesitating before she spoke.

"He got hold of it," Lana said, her voice short. "Anyway, I got him."

"What about the others?"

"They arrived the day before. Tane was on lookout, saw the boat coming. He let me know, I got Hive and Frances on it and they were waiting in the trees with their tasers."

"Tasers?"

"Tasers," Lana confirmed grimly. She didn't raise the corner of her mouth, as Flora half-expected her to. She didn't look proud or joyful or like she had won.

Which made Flora feel infinitesimally better. Because, ultimately, who was Lana? The girl in front of her had ordered the killing of two men. She'd captured another man and was holding him prisoner. She'd ordered people, real people, to be tasered.

Is she a monster?

Flora couldn't match these questions to the Lana in front of her, and so she didn't try. Lana was just a girl who had been through a traumatic ordeal and was trying to deal with the situation with the only resources that she had. The world wasn't split into good and bad; things weren't as binary as Flora was used to.

Night had long since fallen at that point and they could hear soft snores from the other huts. Lana had her own hut.

"You're not like anyone I've ever met," Lana told Flora, as they lay on Lana's bed, looking at the gaps in the ceiling. "And I know that you think you're weird, but the fact that you're different isn't just ok. It's frickin' beautiful."

Lana's door had a lock on it. They were safe. They both sank into that knowledge, clutching onto each other like anchors, like helium balloons.

That was last night; now, Flora and the birds were both

awake and she couldn't believe her luck.

△△△

"Your eggs, New Girl," Lana said, bustling through the door with two plates balanced on one arm. She shut the door firmly behind her and turned to smile at Flora.

"It's Flora, you know," Flora said, smiling lazily.

"Brock," Lana corrected, setting a plate of eggs on toast down in front of Flora. "You're one of us, so Brock it is."

"Shall I call you Skinner then?" Flora teased. Lana reached forward and flicked a lock of hair out of Flora's eyes.

"Never," she whispered, her warm breath tickling Flora's face. Lana kissed her and Flora wished that she could bottle up how happy she felt at that moment. As they pulled back, she noticed Lana's Memorables on her bedside table. Three pieces of straw that had been wound into a plait, a small, silver-framed picture of a man who looked like he must be Lana's father, and a miniature ship. Flora felt her chest ache. She looked at the straw. 'Lana ended up sleeping in a barn for a week and nearly froze to death'; that's what McLarty had told her.

"After I eat these, I need to go and sort something," Lana said, settling herself down on the edge of the bed and putting her own plate on her lap. She picked up a piece of toast, a fried egg swimming on top, and took a bite, releasing a molten flow of yolk.

It's all real. I'm really here, in Lana's bed, and she's made me eggs.

"I thought we missed breakfast," Flora said, taking a bite of her own toast, watching as the egg slopped off of it and back onto the plate. Outside, a blithe bird was chirping a morning song.

"You sounded disappointed that we'd missed it," Lana shrugged. "I couldn't have you going hungry, could I? Not after your day yesterday."

The reminder made Flora pause in her chewing. A thick slab of toast melted on her tongue until it tasted like slushy cardboard.

"Lana," she said, after she'd swallowed the mouthful. It felt painful in her gullet. "You can't keep him in there, you know?"

"I know," Lana replied, straight away, as if she'd been thinking the same thing. She looked ahead, at her neat room. Posters were tacked on the walls: punk bands that Flora didn't recognise.

"So, what's the plan?" Flora asked, gently.

"I'll try and reason with him. See if he'll go away if we let him go."

"Do you think he will?"

"Do we have another option? As much as I hate him, I can't kill him. He's Tane's stepdad. He's Tane's family. Tane would never forgive me."

"What about the others?" Flora asked, feeling bitterness crawl onto her tongue. She couldn't correlate this version of Lana – the loving, strong, kind female that she'd fallen for – with someone who would order the murder of two men.

"That's entirely my fault," Lana said. "I told them to sort them out. I didn't mean kill them, for goodness' sake, but I was distracted, I wasn't thinking. I'd just heard from McLarty that they'd tracked us down, I was still thinking it all through, and then Hive said that Tane had spotted a boat. I told them to take care of it, to *sort it out*: it being the problem, not their lives. Hive takes things very literally."

"Right," Flora said, unsure if she felt any better about the situation. Lana still knew about it; she knew about the murders, the blood that was shed on their own island. "Did you know about Hope and Lennox?"

"Yeah," Lana shrugged, sounding surprised at the new direction of the conversation. "It's nice that she finally gave up on the idea of us." The feathered fingers of a tree scratched against the top of Lana's hut.

"What?"

"It's nice that they've got together. She's been trying to make *us* happen for a long time," Lana said. She shrugged, and a look of humour flickered across her face. "It's been really annoying."

"What?" Flora asked, realisation starting to dawn on her. "So you…she…ah, why weren't you interested in her like that?" *Hope was jealous that Lana liked me.*

"Oh, you know me. I'm *incredibly* fussy," Lana said, shooting Flora a wicked grin. Flora rolled her eyes, trying to find the situation humorous instead of disconcerting.

"No, anyway, I was talking about the fact that they've been harassing me. They… they tried to strangle me." Flora felt her throat tighten at the memory.

"What?"

"Yeah, they told me to stay away from Tane, and then to stay away from you. It got pretty full on," Flora admitted, picking up her abandoned piece of toast and dipping it into the yolk. She took a bite and chewed for a long moment, before she realised that Lana was staring at her.

"Hope and Lennox tried to strangle you?"

"Yeah. It's fine, it's… no big deal," Flora finished lamely, wanting to move on from the conversation. She'd only wanted to know if Lana knew about it.

"It *is* a big deal. Eccles saw you try and kiss Tane, he came back telling us all about it. Honestly, that kid is everywhere; he sees everything that's going on. He calls himself The Oracle. So that explains that whole warning about Tane, maybe, but I don't get why they'd try and punish you."

The moment dripped with awkwardness, as Flora realised how Lana had heard about her and Tane. Eccles was telling them 'all about it'. Flora desperately hoped that the other girl understood that she didn't just go around trying to kiss people. *Well, technically I did, I guess, but that's all over now.*

"I guess Hope was jealous about me and you," Flora said

slowly, trying to explore Hope's feelings. "But why would she warn me away from Tane?"

"That was probably Lennox," Lana said. "He's desperate to keep this life; he was badly bullied back home. He's always trying to stop us getting new people; he went nuts at me when we recruited you. He's worried about upsetting the balance of the camp, whatever the hell that means. If Hope and Lennox are in it together, then it makes sense that they were warning you away from both me and Tane."

Somewhere overhead, an exotic bird made a loud caw.

"Why couldn't you just go after someone simple, hey?" Lana grinned. "Ritchie would make a much more sensible choice."

Flora felt her face burn. She remembered what Hope had said about authority figures. And what Tane had said about her being like the tree on the edge of the cliff, all alone. Perhaps she did seek out power, because she thought that someone might catch her once in a while.

"I'm sorry about Tane," Flora whispered. The motives of Lennox and Hope were clear, but that didn't excuse her trying to kiss Tane in the water.

"It's not been that easy for me," Lana said, looking at her plate. "Seeing you guys, I mean. Seeing how smitten he was from Day One. But I can't stay away any more. Tane will get over it, he'll have to."

"Please never stay away from me again," Flora said, lifting Lana's injured hand and kissing it.

"I won't," she promised. "So, I guess I've got Hope and Lennox to deal with now, too."

"Don't hurt them," Flora quickly pleaded. The last thing that she wanted was more violence. "I'll deal with them, please. Let me talk to them."

"Relax, wild one," Lana said, trailing her fingers up Flora's arm. "It's not your job to be everything everyone needs. You don't have to impress me to be loveable, you don't have to sort out all of the world's problems. Just trust me."

"Fine." Flora breathed out, feeling, for the first time, that perhaps just showing up and being present as herself was good enough. "Don't do anything mad."

"Oh, I won't. But they can kiss goodbye to life on the island." Lana set her empty plate down on the bed next to her. "Right, I'd better go sort something. You gonna be ok?"

"'Course," Flora said gruffly, setting her own half-eaten plate down on the bedding next to Lana's. "I... I don't really know what to say, except that last night was really nice."

"Nice?" Lana looked at Flora and grinned. That look was back; the expression that she always had when she took the mick out of Flora. This time, Flora smiled back and rolled her eyes.

"Yeah, it was really nice."

Lana leant forward, putting her lips gently on Flora's, and she spoke: "I think it was a little more than just *nice*." She kissed Flora deeply, urgently, and Flora felt her heart explode.

She reached out to put her hands around Lana, but the other girl sighed and pulled back. She stood up, shrugged a heavy jacket across her shoulders, cast one final glance at Flora in her bed, and then strode out of the hut. The door swung shut behind her.

Well, life's just got more interesting. The taste of Lana stayed imprinted on Flora's lips long after she'd stopped smiling.

CHAPTER FORTY-SEVEN
LANGUOR

Flora really didn't feel like picking up a task for the day. For one thing, her head was pounding, and her wrists, which had been cut open during the second binding, were causing pins and needles in her hands.

She was filled with a deep sadness, or perhaps it was anger, but for some reason her brain kept telling her: *We'll never be those carefree kids again.* Thinking about Hope and Lennox, about disappointing Tane, about everything that McLarty had done... it had, however briefly, overtaken all thoughts of Lana.

She wanted to track down and confront Hope, but before she had the chance, Tane found her. Flora had been brushing her teeth, thinking about her plans for the day and letting her washed hair drip dry, when Tane burst into the Privy Shack, looking as clean and fresh as anything.

"It's perfect conditions," he announced, as if he were telling a room full of people. Flora, who stood alone in the wooden confines of the silent toilet block, given that everyone else was at their duties, stared.

"Perfect for what?" she asked, spraying globules of toothpaste everywhere.

"For canoeing, of course, Brock," Tane said, hopping up and down on the balls of his feet. "I want to take her out and I can't manage it on my own. You in?"

"I, err..." Flora said, stalling for time by bending down

and spitting out toothpaste into a huge serving bowl, which someone had drilled holes into. "I don't know if I can…"

"Why, what're you doing?"

Waiting in Lana's bed until she's finished with whatever she's up to. "Nothing, I guess."

"Great. Grab your jacket and let's go." Tane bounded out of the door and into the brilliant sunshine outside. *Well then, I guess I'm going canoeing.*

△△△

McLarty found them on the beach. He must have seen them arrive from Poukai; he appeared from the direction of the boat. He ground his feet into the sand to root himself before he talked. "I finished it," he said to Flora, his eyes red and manic. He looked terrible.

He knocked me out. He could have killed me.

Her anger was momentarily replaced with concern; it was hard to be angry with someone who looked so out-of-it.

"Are you alright, McLarty?" she asked.

"I'm on top of the world," he called back, even though he was only a few meters away, blocking their path with his hair stuck on end, his hands shaking slightly. "I finished it."

"Finished what?"

"Lost Grace, obviously," he said, breaking into a sweaty smile, his arms opening slightly as if Flora was going to run into them and hug him. She stayed still. Next to her, Tane was confused.

"Lost what?"

"You finished Lost Grace?" Flora asked. For a moment, she let the words sink in. She suddenly felt numb, empty, as if she'd just fallen into the ocean from height. "That's… amazing."

"I know," he said, grinning manically. He took a step towards them.

"McLarty, this isn't the best time," Tane said, still sounding confused, but firm. McLarty dragged his eyes away from Flora and looked at Tane for a long moment. The sea sucked at the bottom of Poukai, letting out a squelching noise that could be heard all along the beach. Air pockets disappeared.

"Fine," McLarty muttered, and his shoulders descended slightly and his gaze fell to the floor and a look of permanent glumness took up position again. "Anyway, I'm sorry I didn't find the boat, Tane. I thought we were safe." There was a long moment of silence. No one moved.

Tane knows about Scarface's boat. He saw them. But he doesn't know about Axer.

"Ok, thanks McLarty," Tane said slowly, dragging out the words, his voice chilled through. McLarty didn't seem to notice, but he did swing around, back towards the boat, to head back to his gaming room, his Den, his useless spy headquarters, where all of the best coding in the world hadn't beaten a seventeen-year-old boy sitting on a hill.

Flora watched as a long string of flags, strung there erratically by the crew in months gone by, waved uselessly in the breeze.

"Are you ok, Brock?" Tane murmured.

"Fine," she lied, wondering whether she should be doing this.

It wasn't right to go and spend the afternoon with Tane. She'd spent the night with Lana; she knew that it hadn't been easy for Lana thus far. Flora's wrists ached and her hands were shaking and her skull felt as if it had had something drilled into it. *And besides, apparently Tane is 'smitten' with me. Is this what's best for him?*

When they came upon the canoe, past Poukai and further down the beach, her mouth fell open. Even in her foggy state of mind, she could appreciate that the canoe was a thing of wonder.

"It's stunning," Flora whispered.

"Made it myself." Tane whistled, filled with cheer. "I couldn't wait for you to see it."

For me to see it, specifically?

"I'm confused," Flora said, suddenly, looking at the happiness on Tane's face, feeling tiredness pull across her flesh. She felt as if she were a hundred years old. "I don't get you. That night in the sea, you said that we couldn't happen. That it would upset the balance of the camp. That people wouldn't like it. And now, what? It's suddenly ok? Why would you want just *me* to see it?"

Tane looked as if he'd been slapped. His mouth was slightly open, his lower lip slightly purple. For a long moment, he was lost for words.

"Look, Brock," he finally said, pushing the hair out of his eyes and looking around. "It's not easy for us, right. Me and Lana. We can't just go getting distracted, not being there to run the show, to fight off the Lusty's and the McLarty's of the world. Because they'd topple us, or me at least. They'd love to watch me falter, to watch me make one false move, and to take over the camp."

"I get that," Flora said, and she did. "So what's changed?"

"I can't..." Tane ground his foot into the sand and made an aggrieved noise, as if he was in pain. "I can't keep doing this! I can't keep staying away, just because it might upset the balance. Who cares about the balance? It's my camp, I can do what I want." He stilled his foot and looked at Flora. He tapped his palm against his side, agitated, and then strode forwards.

His lips were on Flora's before she had time to react. They were salty and sweet, soft and hard, and wrong, wrong, wrong.

She pushed him off, but a movement caught the corner of her eye. McLarty. He had darted from the ship, where they would have been in full view of him, into the forest nearest Poukai. One streak of his black hair and then there was nothing. Flora was filled with fury.

What was he going to do now that he'd seen them kiss

in broad daylight? Assault her again? Knock her out from a different direction? Her head panged.

"Excuse me a moment," Flora said, and she stormed off towards the ship before Tane could say another word.

△△△

Flora was hellbent on hammering wrath into McLarty's kingdom. "For knocking me out," she spat, as keyboards crashed down on the ground. The adrenaline tasted delicious. Luckily, DeCalbiac was out.

She had remembered the code to get in: 131118. 13th November 2018. Lana had told her what had happened on that date, and she was bestowing more than her own revenge.

"For putting your stupid island 'balance' ahead of my skull." She smashed a computer monitor with a heavy glass bottle. "For not even bothering to stick around and apologise," she continued, as she destroyed the whirring server and the computers and the piles of papers. She threw a computer mouse against the wall and ground it under her foot.

"For wasting all of this time when you could've just been sat on a bloody hill with a pair of binoculars." She crashed and smashed and hurled until the whole computer den was a mass of wires and beeps and flashing red lights. She half expected smoke to emanate from somewhere, but the air remained stagnant.

She had done it. She had destroyed a computer. Something that, in her old life, would have been sacrilege. She wiped her hair out of her eyes, elated. Yes, perhaps a little bit of her anger was also directed at Hope, but what McLarty had done was also unforgiveable, and it wasn't like the computer lab was getting them anywhere.

△△△

"You ok?" Tane asked, as Flora re-joined him, face flushed, eyes bright, skin soaking up the rays of the early afternoon sunshine.

"Absolutely fantastic," she replied, out of breath, empty of anger, feeling jubilant. "Let's do it." She wanted to be on the sea. She wanted the salt spray on her face. She wanted to direct her energy into the depths of the ocean. She wanted to pretend that Tane hadn't kissed her. She wanted to pretend that he didn't feel anything, because she had, literally and metaphorically, now chosen her bed.

And when they came back from a jaunt around the bay, she would no doubt find McLarty freaking out on Poukai. Perhaps crying, pleading, doing anything he could do put everything back together. That room was his baby. Perhaps it was the only way to get him to feel anything.

"Shouldn't we talk about what just happened?" Tane asked, motionless, doubtful.

"Nope," Flora replied, striding over to the canoe. She lifted up one end and dragged it towards the sea. The island had made her strong.

CHAPTER FORTY-EIGHT
OFFING

Paddling away from Taniwha presented a mixture of emotions for Flora to feast on. On the one hand, she felt as if she could finally breathe. The sea air, the safety of being with Tane, the beauty of the wild, undiscovered ocean. The roll of glitter across the curves; the patterns that formed, like clouds, in the spume. She loved the feel of Taniwha; the smell of the breeze, the brilliant colours of the trees, the wild calls from the camp that told her that someone, somewhere, was always having a good time.

But the other part of her mind was replaying everything that she'd found out. They'd murdered people. Her roommates had murdered people. Yes, those people were hunting Tane down in exchange for a reward, and they probably would have killed him without a second of thought. *Probably. We can all die on 'probably'.*

Scarface and his crony deserved some form of punishment, but murder? Was there ever a good reason to murder another human being? And then there was Axer. Flora couldn't stop thinking about the eyeball behind the barbed wire.

Lana was going to try and negotiate with him. *Can you ever negotiate with someone like that?*

And then the other thing, as well. McLarty finished Lost Grace. *He finished my game.* She felt empty. *He could show me how to do it. But it's not the same.* It felt like her only life goal had crumbled to dust. Around her, the clear ocean speckled with brightly coloured fish.

Tane's canoe was quite spectacular to behold, even sat inside. It had been carved like a huge totem pole, with faces and beings and animals intertwined in a sprawling mass of lines and colours. The inner benches were roughly hewn, but topped with vivid, bohemian fabrics: purple, blue, teal. *It's like a magic canoe. Like something out of a game.*

Did I harbour a secret hope of being the first one to finish Lost Grace and therefore Pictopia? Maybe. Even if I wasn't the first, then at least I wouldn't know who it was. But here he is, on Poukai. Someone who is better than me at the only thing that I'm good at.

She sighed. She couldn't care too much. The old Flora was talking in her head, taking centre stage for the first time in a while, telling her the facts: this is what I used to want.

But the new Flora, the tanned, stronger Flora, the Flora who was flying through the open ocean on a hand-carved canoe with a seventeen-year-old billionaire? The Flora that spent the night with the most beautiful girl that she'd ever seen in real life? This Flora didn't have time to worry about Lost Grace. *I'm Lost near Taniwha. Now, there's a game.*

"I must admit," Flora said, laying back and looking at the coruscation of jewels on the ocean, the flecks of blinding sunlight playing on the humped backs of the waves, the mist that rose from the gaggles of rock, "this is a stunning island."

"The best," Tane replied, from the seat in front of her. His mood had picked up immensely since they'd escaped the bay and hit the open water.

"So, I guess you're a bit of an artist yourself," Flora said, running her finger over the carvings on the sides of the boat. Freckles of colourful paints dotted the swirls, curling up over the top and lining the edges.

"Hardly," he snorted, but he sounded pleased.

"You could be the new Esmerelda," Flora said, light, playful. She was thinking about kissing Lana goodbye this morning. About how Lana had told her that it was *more than* nice. If truth be told, she'd all but forgotten that Tane had tried to kiss her.

"Absolutely not, I'm nothing on her. Maybe she would have made better life decisions." He let out a bitter laugh. Flora moved her oar through the clear surface, watching it fall like melted glass back into itself. They'd made it out onto the open sea and everything was smoother, the afternoon sunlight oscillating across the vista.

"That is a really odd thought," Flora said. She didn't have anything else to say. It wasn't her place.

Will I ever game again? She couldn't imagine ever leaving Taniwha. Leaving Lana.

"Are you ok to paddle on the right again? I'll take the left." Tane swooped his oar into the water. Flora obliged and they soon found pace, their oars sweeping through the clear sea, avoiding darting fish and flotsam. "What about you, any unusual family history?"

"Nothing unusual," Flora said, trying to wrack her brain for anything that her parents might have given away. She struggled to remember the facts of back home; it felt like another world, an old dream. "Mum comes from a long line of substance abusers. There's nothing interesting there, it's all a bit sad. Dad probably has some interesting ancestors, but he's not interested in family trees. He hates the idea of dying, and so kind of rejects all history, as if by ignoring the past you can avoid the same happening to you."

"Wow."

"Well, not that interesting."

The gentle slap and swipe of the oar was finally distracting Flora from the pulsing in the back of her skull. She had almost forgotten, however briefly, about being attacked.

"You're really insightful. I don't know many people of any age who know their parents so well. Have you thought about becoming a psychologist?"

"Ha, no," Flora said. "No, not really. I kind of just had to learn about them to get by, you know?"

"And that's why you game, a chance to play?"

"I guess so," Flora said, feeling suddenly uncomfortable with this level of introspection.

"It sounds like you grew up too soon, and you've been desperate to play ever since," Tane noted. Flora found it odd hearing Tane talk so maturely. She'd become used to him being the jolly sort, the kind of guy who laughs easily and doesn't take life too seriously.

"What about you? Surely you were desperate to play when you stole your family's money to buy a pirate ship?"

Tane laughed and Flora saw a fish flip into the air and plunge back down into the water.

"I guess that was less about play and more about escaping," he said, keeping his voice light.

"Escaping with the family jewels," Flora joked. She knew enough now that she could bring these subjects up. And here, where it was only her and Tane, she finally had a chance to ask some of the burning questions.

"How much did you steal?" she asked, matching Tane's pace. They were making their way directly out to sea, towards a never ending horizon, their backs to Taniwha and it's mass of jungle.

"Twenty-five," he replied.

"Twenty-five thousand dollars?" Flora asked, shocked. She hadn't really thought about how much a ship would cost, but that seemed like a lot.

"Try twenty-five million."

"What?"

"Yeah," Tane replied, letting out a nervous laugh. "I know, it's bad isn't it?"

Flora didn't reply. She stopped rowing and stared at the dark blue line where the sky met the sea. She couldn't compute what he was saying; she felt as if she'd dropped into one of her games and was talking about play money. What was the equivalent of 25 million dollars in Pictopia? Probably, like, ten million diamonds.

"What're you thinking?" Tane asked, pulling his oar up into the boat. She felt him lean forwards. The boat lolled to one side and then the other.

"I just don't understand how you can steal that much money."

"What, like, technically? It was no walk in the park, I assure you. I had to create a new offshore crypto coin and then invest it in it over a few months. Pretty much anyone can create one, that's the magic of crypto, but it took an absolute age to get it all to be virtually untraceable. Then dissolved the coin. I owe that to my dad's old accountant, but he took his share. Somewhere in the Bahamas now, I think."

"I don't mean how did you technically steal it. I mean, how are you not going mad with the guilt?"

"I wouldn't have been able to steal it so easily if Axer hadn't taken it straight from my inheritance. That's why he can't report it; it wasn't technically ever his. He had to do his own crooked business to move that money in the first place, and then he lost half of it after a week in Vegas. He told mom that he'd made a shedload, because she never knew about the default rules of intestacy. She's always been incredibly trusting, slash has absolutely no interest in money. 'It's not prudent to talk about finances, Taniel'," he mimicked her voice. "And then the next thing is that he wasn't even telling her about it anyway, it was all buried in offshore accounts and dodgy businesses.

He can't tell mom about me taking back the money any more than he can tell the police, because she'll go ape. So he's just gotta try and track me down. No doubt pull out my fingernails when he finds me. Good luck to the guy, we're a needle in a haystack over here."

Apart from the fact that Scarface and Axer have both found us. Is Tane always so in denial, or does he genuinely have no idea that Scarface was working for Axer? That he obviously alerted him to our whereabouts? He probably thinks that theirs was just a tourist boat. That Lana greeted the tourists and sent them on their way.

She wanted to ask him about it, and vowed to before the end of the boat ride. But she didn't want to just yet. The world was stunning, and Flora was tired. *Let me bask in paradise another minute longer.*

"Taniel?" she asked, to lighten the mood, to try and distract from the hard facts that kept swimming to her in the ocean air. Lana had kept it all secret from Tane. Lana had been protecting Tane this whole time, just like he protected her.

"Crazy name, ain't it? Tane suits me just fine," he said, and let out a howl of laughter. He started bobbing his leg up and down; the boat moved. "Taniel Nuku. Thankfully no middle name to let it down even more."

"Where are we going, by the way?"

"Nowhere and everywhere, baby," he replied, his voice cheerful again.

Flora couldn't believe that he didn't know that his stepdad was on the island. *Perhaps Tane does need to grow up.* The island was clearly his escape, his place to hide away from the reality of back home, of a mother who was disengaged and a stepfather who'd stolen his inheritance and conned a whole society.

The idea of that much money being not only inherited, but actually going into the bank account of Tane, made Flora feel immensely uncomfortable, and she was relieved that Tane was sitting in front of her and couldn't see the flicker of emotion in her eyes. She needed time to digest how she felt about the whole thing.

She'd grown up in a house where every single item in the cupboard was supermarket own. Even now that Abbie lived with them, she got her fruit from the guy at the market who shouted "A pound a bowl" all day. Her mum had been passed from job to job: cleaner, supermarket checkout operative, pub manager, sales rep. On good months, she bought herself Vogue magazine, and read it ten times. She used to have a stack of Vogue magazines by her bed, but it wasn't huge.

Her dad supposedly had been working nights for a few years, although now she knew that that wasn't true. He got a payment from the government every two weeks to help him through the challenges of employment, and he also got something monthly, but she didn't tend to ask questions. Apart from the odd McDonald's breakfast bap, he'd pretty much only eat toast.

When the topic of money was brought up by Abbie, her dad would get instantly stressed, rubbing the back of his neck, closed off to any further conversation. She knew not to mention money, that it was something to be revered and feared.

And now, here was Tane, casually stealing twenty-five million dollars. What was that in pounds? Maybe twenty million? Enough that he could afford to buy her whole city, probably. No wonder Axer was so keen to track him down. At the thought of Axer, she thought of Lana. Lana had taken the chain and padlock to build a prison cell, because she suspected that Axer would eventually track them down. Was she always so nihilistic? Although she'd been right, hadn't she?

Flora wondered where Lana had gone. Would she be standing by his cell, looking through the gaps? Would she watch him sat there, starving, broken, coughing up his innards? How long would she stand there? How long would it take to fill her with the reassurance of power? Flora should get back to her. She didn't want Lana thinking that she'd actually gone on a date with Tane.

McLarty probably told her about the kiss, Flora thought. *But I'll tell her. I'll tell her it was all him; I didn't want it. We've got the rest of our lives to laugh about it.*

"We should get back to camp," she said, steeling herself for another hour of rigorous rowing. Tane murmured in agreement. No doubt someone in the camp would need him for something.

"Sorry about earlier, by the way," Tane muttered, his words laden with shame. "I know it's not cool to kiss someone without consent. I just thought, because last time-"

"It's fine," Flora quickly interrupted. After all, hadn't she tried to kiss him once before too? They were both erring on the dangerous side of non-consent. Tane was silent for a long moment, and the only sound was the sucking and lapping of the oars against the waves.

"You like Lana, don't you?" he asked, eventually. He didn't turn around. Flora felt her heart swell.

"Yes," she said, softly.

"I'm happy for you guys." Tane sounded so alone and morose that Flora couldn't help but grasp on a change of subject. She wasn't ready to talk about her and Lana.

"By the way," she said, her voice almost casual. "I don't understand why you accepted a murderer on board Poukai. I thought you were fussier than that."

Tane stopped rowing.

CHAPTER FORTY-NINE
INCENDIARY

"What do you mean?"

"McLarty," Flora said. She wasn't about to tell him about the other murderers on the island, but he needed to know about this one. "You know that he killed his whole family when he set fire to his house?"

13th November 2018. The day that McLarty killed his entire family.

"What?" Tane asked, his voice cold all the way through. "He never told me that."

"I know," Flora said, not daring start rowing again. Tane wouldn't want a murderer on his island. He saw the crew as his own family. He wouldn't stand for one of them to be a demon.

Lana had told her about McLarty last night. About why he was so desperate to stay. About how he always hid below board when they went back to the mainland. He was wanted for manslaughter. And even with the best coding tricks in the world – and he currently had the police thinking that he was in Colombia – all it would take would be one glance towards a CCTV camera, one sighting from someone who'd seen the articles, and he'd be locked up for life. Life on the island meant evasion.

"How could you forgive him?" Flora asked Lana.

"It was an accident," Lana explained. Flora wasn't convinced. McLarty was an arsonist; he was obsessed with fire.

Even if he'd been trying to create a controlled flame, he started the fire that killed his family, and for that, he was a murderer.

"What the actual..." Tane said.

"I know." The screams of the McLarty family resonated in Flora's head. The smoke, the choking. Did they know that it was him? Were his parents' last thoughts about their son, their monstrous son?

"Leave it with me," Tane said, eventually. "Do you want to go back, or go further?"

He twisted around in his seat to look at her. His face was whiter than before; he looked as if he'd been pushed to his mental limits. Flora briefly wondered if there might be sharks around them.

"Just a little further," Flora said, feeling the universe tilt slightly with her decision. Tane looked miserable; he needed her and the escape that their trip was providing. As soon as they got back to camp, everyone would be hassling Tane again, for instruction, direction, leadership. Besides, they'd already been gone hours, and Flora felt freedom continue to course through her, as if she had been placed on charge. She would go back energised, invigorated, and Lana would be there. *Will we tell everyone about us? Or just let people find out organically?*

They sped on, through time and space, hurtling over the wrinkled ocean towards nothing and everything. The sun was starting to fall low onto the horizon, casting the sky in melted iron and bronze. Discontented birds screeched through the blue patches, hunting fish.

"Tane," Flora said, her voice loud over the movement of the craft.

"Yep?"

"Did you know that they killed them?"

Tane stopped rowing. Flora followed suit and they sat, silently. She watched the back of his head, which was turning into a silhouette against the sky.

"No," he replied, his voice so soft that she could barely hear him over the hushing of the ocean.

"And what about Axer? Did you know that he's on the island?"

"He's not on the island," Tane said automatically, turning violently to look at her, alarm pasted across his face. She found his oblivion infuriating.

"Yes, he is," Flora said, bluntly. "He arrived a day later than the other two. Lana dealt with him."

"There's no way," Tane said, mouthing the words so that Flora was forced to lip read. He shook his head, not breaking eye contact, reading her face, reading the seriousness of the moment. "Then why did you bring me out here?" he yelled, turning back towards the front and yanking his oars so hard that the boat took a moment to spring to life again. "Why are we here if that PSYCHOPATH IS ON MY ISLAND?"

He yelled the last words, pushing his oars so hard that his whole body propelled forwards and then backwards, his arms becoming extensions of the wood: lean, strong, angry. Flora followed suit, almost ripping the oars from their metal hoops, rowing with a fever that didn't match her feelings, because she wasn't worried about Axer. She knew that Lana was capable. *He's locked up.*

"Calm down," she said, over the noise of the ocean. Tane didn't react or slow in his rowing. Low, dark clouds were sitting atop Taniwha, and as they got closer it looked as if there were a tornado in the middle of the island, sucking the dark clouds down, down, into its depths. Or pushing them up into the sky.

"What's going on?" Flora asked, urgency growing within her. *What on earth is that?*

"What is that?" Tane asked sharply, and Flora realised that he'd stopped paddling again and she was starting to hurtle them around in a circle.

"What?"

"That smoke."

Flora looked towards the entrance to the lagoon and saw a plume of thick, black smoke rising up.

"The campfire?" she asked. Hadn't Lana mentioned that the smoke was too thick during her first campfire? If that had been visible then, Flora could only imagine the size of the campfire now, the smoke rising thick and as dark as cigarette ash.

"It can't be," Tane muttered, plunging his oar back into the ocean. Flora followed suit and they sped towards the gateway that would let them into the lagoon, the first hurdle to get past to get back to the campsite. They sailed between the great towering walls at speed, ignoring the murals, the carvings that had clearly been made by Tane. This time, Flora did join Tane in his urgency, her arms straining to keep up.

"Where is she?" Tane asked, and he'd stopped rowing again and his body was frozen, moving with the canoe, emanating a chill that caused panic to fly up Flora's throat. She looked ahead of them and it felt as if she'd been physically hit, because Poukai wasn't there. Poukai was gone.

"No, no, no," Tane said, snapping out of his reverie. "Let's get to camp. This cannot be happening."

The friction of the oars against her blisters caused Flora to wince, but they continued rowing with such ferocity that at first the canoe merely stuttered, before realising what was required and jolting forward at speed. Tane moved mechanically, his eyes always on the shoreline, his arms rippling.

The smell of burning came thick and fast. Tane jumped out of the boat when the shore was still several meters away, splashing through the water, slow until he reached the sand, when the effort his legs had been making nearly toppled him.

"Come on," he yelled, turning around and finding Flora still in the boat. His face was red, sweat dripping from his chin, his eyes wild and rabid. She jumped out, her mind catching up, the water reaching her breastbone. *Where's Lana?*

She waded quickly to the shore, feeling her pulse in the roof of her mouth, willing her feet to move quicker. She could barely hear over her heartbeat, the constriction of her ribs, the panic that crept up her neck. The smoke was choking. It flew through the air from the direction of the camp.

Tane waited until she was a meter away from him before turning and pelting towards the jungle like a wild animal, bare feet slamming down onto branches and pine needles and sticky mud. Flora followed, her feet numb, her hands pushing branches, her breathing manic. They thrummed through the jungle as if they were panthers.

They arrived at the flat rock face and turned left to cut through the thickest part of the woods. There was no birdsong, no small creatures scurrying around the ground. Their jungle was abandoned, and smoke wound between the trees, threatening to trip them up, filling their lungs with black ash.

Out of the blackness came a sudden scream, an inhuman roar that formed the words: "Where is he?" Flora and Tane both stopped running. Flora felt the blood drain from her face.

"Who?" Flora asked, knowing that it was a pointless question, her tongue tripping over the word, afraid. Tane ignored her and took up his pace again, pelting through trees, both of their arms getting ripped apart by thorns and brambles and branches. Eventually Tane stopped, and for a second Flora bent over, wheezing, coughing her innards onto the floor, trying to clear the black spots that clouded her vision.

She straightened up. Took in the full horror of the scene in front of them. It hit her in the gut.

The trees were ablaze. Great clouds of ash and sparks of violent flames rose up around The Kitch. Their kitchen tent had become a moving, roaring monster, the flames from its mouth licking the nearby treetops, howling into the skies, deafening Flora to the crackling, the low level roaring, the billows of sound emanating from the rest of the destruction.

The fire was contained to one side of the camp, for now, and Flora cast her eyes left, towards the Privy Shack and the pathway that led to Axer's cell. Her head stopped moving. Her gaze caught. Because there, on the floor near the shack, was Lana.

CHAPTER FIFTY
NEFARIOUS

"Lana," Tane screamed, as his feet beat the earth. Flora heard only blood; her heartbeat thundering in her ears. The fire heaved, spewing flames like curses.

She was faster. The terracotta mud was her home now; her senses were alive to each rip in the terrain, her bare feet moving like a Cheetah across the savanna.

She crouched down. Shook Lana's body until the older girl's sprained wrist lolled to one side.

Crimson trickled into a pool on the floor. The hot earth looked to be crying.

Flora expelled a guttural, animalistic noise.

Let this be me.

She glanced at Tane. Her hand pushed Lana's hair back, smearing red across that perfect forehead.

Did we do this?

"You're too late," Lana whispered. She opened her eyes; the slits reflected flames. Nearby, a lone giddyfruit rolled from the wreckage, charred, smoking, abandoned from a game of Jungleball, from back when everything was ok.

"What happened?" Flora said, or perhaps she just screamed, because an inhumane noise was rolling from someone's tongue. She tried to pull Lana's hand away so that she could see the damage, see past the blood-sodden t-shirt. It felt as if the remnants of Flora's heart had been peeled and butchered and spliced above Lana's belly button.

Lana's vest had a skull and crossbones on the front. One of the bones had disappeared. Flora's eyes weren't working. She blinked rapidly. A joke, surely. A joke.

"He escaped."

Silence. The blaze raged on. The words were pithy. Cauterised.

"He escaped," Lana repeated. "I'm sorry."

More silence.

"I love you."

Flora blinked. A tear fell. You never know that it's the last time, that you've missed your shot, that there are so many words that should have been spoken, until it's too late.

It had taken Lana great effort to mutter those three magic words. And yet, Flora couldn't speak. Her heart was in her mouth, her skin was wet with tears.

"What's happened to her?" Tane asked, striding around them in a circle, his gaze wild, watching, as if Axer might reappear at any moment. His breathing was loud, quick, punctuated.

"Get Hive," Lana whispered, her throat catching. "Radio call Poukai and they'll come back. They thought everyone was on board, when he saw the fire, McLarty, he…"

"Lan, I don't think Hive can-" Tane started to say.

"Get Hive," Flora screamed at him, her throat red raw, tears spilling into her mouth. *Hell hath no fury like a woman scorned.*

"And Easton too," Lana murmured.

Tane ran over to the nearest radio point, ducking to avoid patches of black smoke.

"He's gone to Sunset Beach," Lana told Flora. "Go. Go and get him, because otherwise he'll come back."

"I'm not leaving you," Flora whispered, tears running down her face. Her hands were covered in Lana's blood as she clutched at the bones on the t-shirt, wishing that she knew what to do, pushing against the wound, trying to build a stopper.

"Seriously, go," Lana said, trying to pull the corner of her mouth up into her signature smile. Flora remembered the gun that she'd hidden under her futon. She stood up. She could hear Tane shouting into the radio; McLarty responding that they were on their way back.

"I love you too," Flora breathed, running away from Lana, towards certain violence.

CHAPTER FIFTY-ONE
EUDAEMONIA

Flora felt feral as she ripped lianas and branches out of her way, jumping from fallen log to dead tree as if she were a wild, angered animal. She made it to Sunset Beach in a matter of minutes, not caring about the cuts on her arms and feet, the thorn that had pierced the skin on her chin so that droplets of fresh, warm blood were coursing down onto her hoodie.

Where is he? Both boats were still there, eerily still.

Flora crept towards them, crouched, listening, all of her senses engaged. She heard a bird cry in the forest. The billowing devastation of the flames in the camp. The muted hush of the sea. The energy that crackled from the surrounding vegetation.

Taniwha felt alive. Taniwha wanted revenge. *Where is he?*

She cocked her head to the side as another noise came into focus. A voice.

"Hello? Hello?" the voice said. A radio crackled. The boat radio.

"Axer," Flora screamed, deciding on the spot to lure him out. She wasn't about to climb onto his boat, to get trapped in small confines with the man who chased Lana out of America.

There was a long, silent moment, as she waited to see if he had heard her. He had. The shell of Axer Nuku-Halliday crawled out of the cabin of his boat and looked at her with a bleary gaze.

"Who are you?" he asked, his voice clean cut and polished, his vowels shuddering through Flora. He looked down her body and noticed the gun in her hand.

"Let's calm down," he said. Flora was shaking. *Can I kill him? Can I kill a fellow human?*

"You stabbed Lana," Flora said, her voice tight, controlled, furious. He lifted both of his hands and slowly showed his palms, as if he knew that she was serious.

"Come on now," he said, slowly. "Let's not do anything stupid. I know that you kids are having fun on this island, but that looks like a real gun for real men. Put it down on the sand and then we can talk."

"Are you serious?" Flora shouted, lifting the gun and pointing it at him. "Are you actually serious? You stabbed Lana and now you want me to show you mercy?"

"Excuse me, hold on for one minute," Axer said. Something switched in his manner, as if he could tell that his current approach wasn't working, and a charming smile worked its way into his eyes. "I know you're upset about Lana. Trust me, I didn't want to hurt her, far from it. She was holding that plastic red knife thing, and I didn't know what to do."

"The filleting knife?" Flora asked, a sinking feeling causing her to lower the gun. *The knife I stole. The knife I left in the cave. That's what he used to stab Lana.*

"That's right," Axer said cautiously. Her attention was distracted, she looked at the sand for a brief moment – *I gave him the knife that he used to stab Lana* – and he disappeared. *Where is he?*

He reappeared from the cabin of the boat wielding a gun of his own. He smiled at her with a sweet, charming, deadly gaze as he lifted his arm.

Flora also lifted her gun, but it was too late; a loud, resounding gunshot reverberated off of the trees, like the crack of a whip, the slap of an oar, Taniwha absorbing another life.

CHAPTER FIFTY-TWO
ZENITH

Axer fell. Collapsed onto his own boat. Flora looked around, bewildered. *What just happened? Did his gun backfire? Am I dead?*

The beach was silent, speechless, overcome, for a long, hollow moment before the whooping started.

"Yesssss," Eccles cried, running out of the forest. Behind him, McLarty appeared, a gun in his hand, his face completely pale, drained of blood. He looked at Flora and she looked at him and it seemed to break the spell that she was under.

McLarty shot Axer. McLarty shot Axer because Axer was about to shoot me.

"We were waiting to see what happened," Ritchie yelled, running out of the forest and putting his arms around Flora. She leant against him, feeling her legs wobble, feeling her body start to disintegrate onto the sand.

"Woah, Flora, it's all good. He's dead. We won, ok?"

"It'll all be ok, Flora," Chan said, as she helped Ritchie to sit Flora on the sand. She stroked Flora's hair back from her face and examined her. "You're a bit pale, but you'll be ok."

"I wasn't going to shoot," McLarty whispered, as he sat down next to Flora and laid his gun on the floor. "Obviously, we have weapons in case we need them, but I honestly wasn't going to shoot, unless he tried to hurt you."

"We were straight here, Brock," Bell said, falling down in front of her. His eyes looked alive. "As soon as Lana told us where you'd gone."

"Lana," Flora said, looking at him. "Where is she?" She started to get to her feet, but her legs felt as if they'd lost all bone and she fell over.

"She's going to be fine," Bell said, in his slow, soothing way. "He didn't hit anything too important. Hive's applied pressure to the wound and has blood transfusion bags. They're on their way to hospital now."

"They've taken Poukai?" Flora asked, numbly.

"Don't be silly," Bell said, laughing. "Easton's style's a bit more radical."

Flora became aware of another sound: propellors, rotating quickly through the air, the sound of trees bending and groaning, the sky coming alive with a shudder. The helicopter sped past them, far overhead, and quickly became a dot on the horizon.

Spin.

"She'll be fine," Chan said, putting her hands around Flora's. She rubbed them, as if Flora was very cold. Flora didn't feel cold. She didn't feel anything. They all became aware of a figure appearing from the trees. The figure stopped. Took in the scene. Walked over to The Esmerelda and stood there for a long moment.

Flora tried standing up again and this time, made it to her feet. She hobbled along the sand, the smell of smoke billowing around her, the feeling starting to come back to her hands with the harshest pain that she'd ever felt.

"Are you ok?" She asked Tane, slipping her bloodstained hand into his.

He was a statue, staring at the bleeding body of his stepfather. Swills of blood ran as rivulets down into the floor of the boat. He squeezed Flora's hand.

"Of course," he replied, his voice at once both sad and hard. "Always am." He flashed Flora a fleeting smile, let go of her hand and turned to the congregation of campmates that had assembled on the sand.

"Today marks the death of Axer Nuku-Halliday," he announced, his voice catching on the words.

No one dared to speak; no one whooped, no one cheered. The group collectively held their breath.

"And the first real day of freedom," Tane yelled, his voice roaring through the Taniwha air. The noise awoke, ripping itself from the throats of all who gathered: screams and cheers, howls and hollers, roars that rebounded off of the trees. The screams of savage, free teenagers sliced their way through the charcoal air.

Flora breathed in deeply, and then joined them.

EPILOGUE

"This is so weird," Tane said, whistling afterwards.

"It's just a small sink next to the main sink." Flora rolled her eyes.

"Ignore him," Lana said, kissing Flora so that her back pressed against the fridge. A postcard of Wales fell onto the floor. "I think it's positively charming." Her lips smiled against Flora's.

"You filing for British citizenship already, Lan?" Tane asked, laughter howling out of him.

"Is the mulled wine ready?" Abbie called from the living room. She sounded happy. Flora's dad had told Flora that he'd stopped working at the meat factory and now worked a sensible supermarket job. Abbie had been happier ever since, and her and Albie went to visit him on his lunch breaks.

"Coming," Lana called back, rolling her eyes and winking at Flora. She left the kitchen, two steaming mugs in her hands, moving slowly. The knife had slid between her ribs, but thankfully hadn't hit any vital organs. Still, she was tender.

Flora missed Taniwha and most of the crew. *I've become a fully accepted member of Planet Belonging.* But still. Tane and Lana were in her dad's house. *They're actually here, in my dad's little house. What the hell?*

"So Lana," Flora's dad said from the living room, "you kids didn't want to go to your own families for Christmas?"

"Nah," Lana replied. "We were after the great British Christmas experience."

"Well, you've come to the right place," Flora's dad said, delighted. He loved Lana; he loved that his house, with the dejected Christmas tree and tattered tinsel, was considered the hub for international Christmas affairs. "And tell me then, Lana, what's this boarding school of yours like? When Flora told me that Jackie was footing the bill, that her mum had sent her for this boarding school tester, I wasn't too happy, but I've been proven wrong. Flora's come back a whole different person."

"How do you mean?" asked Lana, sounding genuinely intrigued. In the kitchen, Flora and Tane stood looking at each other. He raised an amused eyebrow.

"Well, she's... I dunno..."

"Happy," Abbie pitched in.

"Yes, that's it. Happy."

"Well, she makes us very happy too," Lana said, and Flora could tell that she was suppressing a tell-all grin. She hadn't told her dad about the extent of her and Lana's relationship. That could wait. For now, it was enough having two shiny pirates in her little house. Her computer was in a box in the corner of the kitchen.

"Weird present request, mind," Flora's dad said. "When she sent me the link to that second hand bow-and-arrow on Facebook Marketplace I wondered where on earth we were sending her. They do archery, do they?"

"Sure do," Lana confirmed. "She's convinced that she'll be the best in our class, when we go back."

"Good, good." Her dad sounded distracted. "Mrs White, her old teacher, was asking after her in the supermarket. I told her Flora was doing great; she seemed relieved."

Tane started waving the tap across so that water flooded into the main sink and then the smaller counterpart. In the next room, Lana commenced telling her dad about their boarding school, Taniwha Academy, and how they could only stay in Plymouth for a week before they had to head back. That they had to return to their friends; that new people would be joining and that, although she loved Plymouth, they had to get back to their nets.

"Netball? Lovely," her dad said, flicking through various Christmas films on the television. Elves started singing in high pitched voices. "Well, you promise you'll come back here in Summer, won't you?"

"We absolutely will," Lana replied. "That's a promise."

Flora couldn't stop grinning.

GET READY FOR THE NEXT INSTALLMENT...

Coming 1st October 2023 – **Revenge on Taniwha**. Part 2 of the Flora Brock series sees more romance, more danger and one violently angry teenager...

"Paradise is, of course, ruled by loving law. All places good to live in are governed by laws."
'The Islands of Magic; Legends, Folk and Fairy Tales from the Azores' by Elsie Spicer Eells, 1922

See you in October - add it to your diary now! - and thank you so much for reading. You're my world.

Genevieve x

ABOUT THE AUTHOR

Genevieve Flint

Genevieve hails from Somerset in England, where she enjoys exploring the countryside with bare feet and drinking dodgy fermented drinks. She once created a Snail Olympics and caught butterflies all summer (releasing them, of course!) She studied Creative Writing at Bath Spa University and writes fiction, short stories and poetry. She has recently been shortlisted for awards including the Bath, Periscope, Globe Soup and Elmbridge Short Story Awards.

www.vieveflint.com

Printed in Great Britain
by Amazon